AN ENGLISHMAN
IN MADRID

Eduardo Mendoza

AN ENGLISHMAN
IN MADRID

Translated from the Spanish by
Nick Caistor

MACLEHOSE PRESS
QUERCUS · LONDON

First published in the Spanish language as *Riña de gatos*
by Editorial Planeta, S. A., Barcelona, in 2010
First published in Great Britain in 2013 by MacLehose Press
This paperback edition published in 2023 by

MacLehose Press
an imprint of Quercus
Carmelite House
50 Victoria Embankment
London EC4Y 0DZ

An Hachette UK company

Esta obra ha sido publicada con una subvención
del Ministerio de Educación, Cultura y Deporte de España

ISBN (MMP) 978 1 52942 937 4
ISBN (Ebook) 978 1 78206 302 5

10 9 8 7 6 5 4 3 2 1

Designed and typeset in Minion by Libanus Press
Printed and bound in Great Britain by Clays Ltd, Elcograf S.p.A.

*Rosa was by my side
and this fable is for her*

It is part of the strange human condition that
every life could have been different to what it was

JOSÉ ORTEGA Y GASSET, *Velázquez*

AN ENGLISHMAN
IN MADRID

1

March 4, 1936

Dear Catherine,

   Shortly after crossing the border and completing the tiresome customs formalities, I fell asleep, lulled by the rattle of the train wheels. Until then I had spent a sleepless night, tormented by the weight of the problems, alarms and crises our stormy relationship has created. All I could see through the carriage window was the dark night and my own reflection in the glass: the image of a man haunted by anguish. Dawn did not offer the relief often brought by the arrival of a new day. Clouds still filled the sky, and the pale, weak sun only served to render the scenery and my own internal landscape all the more desolate. In this state, on the verge of tears, I finally fell asleep. When I next opened my eyes, everything had changed. A radiant sun was shining in an endless, deep blue sky dotted with a few small, whiter than white clouds. The train was crossing the barren high plains of Castille. Spain at last!

   Oh, Catherine, my beloved Catherine, if only you could see this magnificent spectacle you would understand my state of mind as I write these lines! Because it is not simply a geographical phenomenon or a change of scene, but something more, something sublime. In England and the north of France I have just travelled through, the countryside is green, the fields are fertile, the trees tall; and yet the sky is low, grey and damp, the atmosphere mournful. Here, on the other hand, the land is arid, the fields are dry and cracked and only seem to produce withered bushes, and yet the sky is boundless, the light heroic. In our country we always go around with our heads down, staring at the ground, feeling crushed; here, where the land offers nothing, people hold their heads high, and gaze at the horizon. It is a land of violence, passion, of grandiose individual gestures. Not like us, constrained by our petty morality and trivial social conventions.

That is how I now see our relationship, dearest Catherine: a sordid act of adultery plagued with deceit, doubts and remorse. Throughout the time it has lasted (two, perhaps three years?) neither of us has enjoyed a single moment of peace or happiness. Enveloped in our drab moral climate, we could not see how limited our relationship was: it seemed to us so inevitable that we were almost compelled to suffer. But the moment of our liberation has arrived, and it is the Spanish sun that has revealed it.

Farewell, my beloved Catherine, I am handing you back your freedom, your tranquillity and the ability to enjoy life, all things your youth, beauty and intelligence mean should rightfully be yours. I myself, alone but comforted by the fond memory of our passionate though ill-starred embraces, will seek to return to the path of peace and wisdom.

Yours ever,

ANTHONY

P.S.: I don't think you should trouble your husband with the confession of our adventure. I know how much it would hurt him to learn of the betrayal of a friendship that dates back to our happy days at Cambridge. Not to mention the sincere love he has for you.

"Inglis?"

The question startled him. Absorbed in writing the letter, he had scarcely noticed there were other people in the compartment. From Calais onwards, his only companion had been a laconic Frenchman with whom he had exchanged a few words when he boarded and when he got off again at Bilbao. The rest of the time the Frenchman had slept like a log, as the Englishman had done once he had left. The new passengers had got on the train at several intermediate stations. Apart from Anthony, the train compartment was now filled with what seemed like the members of some travelling theatre troupe: an elderly country priest, a young, fresh-cheeked peasant girl, and the man who had spoken to him. He was of indeterminate age and social condition, with a shaved head and a bushy republican moustache. The priest had a medium-sized wooden suitcase, the girl a bulky bundle, and the man two voluminous black leather cases.

"I don't speak English, you know," he continued, taking Anthony's silence following his first question as assent. "No Inglis. Yo, Espanis. You Inglis, me Espanis. Spain very different England. Spain sun, bulls, guitars, wine. Everibodi olé. England, no sun, no bulls, no enjoyment. Everibodi kaput."

He paused for a moment to give the Englishman time to assimilate this sociological theory, then went on:

"In England, king. In Spain, no king. Before, king. Alfonso. Now no more king. Finished. Now Republic. President: Niceto Alcalá Zamora. Elections. Prime Minister: was Lerroux, now Azaña. Political parties, so many. All bad. Politicians good-for-nothings. Everibodi bastard."

The Englishman removed his glasses, wiped them with the hand-kerchief sticking out of the top pocket of his sports jacket, and took advantage of the pause to stare out of the window. There was not a single tree visible on the ochre-coloured plain stretching as far as the eye could see. In the distance he caught sight of a mule being ridden side-saddle by a labourer wearing a blanket and a broad-brimmed hat.

God only knows where he came from or where he is going to, thought Anthony, before turning back to the man speaking to him. Anthony frowned sternly to show he was in no mood for conversation.

"I am familiar with the vicissitudes of the situation in Spain," he said coldly in Spanish. "Since I am a foreigner, however, I do not feel I have the right to meddle in your country's internal politics, nor to offer any opinion on the subject."

"Nobody here meddles in anyone else's business," said the talkative fellow passenger, somewhat disappointed at the Englishman's obvious command of his own language. "No, sir, not at all. I only said that to make you aware of the situation. Even if you are only passing through, it's no bad thing to know what to expect, should the case arise. For example, suppose I'm in England for whatever reason, and I take it into my head to insult your king. What would happen? I'd be thrown in the clink. It's only natural. Here it's the same, but the other way round. What I mean to say is that things have changed in the past few years."

Not by the look of it, thought Anthony. He did not say so, however: he simply wanted to put an end to this pointless conversation. He slyly turned his head towards the priest, who although he was pretending not to listen could not conceal a disapproving air. The Englishman's ruse had the desired effect: pointing his thumb in the priest's direction, the garrulous stranger warmed to his theme:

"To look no further, here's a perfect example of what I was telling you. Up to four days ago, people like him decided what was what as they pleased. Today they're on their uppers, and if they cause any trouble, we'll chase them out of town. Isn't that so, Father?"

Folding his hands across his lap, the priest looked the republican up and down.

"He who laughs last laughs longest," he replied with equanimity.

The Englishman left them engaged in a duel of proverbs and paraphrases. Slowly, monotonously, the train crawled across the desolate plain, pouring a thick column of smoke into the clear, pure winter air of central Spain. As he was dozing off once more, he heard the republican say:

"Look, Father, people don't burn churches and convents just for the sake of it. No-one has ever set fire to an inn, a hospital or a bullring. If everywhere in Spain the common people have decided to burn churches when they are so hard to set alight, there has to be a reason."

Anthony was awakened by a violent jolt. The train had come to a halt at an important station. A guard in a cape, thick scarf and peaked cap came limping down the platform. An unlit brass lantern swung from his gloved hand.

"Venta de Baños! Passengers for Madrid change here! The express leaves in twenty minutes!"

The Englishman lifted his case down from the net, said goodbye to the other passengers and went out into the corridor. His legs felt numb from sitting still for so many hours, but he jumped down onto the platform. A rush of freezing air hit his face. He looked round in vain for the guard: having made his announcement, the man had scuttled back into his office as quickly as possible. The station clock had stopped and was showing some unlikely time. A tattered tricolour flag hung from a pole. The Englishman wondered whether he should shelter in the express, but instead walked along the platform in search of the exit. He paused outside a glass door covered in frost and soot. Above it was a sign announcing: BUFFET. Inside, a pot-bellied stove gave off little heat and created a fuggy atmosphere. The Englishman took off his misted-up glasses once more and wiped them on his tie. The only customer in the buffet was sipping at a glass of white spirits and smoking a cheroot. A bottle of anisette in his hand, the barman was staring at Anthony, who spoke directly to him.

"Good day. I need to despatch a letter. Possibly you have postage stamps in your establishment. Should that not be the case, perhaps you could inform me if there are postal facilities somewhere in the station?"

The barman stared at him open-mouthed.

"I couldn't say."

Without raising his eyes from his glass of anisette, the solitary customer spoke up.

"Don't be so uncouth, dammit! What impression is this gentleman going to have of us?" Then, to the Englishman: "You must forgive him. He didn't understand a word you said. You'll find a post office where you can buy stamps in the station hall. There's a postbox too. But first you must have a little glass of anisette."

"No, thank you."

"Don't say no, I'm buying. To judge by your appearance, you need a pick-me-up."

"I didn't think it would be so cold. When I saw the sun . . ."

"This isn't Málaga. It's Venta de Baños, in the province of Palencia. When it's cold, you know it. You're a stranger in these parts, by the look of it."

The barman poured a glass of anisette, which the Englishman downed. Having had no breakfast, the alcohol burnt his throat and set his stomach on fire, but he soon felt a pleasant warmth spreading through his entire body.

"I'm English," he said in reply to the other man's question. "And I'll have to hurry if I don't want to miss the Madrid express. If it's no trouble, I'll leave my case here while I buy a stamp. It'll be quicker that way."

Depositing the glass on the counter, he went out by a side door that led straight into the station hall. He walked round it several times without spotting the post office, until a porter pointed out a closed window. He knocked on it and after a short while it opened and the head of a bald, stunned-looking man appeared. When the Englishman explained what he wanted, the clerk closed his eyes and his lips started to move as if he were muttering a prayer. He bent down, then popped up again and placed a huge book on the counter. He leafed through the pages with great determination, disappeared, and came back with a small pair of scales. The Englishman handed him the letter, which he carefully weighed. Afterwards he consulted his book again, and calculated the cost of the stamp. The Englishman paid and rushed back to the buffet. The barman was staring at the ceiling, a dirty dishcloth in one hand. When the Englishman asked how much he owed, he replied that the other man had paid for him, as agreed. The suitcase was still on the floor. The Englishman picked it up, thanked the barman and ran out onto the platform. The Madrid express was already pulling out, amid clouds of steam and puffs of smoke. Sprinting, he just managed to jump aboard the last carriage.

After walking through several carriages in a vain search for an empty compartment, he decided to stay out in the corridor, despite the cold draught blowing through it. He was still hot from running, and the relief at having posted his letter had made the effort worthwhile. The die was cast. To hell with women! he thought.

He wanted to be on his own to enjoy his new-found freedom and contemplate the landscape, but a short while later he saw the man from the bar lurching down the corridor towards him. Anthony caught his eye, and the man came and stood next to him. He was around fifty years old, short, hollow-cheeked, and his face was lined with wrinkles. There were bags under his eyes, which had a wary look about them.

"Did you manage to post your letter?"

"Yes, but by the time I got back to the buffet you had already left. I didn't have the chance to thank you for your kindness. Are you travelling second class?"

"I travel how I like. I'm a policeman. No, don't look at me like that: it's thanks to me nobody stole your case. You can't be so trusting in Spain. Will you be staying in Madrid, or are you carrying on?"

"No, it's Madrid I'm going to."

"May I ask the reason for your visit? Just a personal question, nothing official. You don't have to reply if you don't wish to."

"It's not a problem. I'm an art expert, and more specifically an expert in Spanish art. I don't buy or sell. I write articles, teach classes, and collaborate with a few galleries. I come to Madrid whenever I can, with or without a reason. The Museo del Prado is my second home, or perhaps I should say my first: I have never been as happy anywhere else."

"My, that sounds like a nice job. I would never have thought it," said the policeman. "And if it's not indiscreet of me, does it bring in enough to live off?"

"Not really," admitted the Englishman. "I also have a small private income."

"Some people are born lucky," said the policeman, almost to himself. Then he added: "Well, if you come to Spain so often and speak the language so well, you must have many friends here, no?"

"Not real friends, no. I've never stayed in Madrid for any length of time, and as you know, we English are rather reserved."

"Then my questions must seem like an intrusion. Don't take it badly, it's simply professional curiosity. I observe people and try to deduce their line of work, whether or not they are married and, if I can, what their intentions are. My job is prevention, not repression. I'm part of the state security services, and these are turbulent times. Of course, I'm not talking about you: to be interested in someone does not mean I'm suspicious of them. But even the most ordinary-looking face can hide an anarchist, a spy in the service of a foreign power, a white slaver. How is one to distinguish them from honest folk? Nobody carries a sign round their neck saying what they are. Yet everyone is hiding some mystery or other. You yourself, to look no further: why such a hurry to post a letter you could have sent from Madrid at your leisure in a few hours' time? No, don't say a word: I'm sure there's a quite simple explanation for everything. I was just giving an example. That, in a nutshell, is my mission: to discover the true face beneath the mask."

"It's cold out here," the Englishman said after a pause, "and I'm not as warmly dressed as I should be. If you don't mind, I'm going to look for a compartment with a bit of heat in it."

"Of course, of course. I won't detain you any longer. I myself am heading for the restaurant car for a drink and a chat with the staff there. I often travel on this line and know them well. A waiter is a great source of information, especially in a country like ours where everyone shouts. Have a good journey and a pleasant stay in Madrid. We are unlikely to meet again, but I'll leave you my card, just in case. Lieutenant-Colonel Gumersindo Marranón, at your service. If you need anything, just ask for me at National Security Headquarters."

"Anthony Whitelands," said the Englishman, stuffing the card into his jacket pocket, "also at your service."

2

Despite feeling tired from the long journey, Anthony Whitelands only manages a fitful sleep, and is woken several times by noises that sound like distant gunfire. He has booked into a modest but comfortable hotel he knows from previous visits. It has a small, not very welcoming foyer, and the receptionist seems to take pride in being rude to the guests, but it is warm and his room is large, with a high ceiling, a sizeable wardrobe, a comfortable bed with clean sheets and a pine table with a chair and a bright reading lamp. The wooden-shuttered rectangular window gives out onto the quiet, secluded Plaza del Angel, and above the rooftops there is a view of the dome of San Sebastián church.

All the same, the atmosphere in the city is not a welcoming one. The bitter cold means that the noisy Madrid nights have given way to the mournful howl of the implacable mountain wind, which sweeps dry leaves and waste paper across the glistening hoar frost. Many buildings are covered with torn, dirty election posters and proclamations from all sides of the political spectrum, invariably calling for strikes, insurrection or confrontation. Not only is Anthony aware of the situation, but it is precisely because it is so serious that he has travelled to Madrid. Even so, coming face to face with the reality arouses a mixture of concern and dismay. At times he regrets having accepted the assignment; at others he is sorry he sent the letter putting an end to his relationship with Catherine: though it caused him much heartache, it had also been the only bright spot in his life.

He dresses slowly and with a faint heart, occasionally checking his appearance in the wardrobe mirror. It is not a flattering sight. His clothes are crumpled from the journey, and although he has brushed his jacket thoroughly, he has been unable to remove all traces of soot. Dressed like this, and with his pallid face and weary bearing, he hardly seems in a fit state to visit the people he intends to call on, or be likely to create a good impression.

Leaving the hotel, he walks a few yards and comes out into Plaza Santa Ana. The sky is brightening: the wind has driven away the clouds and it is a clear, bright and icy winter morning. The first customers are entering the bars and taverns. Anthony joins them, going into a café with rich smells of coffee and warm bread. While he waits for a waiter to serve him, he leafs through a newspaper. The headlines and frequent exclamation marks give him a poor overall impression of events. Throughout Spain there have been clashes between rival political groups, with the sad outcome of several dead and many injured. There are also strikes in several sectors. The priest in a town in Castellón province has been driven out by the mayor, and a dance organised inside the church. In Betanzos, a figure of Christ has had its head and feet lopped off. The customers in the bar are commenting on all this with extravagant gestures and emphatic pronouncements as they draw deeply on their cigarettes.

Accustomed to a substantial English breakfast, Anthony finds that the bowl of strong coffee and greasy *churros* neither go down well nor help clear his mind or lift his spirits. He consults his watch, because the hexagonal wall clock seems to be as broken as the one in the station at Venta de Baños. He has more than enough time to keep his appointment, but the noise and smoke are too much for him, and so he pays and goes out into the square.

A brisk walk finds him outside the doors of the Museo del Prado, which has just opened. He shows the woman attendant the document accrediting him as a professor and researcher, and after some consultation and hesitation, he is allowed in free of charge. At this time of year and due to the violent, uncertain situation in Madrid, there are few visitors to the gallery: it is almost deserted. The rooms are ice cold.

Indifferent to everything except the re-encounter with his beloved gallery, Anthony pauses only briefly in front of "Il Furore", the bronze statue of Charles V by Leone Leoni. Wearing a suit of Roman armour, the emperor is brandishing a lance, while at his feet, defeated and in chains, lies the representation of savage violence, its nose squashed against the backside of the victor, who represents order and the will to impose it on the rest of the world at divine command, with little regard to the means employed.

Comforted by this example of valour, the Englishman straightens up and strides towards the Velázquez room. He is so fascinated by this painter's work that he never looks at more than one painting at a time. This was how he studied them years earlier, going to the Prado every day to examine the canvases one by one, jotting down all their details in a notebook as he discovered them. Then, exhausted but content, he would return to his lodgings and copy his notes into a larger book.

This time however he has not come to write anything. Instead he has come like a pilgrim to a saint's shrine, to beg for his protection. This is the feeling at the back of his mind when he comes to a halt in front of a painting, positions himself at the right distance, wipes his glasses and stands motionless, almost without breathing, to contemplate it.

Velázquez painted the portrait of "Don Juan of Austria" when he was the same age as the Englishman now staring at it in astonishment. In its day it was part of a collection of buffoons and dwarves that decorated the royal apartments. That someone could commission a great artist to paint the portraits of these pathetic beings and then convert the canvases into outstanding features of the palace décor might seem shocking to us nowadays, but that cannot have been the case back then, and anyway, what really matters is that the King's strange whim gave rise to these remarkable paintings.

Unlike his companions in the collection, the person known as

"Don Juan of Austria" did not have any fixed employment at the court. He was a part-time buffoon, taken on to fill a temporary absence or bolster the array of sick, crazy or demented people who kept the King and his entourage amused. There is no record of his name in the archives, only his outlandish nickname. To put him on a level with the imperial armies' greatest military leader, someone who was Charles V's natural son, must have been part of the joke. In the portrait, the buffoon, to do honour to his name, is standing upright, while at his feet are an arquebus, a breastplate, a helmet and some iron balls that could have come from a modest cannon. Nobly dressed, he is grasping a staff of command and wearing a hat that is too big for him tilted slightly to one side, crowned by a striking plume of pink and white feathers. This magnificent attire cannot disguise reality, but only serves to accentuate it: the viewer immediately notices the ridiculous moustache and frowning brow that with several centuries' anticipation make him look a little like Friedrich Nietzsche. The buffoon is no longer young. His hands are firm, but his legs are thin and suggest a frail physique. His face is extremely gaunt, with prominent cheekbones. He looks shifty-eyed and wary. To complete the joke, behind him in one corner of the painting there is a glimpse of a naval battle or its aftermath: a ship ablaze, engulfed in a dense black cloud of smoke. The real Don Juan of Austria had commanded the Spanish fleet at the battle of Lepanto against the Turks – as Cervantes tells it, the most heroic battle of all time. In the painting, nothing is clear: it could be a fragment of reality, an allegory, a parody or the buffoon's dream. The intention is satirical, and yet the Englishman's eyes cloud over when he sees the battle portrayed with a technique far in advance of its time, one employed by Turner for the same purpose more than two centuries later.

With an effort, Anthony recovers his composure and glances again at his watch. He does not have far to go, but he ought to be setting off if he is to arrive with the punctuality that is doubtless expected of him, not as a virtue or sign of politeness, but as a picturesque characteristic of his race: the proverbial English punctuality. Since no-one can see him, he nods his head in the direction of the buffoon, turns on his heel and leaves the museum without so much as a glance at the other masterpieces hanging on its walls.

To his surprise, as he steps out into the street he realises that the melancholy feeling induced by his study of the painting has lifted his own low spirits rather than reinforcing them. For the first time, he is aware that he is in Madrid, a city that not only brings pleasant memories but gives him an exciting sense of freedom.

Anthony Whitelands has always liked Madrid. Unlike so many other cities in Spain and Europe, Madrid's origins are not Greek or Roman. They are not even medieval, but date from the Renaissance. Philip II created it out of nothing when he established his court here in 1561. For this reason, Madrid does not have founding myths going back to some obscure divinity, or a Romanesque virgin sheltering it under her carved wooden cloak. Nor does it have an august cathedral casting its shadow over an old quarter. There is no battle-hardened slayer of dragons on its coat of arms; its patron saint is a humble peasant in whose name picnics and bullfights are organised. In order to preserve its natural independence, Philip II built El Escorial, and by so doing spared Madrid from becoming a spiritual centre as well as a centre of power. By the same token, he refused to have El Greco as court painter. Thanks to these prudent measures, the people of Madrid may have many faults, but religious fervour is not one of them. As the capital of a colossal empire supported and held together by religion, Madrid could not always remain aloof, but whenever possible it delegated its darkest aspects to other cities: Salamanca saw the bitterest theological debates, Avila was the backdrop for the ecstasies of Saint Teresa, Saint John of the Cross and Saint Peter of Alcántara, while the terrible *autos da fe* took place in Toledo.

Reassured by the company of Velázquez and the city that had not only welcomed the painter but raised him to the height of fame, and in spite of the cold and wind, Anthony Whitelands walks up Paseo del Prado to the Cibeles fountain, then along Paseo de Recoletos to Paseo de la Castellana. There he looks for the number he has been given, and finds himself confronted by a high wall and an iron gate. Through the bars he can see a two-storey mansion at the end of a garden. It has a portico and tall windows. This unostentatious grandeur reminds him of the purpose of his visit, and his euphoria gives way to his earlier discouragement. Too late now to turn back. He pushes open the gate, crosses the garden to the entrance and rings the bell.

3

Only three days earlier, the offer had seemed to Anthony a wonderful opportunity to change a part of his life that had become intolerable. Whenever he was on his own, he would take a firm decision to end his adventure with Catherine; then, when he met her, his courage deserted him. He adopted a sceptical, tortured position that turned any encounter into an absurd drama: both ran the risk of being found out, and yet all they got from their affair were a few brief moments of anxiety, riddled with reproaches and sour silences. But the more obvious it became that he should end their unhealthy relationship, the gloomier was the thought of returning to normality. Catherine was the only bright spot in a life so carefully constructed that now, at thirty-four years old, he was condemned not to hope for anything beyond a routine that was all the more oppressive for seeming to the rest of the world like the realisation of all his dreams and ambitions.

Born into a middle-class family, his intelligence and hard work had opened the doors of Cambridge to him. There first of all art in general, then painting, and finally Spanish painting from the Golden Age had fascinated him to such an extent that he poured all his intellectual and emotional energy into studying it. He became so engrossed in this that he gave up any other interests and activities, so that while his fellow students were pursuing amorous adventures or becoming involved in the extremist ideologies of the times, he was completely immersed in a world populated by saints and kings, *infantas* and buffoons, created by the palettes of Velázquez, Zurburán, El Greco and a host of other painters who combined an incomparable mastery of technique with a dramatic and sublime view of the world. Once his studies were concluded, and after having spent long periods in Spain and travelling throughout Europe, he settled down to work, and before long his knowledge, integrity and seriousness won him prestige, although not fame and fortune. His name was well respected within a reduced circle of experts, normally more inclined to criticise than to praise. Anthony did not wish for more than this, in his own field or in any other aspect of his life. A friendship which developed into something closer led to his marriage to a young, well-educated woman whose family fortune helped resolve his money worries and allowed him to devote all his time and attention to his great love. Keen to share his enthusiasm with his bride, he took her to Madrid. Unfortunately, they arrived when there was a general strike, and in addition his wife got a stomach upset from the water or the strange food. The experiment was not repeated. Domestic life and a tightly knit circle of friends eventually put paid to a relationship that had never been passionate or particularly stable. When the divorce meant he lost his main source of income, Anthony concentrated still further on his work. When even this began to seem stifling, almost without meaning to he embarked on an affair with the wife of a former student friend of his. Unlike his ex-wife, Catherine was impetuous and sensual. She too was probably only looking to add some excitement to her conventional existence, but the situation almost immediately became impossible for them: too late they realised that the dead weight of social norms they had considered it fun to transgress formed not only part of their consciences, but of their very being.

Several times, finding it impossible to put an end to the affair face to face, Anthony Whitelands had decided to write Catherine a letter, despite the risk that leaving written evidence of their liaison implied. He intended to tell her his mind was made up, and yet after spending long, painful hours trying to write, he always found himself forced to abandon the attempt. Since there were no obvious reasons for his decision, he found it impossible to find the words to make it sound convincing.

One afternoon he was in his study struggling yet again with this arduous task when the maid announced there was a gentleman to see him. She handed him his visiting card on a tray. Anthony did not know his visitor personally, but he had occasionally heard others mention Pedro Teacher, always in a less than complimentary fashion. He was an individual with an obscure background who frequented the world of art collectors, where his name usually cropped up with regard to dubious transactions. These rumours, possibly false and in any case never proven, had meant he was blackballed from the Reform Club, where Anthony himself was a member. This, thought Anthony, must be the reason for his unexpected visit. If he had been absorbed in writing an article on Spanish painting, he would have sent the inconvenient visitor away more or less politely. However, since the interruption permitted him to postpone his letter to Catherine, he put away his writing materials and told the maid to show Pedro Teacher in.

"First of all," said the visitor once they had exchanged greetings, "I must apologise for invading your privacy without any warning in this way. I trust that the nature of the matter which brings me here will serve to justify such a grossly impolite act."

His way of speaking was too correct to be natural; the same could be said of the rest of him. Close to forty, he was short, with child-like features and small white hands that fluttered in front of his face when he spoke. A thin moustache whose ends pointed slightly upwards and his grey, round eyes made him look like a cat. There was a thin film of make-up on his cheeks, and he gave off an expensive, cloying perfume. He wore a monocle, bootees and spats; he was dressed immaculately but in a manner unsuited to his height: his high-quality clothes would have lent a tall man a note of distinction; in him they added a comic touch.

"It's not important," replied Anthony. "Tell me what I can do for you."

"I'll tell you the reason for my intrusion at once. First, however, I must entreat you that nothing we say should go beyond these four walls. I know I may cause offence by calling your undoubted discretion into question, but vital interests are at stake in this matter. Do you mind if I smoke?"

When his host waved his acquiescence, Teacher took a cigarette out of his gold cigarette case, lit it, drew in the smoke, and then went on:

"I'm not sure if you know who I am, Mr Whitelands. As you can tell from my name, I am half English and half Spanish, which means I have friends in both countries. From adolescence I have dedicated myself to art, but lacking all talent apart from recognising that fact itself, I merely act as a marchand or occasionally a consultant. Several painters have honoured me with their friendship, and I am proud to say that Picasso and Juan Gris know of my existence."

Anthony shrugged impatiently, a gesture which did not pass unnoticed by his guest.

"I'll come straight to the point of what has brought me here," he said. "A day or so ago an old and very dear friend of mine got in touch with me. He is a distinguished Spanish gentleman who lives in Madrid. A man of noble descent and wealth, he has inherited and personally acquired a by no means inconsiderable collection of Spanish paintings. I'm sure I don't need to tell you what a crisis Spain is facing at this moment. Only a miracle can prevent that noble nation from rushing headlong into the abyss of bloody revolution. The prevailing violence is alarming. No-one is safe, and for obvious reasons the situation of my friend and his family is little short of desperate. Others who find themselves in similar circumstances have fled the country, or are preparing to do so. Before they do, they transfer large sums of money to foreign banks to ensure their survival. My friends are unable to do this, because most of their wealth comes from country estates. All they have is the art collection I mentioned. I trust you are following me, Mr Whitelands."

"Perfectly, and I can guess where you are heading."

The visitor smiled, then went on speaking, choosing to ignore Anthony's dismissive comment.

"Like every other country, the Spanish state refuses to allow the export of its national artistic heritage, even that part of it in private hands. However, an item that is neither big nor well known could escape the state's vigilance and leave the country, although in practice the operation might present certain difficulties, above all that of establishing the financial value of the work on the international market. To do this would require an expert whom everyone involved could trust. I believe there is no need for me to spell out who I believe would be the perfect person for the matter in hand."

"Me, I imagine."

"Who better? You know all there is to know about Spanish painting. I've read your publications on the subject and can testify not only to your erudition but also to your ability to understand better than anyone the dramatic spirit of the Spaniards. I am not saying there are not equally well-qualified people in Spain, but it would be running a great risk to entrust them with something like this: they could inform the authorities for ideological reasons, out of personal spite or self-interest, or even simply by blabbing it out. Spaniards never stop talking: I am no exception myself, as you can see."

He paused for a moment to show that he could curb this national tendency, then continued in a lower voice:

"I will outline my proposal in a few words: as soon as possible, since days and even hours are of the essence, you will travel to Madrid, where you will make contact with the interested party, whose identity I will reveal if and when we come to an agreement. Once you have made contact, the interested party will show you his collection or part of it, and you will advise him regarding the item most suitable for our purposes. Then you are to value the work according to the best of your abilities: the amount will be communicated by telephone using a password or secret code that will also be revealed to you at the appropriate time. Immediately, and without any demur, the said amount will be deposited in a London bank in the name of the interested party. Once the transaction has been verified, the work for sale will make its way out of Spain. You will play no part in this final stage of the process, so that should any problems arise there would be no legal or other consequences for you. Your identity will be kept secret at all times. Your name will not appear anywhere unless you should wish it to do so. Your travel expenses will be met by the interested party, and as is only logical, you will receive the usual commission for this kind of operation. Once your mission is complete, you are free to leave or to remain in Spain as you prefer. As far as the secrecy that must surround this matter goes, I know I can count on your word of honour as an English gentleman."

He paused again, but in order to forestall any objection from Anthony went on almost at once:

"Two final considerations to allay any scruples or hesitation on your part. To remove a tiny part of Spain's immense cultural heritage in present circumstances should be seen as more of a rescue operation than a subterfuge. If the revolution breaks out, art will be as badly affected as the rest of Spain, and in an irreparable way. The second consideration is no less important, because thanks to your intervention, Mr Whitelands, you will without doubt help save several lives. Think all this over, and make your decision according to the dictates of your conscience."

Three days later, standing outside the heavy oak-panelled door to the mansion with its austere Herreran Renaissance lines, Anthony Whitelands wondered whether his presence there corresponded to the altruistic motives Pedro Teacher had stressed, or to a simple desire to leave dull routine behind and, by giving way to this impulse, put an end to his entangled love affair. While he was trying to instil a sense of adventure he did not feel into his wavering mind, the door of the mansion opened and a butler asked him who he was and what he wanted.

4

"Tell his lordship it is Pedro Teacher who has sent me."

The butler was strangely young for his position. Swarthy, his hair in ringlets and with long sideburns, he looked more like a bullfighter. It would be hard to imagine a greater contrast than that between the Englishman and him. He gave the visitor a hard stare, but just as he seemed about to slam the door in his face, he stepped to one side, urged Anthony to come in, then abruptly shut the door behind him.

"Wait here," he said curtly, more like a conspirator than a servant. "I will inform his lordship."

With that he disappeared through a side door, leaving Anthony Whitelands in a spacious, high-ceilinged hall with a marble floor. There was no furniture, and the place was obviously designed for friends to pass through quickly, and as somewhere to receive anyone else with a minimum of ceremony. The room would have been gloomy were it not for the golden light streaming in through the tall, narrow windows on the garden side.

Oblivious to everything not related to his reduced area of interest, when left on his own Anthony began to study the paintings on the walls. Most of them were hunting scenes, but one in particular attracted his attention. "The Death of Actaeon" is considered to be one of the most important works of Titian's maturity. The painting Anthony was now looking at was a fine copy of the original, which he had never seen, although he knew of it from many illustrations and had read enough about it for him to recognise the canvas at once. The theme came from various sources, although the best known was Ovid's *Metamorphoses*. Out hunting with friends, Actaeon gets lost, and as he wanders through the forest, comes across Diana just as she has taken her clothes off to bathe in a pool. Angered by his intrusion, the goddess changes him into a deer, whereupon Actaeon is devoured by his own dogs. In a seemingly irrelevant passage, Ovid not only names all the dogs in Actaeon's pack of hounds but lists also the names of several of their parents, and their pedigrees and merits. In the end, this wealth of detail lends even greater pathos to a death where everyone knows one another, but do not recognise one another and are unable to communicate. Ovid writes that the first hounds to leap on Actaeon are two that had been left behind but had found a shortcut. The poet concludes that no-one is to blame for this sorrowful event, because choosing the wrong path is no crime. Other versions have it that Actaeon wished to seduce the goddess in word or deed. Still others downplay the cause: nobody can glimpse a deity, dressed or undressed, without suffering the consequences. Titian's representation of the scene is not entirely coherent: Diana is still dressed, and instead of cursing Actaeon it seems as if she is about to shoot an arrow at him, or has already done so. The metamorphosis of the unfortunate hunter has only just begun: he still has the body of a man, but a disproportionately small deer's head is starting to sprout from his shoulders. This does not stop the hounds attacking him with the same ferocity they would have used on ordinary prey, although strictly speaking they should have recognised their master's smell. One might at first put these inconsistencies down to the haste or lack of interest shown by an artist fulfilling a commission, but Titian painted the canvas towards the end of his life, and spent ten years on it. It was still in his possession at his death. It passed through several hands and countries before finally ending up in a private collection in England. The copy Anthony was now examining was slightly smaller than the original, and as far as he could tell had been done in the late 19th century by a competent copyist. Quite how it had reached the hall of this Madrid mansion was a puzzle he was still pondering when he was interrupted by a voice behind him.

"Are you the new English tutor?"

Turning round, he found himself faced by a young girl with long tresses, dressed for school.

"I'm afraid not," he replied. "How did you know I was English?"

"By the way you look."

"It's that obvious, is it?"

The girl came a little nearer to the new arrival, as if wanting to check that she had been right or that he was being sincere. Closer to, she seemed older than her clothes and childish attitude had suggested; she was thin, with delicate features and big, inquisitive eyes.

"My father wants me to learn English in case we have to leave Madrid. I haven't been to school for more than a month now. But I don't like studying languages. The English are Protestants, aren't they?"

"Most of them."

"Father Rodrigo says Protestants will go straight to Hell. Even if they are pagan, good negroes go into limbo. But all Protestants, however good they may be, go to Hell. That's because even though they could have been Catholics, they persisted in the error of their ways."

"Far be it from me to contradict Father Rodrigo. What's your name?"

"Alba María, but everyone calls me Lilí."

"Lilí, at your service, you mean," a firm voice corrected her from behind them.

A tall, sallow-faced man came in. He had a high forehead and grey hair. Taking in the scene at a glance, he passed close by the girl, raising an arm as if to stroke her, then straightening it out to shake the Englishman's hand.

"I'm sorry to have kept you waiting. I am Alvaro del Valle y Salamero, Duke of La Igualada. You are the person Pedro Teacher has sent. I trust that our little tornado here has not embarrassed you with her impudence."

Lilí had moved behind her father. She stood on tiptoe to whisper something in his ear, then ran out of the hall.

"Not at all," said Anthony. "Your excellency's daughter has behaved like a perfect hostess. She predicted my eternal damnation in the most charming fashion."

"Don't pay her any attention," replied the duke, "and don't imagine she is overly concerned about your soul's salvation. She has just told me you look like Leslie Howard. But let's not stay here. Come into my study, if you will."

Passing though two rooms without seeing a soul, they came to a very welcoming library. Instead of heavy Castillian furniture, it was decorated in the English style, with bookshelves of light-coloured wood filled with ancient leather-bound books with gilt edges. On one wall there was a Sorolla seascape, and on another several drawings the Englishman could not place. In addition to the paintings there were several personal photographs in discreet silver frames. The Spanish influence was reduced to the inevitable heavy wooden cabinet in one corner, probably a family heirloom. Everything about the room suggested peaceful calm. A triple window gave onto a part of the garden where slender cypresses and clipped box hedges framed an enchanting corner embellished with statues, a fountain and a marble bench. Going over to consider this delightful scene, Anthony glimpsed a couple standing beside the fountain. Because of the distance and the shade from the trees, he was only able to make out that the man was tall and wore a long navy-blue coat, while the woman was fair-haired and dressed in green. Although they were alone and could only be seen from the mansion (a high wall protected the garden from the street outside) Anthony thought he detected something furtive about their attitude. Aware that he was observing people who did not wish to be observed, he looked away from the window and turned towards his host. A cloud flitted across the duke's face, due either to what was going on at that moment in the garden or to the fact that a stranger had seen it. Neither of them mentioned what they had glimpsed. The duke's face recovered its expression of calm affability as he waved his hand towards a leather three-piece suite. Anthony accepted the invitation and sat on the sofa. The duke took one of the armchairs. Picking a silver box from a side table, he opened the lid and offered his guest a cigarette. When the Englishman declined, he took one for himself, lit it, crossed his legs and smoked in silence for a while. It was plain that the matter which had brought them together was not something that could be quickly dealt with.

"It is not easy," the duke eventually began, "to talk about such a delicate affair with somebody one knows only by reference. Pedro Teacher has been full of praise for you, in regard to both your expertise and your personal qualities. I have known Teacher for many years now, and although our relationship has been a business one rather than a friendship, I have no reason to doubt his powers of judgment or his intentions. The fact that I have to put my trust in people I hardly know is an indication of just how delicate the situation is in which I find myself. You are a gentleman: consider how demeaning it must be for a man like me to have to turn to foreigners for help."

The duke's voice quavered slightly as he said this, but he controlled his emotions and went on, apparently unaffected:

"I am not saying this merely to gain your sympathy, much less to appeal to your sense of solidarity. Quite the contrary: everything happening in Spain now is far from normal and also – why deny it? – extremely dangerous. I am therefore perfectly willing to accept that you could at any moment decide to drop the matter and return home. To put it another way: do this on a professional basis, put your own interests before any others, and don't allow emotions to influence your decision. I don't want to have yet another weight on my conscience."

The duke brusquely stubbed out his cigarette in the ashtray, stood up, and walked over to the window. The sight of the garden appeared to calm him, because he came back, sat down again, lit another cigarette and continued:

"If I am not mistaken, our mutual friend has explained the situation . . ."

Anthony nodded. Then, seeing that the duke was not going to add anything, he said:

"Perhaps without intending to, your charming daughter has told me you may be going to live abroad. I imagine our business has to do with those plans of yours."

The duke sighed, then added in a deep voice:

"My daughter is very sharp. I have not said a word to her about it, but naturally enough, she has guessed my intentions. One only needs go out into the street to see how intolerable things are. For security reasons, I took her out of school more than a month ago. For the moment, a priest is in charge of both her academic and moral instruction."

Crushing his cigarette in the ashtray, he automatically lit another one, then continued.

"It is only a matter of time before the revolution breaks out. The fuse is lit and nothing can put it out now. I'll be sincere, Mr Whitelands: I am not afraid of the revolution. I'm not so blind I cannot see the injustice that has dogged Spain for centuries. The privileges of my class have not prevented me from supporting reform measures on various occasions, particularly with regard to agrarian reform. I have learnt more about that from managing my estates and talking to the tenant farmers than from all the speeches, reports and debates by professional politicians of every stripe. I believe in a modernising of our class structures and economic system that would bring benefits to the country as a whole and more importantly to all Spaniards, rich or poor. What use is one's wealth if our servants are busy sharpening the knife to slit our gizzards? But it's too late for reform. Either from indifference, incompetence or egotism, no settlement has been reached, and so now there is little chance of a peaceful solution to the conflict. A little more than a year ago a Communist revolution broke out in Asturias. It was put down, but while it lasted many outrages were committed, especially against the clergy. The mummified corpses of nuns were pulled out of their coffins and manhandled. The body of one of the many murdered priests was exposed to public scorn with a sign round the neck declaring: 'pig meat for sale'. Such acts have nothing to do with Communism or any other ideology, Mr Whitelands. They are no more than barbarism, the lust for blood. Then when the Army and the Civil Guard intervened, the repression was terrible. We have gone mad, that's all there is to it. In such a state of affairs, my only chance is to get my family out of the country. I have a wife and four children: two sons and two daughters. Lilí is the youngest. I am fifty-eight years old. I am not an old man, but I have led a full and good life. The thought that I might be killed does not exactly enthral me, but nor does it frighten me or cause me anguish. If it were down to me, I would stay. The idea of running away goes against my nature, and not just because it is cowardly. To abandon Spain is like abandoning a loved one in the final stages of an incurable illness. There is nothing to be done, but my place is at her bedside. But I have to consider my family. From a practical point of view, a dead hero is as useless as a dead coward."

With that he suddenly got to his feet, paced around the room, then raised his arms in front of him.

"I beg your pardon: I've been talking too much. My worries are not your concern. I simply wanted to show you that I am not a speculator in works of art. And lately I have had few opportunities to get things off my chest. I try to keep my family out of these matters, and it is not the same talking to someone one knows. People are afraid to express their opinion, let alone reveal their plans. There are no friends anymore, only people who share the same beliefs."

Stupefied, the Englishman began a confused protest at the suggestion that anyone might misinterpret his host's noble, wise decisions.

38

Not he, Anthony Whitelands, at any rate. But before he could get into his stride, the melodious chime of a grandfather clock floated through the blue-tinged air of the library. The Duke of La Igualada sprang up as if he were part of the clock's mechanism. Adopting a cheerful expression, he exclaimed:

"Bless my soul, it's half past one and here we are gossiping away! Time flies, my friend, especially when an old chatterbox like me finds such a polite and sympathetic listener. There is no way we can start work at an hour when any decent person is having luncheon. We can leave that for a more suitable moment. For now, it would be an honour and a pleasure if you deigned to share our repast with myself and my family. Unless, that is, you have other business to attend to."

"Not at all," Anthony replied, "but I have no wish to intrude on your family life."

"Nonsense, my friend! In this house everything is permitted except excessive politeness. You must be impressed by this great barn of a place, but you'll see that we are simple people really."

Without waiting for a reply, the duke pulled on a tasselled bell cord. A few moments later the butler came in and asked gruffly what his lordship required. The duke wanted to know if his son Guillermo had returned. The butler said he had not seen him.

"Very well," the duke replied. "Have another place laid for lunch. And make sure the food is served at exactly half past two. If Master Guillermo is not back by then, he will have to eat heated-up leftovers. And kindly tell her ladyship the duchess that we will take our aperitif in the music room. Guillermo," he explained with unconvincing sternness once the butler had left to carry out his orders, "is my youngest son, and the biggest ninny. He is studying Law in Madrid, but spends part of the year coming and going from our estates. I intend gradually to leave the administration of our affairs in his hands. He has been unable to leave the house here for months, and his mother was desperate to know how things are out in the countryside. And with good reason. I prefer to see the family penned up, but you can't keep young people on such a short rein. After forty-eight hours shut in here he said it was like a prison, and so the day before yesterday he went off hunting on some friends' reserve. He promised to be back before lunch. We will see. My other son is travelling in Italy with two student companions. Florence, Siena, Perugia – lucky fellow! He has a Law degree, but his real passion is art, and I am not one to reproach him for that. Come with me, Mr Whitelands: I will introduce you to my wife and we can have a glass of sherry. The heating system in here is ancient, and it's as cold as any mausoleum. Oh, and when we are with my wife and daughters, please, not a word about what we have been discussing. There is no need to alarm them any more than they are already."

5

Logs were burning merrily in the music room hearth. A white bust of a taciturn-looking Beethoven stood in pride of place on the mantelpiece. A grand piano took up much of the space in the well-proportioned room. A music sheet open on its stand, as well as others piled on the stool, showed that it was put to regular use. The walls were lined with blue silk, while the window looked out onto orange and lemon trees in a corner of the garden.

The two men had scarcely entered the room when the duchess made her appearance. She was a small woman, whose somewhat unbecoming features had been lent an air of dignity by age and a lack of affectation. Her attitude conveyed a sense of intelligence, energy and determination, and when she spoke the trace of an Andalusian accent gave her a natural grace. Her irrepressible spontaneity and candour led her frequently to make mistakes and innocent gaffes which delighted all those who knew and cared deeply for her. It was not hard to imagine that the house revolved around her.

"Welcome to this rambling barn of ours, and especially to this room: it's my refuge and sanctuary," she said in a singsong, faltering voice. "My husband lives for painting; for me, it's music. That means we never argue. He likes things that last, I prefer those that are ephemeral. Are you a music lover, Mr . . . ?"

"Whitelands."

"Goodness, what strange family names you have! What's your Christian name?"

"Anthony."

"Antoñito? Well now, that's better."

"Mr Whitelands," her husband quickly explained in a kind, almost deferential tone, "is the expert on Spanish painting I told you about, Pedro Teacher's friend. He came all the way from England to take a look at our modest collection, but we ran out of time so I asked him to stay to lunch. Is Guillermo not back yet?"

"Julián tells me he returned some time ago, but since he's as filthy as a bandit he's gone upstairs to wash and change clothes."

At that moment Lilí came in, accompanied by a young woman presented to Anthony as Victoria Francisca Eugenia María del Valle y Martínez de Alcántara, the Marchioness of Cornellá, whom they all called Paquita. She was their daughter, Lilí's elder sister. She was willowy, with regular features, but bore a certain resemblance to her mother that paradoxically made her extremely attractive. She took their guest's hand without a smile, and shook it briefly but firmly, in an almost masculine manner. After that she withdrew to a corner of the room and began to leaf through an illustrated magazine. Although she was not wearing green, Anthony wondered if this farouche young woman might not be the enigmatic person he had caught a glimpse of earlier in the garden, dallying with her anonymous suitor. By now though Lilí was beside him, and had clasped his hand with a childish, shameless confidence. When the Englishman turned his attention to her, she said:

"I'm sorry for what I said before. I didn't mean to offend you."

"Oh, it's no offence to look like Leslie Howard."

The young girl blushed and dropped his hand.

"Lilí, let Antoñito drink his sherry in peace, will you?" said the duchess.

"She's no trouble," stammered Anthony. It was his turn to feel his cheeks burn.

A shrivelled, beetle-browed maid who looked slightly simple-minded came in and bawled that lunch was served. They left their drinks and made for the dining room. Without standing on ceremony, Paquita came up to Anthony and took his arm.

"Do you really know about painting?" she asked him point-blank. "Do you like Picasso?"

"Oh," the Englishman said, somewhat taken aback by such a direct approach, "there's no doubt Picasso has great talent. But I must say I have no great enthusiasm for his work, or in fact for much of modern art. From a technical point of view I can understand Cubism and Abstract art, but I don't see where they are headed. If art has to head somewhere, that is. Are you in favour of the avant-garde?"

"No, nor the rear-guard either. I'm part of the musical side of our family. Painting bores me."

"I can't see why. You're surrounded by magnificent works of art."

"Are you trying to say I'm spoilt?"

"No, please, I never said anything of the sort. Besides, that would be preposterous: I hardly know you."

"I thought your profession meant you could spot the real from the fake at a glance."

"Oh, now I see – you're making fun of me, Miss Paquita."

"Only a little, Señor Antoñito."

Anthony was increasingly bewildered. By his reckoning, Paquita must be a little beyond the age when the daughter of a good family, especially if she is attractive, intelligent and vivacious, ought to be married, or at least engaged. Otherwise, as was patently the case here, the young woman either put on a false modesty or exaggerated her carefree independence in a way designed to leave no doubt that remaining a spinster was a matter of choice. He therefore concluded there must be some mysterious reason for the challenging tone adopted by the beguiling young woman who at that very moment was accompanying him into the mansion's splendid dining room.

The dining table could comfortably accommodate as many as thirty guests, although on this occasion only seven places were laid at one end. Two chandeliers hung from the ceiling, while the walls were covered with portraits that immediately caught Anthony's attention, momentarily distracting him from the enigmatic woman who was so keen to mock him. They were obviously a series of family ancestors, from courtly figures from the seventeenth century painted in the manner of Van Dyck to stiff academic portraits from the start of the twentieth. As he contemplated them, Anthony was once again struck by the fact that the Spanish aristocracy had never succumbed to the mannered excesses that the rest of Europe had adopted. The nobility in Spain haughtily rejected the frills, powders, and above all the outsize wigs that would have clashed with their swarthy, ascetic and scowling countenances. At most, they agreed to put their hair up in a ponytail that still left them looking as gruff and ragged as stable boys. Anthony admired this noble refusal. He mentally compared sugary English portraits of fops in their embroidered frock coats, ruddy-cheeked and with full-bodied wigs down to their shoulders, with the individuals Goya portrayed – tough, olive-skinned, dirty, and yet possessing a human, transcendental solidity – and was convinced yet again that he had got the better side of the bargain.

The five of them sat at table, leaving one place for the missing brother and another to the left of the duchess. After rapidly checking that everything was as it should be, she signalled to her husband, who nodded and bowed his head. Everyone apart from Anthony did the same, and the duke blessed the food they were about to receive. When he had finished and they all straightened up, Lilí asked if Protestants also said grace. Although her father scolded her for being so rude, the Englishman replied in a kindly way that Protestants were very keen on prayers and read passages from the Bible whenever and wherever they could.

"But we Anglicans never say grace, and so as a just punishment in England we eat very badly."

This inoffensive joke suddenly seemed a little irreverent, because at that very moment a grim-looking priest joined them. Even before they were introduced, Father Rodrigo had shot an inquisitorial glance in

Anthony's direction, making plain his instinctive dislike for anything that came from outside Spain. He was middle-aged and stocky, with bristling hair and a permanent scowl on his face. Long-standing grease stains on his cassock testified to its wearer's indifference to the vanities of this world.

The tension in the room was dissipated with the arrival of the maid carrying the soup tureen; hot on her heels came a young man obviously freshly washed and dressed, his hair slicked down with brilliantine. Kissing his mother on the forehead, he held his hand out to their English guest.

"This is my son Guillermo," said the duke, a note of pride in his voice.

Guillermo was a handsome young man. He also took after his mother, but in his attitude, like that of many good-looking, rich and intelligent young people, there was an unconsciously insolent edge. He seemed very excited, and launched into a graphic description of what had happened to him and his companions. That same morning, with the sun already high, the tired and frozen hunters had arrived with their tracker at a small village. Desperate for something to eat, a bowl of soup or anything hot that would revive them, they decided to stop and look for an inn. When they reached the main square they ran into the village band, who at that very moment struck up the "Internationale", surrounded by a crowd of villagers. They were cheering and shouting threats at the town hall building and the church, despite the fact that the latter was firmly closed and that a tricolour republican flag was flying from the balcony of the former. It took the hunters some time to realise the danger they were in, and that moment's indecision was enough for one of the villagers to notice them and draw everyone else's attention to this group of young toffs. One of the party made to swing his shotgun down from his back, but their tracker, an old man of great experience, stopped him. As calmly as they could, the hunters edged back step by step, and left the village the way they had come. When they were a couple of kilometres away, they looked back and saw a column of smoke rising in the air, from which they deduced that the rabble had set fire to the church, as was happening in so many parts of Spain.

"That's what you get," the duchess said when Guillermo finished his tale, "for going hunting at this time of year. The mornings are so cold I don't know how you didn't all catch pneumonia or something worse. So much for hunting. What you should be doing at your age is going to classes and studying."

"But Mama," the young man replied, "how can we do that if the University is shut?"

"Shut?" exclaimed the duchess. "What is it doing shut in mid-March? What are they celebrating?"

Lilí laughed to herself, and Father Rodrigo cursed under his breath. In order not to worry his wife, the duke changed subjects.

"Apart from that, how did the hunting go?"

It had not gone very well. First they had been chasing a roe buck, but it had shaken off the dogs by bounding up some crags. Then they fired at a golden eagle, but it was flying too high. In the end, the hunters had come back with only a meagre catch in their satchels: a few hares and a brace of geese. They were all the more disappointed because they had set out with the intention of bagging a great bustard or two.

"You won't see any of them in the hills at this time of year."

Anthony ate and observed while the discussion dragged on. In the middle of the table stood a solid silver centrepiece that was delicately worked; the luncheon service and cutlery were equally elegant. The food served however was simple, nutritious and frugal. Apart from the duchess, who appeared to have a poor appetite, the others ate heartily, including the two daughters. None of them displayed the fussiness of falsely refined people. Although the service was timely and polite, it was so clumsy as to seem almost rustic. Anthony Whitelands could not help comparing this family to the British aristocrats he knew, and once again he was struck by the differences. Here, it was perfectly natural to combine the ease of family life with luxury, the quiet simplicity of the countryside with the thoughtful refinement of the court, straight-forwardness with intelligence and culture. Quite the opposite, in fact, to the stiff, upstart British aristocracy, obsessed with their heredity, their social relations and their income, and so scornful in their behaviour, so arrogant and so lacking in education.

The duchess's voice roused him from these reflections:

"For the love of God, that's enough about your hunting. You're boring our guest. Let's talk about you instead, Antoñito. What brings you to Madrid, apart from a wish to be bored by us? Are you going to give a talk at the Ateneo? I really enjoy the lectures there. If not, I go to sleep. So one way or another, I have a wonderful time. A month ago a German speaker came: he explained that Christopher Columbus was the son of an Eskimo man and a woman from Mallorca. Very interesting. What he did not say is how the two of them ever managed to produce our great Admiral. Do you also have outlandish theories?"

"No, your excellency. I'm afraid I am rather tame. I hardly ever give talks, and only occasionally publish an article in a specialist journal."

"Oh well, you're still young," said the duchess.

The rest of the meal went by in the same relaxed manner. At its close, Anthony presumed that each member of the family would go back to their own business and he could make a start on the task that had brought him here. The duke, however, as though considering tthe day's work to be done, or perhaps because he had forgotten the reason for the stranger's presence in their mansion, decided they should all go back to the music room, where coffee and liqueurs would be served, and where anyone who so desired, he added, pointing to himself, could smoke a decent cigar.

They all followed him, apart from Father Rodrigo, who withdrew, muttering an unintelligible monosyllable that was both an excuse and a farewell. When she had drunk her small cup of coffee, the duchess sat at the piano and began to play some light music. Then Lilí sat beside her and the two of them played a piece for four hands. When they finished, Anthony applauded, and Lilí jumped off the piano stool, ran across to him, flung her arms round his neck and asked if he had really liked it. He tapped her cheek and was murmuring a vague compliment when Guillermo produced a guitar from somewhere, tuned it, and strummed some notes. Paquita sat beside him on the sofa and began to sing in a somewhat husky but tuneful, sensual voice. Anthony was enchanted. Brother and sister took turns to sing and play the guitar for a good while. Lilí, who was still sitting next to him, whispered in his ear: this is a fandango, and this is a seguidilla. The duke was wrapped up in his own world, smoking, and the duchess had dozed off in an armchair. Outside, twilight had softened the contours of the garden. When it became too dark for them to see each other's faces, the duke stood up and switched on a lamp. Startled by the sudden brightness, the spell was broken. They all got up from their seats, and there was a moment's confusion.

"My word," the head of the house said at last, "it's grown rather late. Of course there's still time to work, but there are several urgent matters I have to deal with. As for you, Mr Whitelands, there is no point looking at the paintings now: electric light is no good for studying colour and detail. I'm afraid you'll have to visit us again, if our company does not seem too irksome."

"Oh, it will be a real pleasure," said the Englishman, with sincere emphasis, "if it is not an abuse of your hospitality."

"On the contrary," the duke insisted, "we don't have many guests these days, and we are all delighted to meet you. So that's that. I'll expect you tomorrow morning at whatever time suits you – but not too late, we mustn't let the day slip by again. We have a lot to get through. Lilí, say goodbye to our new friend and go and do your homework. Just because you're not going to school doesn't mean you can neglect your education and turn into a Hottentot. Father Rodrigo is waiting to hear what you've learned, and you know how strict His Eminence is."

They said goodbye one by one. When it was Paquita's turn, she offered to accompany Anthony to the front door. They walked side by side through the rooms between the music room and the hallway, where the attractive young woman paused to say to her companion:

"Don't judge my family too readily. In the present circumstances we all act in an exaggerated fashion, which could seem immature to someone from outside. When the future is uncertain, behaviour and feelings that in normal times would be displayed more calmly and more appropriately are given free rein. I am no exception. In addition, my family is both grasping and feudal: for centuries now it has been accustomed to taking what it likes. And they like you. Perhaps because coming from outside you have reminded our household of another, more cheerful and less cruel reality."

"I'm pleased to have given your family such a good impression," replied Anthony, "but I should like to know what impression you have of me."

"You will have to discover that for yourself, Mr Whitelands. I also like to possess things I want, but I don't allow anyone to possess me."

Anthony opened the front door of the mansion. Standing on the top step, he turned and asked:

"Shall I see you again tomorrow?"

"I don't know. I never make such long-term plans," she said as she closed the door.

Anthony Whitelands found himself alone in Paseo de la Castellana, with only a few cars and no passers-by in sight. Softened by the cold, clear night air of Madrid, the street lamps made no more than small circles of light between the boulevard's trees and hedges. As he set off walking, the tall figure of a man loomed out of the darkness, apparently heading for the duke's mansion. Anthony came to a halt, and the stranger, perhaps realising someone had spotted him, continued on his way past the house, hands stuffed in his pockets and coat lapels raised to cover his face, until the shadows swallowed him up once more. Even though he had not been able to make out his face, the Englishman was certain this was the same man he had seen that morning in the garden, in an intimate tête-à-tête with the mysterious woman in green.

6

Handing Anthony the key to his room, the hotel receptionist told him that a gentleman had been asking after him that afternoon.

"Are you sure?"

"Absolutely. I attended him myself, and he gave your full name. He didn't leave any message or say if he would be back. From his appearance he was probably a foreigner, although he spoke Spanish as well as you, but with a better accent, if you'll permit me to say so."

Anthony went up to his room wondering who this anonymous visitor might be, and how he had found him when he had not told anyone where he was staying. Of course when he arrived he had registered at the hotel, and so perhaps the management had informed the police that they had a new foreign guest. Many foreigners passed through Madrid, but these were uncertain times. But if it had been a policeman, why had he not identified himself? And above all, what interest could the Spanish police, or anyone else for that matter, have in talking to him? Could something have happened in London to make the embassy want to get in touch with him? And then again, why keep everything so secret?

Still pondering this, he took out a book he had tried in vain to read on the train, but found he could not concentrate even in the solitude of his room. After a while he closed the book and went out for a walk.

The cold outside was intense, but the centre of Madrid was thronged with people. Seeing all the passers-by strolling along apparently unconcerned, and caught up in the kind of verbal skirmishes so typical of the quick-witted inhabitants of the capital, he felt infected by the general air of enjoyment, something that always made his stays in Spain so pleasant.

Wandering aimlessly through the streets, Anthony found himself outside a tavern he remembered having visited before. Inviting voices and laughter floated out through its doors. There did not seem to be room for a single extra person inside, but before too long he managed to push his way up to the bar. Despite the tumult, a waiter served him with surprising speed and friendliness: it was as though he were the only customer in the tavern. Anthony ordered a plate of prawns and a glass of wine. While waiting for them to arrive, he recalled previous occasions when he had been in the same tavern. The walls were covered with photographs of bullfighters: this was where a very popular and very argumentative bullfighting supporters' club met. Sometimes the matadors themselves came to share a few glasses of wine with their public. Whenever that happened there was a truce in their bitter arguments, because the bullfighters were authentic idols, and no-one would have dared express an opinion that might have upset them. In spite of the rows, the atmosphere was friendly, and the sessions always went on with songs and music until late into the night. Anthony loved the ambience. One night some years earlier someone had pointed out the presence of a really famous matador, the legendary Ignacio Sánchez Mejías, getting on in years, but still distinguished-looking. Anthony knew him by name, and knew that as well as being a widely admired bullfighter he was an intellectual and a talented poet. Shortly after this chance meeting, Anthony heard he had been killed in the ring. Federico García Lorca had dedicated a heartfelt poem to him, and Anthony, who had been greatly moved by his death, had translated the poem into English in a version that was grammatically correct, but lacked any emotional poetic charge.

This recollection and the thought of his own naivety made him laugh out loud. Seeing this, the man next to him at the bar growled:

"What's so funny?"

"I beg your pardon?"

"You're foreign, aren't you?"

"Yes, indeed."

"And it's obvious you think that what's going on here is funny."

"I'm sorry, I've no idea what you mean. I was laughing because I was reminded of something that has nothing to do with the present."

While he was apologising, Anthony realised the reason for the misunderstanding. Behind his back, two groups were caught up in a violent, unpleasant argument. At first he thought it must be one of the typical quarrels about bullfighting, but on this occasion it was something completely different. The smaller of the two groups was composed of young lads who looked well dressed and well fed. The other group seemed rougher, and to judge by their clothing, their caps and the polka-dot kerchiefs round their necks, they were mostly artisans and labourers. The original row had progressed to the stage of shouted insults. The workmen were shouting "Fascists!" while the others replied with "Reds!" Both sides shouted "Bastards!" at each other. But there was nothing to suggest that words might give way to deeds. Both groups were weighing up each other's strength, with the result that neither side was inclined to go beyond insults. All of a sudden, one of the youngsters made to reach for something in his pocket. Seeing his intention, one of his companions restrained him, shouted something in his ear, and then made for the exit. The others followed suit, never once turning their backs on the workmen, whom they still stared at menacingly.

"As you can see," Anthony's neighbour commented once the atmosphere in the tavern had calmed down again, "people used to come in here to fight over whether Cagancho or Gitanillo de Triana was better . . . bullfighters, that is."

"Yes, of course. I love bullfighting."

"My, aren't you a fine chap! Mateo, another glass of red for me, and the same for this gentleman here. No, don't worry, you can buy the next round and we're all square. Well, as I was saying, that's how it used to be. Nowadays it's: Mussolini's the one; no, it's Lenin; the devil take the lot of them I say, with all due respect to your ideas. Up to now, as you've seen, it doesn't go beyond trading insults. We Spaniards are good at bravado, but are reluctant to come to blows. But the moment we do, not even God can stop us."

Spaniards also have keen hearing when it comes to conversations that are none of their business, and do not hesitate to butt in and give their own opinion, which of course is not merely correct, but the final word on the subject. As a result, within a few minutes a fierce and noisy debate sprang up in which many locals fought for Anthony's attention so as to offer him their irrefutable diagnosis of Spain's ills and their simple solution. Most were workmen, but some were office workers, artisans, tradesmen and cub reporters, all of them united by their devotion to bullfighting in a way that transcended social barriers. The youngsters who had burst in earlier were members of the right-wing Falange. They were doubtless looking for a fight, but the peaceful atmosphere and the apolitical nature of the tavern had taken the wind out of their sails. These Falange activists, Anthony was told, were mostly very young, and therefore impetuous and reckless; their party had fared badly in the recent elections, and now they were trying to stir up trouble. They thought they were the masters of the streets, especially in Madrid, although now and again the socialists or anarchists gave them a roughing up. Recently these confrontations had become more violent, and often ended up with people being wounded or even killed. The Falange, somebody said, were nothing but poor little rich kids; the problem was that their daddies not only gave them money but lent them their pistols. Apparently that same morning a handful of these blue-shirts had broken into a socialist meeting and fired a shotgun at the speaker's platform. Before all those present had recovered from the shock, the attackers had sped off in an automobile. And if at that moment, the man went on, anyone looking like a capitalist or, still worse, a priest, had chanced to pass by, the socialists would have made mincemeat of him. That was how, he concluded, the innocent paid for the guilty.

The problem was, another man asserted, that by now there were no innocent or guilty parties left. It was easy to accuse the blue-shirts of everything that was going on, but you had to remember who had paved the way for it: the attacks, strikes and acts of sabotage, the burning of churches and convents, the bombs and the dynamite – not forgetting the clearly stated aim of all of this disruption, namely the overthrow of the government, the break-up of the family and the abolition of private property. And all this tolerated, out of cowardice or connivance, by the authorities. Given this panorama, it was hardly surprising that certain sectors of society should have decided to take steps to make their voices heard, or at the very least die with their weapons in their hands.

Before he could finish speaking, he was interrupted by a small fellow wearing a threadbare bowler hat. He said his name was Mosca, and that he belonged to the U.G.T. union. According to Señor Mosca, the Catalans were the ones to blame for the conflict. With the excuse of simply modifying the administrative structures of the Spanish state, the Catalans had in fact destroyed Spain's unity, so that now the nation was falling apart like a wall with its cement removed. Since there were no Catalans present, nobody refuted the argument or pointed out that the metaphor did not really apply. This encouraged Señor Mosca to proclaim that with the disappearance of any sense of belonging to a common country, every citizen signed up for the first lot of people marching past their house, and that rather than seeing their neighbour as a fellow countryman, they considered him their enemy. Before he could finish, he was shouted down by several other people, all of them anxious to give their own analysis of the situation. In order to make himself heard, Señor Mosca stood on tiptoe and stretched out his neck, but this only meant that the flailing arms of a neighbour sent his bowler hat flying.

The arguments became increasingly heated. Anthony, whose glass the barman had refilled several times, spoke up to say that in his opinion everything could be resolved through dialogue and negotiation. This set everyone against him, because since he was not defending anyone's point of view, they all thought he must be on the side of their adversary. In the end, a man came up to him and signalled that he should follow him to the door. Tossing some coins on the bar, Anthony did as he suggested. When the two of them had safely pushed their way through the crowd and were out in the street, the stranger said:

"There's no reason you should get into a punch-up."

"You think I would have?"

"More than likely. You're the tallest, and as a foreigner you have no-one to fight on your behalf. If you're not convinced, go back in. As you may imagine, I couldn't give a damn."

"No, you're right, and I'm glad you made me realise it. Besides, it's late, and I ought to be getting back to my hotel rather than poking my nose in where it's not wanted."

He held out his hand to his unknown benefactor, but instead of taking it, the other man stuffed his own hands into his coat pocket.

"I'll accompany you if you like. The streets are dangerous, especially at this time of night. Of course, I'm no guarantee of your safety, but since I'm from Madrid and have knocked about a bit, I know when it's best to change pavements or to take to your heels."

"That's very kind of you, but I don't want to put you to any trouble. My hotel is close by."

"If that's the case, it won't be any trouble to me. And if instead of going directly to your hotel you'd prefer to spend some time in good company, I know a place just round the corner. It's very clean, not expensive, and the girls are first-rate."

"Ah," said Anthony, feeling the effects of the alcohol evaporate and his senses recover thanks to the cold night air and the recent danger, "when I was a student here in Madrid, I occasionally paid a visit to a house of ill repute."

"Well, this should blow the cobwebs away," said the stranger.

They walked up Gran Vía for a while, then turned off down a dark side street. When they reached the front door of a narrow hovel with peeling walls, they clapped their hands until the nightwatchman appeared, staggering and brandishing a bunch of keys. He opened the door ceremoniously, received his tip with a bow and a belch, then disappeared once more. The two of them went into a gloomy courtyard and Anthony's new-found friend said:

"Go up to the second floor on the right and ask for Toñina. I won't go with you because I'm not in the mood for that kind of thing tonight, but I'll wait for you here with no problem, smoking a cigarette. Don't rush, I'm not in any hurry. Oh, and before you go up, I recommend you leave me your wallet, passport and any valuables you've got with you, apart from the price of your session and a bit besides in case you want something special. The girls are honest, but there can be pickpockets in even the best places."

This sounded reasonable to Anthony, so he handed over his money, his documents, watch and fountain pen. Then by the dim light from a lamp flickering in the stairwell, he climbed to the second floor and knocked on the right-hand door. An old woman in a housecoat and shawl opened it for him. Four other women of a similar age were listening to the radio and playing cards round a table with a brazier underneath. The Englishman said he wanted to see Toñina. The old woman looked surprised, but said nothing and disappeared behind a curtain. She returned immediately with a skinny, very pretty young girl, whom they must have been hiding because she was underage. The girl took Anthony by the hand and led him into a tiny room containing a camp bed and washbasin. He emerged a few minutes later, well satisfied. He paid and then went back down the stairs, but when he reached the courtyard his friend had vanished. He was not out in the street either, and everywhere seemed to be locked up for the night, so Anthony hastened back to his hotel and went to bed. As he switched off the light it occurred to him he might have been duped, but he was so exhausted he closed his eyes and went straight to sleep.

7

Opening the shutters the next morning, Anthony was confronted by a murky sky and roofs damp from a fine drizzle. He suddenly remembered the Spanish word for this kind of weather: *calabobos*, literally "idiot-soaker", and felt it applied directly to him. His hangover from the excesses of the previous night did not prevent him from appreciating the drama of his situation. His physical discomfort combined with his anxiety to make him feel sick. He could have done with a solid breakfast and a strong coffee, but knew this was impossible because he did not have a penny, and without a passport could not go to a bank. There was nothing else for it but to turn to the British Embassy for help, however embarrassed he might be at appearing before a disdainful official like the most gullible of tourists.

Trying to shelter from the rain under eaves, Anthony walked down Calle Prado. He wondered how best he could present himself at the embassy when he had no documents proving his identity. If anyone there knew about his work on Spanish Golden Age painting, he would only need give his name; if not, he would have to turn to his friends in the Foreign Office. This made him rather uneasy, as his best friend at the Foreign Office was a former companion at Cambridge who was currently married to Catherine – the woman with whom he had been having an affair in recent years, who, if she had received his letter, was quite likely to have reacted furiously, perhaps even confessing to her betrayal. In either case, it did not seem a good idea to use his friend's name. Moreover, the reason for Anthony Whitelands' presence in Madrid was supposed to demand a maximum of discretion. He wondered whether in fact the nature of his business there did not impose strict professional silence, meaning that he should not even get in touch with his country's diplomatic service. But how could he resolve his desperate situation without the embassy's aid? The only alternative would be to tell the Duke of La Igualada everything, and beg for his protection. Which of course meant that in the eyes of the duke and his family he would lose all respectability and credibility. His face went from white to pink as he imagined Paquita's expression when she heard of his exploits. Everything was conspiring against him.

He had reached the statue of Neptune when the rain came on hard. Not knowing where to shelter, he rushed over to the steps of the Prado, then bounded up to the ticket office. Because it was so early and there were few visitors, the attendant recognised him and, showing a kindness which in the midst of his despair he found quite touching, allowed him in without asking to see his credential, which had also been stolen. Now he was in the dry, and still uncertain about his best course of action, he let his feet take him to the Velázquez room once again. He wanted to look at the "Fable of Arachne", but came to an abrupt halt as he passed in front of the portrait of "Menippus", as though the eyes of this character, half philosopher, half tramp, were forcing him to stay. Anthony had always been puzzled by Velázquez's choice of this subject. In 1640 he painted two portraits, "Menippus" and "Aesop". These were intended to compete for the King's favour with two other very similar portraits by Pedro Paul Rubens, who was in Madrid at that time. Rubens painted Democritus and Heraclitus, two universally famous Greek philosophers. By contrast, Velázquez chose two minor figures, one of them almost unknown. Aesop was a writer of fables, Menippus a cynic philosopher of whom nothing certain has come down to our day, apart from what Lucian of Samosata and Diogenes Laertius tell us. According to them, Menippus was born a slave. He joined the sect of the cynics, made a lot of money by dubious means, and lost all he had at Thebes. Legend has it that he ascended Olympus and descended into Hades and found the same things in both places: corruption, deceit and baseness. Velázquez paints him as a gaunt middle-aged man still full of energy, dressed in rags and without a home or possessions; his only resources are his intelligence and his serenity in the face of adversity. Aesop, his pictorial partner, is depicted holding a thick book in his right hand, in which his famous if humble fables are doubtless written. Menippus also has a book, but it lies open on the ground with a torn page, as though everything he has written is of little importance. What can Velázquez have meant by choosing this evanescent character, who was always setting off without any idea of a goal, apart from his constant, repeated disillusion? In those years Velázquez was the exact opposite: a young painter in search of recognition as an artist and, above all, social advancement. Perhaps he painted Menippus as a reminder to himself, so that he would not forget that at the end of the climb to the pinnacle of fame all that awaits us is not glory but disenchantment.

Inspired by this thought, Anthony rushed out of the room and the museum, determined to resolve his problems in the most practical way possible. The rain had stopped, and the sun was peeping through the clouds. Without hesitation, he made for the Duke of La Igualada's mansion. At the Cibeles statue he had to move out of the way of a sizeable group of workmen in caps and aprons who, to judge by the rolled-up posters and banners some of them were carrying, were going to a march or meeting. Thanks to his lofty stature, Anthony could see a gaggle of blue-shirted young men watching the scene defiantly from the Gran Vía. The workmen scowled back at them. Recalling what had happened the previous night in the tavern, Anthony resolved to avoid any possible confrontations and to return to London as quickly as possible once he had settled his business in Madrid. At the same time, the sensation of violence and danger gave him a shiver of excitement that was highly unusual for a man like him, accustomed as he was to considering himself as methodical, prudent and faint-hearted. When she had said goodbye, Paquita had told him that at moments of great uncertainty, when chance becomes the arbiter of life and death, people behaved with a special intensity. He now understood what she had meant, and wondered whether that beautiful, enigmatic young woman had said it to encourage him to let himself be carried away by his impulses, without stopping to think of the immediate or future consequences.

Reaching the mansion, he knocked on the door with renewed determination. As on the previous occasion, the unlikely-looking butler opened it, let him into the hall, and went to tell the duke he was there. His lordship appeared at once, and greeted the Englishman in the affectionate, natural tone of someone receiving a friend he has seen quite recently.

"Today I will not waste your time," he promised, then said to the butler: "Julián, please inform master Guillermo. We will be in my study." He turned to Anthony. "I want my son to be present, and I am only sorry that my other son is unable to take part too. I have a traditional view of my inheritance. I have never considered that my estates or possessions truly belonged to me, but that they were part of a chain of ownership in which each generation was merely a link. As such, those who benefit from this inheritance need to do their best to preserve it, build it up as much as possible and, when the moment arrives, pass it on to the next generation. Considered in this light, wealth becomes a duty, and the satisfactions it offers are balanced by a feeling of responsibility which robs them of a great deal of their attraction. I am not saying I envy the poor: the happy man who according to legend went shirtless would never have survived our Madrid winter. I am telling you all this for you to understand the anguish I feel at being about to dispose of an important part of my property."

While the duke was talking, they had reached the study where he had outlined his fears during their previous meeting. This time a dozen paintings were lined up against one of the walls.

"My son will not be long," said the nobleman.

Anthony understood that the women in the household would play no part in the decisions taken. This disturbed him slightly, because in his experience women were more down to earth when it came to putting a price on art, possibly because a secret lack of family pride allowed them to accept the compromise needed between the aesthetic value of a work, its sentimental value and its worth on the market.

Guillermo del Valle's sudden entrance interrupted Anthony's thoughts. Greeting each other coldly, both of them turned towards the head of the family.

"Let's get on with it," said the duke with the false cheerfulness of someone about to be operated on. "As you see, Whitelands my friend, in order to help your assessment, we have brought together the works most likely to fit the bill, as I understand it. They are all medium-sized and on decorative themes, and most of them are signed and authenticated. Please be so good as to glance at them and give us your first impressions."

Wiping his glasses on his handkerchief, Anthony Whitelands went over to the pictures. The duke and his heir remained quietly at a discreet distance, but their barely concealed anticipation prevented him from carrying out an objective examination of the paintings. He did not wish in any way to dash the hopes of this noble family in distress, to whom he already felt linked for a variety of reasons, but a first glance was enough for him to realise he would not be able to offer them anything more than kind words. Although his mind was already made up, he paused for a while in front of each painting so as to dismiss the remote possibility that it might be a forgery, judge the quality of the brushwork and examine how well preserved was the paint. All of this only served to confirm his first opinion. In the end, he decided to confront things head on, because he too felt increasingly uneasy, not only at the impossibility of fulfilling the expectations held of him, but because the idea that he had undertaken a useless journey that was proving to be full of difficulties and probably real dangers made him increasingly angry with himself: he should never have listened to a charlatan of the likes of Pedro Teacher.

When he turned towards his host, his face must have betrayed something of these emotions, because before he could open his mouth, the duke exclaimed:

"Do they seem so worthless to you?"

"Oh. No. Not at all. The paintings make a fine collection. And each canvas has its own merits, I'm sure of that. My reservations . . . my reservations are of a different order. I am no specialist in Spanish painting of the nineteenth century, but what little I do know leads me to believe that perhaps this was not the most outstanding period in your country's art. Of course that's unfair, because nothing can compare with Velázquez or Goya . . . but that's how things are: outside of Spain important figures such as Madrazo, Dario de Regoyos, Eugenio Lucas and many more are eclipsed by the great figures of the past. Possibly Fortuny, or Sorolla and . . . not much else . . ."

"Yes, yes, I understand what you are saying, Whitelands my friend," said the duke, gently interrupting him, "and I completely agree, but even so – do you think these works could find a buyer in England? And if that is the case, how much might such a sale raise? I'm not asking you for a precise sum, of course, just a rough idea."

Antony cleared his throat before muttering:

"Sincerely, your grace, I have no idea, and I don't think anyone would be able to judge that beforehand. I don't know who could be interested in this kind of painting outside Spain. In my opinion, the best thing to do would be to hand the paintings over to an auction house such as Christie's or Sotheby's. But that, given the situation . . ."

The Duke of La Igualada waved his hand in the air in a benevolent gesture.

"Don't force yourself, my friend. I thank you for your discretion, but I think I have understood what you are trying to say. This is not how we are going to manage to raise capital." When the Englishman said nothing, he gave a sad smile and added: "No matter. God will provide. Believe me, I am only sorry to have made you waste your valuable time for nothing – although of course your work will be properly rewarded. And I warn you – I won't hear of any refusal. Friendship should never affect what has been agreed, especially where money is involved. You English have made this rule into a positive dogma, and that is what has placed you at the summit of the civilised world. But we'll have a chance to philosophise some other time. Let's put aside this disagreeable business and go and see if our aperitifs are ready. Naturally, we're counting on you to share our modest meal with us again."

Anthony had not been expecting this invitation, and when he heard it he felt as though the heavens had opened for him, not just because it would give him the opportunity to see the enchanting Paquita again, but also because he had eaten nothing all day and was on the point of passing out. Before he could accept, however, he caught a look of annoyance on Guillermo del Valle's face. It was obvious that the young heir felt offended by a foreigner's negative judgment not merely of his legitimate inheritance but of a symbol of the dignity of the family name.

"Papa," he heard him murmur, "may I remind you that today we have a guest."

Casting his son a glance that was a mixture of disapproval and affection, the duke said:

"I know that, Guillermo, I know that."

Much to his regret, Anthony felt compelled to butt in:

"I would not in any way wish to . . . and in fact, I have a prior engagement . . ."

"Don't lie, Mr Whitelands," replied the duke, "and if you must lie, don't so it so badly. And don't pay my son any attention. I am still the one who decides which guests should sit at my table. It is true that today we have a guest, but he is someone we trust, a good friend of the family. Besides, I am sure he will be delighted to meet you, and it will be interesting for you to meet him. So that's that."

He pulled on the bell cord. When the butler appeared, he told him: "Julián, this gentleman will be staying to lunch. And see to it that these paintings are put back as carefully as possible. On second thoughts, I had better supervise that. Guillermo, look after our friend, will you?"

When the duke left the study there was a tense silence. To save the situation, Anthony decided to tackle the subject head on.

"I'm sorry to have disappointed you," he said.

Guillermo shot him a hostile glance.

"You're right in supposing you've disappointed me," he said, "but not in the way you think. I have never had any intention of leaving the country. On the contrary: this is the moment for us to stay at our posts and take up our weapons. We cannot leave Spain in the hands of the rabble. I would have liked to have seen my mother and sisters safe and sound, though. My father too perhaps: he's an old man and, despite himself, a hindrance. Now my family has become a double reason for concern. Firstly on their own account, and secondly because when the time comes they will try to stop me. They think I'm a child, even though I'm already eighteen. Now, if I stay, everyone will think it is not out of choice, but due to a lack of means. That idea mortifies me. Not being Spanish, you wouldn't understand."

After he had got this off his chest the young heir seemed relieved, as if he had rid himself of a great weight.

8

As they approached the music room, the sound of the piano reached their ears, together with Paquita's unmistakable husky voice as she sang a cheerful ballad:

> Rider with your tall plumèd hat
> Where are you going so merrily?

Anthony paused outside the door, and so did his two companions. The Englishman felt increasingly stirred as he heard a chirrup and then:

> The paths that lead to glory
> Are to be trodden warily.

But the passionate listener's enchantment was immediately cut short by a baritone voice that sang the reply:

> Fair maid watering her pot of basil,
> How many stems does your plant have?
> I think it's more than a hundred
> Like the feathers in my hat.

His lordship the Duke of La Igualada opened the door and interrupted the singing. Lilí was seated at the piano. Standing beside it was her elder sister, wearing the same green dress Anthony had seen her in for the first time at the bottom of the garden. Next to her stood a dark, good-looking man of thirty years or so. He had manly features, big, intelligent eyes, a high forehead, black hair and the Spanish aristocracy's easy assurance. The two singers had fallen silent when the others

67

came in, but were still gazing into each other's eyes, lips parted, as if they were caught up in the gallant complicity of their duet. This was only for an instant, until they reacted and turned to look towards the door. The Englishman's gaze briefly met that of the handsome stranger. Before the two men could engage in a duel of looks, Anthony noticed the duchess curled up on the sofa. He went across to pay his respects to the lady of the house, and she held out her hand, saying:

"Praise be to God, Antoñito, we had missed you."

Anthony was unsure whether these words were affectionate or mocking: he thought that perhaps the duchess was put out to see him there again so soon. No great expert in the art of repartee, he lapsed into an embarrassed silence. Luckily for him, Lilí came to his rescue by spontaneously throwing herself into his arms. The duke chided her:

"Alba María, put your favourite Protestant down and behave like a proper young lady." With that he turned to Anthony, and said jovially: "Forgive my ill-behaved daughter, Mr Whitelands, and allow me to present the good friend I mentioned to you just now."

Freed from his innocent admirer, Anthony found himself forced to postpone greeting Paquita and concentrate his attention on the handsome stranger. The duke made the formal introduction:

"In addition to being held in high esteem by my family, the Marquis of Estella is a man of many and varied interests. I am convinced you will have plenty to talk about. Mr Whitelands is a renowned expert in Spanish painting who is visiting Madrid. He has been so kind as to glance at a few works here in order to value them. The Marquis of Estella," he explained, "is aware of our intentions."

The marquis relieved any incipient tension with a hearty handshake and a frank, wholehearted smile.

"My friends here cannot praise you enough," he said. "I'm delighted to meet you."

"The pleasure is mine," replied Anthony, won over despite himself by the man's easy charm.

The butler offered them glasses of sherry on a silver tray.

"Don't be fooled by his manners," the duke observed slyly. "The marquis and I belong to two different generations and apparently to two opposite worlds. I am a dyed-in-the-wool monarchist, whereas he is a revolutionary who would turn the country upside down given half the chance."

"Not a bit of it, Don Alvaro," laughed the other man.

"It was not meant as a reproach," the duke replied. "Age makes conservatives of us all. Youth is radical. Take our friend Whitelands here. Despite all his English phlegm, he is an iconoclast. He would throw everything that isn't Velázquez onto the bonfire, is that not so?"

Taken on an empty stomach, the thick, pungent wine clouded Anthony's mind and left him tongue-tied.

"I said nothing of the sort," he protested. "Every work of art has to be valued on its own terms."

Saying this, he cast an involuntary sideways glance at Paquita, and flushed. The young woman mischievously increased his embarrassment.

"Mr Whitelands is torn between cold erudition and unbridled passion."

The good-looking marquis came nobly to his aid.

"That's only natural. There can be no true conviction without passion. Feeling is the basis and support of profound ideas. In my view, we should be pleased and thankful that an Englishman has given his heart to someone as Spanish as Velázquez. Do tell us about your passion for the painter and how it came about, Mr Whitelands."

"I wouldn't want to bore you with my stories," Anthony protested.

"Oh my boy," the duchess interrupted with her sharp wit, "in this house all we ever hear are arguments about hunting, bullfighting and politics. If I haven't died of boredom already, nothing will kill me now. Tell us straight out whatever you please."

"There's nothing passionate about my story. I'm a researcher, a university teacher. I prefer hidden facts to loud appreciation. The disputes with my colleagues are more like solicitors' letters than political pamphlets."

"That attitude hardly chimes in with a painter as dramatic as Velázquez."

"Oh, forgive me if I disagree. There is nothing dramatic about Velázquez. Caravaggio is dramatic; El Greco is dramatic. By contrast, Velázquez is distant, serene. It's as though he paints only reluctantly: he leaves the canvases half finished, seldom chooses the theme, prefers static figures to movement; even when he does paint movement it looks static, as if frozen in time. Think of the equestrian portrait of Prince Baltasar Carlos: the horse is caught in a leap that will never end, and the figure of the prince shows no sign of the effort a horseman has to make. Velázquez himself was a cold fish. There is nothing spectacular about his life, and he was never interested in politics. Although it's hard to imagine, he spent his whole life at court without ever getting mixed up in palace intrigues. He preferred to be a bureaucrat rather than an artist, and when he finally obtained a top bureaucratic post, he all but gave up painting."

"To hear you talk," said the duke, "no-one would ever think you are describing a great universal artist, an undisputed genius."

Paquita, who until that moment had stayed at a distance and seemed not to be paying any attention, suddenly burst into the conversation.

"I think that Mr Whitelands is doing special pleading," she said.

"What do you mean?" asked Anthony.

Paquita shot him a sly, challenging glance.

"I mean that thanks to all the knowledge you've acquired in museums and libraries, you've taken Velázquez over and shaped him in your own likeness."

His lordship the duke adopted a conciliatory tone.

"Paquita, don't be so rude to our friend. Rude and impudent. Señor

Whitelands is a world authority: what he says about Velázquez is gospel, if you'll pardon the expression."

"It's one thing to read the gospel, another to lay down the law," said the young woman, her eyes still fixed on Anthony. The Englishman was so nervous he had drunk a second glass of sherry, and now the whole room and everyone in it was whirling round him. "It's true I know nothing about Velázquez, but does that mean that Mr Whitelands knows everything? I don't deny that he may know all there is to know. But a man who lived centuries ago, who spent his entire life in the labyrinth of ceremonies, pretence and dissimulation that the Spanish court must have been, and who in addition was a great artist: how can any of us be sure he did not take some secrets with him to the grave, or even that he managed to lead a double life?"

Anthony struggled to overcome his tipsiness and a bewilderment he could not attribute simply to the drink on an empty stomach. Throughout his brilliant academic career he had defended and rebutted arguments with his peers, but always about questions of detail, and always supported by the heavy artillery of an extensive bibliography. Now he was confronted by a beautiful woman attacking him on his own ground and engaging in a hand-to-hand struggle that he saw as a symbol of another more vital, more urgent battle. Something very different from academic prestige was at stake. Clearing his throat, he replied:

"Don't get me wrong. When it comes down to it, I agree far more with what you are saying than with what you suggest I was saying. We can follow Velázquez's life step by step, in even the smallest incidents. As with all the courts of the great monarchs, life in the court of Philip IV was, as you say, a den of falsehood, slander and gossip, but it was also – perhaps precisely for that reason – a rich source of official documents, strict controls, detailed information and rumours. All of this was written down. With a great deal of patience, sufficient resources and a bit of common sense, it's not hard to separate the wheat from the chaff. And yet, however much all this tells us about the everyday reality, nothing and nobody can reveal the final mystery of Velázquez the man and artist. The more I see, the more I study his works and his life, the more I realise what a profound enigma I have before me. In fact, this enigma and the conviction that I will never resolve it is what makes my work so fascinating, and lends some dignity to my life as a humble, painstaking professor."

Anthony's words gave way to a tense silence, as if there was an accusation implicit in what he had said. Fortunately the duke immediately relieved the tension in his good-humoured way:

"I told you not to take him on, Paquita."

Paquita gave the Englishman a look heavy with meaning, and said:

"You've managed to convince me for now, but our swords are still crossed."

"What if we exchange those swords for a spoon and fork?" concluded the duke, pointing towards the dining room door, which had just swung open to reveal the simple-minded maidservant and the announcement that lunch was served.

They all made their way into the dining room. On this occasion however, whether for reasons of protocol or out of spite, Paquita took the Marquis of Estella's arm. As they went in, she whispered something in his ear that no-one else was able to make out.

9

Following a brief moment's silence for the blessing, officiated on this occasion by the scowling, lugubrious Father Rodrigo, and while the maid went round offering the steaming soup tureen, the duchess expressed an interest in the valuation of the paintings. The duke declared himself moderately satisfied.

"Our friend Whitelands here has lived up to his reputation. He was neither carried away nor dismayed by what he saw, and valued them accordingly. He also said that the transaction would be no bed of roses. Correct me if I am misinterpreting you . . ."

"No, no," the Englishman quickly concurred, "it's exactly as your lordship says."

The duchess, who had only heard what she wanted to hear, clasped her hands together, raised her eyes to the heavens and exclaimed:

"Praise be to God! At last we can leave this hell behind. I've prayed for this so much to the Sacred Heart and the Holy Virgin, and my prayers were heard! And all thanks to your intervention, dear Antoñito, a Protestant no less! But even so, an instrument of divine protection. God works in wondrous ways his mysteries to perform, or the other way round. I always get those sayings mixed up. No matter: in the name of my family and myself, allow me to bless you from the bottom of my heart."

Anthony mumbled something he hoped would be taken as a show of modesty or politeness. Even though he was convinced he had acted in a proper fashion, he was feeling the pangs of a first-time traitor, and although the hearty soup was helping restore his spirits, he would gladly have sacrificed it and run from the scene of what he saw as a cruel lie. Sensing his awkwardness, the Duke of La Igualada intervened once more:

"The sad thing is that now our friend has completed his mission he will be going back to his own country, and who knows when we will see him again."

"Don't say that, Alvaro," said the duchess. "Wherever we end up, even if it's in the Americas, Antoñito will always be welcomed by us all."

Nobody seconded this expression of affection, but Anthony thought he caught a hint of sarcasm in Paquita's beautiful eyes, and real sadness in those of her younger sister. Breaking the uncomfortable silence, the Marquis of Estella, who until now had not said a word, suddenly became voluble:

"Well, I too will regret your absence, though for very selfish reasons. Like everyone from a good family in Madrid, I've been going to the Prado since I was a small child – not always willingly, I must admit. I've always preferred poetry. But a tutor used to take my brothers and sisters and myself to the museums as part of our education, although we never learnt a thing. I know next to nothing about art, although Velázquez is as familiar to me as the trees in Retiro park. When I hear you speak, I realise I have a gold mine I could exploit sitting right next to me. Nothing would give me greater pleasure than to explore it in your learned company."

Anthony was pleased at the change in direction this trivial compliment offered him, and so he said as quickly as possible:

"I would be delighted to do so, should the circumstances permit. I can see you are a man of culture, but suspect your life follows a different path. Would it be indiscreet to ask what that might be, your excellency?"

"It's no indiscretion, as my profession is a secret to no-one. I am a lawyer, but for some time now I've devoted myself to politics, partly out of family tradition, partly from personal inclination, and partly out of an almost religious sense of duty towards my country."

"The marquis," explained the duchess, "was until recently a member of parliament for Madrid."

"How interesting!" said Anthony.

"Interesting?" the marquis said doubtfully. "Possibly it is. But also completely sterile, in my opinion. It's true I was a member of parliament, but I have never believed in it or respected it. In Spain the experience of liberal democracy has been a spectacular failure. History has not prepared us for this system of government. I don't deny its merits, as long as it is what it is meant to be, rather than simply an excuse for sectarianism, demagoguery and corruption. Here it has been a failure so spectacular we can witness the consequences every day on the streets of Madrid."

Anthony nodded silently, hoping to avoid a discussion on topics about which he knew nothing and on which he thought that, as a foreigner, he had no right to express any opinion. But Paquita, as mischievous as ever, was not going to let him off the hook that easily.

"You surprise me, Mr Whitelands," she said with feigned innocence. "As an Englishman, surely you ought to defend parliamentary democracy. Or are you as sceptical about politics as Velázquez was?"

"Forgive me, Miss Paquita, but I don't think Velázquez was sceptical," Anthony replied, in all seriousness. "He was simply loyal to a king who in return rewarded him with favours and his personal friendship. In such circumstances, Velázquez's apparently accommodating attitude has nothing exceptional about it – and nor does mine regarding my own country and my king, against neither of whom have I any reason to rebel. I have to admit however that it is easy to be loyal in times of prosperity and social peace."

"You're right in what you say," the Marquis of Estella agreed. "There is a chasm between our two countries, and that's why the political system that England can allow itself has been such a failure here in Spain. Your democracy and egalitarian society are based on social relations that manage to satisfy everyone, and that is only possible thanks to the wealth pouring in from your vast colonial empire. The same could to some extent be said of France. But for those countries not fortunate enough to have this source of wealth, what use is the pantomime of elections? Aren't there more logical ways to decide the destiny of a nation? Take the case of Germany, or Italy . . ."

"You mean you would prefer a totalitarian regime?" said Anthony in disbelief.

"No," said the marquis, "just the opposite. I'm talking about saving Spain from a totalitarianism a thousand times worse than the regimes I mentioned: Soviet totalitarianism, which is striding like a giant towards us, thanks to the connivance of a government and a parliament supposedly elected by universal suffrage."

"What you say is very extreme," said Anthony.

"We're in an extreme situation."

"So would you accept an Italian-style solution?"

"No, a Spanish one."

There was nothing tense or confrontational about their exchange, so that both of them thought this was a good point to change topics, and the rest of the meal passed in polite chitchat. When lunch was over, the marquis apologised for having to leave in a hurry, said goodbye to everyone in the family in his usual affable way, shook Anthony's hand warmly and said:

"It's been a privilege and a pleasure to have met you, Mr White-lands. Any friend of this family, which is as dear to me as my own, will always be a friend of mine. I would love to see you again, and I trust we will have the opportunity. If, however, you must return to your own country, I wish you a good journey and the best of luck. Don't forget to reflect further on what we were discussing."

Anthony stayed on at the luncheon table. Unlike the previous day, this time there was no music or animated conversation. The marquis' withdrawal had left a gap that none of the others seemed capable of filling. It was as though when he departed their illustrious guest had taken all the oxygen in the room with him, leaving a rarefied atmosphere. The duchess, who until then had seemed so pleased at the thought that she would soon be leaving the country, had fallen into a melancholy silence, as if she were already experiencing the sad fate of an exile. The duke's mind was elsewhere. His son Guillermo, who seemed both nervous and irritated, left after a few minutes, muttering an incomprehensible excuse. The two girls also seemed downhearted. From time to time Lilí shot fleeting languid glances at the Englishman, while Paquita could not hide a look of intense preoccupation. Anthony imagined she probably felt a love for the good-looking marquis that was not requited. There was nothing odd about that: the marquis was handsome, distinguished, brilliant and doubtless of a fiery nature. He would cut a swathe through Cambridge, he thought. Then, although still admitting this possibility, he told himself that what little he knew so far about those involved made any such supposition extremely uncertain. A woman of Paquita's intelligence and social standing probably had more than enough reasons to be concerned in the current situation, and none need be of a romantic nature. And in the end, he told himself, what do I care? This time tomorrow I'll be on the train, en route to Hendaye, and I will never see these people again. But however true and reasonable these thoughts were, they left Anthony feeling thoroughly depressed. Once back in the safety and comfort of his London home, how would he assess a journey marked by professional failure and the realisation of his own stupidity? What opinion had they gained of him, especially Paquita? And, above all, what would they think of him when they learned that his judgment of the paintings would not help save the family? Like a doctor diagnosing a serious illness who knows that through no fault of his own he cannot expect any sympathy from the patient, Anthony had no illusions about Paquita's feelings towards him in the unlikely event that they met again. Bah, he told himself. When it comes down to it, why do I care what that woman thinks of me, even if I find her attractive? It was absurd to speculate on what he felt for Paquita at the very moment when he had just put an end to his relationship with Catherine. By now not only the best but the only reasonable solution was to leave this house as quickly as possible, wind up his ridiculous Madrid adventure, and try to forget what had happened. Let the Spaniards sort it out among themselves as best they could, he thought; even if they end up killing each other, once the storm has passed Velázquez will still be there waiting for me.

Determined to end the situation and his speculation, Anthony began his farewells. He thought they would be prolonged, but they proved very brief. Only the duchess kept his hands between her own fingers, chilly despite the warmth of the room, and murmured:

"If we don't meet again in Madrid, we'll expect you on the Côte d'Azur. That's where we'll be until all this has blown over, isn't it, Alvaro?"

His lordship the duke nodded gravely. Paquita stretched out her hand, and Lilí planted a moist kiss on his cheek. The duke offered to accompany him to the front door.

"Come and see me early tomorrow and we can settle up. No, don't say anything. A deal is a deal. You have done your job well and I always keep my word. I especially thank you for your discretion: I know the English do not like white lies."

Anthony walked away from the mansion wearily and with a heavy heart. If he had had any money, he would have caught the first train back to England. But that was impossible. He was penniless and he had no documents. He cursed himself a thousand times for his stupidity. Then, realising this was getting him nowhere, he resolved to do all he could to recover his wallet and papers. If, as seemed likely from his methods, the person who had taken them was a professional criminal, he probably plied his trade within a limited area, where he knew the streets and those who lived in them. Night had fallen, and the taverns were beginning to fill up. Although he knew he was unlikely to find him in the same place again, Anthony decided to start his search in the bullfighting bar where he had run into the thief as a result of the brawl started by the Falange youngsters.

Anthony did not discover him there or in any other of the countless establishments he visited. Determined to carry out his search methodically, he went in wherever he saw there were people. The customers in a number of bars looked distinguished; in others they were mainly office workers, and in a few they were frankly sinister-looking; most, however, had a varied and democratic clientele. They were all deafeningly noisy, and there was a constant toing and froing of an incredible assortment of wines and plates of food. Everyone seemed to be predicting an imminent outbreak of violence. Anthony had no reason to doubt the accuracy of these predictions, but until the tragedy actually occurred, the people of Madrid seemed determined to enjoy themselves.

This was the only conclusion Anthony was able to draw from his lengthy tour of the city's nightspots. Trying to visit as many places as possible, but having no money to buy anything, each time he went into a new bar he headed straight for the manager, a waiter or one of the customers and asked them if they knew anyone fitting the description of the person who had robbed him the night before. His brusque manner, his accent and the fact that he could not pay meant he had no luck whatsoever. His questions aroused suspicion, and in some cases open hostility. On more than one occasion he was forced to beat a prudent, if not humiliating, retreat. In the end, he decided to return to his hotel.

On his way back, he resolved to make one last attempt, and turned his steps towards the scene of the crime. It did not take long for him to find the crumbling gateway, where he clapped his hands and waited for the nightwatchman to appear. When he came staggering into view, Anthony asked him:

"Do you remember me?"

"From when?"

"From last night."

"What happened last night that was so important?"

"Nothing. Open the gate, will you?"

The same blowsy old woman seemed pleasantly surprised to see Anthony again. There could not have been many such assiduous clients. Her attitude led Anthony to dismiss any idea that she might be in league with the pickpocket. Ushering him in, she closed the door, and before he could say anything shouted down the dark corridor.

"Toñina my girl, come here quickly. Your beau is back!" Then, turning to Anthony, she said, "She won't be long, sir. She must be doing herself up. The poor thing is crazy about you, anyone can see that. You've no idea how much she likes Catalans. Toñina, for Chrissake, get a move on! And put on that black petticoat the salesman from Sabadel in Catalonia gave you!"

"But I'm not Catalan," Anthony explained. "I'm English."

"Heavens! I'm so sorry. What with your strange accent and the fact that you didn't leave a tip . . . But here's the little darling. By Jesus, isn't she beautiful?"

In his sober, crestfallen state, Anthony noticed for the first time the starving gleam in the young girl's eyes.

"I'm sorry, but I haven't come for what you are expecting," he said.

He embarked on a confused explanation of what had happened, doing his best to reassure the two women as to his intentions. He in no way suspected the inhabitants of this distinguished dwelling, nor did he have any thought of going to the authorities. He simply found himself in a fix, being a foreigner with no papers, and wished to enquire if they knew the individual who had fleeced him. As was to be expected, his words did nothing to reassure the two women. They swore they knew nothing about the person in question, and the older woman insisted it was a strict house rule never to ask questions or to remember faces. Anthony thanked them and took his leave. Before he could get out of the door, the woman said:

"If you've got no coin, you won't have eaten."

"No, that's true."

"Well, here we give nothing away for free, but who can deny a fellow human being a bit of bread? Even if they are English. Is it true that in your country the men wear skirts?"

"In Scotland, and only when there are celebrations."

"Aha, I can imagine what kind of celebrations they are," she laughed.

A few moments later Toñina came back with an earthenware bowl full of greasy soup, a wooden spoon and a glass of water. As he ate, Anthony Whitelands could not help recalling Velázquez's painting "Christ in the House of Martha and Mary".

10

Early the next morning, relying on his fellow countrymen's reputation for hard work, Anthony Whitelands headed for the British Embassy on Paseo de Recoletos. When an employee stopped him at the entrance and asked to see his papers, he explained it was precisely because he had lost them that he was there. The man hesitated. Could he not prove he was a subject of the Crown? Then unfortunately he would not be allowed in. Irritated that his appearance and unmistakable Oxbridge accent were insufficient, Anthony demanded to see the ambassador in person, or at the very least one of the senior diplomats. The attendant told him to wait in the entrance hall while he went to consult on the matter.

The man left. In a room next to the entrance hall, Anthony saw a smartly dressed old lady doing her knitting. Seeing him looking at her, the woman gave a faint nod of greeting. While the two of them were exchanging pleasantries about the weather, the attendant came back. With a haughty chill in his voice, as if this interloper had led to him being reprimanded, he told Anthony to follow him. They climbed a wide, carpeted staircase up to the first floor, then walked down a short corridor. The attendant knocked on a door and, without waiting for a reply, opened it and stood to one side.

Anthony found himself in a medium-sized office lined with bookshelves filled with legal tomes, a heavy desk and some upholstered chairs. A young man got up from the desk and greeted him with a show of enthusiasm.

"Harry Parker, counsellor at the embassy," he said, extending a limp hand to his compatriot. "What can I do for you?"

He looked meek, but his apathetic air and a certain vague look of apprehension in his eyes suggested the unease of an official who only feels secure when everything follows a clear, well-established pattern. Although he was still fresh-cheeked, it was not hard to see the thinning hair and bulging waistline that the future held in store for him. On one corner of the desk stood a framed photograph of Harry Parker shaking hands with Neville Chamberlain. That and a photograph on the wall of His Majesty Edward VIII were the only clues in the room as to the nature of its occupant.

"Delighted to meet you. My name is . . ."

"Anthony Whitelands," the young diplomat cut in hastily. "And you've lost your wallet. An awkward situation, truly awkward. The fact is, we were expecting you yesterday, as soon as we learned what had happened. I wonder how you managed to get through the whole day without a penny. Remarkable. Luckily, all's well that ends well, isn't it?"

As he spoke, he rummaged in one of the desk drawers. Eventually he pulled out Anthony's wallet, his passport, watch and fountain pen, and handed them to him.

"Please check everything is there. Naturally that would not be necessary between the two of us, but the embassy signed a receipt and we need your countersignature. If you are in agreement, of course."

Recovering from his astonishment, Anthony examined the contents of the wallet, saw that nothing was missing and told Parker so. Then he asked how all his things came to be there.

"Oh, nothing simpler," said the youthful diplomat. "Yesterday morning a fellow with Spanish nationality came here and handed them over. According to him, you yourself had given them him for safe keeping when you went into a brothel. He said he was waiting for you out in the cold for a long while, but seeing that you did not reappear and he was frozen stiff, he decided to go back home, at some distance from the centre, and return everything to you the next day. It was only when he arrived that he realised he did not know where you were staying. Not knowing what to do, it occurred to him to bring them to the embassy, because he was sure you would come here sooner or later. Of course, we ourselves would have got in touch with you straightaway if we had been informed of which hotel you were staying in."

"Goodness," exclaimed Anthony, "I'd never have imagined this was how things would turn out. And did this person leave his name and address? I'd like to give him my thanks and reward him for his honesty."

"His name is on the receipt: Higinio Zamora Zamorano, but not his address. I seem to remember he mentioned somewhere by the name of Navalcarnero; could that be right?"

"Yes, it's a village quite a way from Madrid. I don't think my benefactor can live there. Perhaps he used to, or possibly that's where he is officially registered. However that may be, I don't see how I can get in touch with him, because now I've got my wallet and passport back and there is nothing keeping me in Madrid, I intend to return to England today if possible. If I'm not mistaken, there's a train that leaves at half past one this afternoon. If I hurry, I could be in Hendaye tonight."

Anthony had taken this decision hastily and almost without thinking, but the young diplomat agreed as if he had been counting on it.

"Of course," he said, "with the way things are in Spain at the moment, it's not wise to prolong your stay without good reason. And while we're on the subject, could I enquire as to the reason for your being in Madrid, Mr Whitelands?"

"Private business. I came to see friends."

"I understand. Of course, it's none of my affair. Absolutely. I wish you a pleasant journey. Just one question, if you don't mind. Do you know someone called Pedro Teacher? I can spell the surname if you like."

"There's no need. Pedro Teacher is an art dealer in London. I'm an art expert and as a consequence it's natural I should know Mr Teacher by name. Is there anything else you'd like to know?"

Harry Parker looked out of the window framing the blue, cloudless sky. He shrugged as though considering the matter at an end and then, still staring out of the window, he said:

"Everything leads me to believe, Mr Whitelands, that you know this country well. That being the case, you cannot fail to have recognised the dangerous situation in which Spain finds itself. I'm sure I do not need to tell you either how concerned His Majesty's government is about the possible outcome of events, inasmuch as they could have serious consequences for the whole continent. This concern particularly affects our embassy. Firstly, because of the repercussions for the safety of the many subjects of the Crown who reside in or are visiting Spain; and secondly, because of the effect on both our strategic and economic interests. Naturally, these grave matters are the domain of our ambassador and the different attachés. I am responsible for less important but still significant issues. And in my area I need to stay informed, don't you agree?"

Turning back from the window, he fixed his still-innocent eyes on Anthony.

"It's no secret," he went on, "that in these uncertain times many families are trying to safeguard their possessions in case they find themselves forced to leave the country. Which of course is completely natural. Completely natural. But precisely in such uncertain times, His Majesty's government is anxious to avoid any possible friction over anything to do with contraband, if you follow me. I can tell you in confidence that some time ago we were informed that Pedro Teacher, as you know a Mayfair art dealer, had been sounding out . . . Of course, no-one is calling Mr Teacher's honour into question. However, Mr Teacher is not . . . how shall I put it? He is not one hundred per cent English. Nothing wrong in that either: no-one can choose their origins. I was simply referring to – you know – divided loyalties . . . moral dilemmas, if we could call them that. It's true that moral dilemmas are not part of my brief either. You've just told me you are an art expert . . ."

"Listen, Mr . . ."

"Parker. Harry Parker."

"Mr Parker, I give you my word as a gentleman that I am not involved in any dealing in artworks in Madrid, and still less in illegal dealing in paintings."

"Oh, of course," said the young diplomat, a look of alarm on his face, "of course. I didn't mean to suggest anything of the kind. One thinks, you know – yes, one sometimes thinks that the boundary between what's legal and what's . . . slightly illegal is far from clear. That's just a hypothesis, mind. It doesn't apply to you, of course, especially if you didn't come to Madrid to make any deals, legal or illegal. Did you say you were returning to England today?"

"If I don't run into any obstacles."

"There's no reason you should. Spanish trains may not be punctual, clean or comfortable, but they work quite well when there are no strikes or sabotage. In any case, if for whatever reason you decide to stay on in Madrid, I should be obliged if you kept me up to date. Here's my card. Harry Parker. The telephone number is the embassy here; you can call at any time of the day or night. There is always someone on duty, and that person will get in touch with me. Don't hesitate to call at any time, Mr Whitelands."

As he left the embassy, Anthony heaved a deep sigh of relief. All his problems had been resolved in an instant. He had been able to conceal the reason for his trip without breaking his promise, since strictly speaking he had not taken part in any transaction, and since he once again had his passport and money, he could go back to England without the need to accept the fee that the duke had so gallantly offered him. Leaving Madrid without seeing the duke's welcoming family again made him feel sad, but above all he felt relieved. He mentally gave thanks to the exemplary honesty of that humble representative of the Spanish people (whose name he had already forgotten) who could have made money without the slightest risk, but had preferred to return all of Anthony's belongings, and who had proved sufficiently intelligent to think of going to the embassy, taking the trouble to go in person without any thought of reward.

It was a cold morning; people walked by quickly, hands in pockets, caps pulled down and their coat lapels turned up. The snowy peaks of the Sierra de Guadarrama stood out clearly on the horizon. It was half past ten: he had more than enough time to return to the hotel, pack his things and go to Atocha station to catch the train.

When he reached the hotel, he told the receptionist he was leaving the room. The man noted this down in his register, then gave him his key and a letter.

"This came for you a short while ago."

The envelope was sealed, and there was no indication of who the sender was.

"Who brought it? The same man who came yesterday asking for me?"

"No. This was a young, swarthy type; he could have been a gypsy. He didn't give his name or say much else, just that I was to hand the letter directly to you when I saw you. That it was important. That's all."

"Alright then," said Anthony, stuffing the letter into his pocket. "I'm going to pack my bags. Prepare my bill, would you: I've no time to lose."

With that he went up to his room. Placing his suitcase on the bed, he opened the wardrobe door to survey his few belongings. Before starting to transfer them to his case, he went over to the window, took the letter out of his pocket and opened it. Inside was a sheet of paper with large, educated female handwriting on it. The letter read as follows:

Dear Anthony,

I know that my father and you have agreed to meet this morning, but the noble character I have been able to discern in you during our brief acquaintance leads me to fear you will decide not to come. Please don't do that: it's absolutely necessary I see you again. Necessary for me, and, if my instinct and my reason do not deceive me, for you too.

This is the pressing motive that leads me to write to you. Our butler, whom you already know, will bring it to you, although he has no idea what it contains, or even who wrote it. If he sees you, don't read it in his presence or ask him anything. Tear up the letter as soon as you have read it.

When you come to the house, don't use the front door. Follow the wall into the small side street until you come to a narrow iron door that gives onto the garden. At exactly twelve o'clock, knock three times and I will open it for you. When you come, make sure you are not followed or seen. I will explain the reason for these precautions in good time.

Your ever-trusting friend,

PAQUITA

Anthony read the letter a second time, but still did not fully understand it. Even so, despite the fact that it ruined all his plans, he could not ignore such an urgent appeal. He went down to reception and announced he would be staying another day. Scratching out his previous note, the receptionist changed the date in the register without a word. This immediately aroused Anthony's suspicions: the caution advised in the letter had left him feeling extremely nervous.

He went back up to his room, put the suitcase away and closed the wardrobe. It was eleven. He had more than enough time to keep the appointment, but he was far too much on edge to stay indoors, and so he left the hotel. Realising he had not eaten breakfast, he had a beer and a plate of squid in a bar in Plaza Santa Ana. Then he set off for the mansion by a very roundabout route. By the time he entered the side street running alongside the duke's mansion he was certain he had not been followed, or had managed to throw any possible pursuer off track. Once he was in the street it was easy to find the small iron door described in the letter. Tapping on it with his knuckles, he heard the metal reverberate dully. At once a key turned in the antiquated lock and the door creaked open. Anthony stepped inside and it was quickly closed behind him. He found himself confronted by a female figure protected from the cold and prying eyes by a voluminous hunting cape; her face was hidden by a shawl. Through its folds Anthony could glimpse a bright glint of adventure deep in Paquita's eyes. He saw a rosary wrapped around the knuckles of the hand grasping the huge key, as if it were a talisman.

"Don't worry," he said, "no-one followed me."

"Ssshhh!" Paquita whispered, raising a finger to her lips.

Taking his hand, she led him gently but swiftly along the garden path to the house. Anthony had only caught glimpses of the garden from the mansion windows. Seen from ground level, it seemed much bigger and more mysterious. The wet earth where next year's plants were hibernating gave off a melancholy smell. Moss-covered stone benches peeped out between dry myrtle and skeletal rose bushes. Through the bare tree branches he could see the pale golden sun reflected in the mansion's windows. A dog was barking in a nearby garden. They came to a halt outside an arched doorway. Paquita opened it, revealing a dark passageway. Before going in, on a sudden impulse, she flung her arms round him. Anthony felt her burning cheek on his, and her freezing lips brushed against him. "My life is in your hands," he thought he heard her say above the whistling wind. What on earth did she mean by that? A fleeting idea, the last vestige of common sense, raced through his mind: by now I ought to be boarding the train for Hendaye. This sobering thought won out over his outlandish fantasies, and he told himself he should keep all his wits about him while he watched how this extraordinary situation developed. Still clutching his hand and not allowing him any further opportunity for thought, Paquita set off down the passageway. As the door closed behind them, they were engulfed in darkness until their eyes became accustomed to the dim light from a bare bulb hanging from the ceiling. The passageway was cold and dank. Before long they reached another door, which the young woman opened with brisk, determined movements. She went in, and Anthony followed her. He found himself in a large basement crammed with antique furniture, chests, bundles of different sizes covered in blankets and several spectral statues. When Paquita said and did nothing, he asked:

"Where are we? Why have you brought me here?"

A deep male voice answered from a dark corner of the room:

"Don't be afraid, Mr Whitelands, you're among friends."

As he said this, none other than His Excellency the Duke of La Igualada appeared from among the heaps of furniture. He was wearing a thick dressing gown and a green velvet cap with a tassel. Seeing him, the Englishman was stunned: the emotions Paquita's behaviour had aroused in him had led him to forget the reason for his presence in the mansion.

"I'm very grateful to you for coming," the duke went on. "I thought perhaps your pride might lead you to refuse us. And as for the secrecy surrounding our meeting, let us say that we have erred on the side of caution. It is important no-one should know of your presence here, and above all, of what we are about to discuss. You will also have to excuse me for how uncomfortable it is down here. And now, if you allow me, and without further ado, I'll give you the explanations we most certainly owe you. If you are patient enough to listen to them, you will understand and forgive such melodramatic behaviour. First and foremost, Whitelands my friend, I must ask you a thousand pardons for the deception I have deliberately inflicted on you until now. I have had to struggle against my natural openness to put on an act for you, and harder still against my sense of decency, in the knowledge that in so doing I was abusing your confidence and sense of fair play. My remorse is only assuaged by the thought that in the end you will receive a moral reward as great as the affront I have committed."

The duke came over to his perplexed guest. Putting a hand on his shoulder, he continued in a lower, more confidential tone:

"Although I am no expert when it comes to works of art, I am not so stupid or presumptuous as to imagine that the paintings I showed you yesterday could have any great value on a foreign market. I would never have asked such an authority as yourself to come and assess the modest collection of a simple art-lover. Don't be offended if I tell you that I had you visit us twice and share in our family life simply in order to observe you. All the references I had for you were excellent, and I had no reason to doubt your honesty, but the nature of our business requires a trust that can only arise from personal contact. It goes without saying that the results of my observation have not only been satisfactory, but have gone far beyond my most optimistic expectations. I now know you to be an intelligent, upright and level-headed person; I would not hesitate to put my life and that of my family in your hands. And in all truth, that is what I am doing."

He choked, as if mentioning the danger closing in round his loved ones stole his breath from him. Although he kept casting fearful sideways glances, it was plain he was almost enjoying the situation.

"No-one in my family has any idea of what I am now telling you. Except for Paquita here, of course: she has great discernment and courage for a woman. All the others think that everything that has happened since your arrival, including the white lie about the possible value of the paintings (which they will soon be disabused of), is the simple truth. I am trying not merely to shield them from any unfortunate consequences, but to do something more important still: if, as I suspect, we are being spied upon, whoever is doing so will reach the same conclusions as my family and as you must have done until now. Having said all that, Whitelands my friend, I will show you the painting that is the reason for your visit to Madrid. No-one knows of its existence and, out of the same sense of caution I expressed earlier, I cannot show it to you outside this basement, where I know there is not enough light. I will bring another lamp in due course. For the moment, you will have to make do with a single wretched bulb. There was no way I could postpone this conversation any longer, or neglect to show you the object of all the subterfuge and mystification."

Falling silent, the duke did not wait for Anthony to reply, but went over to the far side of the room. The Englishman followed him, more confused than when he had heard his host's explanation. Paquita, who had not said a word, walked across beside him, head lowered and with an enigmatic smile on her lips.

Leaning against an old mirrored wardrobe was a medium-sized rectangular object covered in a thick brown blanket. The Duke of La Igualada carefully started to unwrap it, until a remarkable canvas was fully revealed to Anthony's incredulous eyes.

11

Anthony scrawled a telephone number on a page of his notebook and asked the operator at the Ritz to put him through. Because he was speaking a hasty jumble of English and Spanish he had to repeat his request several times. He had gone into the hotel not only to make the call, but also in search of the protection that the calm, impersonal luxury of the hotel seemed to offer. For a brief moment, he felt sheltered from the real world. In order to calm his spirits and sort out his ideas, he made for the bar and ordered a whisky. Once he had drunk it, he sensed the turmoil die down inside him, but was still no clearer as to the direction he should take in these unprecedented circumstances. A second whisky did nothing to resolve his doubts, but made him even more determined to take the risk. Accustomed to the eccentricities of some of the members of the hotel's select clientele, the telephone operator dialled the number, waited a few moments, then pointed him towards a booth. Anthony shut the door behind him, lifted the receiver, and when he heard the secretary's weary voice, said:

"I'd like to speak to Mr Parker. My name is . . ."

"Stay on the line," the secretary cut in, suddenly wide awake.

A few seconds later, he heard Harry Parker's voice:

"Is that you?"

"Yes . . ."

"Don't say your name. Where are you calling from?"

"From the Ritz Hotel, opposite the Prado."

"I know where it is. Have you been drinking?"

"A couple of whiskies. Is it that obvious?"

"Not at all. Have another one while I'm on my way. And don't talk to anyone, is that clear? Not to anyone. I'll be there in under ten minutes."

Anthony went back to the bar and ordered another whisky. He felt pleased and yet somehow sorry that he had made the telephone call. He had just finished his drink when he saw Harry Parker come into the bar. Before greeting his compatriot, Parker left his hat, coat, scarf and gloves on the back of an armchair and called a waiter. When the man came over, he slipped a banknote into his hand and told him:

"Bring me a glass of port and another whisky for this gentleman. My name is Parker – like the fountain pens. If anyone asks for me, come and tell me in person, without calling out my name. I don't want my name called out loud for any reason. Is that clear?"

The waiter stuffed the banknote into his pocket, nodded briefly, and moved off. The young British diplomat turned to speak to Anthony:

"Everybody here keeps an eye on everyone else: Germans, French, Japanese, Ottomans. It's a joke, of course. Luckily, a tip solves any problem perfectly well. When I first arrived I found it hard to understand, but now it seems to me a wonderful system: it allows the Spaniards to keep wages low, while at the same time making social hierarchies plain. Workers earn half what they should, and have to thank their employers for the other half: that way their subordinate position is reinforced. Anyway, what can I do for you? If I remember rightly, the last time we met you were about to take the train back to London. What made you change your plans?"

Anthony hesitated before answering:

"Something happened . . . I don't know if I did the right thing by calling you."

"That we will never know. What would have happened if we had behaved differently, eh? That's an unanswerable conundrum. For the moment, all we can be sure of is that you did telephone me, and here I am. Take your time, and tell me from the beginning why you called."

The waiter brought their drinks. Once he had moved away again, Anthony said:

"I won't ask for your word as a gentleman that everything I'm about to tell you should remain a secret. But I would like to beg you to treat our meeting in the strictest confidence. I'm not turning to you in your capacity as a qualified diplomat, but as a compatriot, and as someone capable of understanding the utmost importance of the matter. I'd also like to add," he said after a moment's pause, "that I was not lying this morning when I said I wasn't involved in any commercial transactions. To tell you the truth, I was asked to come here to advise on the sale of a collection of paintings, but the operation fell through before it had even started."

"What was the name of the person who contacted you? What nationality is he?"

"Oh, Mr Parker, you know I can't reveal that person's identity. It's a professional secret."

The diplomat took a sip of his port, closed his eyes, and murmured:

"I can accept that. Go on."

"The reason I was invited to Madrid was as you suggested: to help sell paintings outside Spain in order to deposit money abroad so that the person in question and all his family could go into exile if the political situation here demands it."

"But you just said that the operation never even got started."

"That's right. At first I myself advised against the sale of the paintings, not so much for legal reasons as because I thought there was only a remote possibility of them finding a buyer in any country in Europe or America. At midday today though, things changed . . . in a radical manner."

"In a radical manner?" the young diplomat said sceptically. "What does 'in a radical manner' mean?"

Before replying, Anthony cleared his throat and stared intently at his whisky glass. He was on the verge of making the most important revelation of his life, and was sorry he was having to do it to a person he did not know, someone who clearly lacked the necessary finesse to appreciate the magnitude of what he was about to say, and in very different surroundings to those he had imagined for his moment of glory.

"It involves a Velázquez," he said finally, with a lengthy sigh.

"Oh, indeed," replied Harry Parker, without showing the slightest enthusiasm.

"Not only that," Anthony went on, discouraged, "but it's a Velázquez that hasn't been catalogued, one that was totally unknown until now. No-one knows of its existence apart from its owners, and now you and me."

"Does that make it more valuable?"

"Of course, much more valuable. And not just from an economic point of view – because there's more. Are you an art expert, Mr Parker?"

"No, I'm not, but you are: tell me everything I need to know."

"I'll try to explain the essential as briefly as possible. Everything is known about Velázquez's public life: he was born and brought up in Seville, came to Madrid as a young man and was appointed the court painter by Philip IV. He died of natural causes aged sixty-one. He never took part in any palace intrigues; never had any problems with the Inquisition. All this, as I said, relates to his professional life. By contrast, little is known of his private life, although it appears there is not much to know. He was married in Seville at nineteen to the daughter of his master, and had two daughters; his marriage was exemplary, and there is no evidence of any dalliances. If Velázquez had gone astray in this or any other way, his rivals – those who envied his fame and privileges – would have quickly broadcast the fact in order to undermine him. In addition, unlike many other painters of his kind, Velázquez never painted his wife, or used her as a model. Not even at the start of his career, when he painted everyday scenes using people around him. He visited Italy twice: the first time he was away for a year; the second, almost three. He did not take his wife with him, nor has any correspondence between them been found. Velázquez was a good-looking man with many advantages, and, as is plain from 'The Toilet of Venus' in our National Gallery, he had an eye for female beauty."

Anthony paused to make sure the other man was following his explanation, but Parker had half closed his eyes and appeared to have dozed off.

"I say," Anthony exclaimed in astonishment, "aren't you interested in what I'm telling you?"

"Oh, yes, yes, forgive me. I've just remembered some business I have to attend to tomorrow, tomorrow morning . . . you know how it is, work and all that . . . but I'm listening, I'm listening. What did you say about the National Gallery?"

"Don't talk nonsense, Parker. I'm describing Diego de Silva Velázquez's private life to you. "

"Look here, Whitelands, have you really made me leave my home in such a great hurry at an inconvenient time in the depths of winter, simply to suggest that perhaps Velázquez was not the perfect husband his biographers claim? I have to admit that we diplomats never disdain the secrets of the bedchamber, but honestly, I can't see what interest there can be in the womanising of some good-for-nothing who kicked the bucket three hundred years ago."

Carefully placing his glass of whisky on the table, Anthony White-lands straightened in his seat.

"I find your attitude deplorable, Parker," he protested. "I will not allow you to be so scornful about my knowledge, or to question my assertions – and least of all, to call someone like Velázquez a 'good-for-nothing'."

"What assertions?"

"My assertions as to the importance of the painting. Look here: what I saw a few hours ago is not only an authentic Velázquez of the highest quality, which by itself would be a sensational discovery, but it is an extraordinary addition to the history of painting in general. I'll give an example to help you understand. Imagine that one fine day a Shakespeare manuscript falls into your hands: a work comparable in quality to *Othello* or *Romeo and Juliet*. One which in addition contains biographical elements that can resolve the enigmas surrounding the Bard's life? Would that be of interest to you, Mr Parker?"

The young diplomat, who had sat through this diatribe gazing at the floor, raised his eyes and peered round the room. Then, still without looking at Anthony, he replied:

"Mr Whitelands, what does or does not interest me is irrelevant. I have not left the comfort of my home to acquire new interests. I'm here to discover what you are interested in. And don't be so sensitive or hot-headed, if you don't want to tell everyone what they should not be hearing. For the love of God, even a child could see I'm merely putting you to the test. If you lose your calm, you don't stand a chance. And now, if you can turn your thoughts away from your beloved painter for a few moments, tell me what it is you want from me in all this."

Anthony paused to try to clarify his thoughts. The bar had started to go round and round to the rhythm of the music. He would gladly have given in to this pleasant sensation, but knew he had to express himself as clearly as possible in such a delicate matter.

"Look, there's someone, a curator at the National Gallery. His name is Edwin Garrigaw; from a good family, highly respectable; he was my tutor at Cambridge, and by now must be getting on in years. At Cambridge he was known as Violet or something similar, but if you tell anyone that, I'll deny I ever said it . . . Well, this gentleman, Edwin or Violet or whatever, is an expert in Spanish painting: Velázquez, Murillo, Ribera, that sort of thing. This means that in the past we have clashed on several occasions – though not personally, of course: articles in specialist reviews; an exchange of letters to *The Times*. Our arguments were always polite, although occasionally he was both sarcastic and mocking, because he doesn't like me. I suspect he thinks I would like his job, and I won't deny that a few years ago the idea did occur to me

. . . but it's not about that now. In the end, I don't like him much either: if you want my opinion, I think he's a snobbish old fuddy-duddy, and yet I have to admit he knows his stuff, and so I . . . I've written him a letter . . ."

Taking a bulky envelope out of the inside pocket of his jacket, he made as if to hand it over to his companion. At the last moment however he drew back and stared at it. Tears started to brim in his eyes.

"For goodness' sake, Whitelands, get a grip," muttered the diplomat when he saw the other man's sudden outburst of emotion. "Your attitude is embarrassing. Would you care for another whisky?"

He signalled to the waiter, who, correctly interpreting his gesture, went to bring them another glass of whisky as quickly as possible. By the time it arrived, Anthony had recovered his composure, and was wiping his glasses on a handkerchief.

"I'm sorry, Parker," he said, his voice still shaky. "It was . . . it was just a moment's weakness . . . I'm alright now. The letter," he went on, sipping his drink, "the letter is addressed to Edwin Garrigaw, and is only to be handed to him if something should happen to me. You understand, I'm sure. I'm giving it you on that condition. If I should . . . if anything should happen to me, if unforeseen circumstances prevent me . . . I'm referring to the Velázquez. It is not to stay hidden any longer for any reason whatsoever; the world has to know of its existence, and by hook or by crook it must end up in England. Edwin will know how to do that. And if he can't, then make sure they dig up Lord Nelson or Sir Francis Drake, because we have to have that blasted painting at any cost – do you understand, Parker? At any cost. That painting is worth more than all the Rio Tinto mines. Have you got it, Parker? Have you understood the nature and importance of your mission?"

"Yes, my good man. It's not complicated. I have to give this letter to a chap in London."

"But only if something happens to me, right? Otherwise, definitely not. And if, for whatever reason, you have to give Violet the letter, don't forget to tell him I was the one who discovered the painting and verified its authenticity. Don't allow him to keep the painting and the glory all for himself. If something should happen to me . . . then at least, Parker, at least I'll be remembered with dignity . . ."

"Don't worry, Whitelands," the young diplomat cut in hastily, seeing tears well up again in his companion's eyes. "Your letter is in good hands. And let's hope I never have to deliver it. But now, tell me, what are you thinking of doing?"

"The letter . . ."

"Yes, yes, the letter; if something calamitous should happen to you; I've got all that. But for the moment you are still alive, and nothing will happen to you if you don't go sticking your nose in where it's not wanted. That's why I'm asking: what are you thinking of doing now? About the painting, I mean."

Anthony stared at the counsellor blankly, as if the question were completely absurd. After a while he drew his hand across his face and said:

"Do? I . . . I don't know. I haven't thought about it yet."

"I follow you. Anyway, what you do is none of my business. But, since you called me and have put your trust in me, I think it is my duty to return that trust with a word of friendly advice."

"Oh, I know what you're going to say. But I'd prefer not to hear it. Don't be offended, Parker. You're a good man, and I'm really grateful for your coming out like this. In fact . . . in fact you're the only friend I have in the world . . ."

Seeing his emotional compatriot about to burst into tears again, the young British diplomat gently picked up the letter from the table and slipped it into his pocket. He got to his feet and said:

"If that's the case, Whitelands, I'll give you my advice anyway. Go back to your hotel and sleep it off. You'll see everything more clearly in the morning, and tonight it's best if you don't talk to anyone else."

12
~

With the weaving but ceremonious gait of the decidedly tipsy, Anthony Whitelands was making his way back to his hotel along the cold, deserted streets of a wintry Madrid when he heard a voice calling him. An individual looking like a beggar and wearing an old-fashioned broad-brimmed hat fell in step alongside him. He seemed so like a figure who had just stepped out of a painting that Anthony thought he must be hallucinating, and so carried on walking without saying a word or even looking in the other man's direction, until his unlikely companion took him by the arm and halted him beneath the cone of light from a street lamp. He said in a reproachful voice:

"Don't tell me you don't recognise me? Take a good look: it's Higinio Zamora Zamorano. I'm the one who looked after your wallet the other night."

As he spoke, he raised the brim on his hat so that his scrawny features were lit by the street lamp. Finally realising who he was, Anthony gave a start and exclaimed:

"Gracious me, Don Higinio, you must forgive me. The street lighting isn't very good, and I seem to have left my glasses in the Ritz."

"No, my friend, you're wearing them. And don't call me Don Higinio: simple Higinio is quite enough. Are you feeling alright?"

"Oh yes, perfectly fine. And I'm really glad about this chance encounter of ours, because it gives me the opportunity to thank you. I've tried without success to discover where you live, so that I could offer you a reward for taking my things to the embassy."

Higinio Zamora Zamorano swept his hat off in an extravagant gesture, replaced it, and said:

"I wouldn't hear of it. But tell me, where are you headed at this time of night, in such a merry mood? If you don't mind telling me, of course."

Anthony pointed up the street and said resignedly:

"Back to my hotel, to sleep it off."

"Aha . . . is it far?"

"No. If I haven't lost all sense of direction, it's somewhere along there."

Squeezing his arm again, Higinio Zamora said:

"Well, if I were you, I wouldn't go that way. I've just come from there, and I heard people shouting and running. The C.N.T. union members and the Falangists are fighting a pitched battle. We'd do better to wait for the storm to pass. Listen, why don't we go for a while to the place I took you to the other night? Doña Justa is bound to still be up, and we can always wake the young girl, if necessary. At least there we'll be out of the cold and the ruckus, and we can have a few glasses of rum to warm us up. What about it? The night is young."

The Englishman shrugged.

"Well," he said, "the truth is I didn't really want to go back to the hotel. Have you ever been told how much you look like the Menippus painted by Velázquez?"

"Never," replied the other man. "Come on, we can make a detour avoiding the main streets: that's where the fighting is."

Although even by straining his hearing Anthony could not make out any of the sounds of battle his companion had warned him of, he let himself be led along by the arm, unwilling to see such an extraordinary day come to an end. They walked arm in arm across the Plazoleta Vaquilla – empty now, but so busy in summer with its second-hand dealers under their parasols – and plunged into a maze of dark, twisting side streets. Soon, Anthony was completely lost. This made him understand how little he knew Madrid, despite having spent relatively long periods of time there. He felt doubly foreign now, and this sensation gave him a feeling of deep melancholy mixed with the thrill of the unknown. His mood swung uncontrollably between infantile enthusiasm and a sadness bordering on despair. He was so stunned at both extremes that he would have let himself be led anywhere. But Higinio Zamora Zamorano only wanted to take him where he had promised, and after many twists and turns they once again found themselves outside the tumbledown old gateway. He clapped his hands furiously until the watchman appeared, wrapped up in his cape, dragging his feet and shivering with cold. Beneath his cap his eyes were rimmed with red, and a sticky drip hung from the end of his nose.

They went up to the second floor and rang the bell. After some time, they heard shuffling footsteps, and the owner appeared, dressed in a felt housecoat, slippers and mittens. When she saw the Englishman, she stood with her hands on her hips and said gruffly:

"My, my, don't you 'ave anywhere else to go in Madrid? This is no time to come visiting, for heaven's sake! And if you've got nothin' to eat, get back to your own country, or to Gibralta' – it must be worth somethin' for your lot to steal it from us."

Anthony bowed, but only succeeded in banging his head against the doorframe.

"You misinterpret my intentions, Doña Justa," he muttered, recalling the name Higinio Zamora had mentioned a short while earlier. "I'm not poor as I was the other night, and I've not come for my bowl of gruel. I recovered my wallet with all the money in it, thanks to the honesty of my friend, who is here at my invitation."

It was only then that Justa noticed Higinio Zamaro. Her attitude softened.

"Why didn't you say so to begin with? Higinio's friends are always welcome in this house. But come in, don't keep yoursels standin' out on the landing, or you'll catch your death. Tonight's real brass monkey weather. Although ourselves is makin' do with a brazier at the table 'ere."

The two men went into the small reception room Anthony was

familiar with from his previous visits. On the round table, an oil lamp shed a dim light on a half-empty bottle, two glasses and a plate covered in crumbs. An old woman with a dry, wrinkled face was sitting at the table. She was so slight and wore so many layers of clothing it was hard to tell her apart from the cushions and coarse blankets strewn around the room to conceal the battered furniture. In the silence of the night the only sounds were a dripping tap and a cat mewling out in the shared courtyard. Higinio hung his coat and hat on a stand, then helped the Englishman off with his things. They went over to get warm round the brazier under the tablecloth, while Doña Justa fetched another two glasses from the sideboard and poured a drink for the new arrivals.

"I'll go and wake the girl up," she announced.

"Oh, no, don't bother her if she's sleeping," murmured Anthony in a faint voice. "Not on my behalf . . . I didn't come here to . . ."

Higinio came to his friend's rescue:

"Forget it, Justa. We just came to pass the time: there's been shooting again on the streets."

"Damnation politics!" the woman grunted, coming over to the table and addressing the Englishman. "Before, we had students who came 'ere. They were very noisy and didn't have much coin, but it was something. Now though they prefer to go and beat people up, or get beaten up themsels, if not somethin' worse. The long and the short of it is that what with the freezing weather and all the disturbances, we never see a soul 'ere anymore. The country is going to the dogs, damn an' blast Don Niceto and Ortega y Gasset."

"They're not to blame, woman," Higinio insisted. To change the topic of conversation, he turned to the old woman and, raising his voice as loud as he could, asked after her health. She seemed to come back to life, and opened her toothless mouth as if she was about to say something. Almost immediately however, she closed it again, and dozed off once more.

"You'll have to forgive 'er," Justa said to Anthony. "Doña Agapita lives all alone next door, and at 'er age she's a bit out of it. She's as deaf as a post, half-blind, hasn't got a penny or anyone to look after 'er. When it gets so cold I ask 'er in, because she doesn't even have a brazier to keep 'er warm in 'er place."

Anthony looked pityingly at the frail old woman. As though realising that for an instant she had become the centre of attention, she suddenly squawked:

"*Churros*, rum and lemonaaade!"

"What was the shooting about?" asked Justa, ignoring her neighbour.

"Who knows!" said Higinio. Turning to Anthony, he explained: "In Spain things have been going badly for centuries, but in the last few months it's become a madhouse. The Falangists are scrapping with the socialists, the socialists with the Falangists, the anarchists and, every now and again, amongst themselves. And they all insist they're going to lead the revolution. Fat chance. To stage a revolution, either on the right or on the left, the first thing you have to do is take things seriously: unity and discipline."

Taking a sip of his drink, Anthony felt as if his throat was on fire. He coughed and said:

"It's better not to have a revolution, even if it's only through not being serious enough."

"There won't be any revolution," Higinio said. "What there will be is a coup. Led by the military – that's as clear as the nose on your face. The only thing we don't know is when: tonight, tomorrow or in three months; time will tell."

"Well," said Justa, "perhaps the military can sort things out. We can't go on as we are."

"Don't talk nonsense, Justa," replied Higinio in a very serious tone. "If there is a military coup, all hell will break loose. The whole country will take up arms to defend what is theirs."

Sweeping her arm disdainfully around the room and its occupants, Justa said:

"To defend wha'? This filth?"

Downing the rest of his drink, Higinio put the glass back on the table with a thump.

"To defend freedom, damnit!"

"*Churros*, rum and lemonaaade!" Doña Agapita roared, woken up by their argument.

Justa burst out laughing and filled their glasses again. A bell chimed twice in a nearby convent.

"Don't listen to 'im," she said to the Englishman. "To hear 'im talk, you'd think he loved violence, but deep down he's a little lamb. And he's kindness itself."

"Don't start, Justa. Those stories don't interest strangers."

"They interest me," Justa insisted, "and we're in my 'ome. So keep your trap shut."

Ignoring Higinio's reproaches, and interrupted every now and again by the senile cackling of her ancient neighbour, Justa launched into a long, confused story the point of which Anthony struggled to grasp. In her childhood, she said, like so many village girls lost in the hustle and bustle of the big city, she made a mistake and ended up streetwalking. One day her path crossed with that of a good-looking, honest and upright young worker who, in an act of defiance against bourgeois morality, took her off the streets and to the altar. After several years of happiness (and a few disappointments), the workman died of natural causes (or not – Anthony could not quite follow that part of the story), leaving Justa and the little girl born of their union utterly abandoned. Just as the world seemed to be collapsing around their ears, Higinio Zamora turned up out of the blue. She had never seen or heard of him before, but he said he had been a comrade-at-arms of her dead husband during the war in Morocco, where like so many young lads they had both ended up as conscripts, and where the former had saved the latter's life, or vice versa. This was why Higinio, when he got wind of the situation that the widow and daughter of his former comrade had found themselves in, had come to settle the debt or to keep the promise made on the battlefield or the night before battle, or on many other occasions throughout that ill-fated campaign.

While Justa was telling her story, Higinio smiled and shook his head, as though trying to downplay his virtues and diminish the role he had played. After all, he had only done what anyone would have done in his place, especially since at that time he earned a fairly good living as a plumber's assistant, and had no-one else to look after. His parents had died, his two brothers had emigrated to Venezuela and he had no partner, even though with his talents and earnings there was no shortage of candidates. He swore he did not belong to a trade union or political organisation but firmly believed that the proletariat had a duty to help each other. Justa hastened to explain that Higinio never asked for compensation of any sort in return for his kindness. At that moment, as though she had been listening to the tale or at least part of it, Doña Agapita woke up again and declared that there was nothing like a soldier for romance, just like a boyfriend she once had.

"I can still see him now," she said with sudden eloquence, "with his moustache and his blue and red jacket. When I met him he was serving Isabel the Second. I don't know if he was in her household regiment, he never told me. But he did serve her ladyship, that he did! A Queen's Hussar! When I hugged him his braid got caught in my flesh, and his sabre . . . his sabre . . . *churros*, rum and lemonaaade!"

Tapping her temple with a finger, and smiling more out of pity than mockery, Justa said:

"Don't pay 'er any mind. She's not all there, you know. She 'ad a kidney problem and then got hooked on morphine. Poor Agapita, if only you'd seen 'er in 'er better days! As for that boyfriend of 'ers, she 'ad one right enough, but as for serving the queen, that's fiddlesticks. They threw 'im out the Army for being a drunkard and a trouble-maker."

The drink and tiredness were taking their toll on Anthony. He could no longer follow anything that was being said, and it was a great effort to get up and ask to go to the toilet. When he had finished, he filled the washbasin with freezing water and splashed some on his face. This cleared his mind a little, but did nothing to curb his physical exhaustion. As he was drying his face on a dirty rag, he thought he heard a baby crying on the other side of a partition. He was not surprised, but when he returned to the main room he found Toñina with the others, cradling the tearful creature in her arms. She seemed more sickly-looking than on his previous visits, perhaps because she was still half-asleep. She was covered from head to toe in a rough woollen nightdress, and her feet poked out of a pair of thick men's socks. None of them bothered to explain what the baby was doing there, and Anthony had not the slightest interest in finding out. To avoid collapsing, he thrust his hands on the tabletop, making the bottle and the lamp shake violently. He announced that he was leaving, at which the child abruptly stopped crying, while the others raised their voices in unison: what was he thinking of, going out again at that time of night? That was folly! He shouldn't even consider it! They weren't going to let him! He was in no state to be walking the streets on his own! Handing the child to Justa, Toñina came up behind him and wrapped her arms round his waist.

"Stay here and get some rest," she whispered in his ear. "What's your hurry? There's nobody waiting for you at the hotel."

"The girl is right," Higinio added. "You're among friends here."

Anthony tried unsuccessfully to wriggle free from Toñina's skinny arms.

"I thank you most sincerely for your hospitality and your concern. I don't wish to seem impolite, but I have an appointment I cannot miss early tomorrow morning, and I need to sleep a few hours beforehand and to make myself presentable."

"Tha's no problem," Justa said. "You can sleep 'ere an' we'll wake you up whenever you say. You can 'ave a nice coffee an' a crust o' bread, then be on your way."

"No, no," insisted the Englishman. "You don't understand. I have to leave right now. What I have to see to . . . what I have to see to is really important. A really crucial business transaction. You are simple people and would not understand. It involves a painting . . . an incomparable painting, both because of its quality and its historical significance. It has to be got out of Spain as soon as possible . . . by whatever means. You would not . . . you would not understand . . ."

At this point, Anthony lost consciousness. When he came round he was in complete darkness, lying flat out on a hard bed and covered with a furry, smelly blanket. He could hear someone else breathing alongside him. He reached out and was relieved to feel Toñina's youthful outline. Moving his hand further, he was astonished to come into contact with the tiny shape of a baby beneath the covers too. How right Higinio is! There really is no hope for Spain, he thought, before falling fast asleep once more.

13

The shock of the freezing morning air helped Anthony find the way back to his hotel, walking uncertainly but without getting lost. His stomach was heaving, his mouth was dry and his throat was on fire: his whole body felt sluggish, and he had no clear recollection of the previous night. He was surprised not to have lost any of his belongings, not even his coat, hat or gloves. The sky was leaden and snow was in the air.

As he entered the hotel he saw a man leaning against the wall reading a newspaper. He was made even more conspicuous by the fact that he was doing so in a pair of sunglasses and with his hat and raincoat still on. On seeing the Englishman he abandoned all pretence, folded the newspaper, came up to him and said in a brisk, urgent tone:

"Are you Antonio Vitelas, by any chance?"

This approximation of his name did not upset Anthony, but something about the man's behaviour troubled him. He cast a sideways glance at the receptionist, who simply raised his eyebrows, rolled his eyes, and spread his palms, clearly signalling that he wanted nothing to do with anything not strictly related to his job. Meanwhile, without waiting for a reply to his question, the stranger had gripped Anthony's forearm and was guiding him towards the exit. He muttered:

"Be so kind as to accompany me. Captain Coscolluela, ex-infantry officer, currently attached to National Security Headquarters. If you cooperate, there is nothing to be afraid of."

He had a pronounced limp, and this gave his face a contorted, painful expression. It was plain his pride was hurt by his physical defect.

"Am I being arrested?" asked Anthony. "What am I accused of?"

"Nothing," replied the officer, still urging him forward. "You're not under arrest, and that being so, you are not charged with anything. I asked you to come with me, you're doing just that, so all's well that ends well."

"At least let me go up to my room to wash and change. I can't go anywhere like this."

"You can where we're going," the man in the raincoat declared brusquely, still gripping his arm.

Parked outside the hotel was a black car with a driver inside, its rear door open. They got in, the car sped off, and a short while later they came to a halt outside the National Security Headquarters building, situated on Calle Victor Hugo on the corner of Infantas. Anthony breathed a sigh of relief: he had been so taken aback he had not asked the man for any proof that he was, as he claimed, a policeman, and during the journey he had suddenly felt afraid that he might be being kidnapped – although he had no idea why or by whom. His anxiety lessened when they got out of the car and walked straight past the armed guards on the door, who made no attempt to stop them.

The entrance hall was dimly lit and, contrary to all expectations, was completely calm. At one end several men and a plump woman dressed in mourning and carrying a folder were whispering in a huddle. The rancid smell of stale tobacco hung in the air. Anthony and his companion crossed the hallway, but before they came to the main staircase turned and went through a side door, then up a narrow, gloomy set of stairs to the first floor. There they walked down two or three corridors before reaching the door to an office they entered without knocking. Anthony found himself in a tiny square-shaped room, scarcely big enough for the wooden filing cabinet, enormous desk and chairs, coat stand, porcelain spittoon and wire waste-paper basket it contained. A small barred window gave onto a dark courtyard. A yellowing, sagging map of Madrid was fixed to the wall with drawing pins, its middle section worn with use. The desk was strewn with heaps of documents. It also held a table lamp, an inkstand, a telephone and an unseasonable fan. Absorbed in reading one of the pieces of paper in the midst of this chaos was someone who, although his face was in darkness and at an angle, seemed strangely familiar to Anthony. He had no idea where or when, and yet he was sure he had already seen the man who had brought him in for questioning.

After a few moments when nobody moved, the engrossed reader raised his eyes from his sheet of paper, studied the Englishman carefully and said:

"Sit down."

Then he addressed the man in the raincoat, who was making to leave the room.

"Don't go, Coscolluela. Or rather, do me a favour and go and find Pilar. Tell her to come back with the dossier I've just given her. And if you would be so kind as to bring me a cup of coffee with *churros*, I'd be very grateful."

Nodding briefly, the man in the raincoat left, closing the door behind him. When it was just the two of them, and seeing that the man behind the desk was still observing him without saying a word, Anthony spoke up:

"Might I enquire as to the reason why I've been brought here, señor . . . ?"

"Marranón. Lieutenant-Colonel Gumersindo Marranón. I thought possibly you would remember me, as I do you. But I don't blame you for not doing so: remembering faces is part of my job, but not yours. If it's any help to you, we met a few days ago, on the train. You were travelling down from the border, and, so you informed me, had come from your native England. We met in Venta de Baños station and had a short but friendly chat. That was why, when I learnt by chance of where you were staying in Madrid, I went to your hotel last night to say hello and offer my services. I waited for you and in the end, since you didn't return and I was unable to leave my office a second time, I decided this morning to send one of my colleagues to ask you to come in. I myself am up to my ears in work. I consider Captain Coscolluela to be a bright, well-educated fellow. We fought alongside one another in Africa. A wounded leg meant he was dismissed from active service. A brave man: they came within a whisker of awarding him our highest award, the Laureate Cross of Saint Ferdinand, but his political ideas . . . well, you know how it is. I trust he treated you with all due respect."

"Oh yes, yes, of course," Anthony hastened to say. "Yet this . . . visit . . . although very pleasant, is in fact extremely inconvenient for me at this time. You see, I had arranged to meet some people . . ."

"Caramba, I hadn't thought of that. An oversight on my part, which I beg you to forgive. Luckily, we can sort it out at once. Use my telephone, call your friends and tell them you're going to be a bit late. They'll understand: unfortunately here in Spain we're not as strict about punctuality as in your country. And if you don't know the number, just tell me the name of the person or persons in question, and I can find it in a flash."

"No, thank you," Anthony replied hurriedly. "It wasn't really a firm appointment. I wouldn't want to put you to any trouble."

The telephone jangled on the desk. The lieutenant-colonel picked it up and put it down again without answering, never once taking his eyes off the Englishman.

"As you prefer," he said cheerfully. "Oh, here's Pilar. Pilar, let me present Mr Vitolas. He's English, but he speaks Spanish better than you and me put together."

Anthony realised that Pilar was the plump woman he had seen in the entrance hall, and that the folder appeared to be the same one as well. From this double coincidence he deduced that the pantomime he was being put through had been carefully prepared beforehand. As Pilar left the folder on her boss's desk and he untied the ribbons and started to leaf through its contents, Captain Coscolluela came in again carrying a tin tray containing a steaming bowl and a paper cornet over-flowing with greasy sugared *churros*. They all helped shift papers to make room for the tray on the desk. Then Coscolluela took off his raincoat and hat and hung them on the stand. He immediately sat down, and Pilar did the same. She took a shorthand notebook and a pencil out of her bag, as if she were going to take notes on the conversation. Once all these preparations were complete, the lieutenant-colonel stared at Anthony and said:

"I'm not sure whether Captain Coscolluela explained clearly enough that your presence here is not for any official reason. Or that your being here is entirely voluntary: to put it another way, this is simply a friendly visit. That needs to be clear from the start. There will be no record of whatever is said within these four walls," he added, as if he had not noticed the preparations made by his secretary, who in any case was sitting there with her pencil raised, but without taking any of this down. "From what I have just said," Marranón went on, "it is obvious you are perfectly entitled to leave whenever you wish to do so. And yet I would ask you to devote a few minutes of your time to us. Among friends, of course. In fact, the coffee and *churros* that Captain Coscolluela has so kindly brought are for you. As soon as I saw you come in, I said to myself: that man has had no breakfast. Tell me if I'm wrong. No, of course, that kind of thing never escapes a policeman. So don't stand on ceremony, Mr Vitelas, and dig into this modest snack right away."

Anthony's sense of dignity suggested he should refuse the offer, but he was faint from hunger and thought that the milky coffee and *churros* could help collect him his thoughts for the interrogation they seemed bound to submit him to.

"That's what I always say," exclaimed the lieutenant-colonel as he watched him tucking into the breakfast. "Nowhere in the world can you find *churros* like the ones here in Madrid."

While saying these friendly words, he had taken a single sheet out of the dossier. He now showed it to the Englishman. It was a photograph of a man giving a speech, arm raised in a dramatic gesture. Although it was not a good photograph and had not been carefully printed, Anthony immediately recognised the man he had met in the Duke of La Igualada's mansion. Fortunately his mouth was full at that moment, which gave him an excuse to disguise his confusion and delay any reply. Trying to appear calm, he took out his handkerchief, wiped the grease off his lips and fingers and said:

"Who is he?"

"Your question makes mine unnecessary, because it leads me to understand you don't know him and have never met him," said the policeman, without taking the photograph away from Anthony's eyes. "No matter; I didn't think there was any link between you and this gentleman. Sometimes though, I don't know, perhaps in a café get-together, or at mutual friends' houses . . . you know, a chance meeting . . . As far as his identity goes," he added, putting the photograph back in the dossier and closing it, "it is natural that you haven't heard of him, but I can assure you there are few Spaniards who would have to ask."

Winking at Captain Coscolluela and Pilar, he outlined a brief profile of the person in question.

He was none other than the eldest son of Miguel Primo de Rivera, an anti-constitutional general, dictator of Spain between 1923 and 1930. José Antonio Primo de Rivera y Sáenz de Heredia often used the title of Marquis of Estella in the aristocratic circles in which he moved; his supporters called him José Antonio for short, or simply The Chief. Born in Madrid, a lawyer by profession, unmarried; thirty-three years old at the present time. Stripped of his rank and cashiered from the Army for having assaulted a general in public when both were in civilian clothes. In 1933 he founded the Spanish Falange, a political party with fascist tendencies. A year later the party merged with the group led by Ramiro Ledesma Ramos known as the Assemblies of the

National Syndicalist Offensive or more usually the J.O.N.S. They have similar leanings, but are more radical in their approach. Shortly afterwards the two split up: Ramiro Ledesma pulled out, and either out of conviction or spite, launched a bitter campaign against the Falange and its Chief, accusing them of having appropriated the ideas and symbols of the J.O.N.S. This move failed dismally, because most of the J.O.N.S. activists chose to abandon their former leader and stay as part of the Falange, but the split was a difficult one, and emphasised many as yet unresolved contradictions. Later, when José María Gil Robles seemed destined to become the Spanish Mussolini, José Antonio Primo de Rivera offered the support of the Falange in carrying out the coup, but Gil Robles could never make up his mind to take the decisive step, and declined the offer. These two reversals convinced José Antonio of the need to take the Falange into battle on its own. Soon afterwards, this conviction led him to reject a possible alliance with José Calvo Sotelo, an authoritarian monarchist, brilliant orator and powerful personality who had become the champion of the most conservative elements on the Right and aimed to lead the Spanish fascist movement. Relations between the Falange and those members of the armed forces in favour of a coup were cordial but uncertain: on the one side was José Antonio's distrust of the Army, whom he blamed for having abandoned his father; on the other, the Army's suspicion of a party with a confused ideology and erratic behaviour. Violence had been part of the Spanish Falange's activities from the outset, and it had been involved in a succession of clashes with left-wing groups. In the 1933 legislative elections, Primo de Rivera had won a seat in parliament; in the 1936 elections he lost it. From then on, violent actions had been renewed, and so had reprisals against them.

"We don't know what he is up to at the moment," the lieutenant-colonel concluded, "but he has been constantly calling for armed rebellion, and it's not out of the question that he may try to stage a coup d'état."

Rubbing his hands, Marranón continued speaking:

"You will be asking yourself, Vitelas my friend," he said slowly and deliberately, "why we are telling you things which as a foreigner simply visiting our country are irrelevant to you. I would find it hard to give an adequate reply to that question. And yet from that first day when we spoke on the train, I am convinced that despite being English you have a very special affection for Spain and would not like to see her go up in flames, as it were. Am I wrong?"

"No," Anthony replied, "you're quite right. Spain is very close to my heart. Not that this means I should get mixed up in your country's affairs, especially when it comes to high-level politics. But, since that is what we are talking about, tell me something: do you really believe this Primo de Rivera fellow could carry out a coup?"

Marranón and Captain Coscolluela glanced at one another, as if each was expecting the other to take the lead in giving his view. In the end, it was the lieutenant-colonel who spoke.

"It's hard to say. He could try, of course. Would he succeed? I doubt it. Unless he has help from outside. He would not get far with the Falange alone. When it comes down to it, neither the Falange nor the J.O.N.S. amount to much. Their founders are poor little rich kids with nothing better to do; their followers a handful of students and more recently half a dozen paid gunmen. Their backing comes from a sector of old-fashioned reactionaries, and the only people who vote for them are snooty young women and daddy's boys from Puerta de Hierro. But there's no denying their organisational ability. Tell him, Coscolluela."

Captain Coscolluela cast him a sideways glance. His expression changed from submissive to authoritative as he began to explain:

"José Antonio's Falange is organised in the form of a pyramid: platoons, squadrons, phalanxes, centuries, companies and legions. The smallest unit, the platoon, consists of three men, a leader and his deputy. The largest, the legion, is made up of about four thousand men. This system gives them great flexibility in all kinds of armed combat, as guerrillas and as shock troops, and it can be adapted to any situation, apart from open battle. It's hard to know the exact number of Falangists. Everyone exaggerates, some by over-estimating, others by minimising the numbers to suit their case. Whatever the truth, there are not enough of them to be able to seize power on their own. Primo de Rivera has offered on several occasions to give his support to the Army if it – or part of it – decides to stage a coup. Naturally enough, the generals have slammed the door in his face. They will do as they wish when they consider the moment has come, and neither then, before then or afterwards do they want anything to do with an armed faction that does not recognise the military hierarchy and only obeys a leader who once punched a general and is seeking to impose his political objectives on the Army itself if they take power. Despite this, it is quite likely that if there is a conflict the Army will use the Falangists as an auxiliary force or for some of the dirtier business. The Falangists are not exactly squeamish. In short, we do not know what might happen. Beyond any logical considerations, we should not forget that José Antonio is an irresponsible fool, and that his supporters are fanatics who will do anything he asks without stopping to think. Most of them are hotheaded, romantic children. At that age they have no fear of death because they have no idea what it means. And their Chief has fried their brains with all his nonsense about heroism and sacrifice."

The lieutenant-colonel raised his hand politely.

"That's enough, Coscolluela. We mustn't bore our guest. You've given him a clear picture, and he has other things to attend to. You must excuse our over-eagerness, Mr Vitelas."

Anthony's reply was a vague murmur. After a brief silence, the lieutenant-colonel spoke again:

"When it comes down to it," he said in his usual agreeable way, "I think the same as you. I'm not interested in politics either. I don't belong to any party, union or lodge, and I have no sympathy or respect for any politician. But I am a paid servant of the state; my task is to keep public order, and in order to do that I have to keep ahead of events. I can't just sit here with my arms folded, because if the whole thing explodes, as it could well do at any moment, then, Mr Vitelas, neither the police nor the Civil Guard nor even the Army itself will be able to prevent a catastrophe. I can. But to do that, I need to know. What, who, how and when. And to act at once, without treading too carefully. To discover the conspirators and arrest them beforehand, not afterwards. And the same with their accomplices. And those covering up for them. It's not a crime to know José Primo de Rivera, but lying to the police is. I'm sure you would do no such thing. Having said that, I won't keep you any longer. I have just one request. Or rather, two requests. The first is that you keep me informed of anything you think might interest me. You are intelligent enough to grasp my meaning. My second request is that you stay where we can reach you while you are in Spain. Don't change hotels; and if you do, tell us. Captain Coscolluela here will pay you a visit from time to time, and if you should wish to contact us, as you know, we're open twenty-four hours a day."

14

Stepping out of General Security Headquarters, Anthony was surprised to find himself in a cheerful, well-known place, full of people rushing about as though spurred on by the cold. The overcast sky had taken on a metallic hue, and in the stillness that precedes intense natural phenomena, the usual hustle and bustle of the city seemed far off. However, none of this made any great impression on Anthony, who was still bewildered by his recent interview. He knew he was facing a moral dilemma, but was so perplexed he could not even work out exactly what this was. As he made his way through the crowd, he wondered why he had been arrested in such a bizarre fashion. It was obvious the police knew about his movements and connections in Madrid, but from what they had said, it was impossible to tell just how much. In all likelihood, very little, or they would not have gone about things in such a roundabout way. Perhaps they knew nothing, and were merely sounding him out. Or trying to scare him. Or to warn him: but about what? About the danger involved in any contact with José Antonio Primo de Rivera? If that was the case, they must know about his meetings with the Falange Chief in the Duke of La Igualada's mansion. Who could have informed them? As far as José Antonio himself went, he had always mistrusted that mysterious individual, even if direct contact with him had left Anthony agreeably surprised. At any rate, the important thing was not his personal impression, but the role the Falange leader might be playing in this affair. Did José Antonio know of the duke's plans? Was he in league with him? Was his apparent interest in Paquita real, or did it simply conceal other interests? And when all was said and done, what was an English expert in

Spanish painting doing mixed up in this mess? These were unanswerable questions, but ones that affected his view of what to do: he could not continue to behave as if he knew nothing. Before taking his next step, he had to clarify things so that he knew exactly where he stood. Common sense clearly indicated the most sensible course of action: to leave it all behind and return to England without delay. But that meant missing out on a once-in-a-lifetime professional opportunity. For the moment, there was nothing to suggest any direct link between the police's explanations and insinuations and the sale of a painting, the possible illegality of which was an administrative affair without any political or other kind of implication. Added to which, that illegality in no way concerned a person who had merely certified the authenticity of a work of art. What happened beyond that was none of his business, and the more Anthony uncovered, the more involved he would become in something that had nothing to do with him. He had no proof that a crime was about to be committed. He was a foreigner in a country plunged into chaos, one whose activities, in addition, were protected by professional secrecy. Far better not to dig any deeper.

Besides all this, Anthony had more pressing and prosaic concerns: he had to meet his appointment with the duke without any further delay, and to justify his late arrival so that it would not be seen as a betrayal at the very moment when the matter had reached such a decisive stage. First though he had to shave, wash and change clothes. To make matters worse, the first snowflakes had begun to fall, leaving damp black marks on the pavement.

Anthony hurried back to his hotel. He carefully wiped his shoes on the doormat in order to avoid a scolding from the receptionist who, when he saw him come in, had adopted the aggrieved expression of someone who has just seen a client of his establishment led away by the police. Anthony casually asked for the key, and asked whether anyone had enquired after him during his brief absence.

"Well now, let's see," the receptionist replied curtly. "You seem to give us more work than all the other guests put together."

Shortly after he had left, a man had telephoned the hotel asking if the English gentleman was there or had gone out. When the receptionist had replied that he was out, the man had wanted to know when he left and if he had said where he was going. The receptionist said he knew nothing: he had no wish to get a client into trouble, and still less to get mixed up in anything. However, the caller had seemed disturbed or alarmed, or perhaps both. He did not want to leave his name or a telephone number where he could be reached, as the receptionist suggested. Then, scarcely half an hour later, a very pretty young girl had appeared with a letter. The receptionist frowned as he reported this: he did not like the idea that a girl should come to the hotel with a letter for a guest, still less to have to handle the correspondence. Anthony could not think of any reasonable explanation, and so said nothing. Still scowling, the receptionist handed him the letter.

Back in his room, Anthony opened the envelope and read this short message on a sheet of notepaper:

Where did you get to? For the love of God, call 36126.

As there was no telephone in the room, Anthony went back down to reception and asked to use the public one there. The receptionist pointed to the apparatus on the counter. Anthony would have preferred something less conspicuous, but in order not to arouse any further suspicion he accepted, and dialled the number. Paquita answered at once. When Anthony identified himself, she replied in a hushed voice, as if frightened of being overheard:

"Where are you calling from?"

"I'm in the lobby of my hotel."

"We were very concerned at you being so late. Has something happened?"

"Yes, my dear sir. I'll give you the details at our next meeting," said

Anthony, trying to adopt the natural tone of a tradesman going about his business.

There was a silence, then Paquita said:

"Don't come here. Do you know the Medinaceli Christ?"

"Yes, it's a seventeenth-century Seville carving."

"I mean the church."

"I know where it is."

"Well, go there as quickly as you can and sit in one of the last pews on the right. I'll see you there as soon as possible."

"Give me half an hour to wash and change my clothes. I look like a tramp."

"All the better. That way you won't attract attention. Don't waste time on such childish nonsense," snapped the young woman, who by now had recovered her usual pertness.

Pretending not to notice the receptionist's sour expression, Anthony put the telephone down, thanked him, went up to his room once more, put on his overcoat, picked up his umbrella, came back down again, left the key on the counter and went out.

Walking down Calle Huertas he soon reached the agreed meeting point. The snow had continued to fall, and was starting to settle in the spots where people's footprints had not erased it. When he reached the pompous, unharmonious facade of the church, Anthony paused a moment to recover his breath and his calm. His heart was pounding not only because he had rushed there, but also because of the risk he was running and the fact that he was about to meet the enigmatic Marchioness of Cornellá once more. From the opposite pavement, he studied the lengthy queue of the faithful who, refusing to be intimidated by the harsh weather, had come to pray and appeal to grace. The doleful group was made up of people of all ages and every social class. Anthony grasped what a wise choice Paquita had made in having them meet there, where nothing and nobody could attract attention. Crossing the road, he instinctively went to the end of the queue to patiently wait his turn, but soon realised how inappropriate his civic concern was, and decided to slip into the church through a side door, trusting that his foreign appearance would excuse this slight transgression. In order to reach it he had to cross the atrium, which was crowded with blind and maimed people, as well as a flower-seller wrapped up in a black shawl to protect herself from the cold and snow. The laments and entreaties of these supplicants made a tuneless, mournful sound. Navigating these obstacles safely, the Englishman was relieved when he found himself inside the church itself. The flickering light from thousands of candles lit up the garishly coloured walls. Heavy with the smell of sweat, smoke, incense and melted wax, the air seemed to vibrate with the constant murmur of prayers. Anthony had no difficulty finding room on one of the agreed pews, because most of the faithful wanted to approach the altar to leave ex-votos or get as close as possible to whisper their entreaties to the venerated image. The throng in the church was a sure sign of the deep anxiety felt throughout the city.

Because of his interest in Spanish art of the period, Anthony had studied the carved statue on several occasions. It had always inspired a distaste bordering on repugnance. While there was no denying the artistic merit of the piece, the Christ's attitude, his sumptuous attire and above all his flowing real hair gave him the look of a seducer and confidence trickster. At that time Anthony had thought it was perhaps this which made the figure so popular among the common people of Madrid: God made flesh as a vulgar spiv. In his undergraduate days at Cambridge he had heard an expert explain that the Catholicism of the Counter-Reformation had been a revolt by the more sensual southern Christians against the cerebral Christianity proposed by the men of the north. In Spain this had meant a Christianity of beautiful virgins, black-eyed and with their lips open in an expression of carnal theatricality. The Christ of these believers was the Christ of the Gospels: a Mediterranean man who lives his life eating, drinking, chatting with friends and enjoying relationships with women, and dies suffering real physical torment. Someone whose ideas go from good to evil, pleasure to pain, and from life to death without any shadow of metaphysical doubt or ambiguous reasoning. It was a religion of colours and smells, brightly coloured clothing, processions, alcohol, flowers and songs. At the time, Anthony, a non-believer by nature and conviction, a positivist in terms of education and suspicious of the slightest hint of mysticism or mumbo-jumbo, had considered the explanation satisfactory but irrelevant.

Lost in these thoughts, Anthony jumped when he felt the soft touch of a gloved hand on his forearm: for an instant he thought the police were arresting him again. But no, it was a woman dressed in mourning, her face covered by a thick lace veil. She was holding a rosary of jet beads in her other hand. Even before he heard her voice, Anthony knew it was Paquita.

"Goodness, you gave me a fright," he said. "No-one would recognise you like that."

"That's the idea," replied Paquita, with a mischievous note to her voice. "And you're a bundle of nerves."

"With good reason," said the Englishman.

"Kneel down so we can bring our heads closer together," she whispered.

Bent over on their prayer stools, their heads almost touching the rail in front, they looked like a couple of devout souls fervently reciting their Hail Marys. Only too conscious of the young woman's body pressed against him, Anthony told the marchioness of his recent experience in the National Security Headquarters. Paquita listened in silence, occasionally nodding her bowed head.

"I lied to the police for no real reason," the Englishman said at the end of his account. "I broke the law on an impulse. Tell me I wasn't making a mistake."

"No, you did the right thing," Paquita said after a moment's pause, "and I thank you for it. Now," she went on slowly, as if having trouble finding the right words, "now I have to beg a huge favour of you."

"Tell me what it's about, and if it is in my power, I'll—"

"It is. But it means you making an enormous sacrifice," she replied. "That object we showed you yesterday . . ."

"The Velázquez?"

"Yes, that painting. Are you sure it's authentic?"

"Oh . . . of course I have to examine it more thoroughly, but I'd put my hand in the fire—"

"What if I told you it was a fake?" Paquita interrupted him.

Anthony had to stifle a cry of protest.

"What? Fake?" he exclaimed, keeping his voice low and containing his sense of shock. "Do you know that for a fact?"

Still with a sense of drama, but allowing a note of mockery to creep back into her words, Paquita said:

"No. I think it's authentic. But that's the favour I'm asking of you: I want you to say definitively that it's a fake."

Anthony did not know what to reply. When Paquita spoke again, she was completely serious once more.

"I can understand your astonishment and resistance. I warned you it would mean an enormous sacrifice. I've not lost my mind: there are powerful reasons for my request. Naturally enough, you want to know those reasons, and I will tell you them all in good time. But for the moment I cannot. You'll have to act simply trusting me. Of course, I can't oblige you to do this or anything else. I can only beg you, and swear in the presence of almighty God, in whose house we find ourselves, that my gratitude will be boundless, as will my wish to repay your generosity. Engrave this on your mind, Anthony Whitelands: there is *nothing* I would not do to compensate you for your sacrifice. Yesterday, in our garden, I told you my life was in your hands. I'm repeating that now, with renewed belief. No, don't say anything, just listen carefully. This is what you have to do: go to my house this afternoon and make up some excuse to my father for not keeping your appointment this morning. Whatever you do, don't tell him what you've just told me. Don't mention National Security Headquarters, and still less José Antonio. Don't say any more than that the Velázquez is a fake and is therefore worth nothing. Be convincing: my father trusts you, but he's no fool. He has no doubts about you as a person or as an expert: if you are convincing, he will believe you. And now, I'm sorry, but I have to go. No-one in my family knows I'm here, and I don't want my absence to be noticed. Stay in the church for a few minutes. There are a lot of people in here; someone might recognise me and I don't want us to be seen together. If as seems likely we meet each other at home this afternoon, behave as if you had not seen me since yesterday. And remember: I'm in your hands."

Paquita crossed herself, kissed the cross on her rosary and put it away in her bag. She stood up, then moved slowly away from him. Anthony was left in a fog of confusion.

15

Still stunned, and with an anguished look on his face not dissimilar to that of the Christ that gave the church its name, Anthony Whitelands stumbled out into the street, pushing his way through the endless flow of the faithful. Beyond the entrance to the church the snow was coming down hard, and he was soon lost in a whirling mass of heavy snowflakes so thick and white they seemed to leave the rest of the world in impenetrable darkness. This phenomenon seemed to him to reflect his state of mind, now the scene of a desperate battle. No sooner did he decide to surrender his will to Paquita's disconcerting entreaty than part of him rebelled against such a cruel imposition. There was no doubt that the daring if tacit way she had offered herself to him aroused his desire, but he thought it might be too high a price to pay. Did he have to give up on worldwide recognition just when it was within his grasp? And she had not even offered him an explanation, simply appealing to his weakness for her. It was outrageous!

The cold and snow cleared his mind, at least to the extent that he realised he could not stay out in the storm talking to himself like a madman. His mind still in a turmoil, he went into a nearby tavern, sat on a stool and ordered a glass of wine to warm himself up. The innkeeper asked if he would like something to eat.

"My mother-in-law makes tripe like . . . how can I put it? Between you and me, she doesn't have much to recommend her, but when it comes to cooking she's a goddess. Her tripe could raise the dead, and if you don't mind my saying so, you look as though you've just seen a corpse."

"You're not far wrong there," said Anthony, pleased that the other man's chatter was helping him forget his bewilderment. "I'll have the tripe. And bring me a plate of ham, some squid *a la romana* and another glass of wine."

After his lunch, Anthony felt better. He had not come to any decision, but he was no longer wracked with doubt. The snowstorm had slackened off, the wind had died down and the streets were covered in snow that crunched beneath his unsteady footsteps. He reached the hotel surrounded by silence, went up to his room, took off his coat and shoes, collapsed onto the bed and fell fast asleep.

Against every expectation, he slept for a good while without a single nightmare or moment of panic. By the time he awoke, night had fallen. Outside the window, the sky had taken on the pearly sheen of the snow. Looking out, he saw all the rooftops covered in a layer of white. Down in the street the cars and carts had dug black furrows, and slush was collecting in the kerbside gutters. Anthony washed, shaved, put on a change of clothes. He left the hotel and headed for the Duke of La Igualada's mansion. He had not thought of an excuse or resolved his terrible dilemma, simply trusting to instinct and allowing his decisions and actions to be dictated on impulse.

Anthony walked to the Castellana avoiding the busiest streets, where the effects of the snowstorm were holding up vehicles and pedestrians. These precautions did not prevent him from arriving with soaking shoes and wet, sagging trouser turn-ups.

The butler showed him in, took his coat and hat, then disappeared to announce his arrival to the master of the house. Left alone in the spacious hallway, in front of the copy of "The Death of Actaeon", Anthony's foolhardy euphoria quickly evaporated. He tried to think of a convincing excuse for not having appeared that morning, but could not come up with any. In the end he decided to say he had not been well: after the excesses of the night before and the disturbing events of that day, his appearance would back him up. Even so, he hated having to lie. In his affair with Catherine he had frequently found himself obliged to employ this kind of deceit, and this had finally poisoned the relationship and turned it into something he despised. By ending it, Anthony thought he was also leaving behind that painful but necessary servitude, yet now, after only a few days, here he was once again fabricating a lie that was not merely unnecessary but could rebound against him. The butler's return offered him some respite.

"His excellency is with another guest, and the rest of the family is out. If you would care to wait, you may accompany me to the drawing room."

Anthony found himself alone in the room where previously he had taken coffee with the family and where Paquita had enchanted him with her singing. Now the piano was closed, and there were no music sheets on the stand. Uneasy, he paced round like a man in a cell. Damp had seeped through his shoes, giving him an unpleasant sensation in his feet and ankles. The rococo clock struck six. When it went on to chime the quarter hour without anyone appearing, Anthony's nervousness became more like anxiety. Something important must be going on for the duke to keep him waiting, especially after his insistence the previous evening that he give his final verdict on the painting. When Anthony had had the good sense to refuse to give his opinion on the spot, and suggested he return the following morning to make a calmer inspection of a work that had completely dazzled him at first sight, the duke had understood and accepted the postponement, but had not hidden his impatience to conclude the matter without further delay. What could have happened in the interim to produce such a drastic change of attitude? Whatever it might be, Anthony could not spend the whole evening cooped up like this.

Stealthily opening the drawing room door, he peered out into the hallway. When he saw it was empty, he ventured down the corridor leading to the duke's study. At the door he heard voices. Thankfully, Spaniards always shout when they are talking, he thought. He recognised the duke's voice and that of his son Guillermo, but not the third speaker, and he could not make out what they were saying. As there was no chance of him discovering what they were discussing, and since he was afraid of being found out, he went back to the drawing room with the intention of calling for his coat and leaving. He was stopped at the door by the sound of a female voice.

"Anthony! No-one told me you were here. What are you doing?"

It was Lilí, the duke's youngest daughter. Anthony cleared his throat.

"Nothing. I was waiting for your father, but since he hasn't come, I was looking for a servant."

"Don't lie. There are footprints all over the house. You've been sniffing around."

By now they were both in the drawing room. Lilí shut the door behind them and sat modestly on the edge of a chair. She smoothed down her skirt and said:

"I'm really sorry my father has stood you up. It must be something serious for him to behave in such a rude manner. When I came past his study I could hear them arguing. I don't dare go in and ask, but I can keep you company."

"It will be a pleasure," the Englishman replied with a hint of irony. He was not at all pleased at the idea of spending time alone in a room with this headstrong young thing who had obviously inherited the family's ability to disconcert him.

"I can see it won't," she said, "but I don't care. I'll keep you company because I like you, Tony. Do they call you Tony in your country?"

"No, Anthony."

"A cousin of mine in Barcelona is called Toni. Tony suits you: it makes you sound nicer. Not that you aren't nice when you're called Anthony, don't get me wrong," Lilí chattered on. All of a sudden she turned serious and added: "This morning I went to your hotel to give you a letter. That man in reception is very rude."

"That's something we agree on. And thank you for taking the trouble."

Lilí fell silent. Gazing down at the floor, she said in the faintest of voices:

"Are you sweet on my sister?"

"No! My, what ideas you get! You know I have professional business with your family. That was what the letter was about, nothing more."

Raising her eyes from the floor, Lilí stared at him in anguish.

"Don't treat me like an idiot, Tony. My sister personally entrusted me with the letter, and to judge from her face and what she said, I could tell it wasn't just business."

Anthony realised he was not dealing with a girl, but a person on the verge of becoming an intelligent, sensitive young woman of disturbing beauty. Flushing despite himself, he said:

"Don't be angry. I've never thought you were an idiot. Quite the opposite. The thing is that the matter your family and I are involved in is far from simple. It does have material aspects, but also others that go beyond the strictly commercial. You must understand that I can't reveal details your own father hasn't spoken of to you. But I can assure you that there's nothing between your sister and me. Besides, what's that got to do with you?"

In reply, Lilí went slowly over to the piano, lifted the lid, and played two high notes with a finger. Still staring at the keyboard, she said:

"Before very long I'll have a title too. I'll be able to count on my share of Grandmother's inheritance. Then I'll be properly grown-up, and Paquita will be an old woman."

Snapping the piano lid shut, she laughed when she saw how bemused the Englishman looked.

"But you don't have to worry: as of now I'm still a foul-mouthed brat."

The entrance of the butler spared Anthony any further torment.

"His grace asked me to give you this," said the butler, holding out a folded note.

Unfolding it, Anthony read: "Powerful reasons prevent me from seeing you today as we agreed, and as I could wish. I will be in contact with you soon. Forgive me for any trouble caused, and with all my best wishes." The signature was a florid scrawl. Anthony folded the note up again and put it in his pocket. He asked for his coat and hat.

"You're not leaving already are you, Tony?"

"Yes. Your company is delightful, but it's obvious I'm not wanted here."

Lilí opened her mouth to say something, but closed it again almost immediately, and rushed out through the door leading to the dining room. In the hall, Anthony put on the clothes the butler proffered him, said goodbye with a curt nod of the head and stepped out into the street. The door was closed behind him with what seemed like excessive zeal. An icy wind had swept away the clouds, and stars shone brightly in the night sky. The snow had begun to freeze, making the pavement very slippery. Turning up his coat lapels and taking short, careful steps, Anthony looked around for a taxi. When he reached the end of the side street, a terrible idea brought him up short. Trying to find a reason for the duke's surprising behaviour, it suddenly occurred to him that he might have brought in another expert. Perhaps Mr Whitelands had not lived up to his expectations, though Anthony could not see what he had done wrong, either professionally or on a personal level. Of course, there might be other reasons: perhaps the strict duke had become aware of his meeting with Paquita in the church – a harmless episode that had been none of Anthony's making, but which, to judge by Lilí's question, could have given rise to a misunderstanding. Lilí herself, who made no secret of the attraction she felt for Anthony, might have given them away so as to provoke her father's wrath and put a stop to an idyll that existed only in her imagination. Not only was this a wild idea, but it presupposed in Lilí a desire to do harm that was not justified by anything he had seen so far. However, it is well known that children are by nature selfish creatures, and that their lack of experience often means they are unable to gauge the consequences of their actions. Of course, even if this were what had happened, it was absurd to think the duke would have had time to replace Anthony with someone else as highly qualified. If this was in fact what the duke had done, it was both an over-hasty and a rash act: the transaction had to take place in the utmost secrecy, and a resentful scholar is a dangerous animal.

Anthony realised that his suspicions were unfounded, childish, and even dangerous for his health: if he stayed out in the cold without moving much longer, he could become seriously ill. None of this served to allay his fears. I'm not going to budge from this spot until I find out what's going on in that house, he told himself.

Fortunately he did not have to wait long. A few minutes later, the front door to the mansion swung open. The lighted rectangle showed the silhouettes of two men saying effusive goodbyes. Against the light, and only dimly illuminated by the street lamps, Anthony found it impossible to identify them, although he took it for granted that one must be the head of the house. The other man set off on foot. Hidden on the far side of the street, Anthony let him pass by. Once he was at a safe distance, he began to follow him.

Pursued and pursuer advanced slowly over the treacherous terrain. They had only gone about twenty metres when two shadowy figures leapt out from behind the trees lining the avenue and intercepted Anthony. When he stopped, one of the strangers punched him on the jaw without warning. Although his coat lapel softened the blow, Anthony was taken by surprise. He lost his balance and fell on his back on the ice. He watched from the ground as the other man took out a revolver, flicked off the safety catch, and pointed it straight at him. No doubt about it, things were going from bad to worse for the Englishman.

16

Solemn-faced, Edwin Garrigaw (alias Violet) strides round his domains. Late in the afternoon he has received a phone call of transcendental importance, and now he is trying to stay calm by contemplating all the beauty around him. There is only a short time to go before the National Gallery closes, and there are no more visitors in the rooms, which are never crowded anyway at this time of year. Without a public, the building's heating system is insufficient, and it is cold in the spacious rooms. The elderly curator's firm footsteps echo from the lofty vaulted ceilings. The phone call ended with a strict instruction: have everything ready for when the moment comes. There was no need to specify what moment that was: Edwin Garrigaw has been desiring and fearing it for many years. Finally it seems to have arrived or to be on the verge of arriving, and he is convinced he will not have long to wait. At his age though, any change means upheaval. Absorbed in these thoughts, he has allowed his steps to take him to the galleries of Spanish painting, of which he is the undisputed master: nobody within this venerable institution questions that. Outside the gallery walls, things are different, of course. Young whippersnappers who think they have reinvented the wheel, and take him to task for everything. Nothing serious in the grand scheme of things: storms in the tiny teacup of British academe. The elderly curator is not worried on that score: however old he may be, neither his job nor his prestige are at stake.

He comes to a halt in front of one particular painting. The label reads: "Portrait of Philip IV in Brown and Silver", commonly known as "Silver Philip". The portrait depicts a young man, with noble but unattractive features, the face framed by long golden curls. His eyes have the wary, anxious look of someone who is trying to demonstrate majesty when all he feels is fear. Destiny has placed a heavy burden on weak, inexpert shoulders. Philip IV is wearing a brown doublet and breeches richly embroidered with silver: hence the painting's name and sobriquet. One gloved hand rests boldly on the pommel of a sword; in the other he holds a folded piece of paper on which the name of the artist appears: Diego de Silva Velázquez. The painter had arrived in Madrid in 1622, in the wake of his fellow countryman the Duke of Olivares, a year after Philip IV had ascended the throne. Velázquez was twenty-four, six years older than the King, and had already demonstrated great skill as an artist, although as yet with provincial overtones. As soon as he saw the works of this aspiring court painter, Philip IV, inept regarding affairs of state but not with regard to art, realised he was in the presence of genius and, paying no heed to the experts' opposition, resolved to trust his and his family's image to this lazy, audacious young man who was so insultingly modern. In so doing, he ensured his triumphal entry into history. Possibly the two men's relationship was limited by the etiquette of the Spanish court. But in the complex world of palace intrigue, the King's support for his favourite painter never wavered. They both shared decades of loneliness, when fate seemed against them. The gods had granted Philip IV all imaginable power, yet he was only interested in art. Velázquez was born with a gift, as one of the greatest painters of all time, yet all he wished for was a little power. In the end, both of them fulfilled their desires. At his death, Philip IV left a ruined country, a decaying Empire and a sick heir destined to liquidate the Hapsburg dynasty, but he bequeathed to Spain the most extraordinary art gallery in the world. Velázquez subordinated his art to his desire to get ahead at court, his ambitions sustained through talent alone. He painted little and with bad grace, only to obey and please the King, his sole aim being to win social advancement. Towards the end of his life, he was rewarded with his coat of arms.

In the same room and on the same wall, only a few metres from this magnificent painting, there is another portrait of Philip IV, also by Velázquez. This one was painted thirty years later. The first measures almost two metres by a little over one and is a full-length portrait; the second measures scarcely half a metre wide and only shows the King's head on a black background, with his doublet barely sketched in. Naturally, the features are the same in both paintings, but in the later portrait the flesh is pale and dull, the cheeks and jaw are slack, and there are bags under a pair of sad, lacklustre eyes.

Velázquez, who only painted when encouraged by others and had not the slightest appetite for work, seldom did self-portraits. As a young man, he is perhaps there as a sceptical witness to the fleeting surrender of Breda; later, in the final stages of his career, he depicts himself in "Las Meninas". In this work the Order of Santiago confirming him as a gentleman is displayed on his chest, but the image is also that of a weary man who has achieved his dream following a lifetime of struggle and disappointments and who wonders if it was all worth it.

Edwin Garrigaw is asking himself the same question. Perhaps the moment has arrived, but when he looks in the mirror (something he does every day, with obsessive frequency) he no longer sees the face of the young man who had the dream and began his patient vigil. Back then he had smooth, pink skin, his eyes were bright, his hair thick and wild, his features somewhere between childish and feminine. An emeritus professor sent him anonymous sonnets in Latin and small bouquets of violets, in honour of his nickname. Cambridge was the backdrop to his academic triumphs and amorous adventures that were only made adventurous by repeated betrayals. He wasted his youth in games of this sort; his mature years were lost in professional struggles. Now he too has sagging cheeks and wrinkled skin; his hair is going grey at the temples, and is receding dramatically but inexorably in a way no treatment can forestall. Of late he has repeatedly asked himself whether he should not try to find a stable partner to avoid a lonely old age with only mercenary palliatives, but this is nothing more than a rhetorical question. Although it is plain he will soon have to give up his post in favour of a younger man, the idea does not upset him: his work is no longer an end in itself. At most, he may add a few additional, probably pompous observations to his scant bibliography, which will immediately be challenged, if not ridiculed, by the rising generation. Not that this is of much concern to him either: previously he was afraid of being discredited; now he is terrified of becoming decrepit. In any case, he has no wish to become embroiled in a bitter, lengthy battle if it is not over something exceptional, and he doubts whether anything truly exceptional or even merely curious will come his way at this stage. The beauty he has dedicated his life to has betrayed him by not ageing alongside him. After three hundred years, "Silver Philip" is still as youthful as when he first saw it, and will go on being so when he is no longer there. What will he leave behind of his passage through these grand, empty rooms? If at least his labours were to receive some form of recognition, perhaps a title: but Sir Edwin did not exactly chime with his ideas. Possibly, Sir Violet . . .

The bell rings to signal that the gallery is about to close. The elderly curator returns to his office. He asks the secretaries if anyone has telephoned while he was out. On being told no-one has, he puts on his coat, picks up his umbrella, briefcase and bowler hat, says goodbye and leaves with that slightly mincing gait of his. He knows the way, and so is not hampered by the gloomy corridors or the dimly lit staircase. As he steps outside, he finds the city shrouded in fog. This does not surprise or bother him either. On his way to the Underground, he thinks he sees someone he knows, and pauses. The fog prevents him from identifying him properly, but also means the other person does not recognise him either. Garrigaw makes a detour: the last thing in the world he wants is to meet up with that man, whom he detests. He soon loses sight of him, and gets back on the right path, lost in thought. He is certain the man was heading for the gallery, doubtless to go and see him. Fortunately he has left earlier than usual, so the meeting cannot take place. Garrigaw is pleased at this, but it means he cannot know what on earth Pedro Teacher might want, and why he has come to see him today of all days, just when he has received the call.

At the same time, but far from there, his former student, colleague and adversary in many disputes is lying on the Castellana pavement, knocked flat by a punch and staring up at the sinister barrel of a gun. The situation is so absurd he feels indignant rather than frightened.

"I'm English!" he cries in a high-pitched lament.

Before his attackers can react to this information, a command halfway between peremptory and amused rings out.

"Let him go. He's no danger."

The attackers freeze, then respectfully withdraw as the man Anthony has been following comes over and offers him a firm hand to help him back up. Under the street light he recognises the athletic figure, noble bearing, virile looks and frank smile. He gets up and flaps at the slivers of ice and mud stuck to the folds of his coat. As he does so, he realises he is visibly trembling.

"I demand an explanation," he mutters, to disguise his sense of weakness and to recover at least a fraction of his lost dignity.

"And you shall have one," his adversary replies, a note of irony in his voice. He stares at him, and adds in a friendlier tone: "I don't know if you remember me. We met a couple of days ago in the house of our mutual friend—"

"Yes, of course, I don't have problems with my memory," the Englishman interrupts him. "The Marquis of Estella."

"José Antonio to my friends. Unfortunately, to my enemies as well. And that is the reason for this regrettable incident. I've been attacked several times, and so am obliged to have an escort. I beg you to forgive my hasty companions. They were simply being over-zealous. The sad truth is that the present situation does not leave room for courtesy. We've suffered many casualties, and the violence is on the upsurge again. Are you hurt?"

"No, I'm fine. And I accept your apology. Now, if you don't mind . . ."

"No, I won't hear of it." José Antonio silences him in a rush of friendliness. "I have to make amends, and can think of nothing better than to invite you to supper. I've seen you eat and know you won't turn your nose up at good food. This way we can get to know each other better. I'm aware that we have shared interests."

"I'd be delighted," replies Anthony, partly because he thinks it unwise to contradict people who carry weapons and are quick to use them, and also because he is intrigued by what that last sentence might mean.

"In that case, there's nothing more to discuss," says José Antonio. "But first I must drop in at our headquarters to see what news there is and to give some instructions. It's not far, and it is still early. If you don't mind accompanying me, you will have the chance to meet some worthwhile people and to see a little of how our party functions – if we are still allowed to call it a party, that is. Come on, Whitelands my friend, my car is just round the corner."

17

With the casual arrogance of someone who has centred his life on danger, José Antonio Primo de Rivera pressed his foot down on the accelerator of his small but powerful yellow Chevrolet, ignoring the patches of ice on the road. They turned off the Castellana down Calle Zurburán as far as Calle Nicasio Gallego, where the car pulled up outside Number 21. The pair of faithful bodyguards leapt out first, pistols in hand, to make sure the coast was clear. José Antonio and Anthony followed. Two men wearing leather jackets and berets on guard outside the doorway let them in after they had said the password, raising an arm and shouting "Arise, Spain!" as they did so.

The Centre, as the headquarters of the Spanish Falange and the J.O.N.S. was called, was situated in a large detached house. Until a short while earlier, it had been on a single floor of a building on Santo Domingo hill, but to the neighbours' great relief, the owner had thrown them out for not paying their rent: the movement's coffers were not exactly overflowing. Eventually the Falange had come to rest in this new location thanks to a stroke of fortune and the painful recourse to intermediaries and subletting. Even so, their position was precarious. There was nothing they could do when those in power lavished resources on silencing their voices, José Antonio had explained as they sped there. Anthony listened without comment, more worried about a possible traffic accident than any plot being hatched against the lunatic driver and his underlings. They skidded several times, and only José Antonio's skill and good luck prevented them crashing into a lamp post. Anthony was naturally phlegmatic, but saw no reason to run unnecessary risks, and was afraid he had put his physical well-being in the hands of a blithe idiot.

Despite the late hour and foul weather, the Centre was swarming with people. Most of them were smooth-cheeked adolescents. Some of them were wearing royal blue shirts with a red insignia. The same insignia, a yoke crossed vertically by a fistful of arrows, appeared in the centre of a flag with red and black stripes draped across one wall. However busy all those present were with their own tasks, as soon as they saw José Antonio come in, they all left what they were doing, stood to attention, clicked their heels and raised an arm in salute. This attitude of respect and devotion towards the Chief impressed the Englishman; although he was averse to any great show of emotion, he could not help but feel the sense of fanatical energy in the atmosphere. Glancing sideways at his companion, he could see that he was transformed the moment he crossed the threshold of the Centre. The cheerful, courteous and slightly shy aristocrat he had known and talked to in the duke's mansion had turned into a resolute leader, with an imposing aspect and resonant voice. Straight-backed, his eyes glinting and cheeks aflame, José Antonio was giving orders with the authority of someone who expected nothing less than blind obedience. As Anthony watched him, he recalled the images of Mussolini he had seen at the cinema, and wondered how much of this display was imitation or show; he also wondered whether Paquita had seen him transformed in this manner, or if she only knew his private persona. Perhaps, he thought, it is me he wants to impress, not her. If he is afraid of me as a rival, this is the best way to put me off.

But these thoughts did not completely distract him from his own situation. It had been reckless of him to come alone to a place like this, which seemed dominated by a thirst for primeval, irresponsible violence, a violence which in addition could be met with similar force from outside. He was careful not to stray far from José Antonio's side, seeing this as his only protection while he decided if he was surrounded by idealists, madmen or criminals.

A burly man of medium height and with a bulbous forehead came over. He went up to José Antonio to tell him something important, but stopped short when he saw the stranger, and frowned deeply.

"He's with me," said José Antonio, noticing his comrade's reticence. "He's English."

"Well, well," said the other man slyly as he held out his hand, "so Mosley is sending us reinforcements."

"Mr Whitelands has nothing to do with politics," José Antonio explained. "In reality, he's a great expert in Spanish painting. What did you want to tell me, Raimundo?"

"Sancho called from Seville a while ago. Nothing urgent – I'll explain later."

José Antonio turned to Anthony and said:

"Sancho Dávila is the leader of the Falange in Seville. It's always important to stay in contact with our different centres, and now more than ever. The comrade here is Raimundo Fernández Cuesta, a lawyer and a friend and companion from the start. Comrade Raimundo Fernández Cuesta was one of the Falange's founding members, and is currently our secretary-general. That man over there, who looks like me only with a moustache, is my brother Miguel. And what you see around you is the cage of the wild beast. This is where the University Union, the Press Department and the Militias are based."

"It's all very interesting," said Anthony, "and thank you for the trust you've shown by bringing me here."

"It's no such thing," said José Antonio. "For good or ill, our noto-riety means we don't have to keep secret either who we are or what we get up to. Nor even our intentions. The police have files on all of us, and doubtless there are informers within our ranks. It would be naïve to think otherwise. If you'll allow me, I'll just deal with a few bits of business and then we can go and have supper. I'm ready to die for the Fatherland, but not of hunger."

Several Falange members had come up to speak to the Chief. José

Antonio introduced them all to the Englishman, who struggled to remember their names. Although they spoke in short bursts, parodying the brusque precision of military parlance, their diction, vocabulary and attitude betrayed their elevated social origin and a considerable level of education. Those in positions of responsibility were, like José Antonio, around thirty years of age; the others were very young, probably university students. This meant that Anthony's initial concern gradually gave way to a sense of feeling at ease, especially as everyone seemed so well-disposed towards him. Possibly they thought he shared their ideology, and since it was the Chief himself who had brought him there, he felt under no obligation to disabuse them. If he was asked anything about the British Union of Fascists, he said only that he had never had the opportunity to meet Oswald Mosley personally, and to mutter vague generalities that his condition as a foreigner helped sound convincing.

After a while, José Antonio, without losing his cordial and energetic demeanour but beginning to show obvious signs of impatience, cut short the endless stream of enquiries and exhorted them all not to let up in their efforts or to lose faith in their project, which was on the verge of bearing fruit. Then he took Anthony by the arm, saying:

"Let's leave while we can or we'll never get out of here."

He raised his voice to ask his brother if he wanted to go with them. Miguel Primo de Rivera excused himself, saying he had other things to do. Anthony reflected that possibly, consciously or unconsciously, he had no wish to be seen with his elder brother, to avoid the domineering personality of the taller, better-looking and more brilliant firstborn overshadowing his own. It was natural for Miguel to be devoted to José Antonio, but also for him not to want to risk comparisons that would in all likelihood be unfavourable.

Since the invitation had been directed towards Miguel, but José Antonio seemed to be including anyone else interested, Raimundo Fernández Cuesta joined them, together with a reserved, rather gaunt individual whose round-framed glasses robbed his appearance of any possible air of nobility. Rafael Sánchez Mazas was an intellectual rather than a man of action. In spite of this, as José Antonio explained to the Englishman while they were on the way out, he had been a founding member of the Spanish Falange and was on its central committee. He was the one who had coined the phrase they had all adopted: "Arise, Spain!" Anthony took an immediate liking to him.

Together with the two bodyguards, the four of them crammed into the yellow Chevrolet and headed for a Basque restaurant called Amaya in Carrera de San Jerónimo. As they entered, the owner raised his arm to them.

"Don't pay him any attention," José Antonio joked, slipping easily into the familiar form of Spanish to address Anthony. "If that socialist Largo Caballero comes in, he'll raise his left fist. What's important is that you can eat well here."

They were served a hearty meal and as much wine as they could drink. José Antonio ate heartily and before long they were all very lively, including Anthony, more relaxed now that he was on neutral territory. He no longer felt obliged to conceal his opinions. In addition, José Antonio was friendliness itself, which meant that the other two treated him, if not exactly cordially, at least with respect. Halfway through a first course of scrambled eggs with peppers, the Chief said:

"I trust, Anthony, that when you get back to London you will report on what you have seen and heard here objectively and accurately. I know there is a lot of nonsense said about us, and we're never judged on our version of the story. In most cases, the people giving this misinformation are not doing so deliberately. The Spanish government does all it can to silence us. That means people hear their version, not ours. The government censors and seizes our publications, and if we ask permission to hold a meeting, it is systematically refused. Then, since in accordance with the democratic convictions they claim to profess they cannot deny us our constitutional right, they give us permission at the very last minute, so that we don't have a chance to organise the event, or to publicise it properly. Despite this, many people turn up, the meeting is a success, but the next day the press only publishes a short article in which the newspaper expresses its disapproval and adds three or four garbled quotes from the speeches. If, as usually happens, there is trouble, they only report the casualties the others suffered, not ours, and they invariably blame us for what has happened, as if we were the only ones looking for trouble, or as if we were encouraging the violence of which we are the main victims."

"And in these last months," Sánchez Mazas added dispiritedly, "with the party declared illegal, we can't even hope for that."

Anthony thought this over for a moment, and said:

"Well, if everyone is against you, there must be some reason for it."

His words led to a moment's stupefied silence. Sánchez Mazas' eyes widened behind his glasses, and Raimundo Fernández Cuesta's hand moved towards his pistol. Fortunately, José Antonio resolved the situation by bursting out laughing.

"Ah, the famous fair play of the English!" he cried, clapping Anthony on the shoulder. Then, turning serious once more, he added: "But there's no such thing here, my friend. They attack us because they're afraid of us. And they're afraid of us because reason and history are on our side. We are the future, and the weapons of the past are useless against the future."

"That's right," said Sánchez Mazas with cautious conviction. "If here and now, repressed and gagged as we are, we continue to grow and go from strength to strength, what would happen if they left our hands untied?"

"We would do away with the political parties in a flash," concluded Fernández Cuesta.

"Well, if you want to get rid of them," said Anthony, plucking up courage, "it's logical that the political parties try to defend themselves."

146

"You're missing the point," Sánchez Mazas retorted. "We want to get rid of the parties, not the people in them. We want an end to all that's false and obscurantist in the parliamentary system and to offer Spaniards the possibility of joining a single great common cause."

"They already have one," said Anthony.

"No," José Antonio insisted. "What exists in Spain today is not a project. It's a soulless mechanism lacking in all faith. The Liberal state does not believe in anything, not even itself. The socialists are bandits, the radicals are taking advantage, the Confederation of the Autonomous Right tries to please everyone. This means that the National Assembly, which is supposed to legislate, has degenerated into a den of the most disgusting intrigues and the most shameful deals. It's become a cheap spectacle, nothing more. With things as they are, republicans are nothing more than puppets for the unruly masses of the violent workers' organisations. The times we live in give no quarter."

As he spoke, José Antonio gradually raised his voice, and a respectful silence fell over the room. The two bodyguards kept a watchful eye on the other patrons, none of whom moved. José Antonio noticed the effect his harangue had produced, and smiled with satisfaction. Anthony was impressed by his conviction and energy. He himself had not the slightest interest in politics. In the last English elections he had voted Labour at Catherine's insistence; in the previous ones, Conservative to please his father-in-law. In neither case did he know anything about the candidates or their party manifestos. Educated in the principles of Liberalism, he considered it a good system as long as it did not show itself to be too inefficient, and felt no attraction towards any other ideology. During his years at Cambridge he had instinctively rejected the Marxist ideas so fashionable among the students. He thought Mussolini was a charlatan, although he credited him with having brought discipline to the Italian people. Hitler on the other hand inspired nothing but aversion. Not so much for his ideology, which he saw as more bluster than anything else, but because of the threat his posturing represented for Europe. Too young to be called up between 1914 and 1918, Anthony had seen the consequences of the Great War with his own eyes, and now he looked on as the nations which took part in that butchery rushed headlong towards a repetition of the same madness. Deep down, all Anthony wanted to do was to dedicate himself to his work, without any further complications than those created by his turbulent private life. Even so, he had not been able to resist José Antonio's magnetism, and if the Falange Chief was capable of provoking such a reaction in a sceptical foreigner busy tucking into a plate of stew, what might he arouse in well-disposed crowds in an atmosphere that lent itself to exalted, passionate feelings?

Before he had time to answer this question, it was José Antonio himself who eased the tension by raising his glass and saying jovially:

"Let's make a toast to the future, but let's not forget the present. It would be a crime to let these tasty dishes grow cold, and an even greater crime to bore a stranger with our domestic problems. Let's eat, drink, and talk about more pleasant things."

Rafael Sánchez Mazas followed up this proposal by asking Anthony if his knowledge of Spanish painting of the Golden Century extended to its literature. Happy to return to territory about which he felt less ignorant and insecure, the Englishman replied that, although the main object of his research and interests was in fact painting, and more precisely the work of Velázquez, he would be hard put to assess that without being aware of other manifestations of the extraordinary Spanish culture of that glorious period. After all, Velázquez was the exact contemporary of Calderón and Gracián, and there was ample proof of his contacts with literature. He had painted Góngora, and although the portrait of Quevedo could not be attributed to him, as some people had done, this mistake in itself proved that he could have done so. In the Madrid of his day, Velázquez must surely have crossed paths with Cervantes, Lope de Vega and Tirso de Molina, and the intellectual atmosphere was filled with the poetry of Saint Teresa, Saint

John of the Cross and Fray Luis de León. To show his competence in the matter, Anthony recited:

> *Del monte en la ladera,*
> *por mi mano plantado tengo un huerto,*
> *que en la primavera*
> *de bella flor cubierto*
> *ya muestra en esperanza el fruto cierto.* *

He did not do it very well, but his willingness and his obvious love for all things Spanish – and above all, his picturesque accent – meant that not only his table companions but a number of other guests and several waiters all burst into applause. So the meal ended with laughter and in an atmosphere of pleasant comradeship.

The cold night air outside refreshed and enlivened the cheerful group. When Anthony announced he was retiring, José Antonio refused to hear of such a reasonable idea. The Englishman, unable to resist the Chief's irrepressible energy, admitted defeat and squashed inside the car with the others once again.

Driving back the way they had come, they sped along Cedaceros and out into Alcalá. After passing the Cibeles fountain they parked the car and walked to the basement of the Café Lyon D'Or. José Antonio and his followers often went to a literary gathering in this small, noisy and smoke-filled room, known as the Happy Whale, where the walls were decorated with paintings of sailors. The new arrivals greeted all their friends, briefly presented the stranger they had brought with them, and then without more ado joined in the debate. José Antonio seemed at home in the midst of this din, and Anthony, who was used to this kind of Madrid reunion, soon found his own discreet but amiable place. As well as being poets, novelists or playwrights, most of

*On the side of a hill / planted by my own hand I have a garden / which shows in spring / covered in beautiful flowers / the hope of certain fruit.

those present were fervent members of the Falange, but in that relaxed atmosphere there was no respect for hierarchies when it came to giving opinions or refuting an adversary. Anthony was pleased to discover that José Antonio was more flexible in his ideological stance than his companions when it came to the cut and thrust of argument. At that moment, a play by Alejandro Casona called *Our Natacha* was all the rage. According to the patrons of the Happy Whale, its success with public and critics alike was due mainly, if not entirely, to its explicit Soviet propaganda. José Antonio admitted he had not seen the work in question, but praised *The Beached Mermaid*, an earlier play by the same author. A short time later, once more against the general view, he expressed his unreserved enthusiasm for the Charlie Chaplin film "Modern Times", despite its overtly socialist message.

And so between whiskies and heated disputes, two hours flew by. When everyone finally left, they followed the custom in Spain by lingering a long while out on the pavement giving one another farewell hugs or shouting at the tops of their voices as though they had not seen each other for ages or were saying goodbye forever. A painfully skinny woman dressed in rags came up and offered them lottery tickets. Sánchez Mazas bought a strip. As she moved on, the lottery seller smiled at him.

"If I win, the money will go to the cause."

"Don't tempt fate, Rafael," said José Antonio, tilting his head to one side.

Eventually, the group split up.

Feeling quite merry, Anthony started to walk back towards his hotel. He had gone some distance along the deserted Calle Alcalá when he heard the sound of hasty footsteps behind him. His alarm was only half relieved when he realised his pursuer was Raimundo Fernández Cuesta. Anthony felt uncomfortable in his presence – he had been taciturn all night, and now his expression was even darker.

"Are we heading in the same direction?" he asked.

"No," replied the other man, panting from the effort to catch up with the Englishman.

"What can I do for you, then?"

Before replying, the Falange secretary-general looked all around him. When he saw they were alone, he said slowly:

"I've known José Antonio since he was born. I know him as well as I know myself. There has never been and never will be another man like him."

Seeing that this ringing pronouncement was followed by a prolonged silence, Anthony thought that perhaps this was all he had to say, and was about to make some anodyne comment when the other man added in a confidential tone:

"It's obvious he feels a sincere, fraternal affection towards you. At first I could not understand why, but finally I have understood that José Antonio and you share something of great value to him, something both sublime and vital. In other circumstances, you would be rivals. But the circumstances are not normal, and his noble soul knows nothing of rancour or egotism."

He fell silent again, then after a pause added gruffly:

"My only wish is to respect his feelings and to give you some advice: don't betray the friendship he honours you with. Nothing more: goodnight and Arise, Spain!"

With that, he turned abruptly on his heel and walked off at a brisk pace. Anthony was left pondering the meaning of the strange message and the vague threat it contained. He was a woeful psychologist, but he had dedicated his life to the great masters of portraiture, and so was able to infer something from other people's facial expressions. Raimundo Fernández Cuesta did not seem to him to be behaving with the impulsiveness typical of the Falangists. Rather, he possessed a cold, calculating ideology. Anthony realised that if the Falange did turn to action, not only would they be unpredictable, but some of them would also be implacable.

18

Anthony was awakened by a distant crash, like the sound of heavy artillery. Startled, he thought something terrible must have just started. Then, when the first detonation was not followed by any further ones, he thought perhaps it had been nothing more than part of a bad dream. To drive it away, he went over to the window and flung open the shutters. It was still night, and the sky was too uniformly purple to suggest that day was dawning. There were no vehicles or people down in the square. If Madrid were burning there would be shouting everywhere, he told himself, not this ominous silence. Everything was calm, as they say it is in the eye of a storm.

Anthony crept back into bed, tired and frozen, but he was too unsettled to get back to sleep. He had left the shutters open, and soon saw the rectangle of the window growing lighter. He got up again, put on a thick flannel dressing gown, and looked out. The square was still deserted, and from the adjoining streets there was no roar of lorries or rattle of carriages on the cobbles, no car horns or any of the other usual noises.

Behind the shutters, the royal city is silent, waiting.

With the first light of day the lights that have been burning all night in the National Security Headquarters go out. Don Alonso Mallol is there, waiting for the arrival of the Interior Minister, who has been closeted with the Prime Minister for several hours.

The surprise results of the February 18 elections have made it a difficult moment for Señor Mallol to be taking over as Director-General of National Security. Conflicts are multiplying. His instructions from the government are hesitant and contradictory, and he is not even sure he can trust his own subordinates, whom he has inherited from the previous government, which in turn inherited them from the previous one, and so on ad infinitum. Trusting to instinct, he has placed men he only half knows in the key posts, ignoring advice and refusing to read reports that are probably tendentious anyway: he knows that in Madrid every report is one part truth to three parts tittle-tattle. As for the rest of his staff, he is relying more on the inertia of civil servants than on their loyalty.

On the stroke of eight an assistant announces the arrival of Lieutenant-Colonel Don Gumersindo Marranón. The director-general asks him come through at once, and he comes in accompanied by the limping Captain Coscolluela. They exchange lengthy greetings, and the newcomers give their reports in a few dry sentences, as though a lack of enthusiasm were the guarantee of objectivity. Don Alonso listens carefully: the lieutenant-colonel is one of the few men he can trust.

His report may have been monotonous, but it is hardly reassuring: in Madrid and the rest of Spain, churches have been set on fire. Thanks to the late hour at which the attacks took place, there were no worshippers in the affected buildings, and damage was minimal. In some cases, the agitators simply burned papers and rags in the church atrium, creating more smoke than anything else. Symbolic acts, although it is also possible that right-wing agents provocateurs were responsible. If that is the case, they have succeeded, because a fireman has died in Madrid attempting to put out one of the blazes, and a protest march is being organised, which the Falange is certain to take part in. To make matters worse, the Falange has called a meeting at the Europa cinema for the following Saturday at seven in the evening. A month earlier, prior to the elections, they held a meeting in the same place, and crowds of people had turned up. On that occasion the event had passed off without serious disturbances. But back then all the political parties were busy with their own campaigns. Don Alonso asks what the meeting is for. The lieutenant-colonel shrugs. He doesn't know, but he supposes it must be to justify their crushing defeat in the elections, where the Falange did not win a single seat, and to explain their future strategy to their followers. The Falange does not seem inclined to disappear, and if it wants to play a role in Spanish politics, it will have to come up with something. Whatever the reason, the meeting promises to spark trouble.

The lieutenant-colonel pauses and looks enquiringly at his boss, who nods in response: authorising the march and the meeting are as dangerous as banning them; the slightest thing could light the fuse that sets off the explosion. Better to leave the decision in the hands of the Interior Minister, who will probably consult with the Prime Minister. This delegation of responsibility is not so much a sign of cowardice or deference as merely common sense: in the whole of Spain, the Prime Minister is the only person who still believes there is a peaceful way out of the current situation.

This cautious optimism is not gratuitous. Don Manuel Azaña has many years of experience in government, and, as is often said, he has seen everything. When the Republic was first proclaimed in 1931, he became Minister of War; shortly afterwards he was appointed Prime Minister. In 1933 he went into opposition, and now he is back as Prime Minister, when the panorama is not merely gloomy, but desperate. But not to him: an intellectual first and a politician second, he has reached the pinnacle of power thanks to the swift, unpredictable twists and turns of history rather than through his own efforts. This has meant he does not know or want to know anything of the murkier recesses of real politics, something that both his adversaries and his supporters accuse him of. Perhaps also for this reason he believes in a loyal opposition, one that will not seize power without thought for the consequences. Even now he thinks that dialogue and negotiation can provide an answer to Spain's pressing problems: strife among the workers, agrarian reform, armed confrontation, the Catalan question.

Very few others share his view. Unlike what happened in the early days of the Republic, the workers' organisations have turned their backs on the politicians. It is only indecisiveness and internal wrangling that is preventing them from descending into the streets and seizing power by force. There is no shortage of reasons for them to do so: the right-wing government that preceded the current one did all it could to invalidate the progress they had achieved up to then, and repressed all protests with unusual brutality. Now the Popular Front is trying to redress the situation but is meeting formidable obstacles: the opposition, led by Gil Robles and Calvo Sotelo, is torpedoing the new government's social reform programme in parliament, while the owners of the large fortunes in Spain are manoeuvring on the European stock exchanges to bring about a devaluation of the peseta, mass unemployment and a collapse of the economy. The Church and the press, largely in the hands of the Right, are stirring people up and spreading panic; the most influential intellectuals (Ortega, Unamuno, Baroja, Azorín) are renouncing the Republic and calling for drastic change. Anticipating a coup by the military or the fascists, the trade unions are collecting money to buy weapons, while the workers' militias are on standby day and night, ready to intervene at the first alarm signal.

Don Manuel Azaña is aware of all these factors, but disagrees with everyone else as to their importance. In his opinion, the workers will not decide to take to the streets: the socialists and anarchists will not unite, and the Communists have received strict orders from the Komintern to stay on the alert and wait; the moment is not ripe for revolution, and to try to impose the dictatorship of the proletariat would be an error of judgment. For the same reason, he does not believe there will be a right-wing coup. The monarchists have already asked Gil Robles to proclaim himself dictator, and Gil Robles has refused.

That leaves the Army, of course. But Azaña knows it well: not for nothing was he Minister of War. He is aware that beneath their threatening exterior, the military are inconsistent, changeable and manipulable. On the one hand they huff and puff and criticise; on the other they whine about promotion, postings and medals. They are desperate for privileges and jealous of anyone else having them. They all think that others with less merit have stolen a march on them; in short, they can be sweet-talked like children. Accustomed by their strict hierarchies to do only what a superior has decided, they cannot reach any agreement on joint action. All the different arms (artillery, infantry, engineers) are at daggers drawn with each other, and it is enough for the Navy to do something for the Air Force to do the opposite. After the Popular Front's recent electoral triumph, General Franco went to see the then Prime Minister Portela Valladares and urged him to put a stop to the reigning disorder, with the Army's help, if necessary. Francisco Franco is a young general; he possesses a lively practical intelligence and has proved his worth: in Africa, he enjoyed a meteoric rise which gained him a merited reputation among the officer class. His personal qualities and influence might make him one of the leaders of the rebellion, were it not for the fact that his genial character and his natural reserve inspired mistrust among the other generals. It is doubtful whether Franco's veiled threat to the prime minster enjoyed the backing of the entire Army, but his visit so terrified Portela Valladares that he resigned on the spot. It was the vacuum created by his resignation that led to Don Manuel Azaña taking over as Prime Minister once more.

An assistant knocks and comes into the director-general's office carrying a tray with a steaming jug of coffee and a basket of rolls on it. Another man brings in cups, plates, glasses, knives and forks, napkins and a jug of fresh water, then sets the table for the snack. Just as they are finishing their breakfast, two other men make their appearance: Don Amós Salvador, the Interior Minister, and his deputy, Don Carlos Esplá. Laughter and greetings. Mallol and Esplá, who are both masons, quickly exchange signs. They are accompanied by assistants, officials, inspectors and a civil governor who happens to be passing through Madrid. Briefcases are piled high on the desks; the coat rack sways from the weight of overcoats thrown on it. Cigarettes are rolled, pipes and a few cheroots are lit. The air in the office becomes dense with smoke.

As expected, the director-general decides to authorise the Falange meeting at the Europa cinema. Precautions will be taken, and matters will take their course. If the Falange supporters turn up and cause trouble, it will give the government an excuse to declare the party illegal and to throw the main leaders in jail. If need be, a curfew can be imposed. In his usual succinct way, and with occasional help from his colleague Captain Coscolluela, Lieutenant-Colonel Marranón reports on the latest movements of Primo de Rivera and his entourage in the capital and provinces. Then they turn to other matters.

According to reliable information, the secretary of the Communist International, Georgi Dimitrov, is still determined to defend the Republic at any cost. From that side at least there is no danger. Of course, the military are still plotting; many of them are in close contact with the Falange or the Traditionalist Communion headed by the Carlist Manuel Fal Conde. As a preventive measure, the most troublesome generals have been posted to commands on the margins, well away from the strategic centres.

News censorship is to be maintained, both about acts of violence, including the burning of churches, and strikes in different sectors throughout the country. The civil governor raises the possibility of using the Army to cover basic services and supply problems caused by the strikes. In principle this does not seem like a good idea, but it needs to be studied on a case-by-case basis. For the moment, Catalonia is quiet, but Andalusia is very restless.

Another hour of their busy schedules is taken up with matters that are less important but vital to the smooth running of the administration. After that, red-eyed from the smoke and lack of sleep, the officials leave the office one by one and return to their own departments.

When the director-general is once more alone with Lieutenant-Colonel Marranón and Captain Coscolluela, he stifles a yawn, rouses himself and murmurs wearily:

"What news is there of the Englishman?"

The lieutenant-colonel was already rising to leave, but now sits down again. Glancing out of the corner of his eye at the captain, he says in his flat voice:

"Nothing definite for the moment. He seems like a halfwit, but that can't be the case. He lied deliberately when we interrogated him."

He briefly refers to the dialogue he had with Anthony Whitelands the previous evening, pauses for a moment for his superior to absorb the information, then adds:

"Last thing yesterday I received a telephone call from our informants in London, whom I had already been in contact with. Everything appears to confirm that Whitelands is what he says he is: a paintings expert. He has published articles and is well respected in his field. Even though he studied at Cambridge, he is not a queer or a Communist. He has not had any contacts with fascist or other groups, and until now has been apolitical. He has no personal fortune. In recent years he has been cuckolding a Foreign Office official. He has a small private income, but what he earns from his work wouldn't keep him in peanuts."

"That could explain why he came to Spain," the director-general suggests. "Money is important."

"Yes, that's a possibility," the lieutenant-colonel agrees. "He's been seen coming and going from the Duke of La Igualada's place."

Mallol grunts and mutters:

"Can that old fogey be up to something?"

"I wouldn't put it past him. Primo de Rivera often visits the house."

"That will be for the girl."

"Bah! That won't get anywhere. Although, of course, you never know with women . . . All we know for sure is that last night the

Englishman was out on the town with Primo and his henchmen at the Happy Whale."

Don Alonso Mallol waves his hand in the air. He is tired, and wants to settle the matter without more ado:

"Don't let him out of your sight," he says, by way of dismissing them.

A pale sun is shining in through the window. The muffled sounds of the city rise from the streets. At that same moment, oblivious to the scrutiny he is under, Anthony Whitelands is breakfasting on a milky coffee with fried pastries in a bar in Plaza Santa Ana. He skims through the daily press with a worried look. He has been infected by the uncertainty all around him, but as a true Englishman cannot understand why the media is silent about matters that have the country on tenterhooks. He is aware of the strict censorship imposed by the government, because the newspapers themselves devote front page headlines to the attacks of which they are victims, but he cannot understand the point of a measure which weakens the government and produces the opposite effect to the one desired. Because of the lack of proper information, endless rumours are flying around, which are transformed and exaggerated out of all proportion by the popular imagination. Everybody claims to have sensational news on good authority, and to know important secrets which they have not the slightest compunction about broadcasting to the four winds. The channels through which this kind of information circulates are as varied as they are complex, since there are no bounds to Spaniards' sociability. With great assurance, in taverns and cafés, offices and shops, on public transport and in courtyards, ordinary people discuss, dissect and hotly debate with friends and complete strangers the present and future of the turbulent Spanish reality. The same occurs at higher levels of society, but here there is an extra element of confusion, because political sympathies vie with family circles, sports clubs or whatever cultural or leisure centre these people belong to. The dyed-in-the-wool right-winger and his equally convinced left-wing counterpart may meet at a bullfight or a football match and exchange news and gossip about such and such a topic, such and such a person or such and such a scandal; and the same happens at the Ateneo, when leaving church or at the Masonic lodge. By all these means, Spaniards in general and the inhabitants of Madrid in particular receive information that may be either true or false, without being able to distinguish in any way between the two.

Anthony Whitelands has a vague notion of all this, but although his knowledge of Spain is profound in some areas, it is very superficial in others, so that he easily becomes lost in the labyrinth of facts, conjectures and fantasy in which he finds himself immersed. Above and beyond this, he is also preoccupied with his own situation.

The editorial in the *A.B.C.* newspaper denounces the government's lack of response to the acts of vandalism committed in churches and convents. How much personal misfortune and how much damage to the nation's artistic heritage will we have to suffer before Señor Azaña deigns to take decisive action against those responsible? Are we going to have to wait for the rabble to show its hatred of other sectors of society by burning innocent people's houses with them inside?

This possibility suddenly leaves Anthony gasping for breath. In the current situation, he would not rule out an attack on the duke's mansion. If that happened, what would become of the painting which at that very moment is in the basement awaiting his verdict?

19

Without stopping off at his hotel or announcing his visit beforehand, Anthony Whitelands walked briskly to the mansion on Castellana and rang the bell. When the butler opened the door, he did not apologise for appearing in this way, or try to hide his nervousness.

"I have to see his excellency the duke at once," he said.

The butler parried his outburst with all the scorn of a Seneca.

"His excellency would doubtless see you if he were at home," he said, "but as he isn't, I'm afraid that's impossible. His excellency left early this morning without giving any indication when he would return. The duchess is at home, however, but she does not receive guests until after twelve o'clock. If you wish, I can advise the young master Guillermo that you are here."

His impetuousness quelled by this reverse, Anthony adopted a distant tone.

"I have no wish to speak to the young master Guillermo," he replied curtly, making it clear he did not deal with spoilt brats. "Is Señorita Paquita available?"

The butler gave the half-smile of someone who, although inferior in rank, knows he is in command of the situation.

"I shall go and see," he said, stepping to one side to allow the Englishman in. His face now showed the meek look of someone preparing the way for a polite dismissal.

Anthony once again found himself on his own in the large hallway, standing in front of the copy of "The Death of Actaeon". This violent, confused scene showing a sudden, irreparable act produced in him an equal measure of admiration and revulsion. Titian had been commissioned to paint the picture by the Spanish crown, but for reasons unknown to Anthony, it had never reached its intended recipient. Possibly Philip II learnt of the subject and decided it was inappropriate. Despite the passionate nature associated with Spaniards, anger and vengeance have no place in Spanish painting. Velázquez would never have painted a topic of this kind. His world was made up of everyday events imbued with a vague sense of melancholy; a serene, understated acceptance of the inevitable failure of our hopes in this world. Anthony was still puzzled that this Titian copy had ended up in such a prominent position in the duke's austere home, although the choice could be explained by the prestige of a signature and the passage of time. There could also be other reasons: Anthony had seen horrible scenes of slaughter presiding over salons where canapés were served and people danced or chattered, simply because the canvas in question had been purchased for a high price, or had been inherited from an illustrious ancestor, and now was nothing more than another demonstration of wealth and noble lineage. Anthony detested this perversion of art. To him, the content of a painting was essential. The artist's intention was not only vital even centuries later, but this spirit, when a true work of art was involved, was more important than any other technical, historical or monetary considerations.

Engrossed in his thoughts, Anthony had gone right up to the painting and stroked it with his fingertips. Then he took a few steps back and contemplated the impressive composition from the middle of the vestibule. He smiled faintly. "Oh! he said to himself. It's the old story of the hunter hunted."

"What are you muttering to yourself, Señor Whitelands?" Paquita said from behind him.

Anthony turned round unhurriedly. He was not in the least flustered.

"I'm sorry," he said, "I didn't hear you come in. I was studying this picture."

162

"It's only a copy."

"Yes, I know, but that doesn't matter. It's a good reproduction: the copyist not only captured the essence of the original, but was able to retain its mystery. I wonder where he copied it from, and how it comes to be here? Perhaps you know?"

"No, I don't," she said, waving her hand behind her, as though indicating a lengthy trail into the past. "I guess it must come from the family collection. Julián said you wanted to see me."

"That's right," said Anthony, suddenly abashed. "In your father's absence, you are the most appropriate person. Look, I read in the newspapers . . . about the fires, I mean . . . this mansion is not properly protected . . . there are more and more disturbances."

"Yes, I see what you are aiming at: this house could be attacked by a mob, in which case what worries you is the fate of the painting, not what happens to us."

"Señorita Paquita," Anthony replied, offended, "this is no time for parlour games. You know very well what worries me. In fact, what I would say torments me. It seems to me unworthy of you to rub salt in the wound. I was talking in practical terms: if there is a fire, people can escape relatively easily, but a canvas would be destroyed in a matter of seconds. I'm convinced you know the value of the painting and that you not only understand but share my concern."

Placing her hand on his forearm, Paquita looked him in the eye with a serious expression, and then immediately withdrew her fingers.

"I'm sorry, Anthony, I shouldn't have made fun of you. I told you the first time we met that all our nerves are frayed, and that makes us inconsiderate. But as far as that blasted painting is concerned, I would not mind in the least if it were reduced to ashes. I told you the other day, and I repeat it now: authentic or fake, leave that painting in peace. And stop suffering on its behalf: it's in a safe place. You can go back to England with your mind at rest."

"Could I see it again?"

"You're as stubborn as a mule. Alright, I'll go to the basement with you. I'll just fetch the keys and something to put on: it's freezing cold down there. Wait for me here, and don't say a word to anyone. The servants don't know what's in the basement, and there's no reason why they should."

This stern warning contrasted sharply with her mood, which seemed more light-hearted than anxious. She flitted out of the hall like an adolescent, and Anthony thought to himself: how young and beautiful she is! She shouldn't be caught up in this mess. But she is, and so am I.

Paquita soon returned. Making sure no-one saw them, the pair hurried down a corridor. At the far end, under a staircase leading up to the first floor of the mansion, there was a low doorway. Paquita picked out a large black key from the bunch. As she was inserting it in the lock, she said:

"This key always reminds me of the story of Bluebeard. Do you know it in England?"

"Yes, of course," he replied, quickly glancing at the door to judge its thickness.

Beyond the door, a flight of steps led down to the basement. Paquita switched a light on. After she closed the door behind them, they were enveloped in gloom. The only light was provided by a naked bulb above; the shutters on the basement windows were tightly closed. A rush of cold air from down below brought with it the smell of dust and mothballs. Anthony hastily put his coat on again. As they slowly descended the narrow steps, Paquita said:

"The basement is part of the house's original structure. It wasn't designed as a storeroom, but as the servants' quarters. That is why it is protected from damp and flooding. There aren't any rats or harmful insects either. If that weren't the case, we wouldn't use it to store our furniture. Even so, the painting has always been somewhere else. It was brought here not long ago."

They had reached the large room, crammed with pieces of furniture. The painting was under its blanket in the same place.

"Who brought it?" asked Anthony. "It must be heavy."

"I've no idea. Some of my father's employees, I suppose. With proper precautions, and without them seeing what they were carrying, because the canvas was crated up. Once it was here, my father and I unwrapped it and covered it in the blanket. He and I are the only ones who have seen it – and now you, of course."

"Help me lift the blanket," said Anthony. "The last thing I want to do is damage it."

The two of them uncovered the painting. Anthony said nothing, and showed no emotion. He stared at the picture, his eyebrows raised, his eyes half shut, his lips pursed. In the basement's sepulchral quiet, all that could be heard was his deep, regular breathing. Paquita watched him closely, drawn in by the magnetic quality that emanates from someone who, oblivious to everything around him, applies himself completely to an object he knows, values and respects. This went on for some length of time. Finally, the Englishman appeared to emerge from a dream. He smiled and said quite calmly:

"The painting has been well preserved. Neither the canvas nor the paint has suffered irreparable damage. Nothing that careful restoration could not deal with. It's a truly magnificent work."

"Do you still think it's authentic?"

"Yes. How did such an important work end up in your family? You must know that at least."

"Not entirely. As I told you the first day we met, I am not particularly interested in painting. We must have inherited it from some distant branch of the family. Like every noble house, we are related to all the rest of the Spanish aristocracy. Our family tree is more of a forest, which explains a large part not only of our inheritance, but of our failings as well."

"What are yours?"

"The usual: selfishness, laziness, arrogance and a lack of common sense."

"Good God! . . . Who else knows about this painting?"

"No-one. However strange it might seem, the painting has been stored away for generations. Most likely because of the subject. In addition to what I said earlier, my family is prudish and God-fearing."

"But it must have been recorded," said Anthony.

"The earliest transfers would have been registered. But after that, it was handed down in private, for obvious reasons. If there are any documents, they will be in an archive in the attic of one of our family homes, though God knows which one. They could be found, with time; I'm sure they will turn up if needed. For now, unfortunately, we only have your suppositions. Aren't you cold?"

"Yes, I am. But I need time. You can leave me on my own if you like."

"Why don't you tell me what you're thinking?"

"I'd be happy to, once we get out of here. I'm really grateful that you let me see the painting and have given over so much time to me."

"Don't thank me," replied the young woman. "I also have a favour to ask you."

"Rely on me if it's something in my power," said Anthony. "And perhaps you could clear up a doubt I have. Did any of your forebears ever hold an important position in Italy?"

"I once heard that someone on my father's side of the family was a cardinal. Does that help?"

"Indeed it does. Let's cover the painting again."

Between them, they pulled the blanket back over the frame. As they were leaving the basement, the light bulb began to sway, and then fizzled out. They were plunged into complete darkness.

"What a bore!" Paquita said, unruffled. "The bulb must have gone. Or there's another blasted strike. It could be hours before the lights come on again; if we don't get out of here we'll catch pneumonia. Don't move, you could hurt yourself. Give me your hand and we'll try to reach the door to the garden. I know this place better than you."

The Englishman had no difficulty finding her hand. It was icy. He squeezed it as hard as he could.

"Aren't you scared of the dark?" he asked.

"The same as anyone," she replied firmly. "Less, if I have someone with me."

They edged their way across the room. The darkness intensified the cold; it was as though time stood still.

"Feeling your way makes everything seem further off," said Paquita.

"Be careful you don't make a mistake, or we might end up in a wardrobe."

"That's where they should put you, you're so silly," she said.

They soon reached the door out to the garden. Letting go of Anthony's hand, Paquita fumbled with the bunch of keys and finally opened the door. Accustomed by now to the darkness, the bright light outside dazzled them. Wrapping herself in her shawl, Paquita poked her head out to make sure no-one was in the garden. Anthony recalled that it was in this same spot that she had embraced him two days earlier. He reached out impulsively and drew her to him. Paquita did not resist, but turned her face away and said:

"Don't think I make a habit of it."

They pulled apart and sneaked across the garden. When they reached the iron gate, Paquita said:

"On the other side, in Calle Serrano, there's a café called Michigan. Wait for me there. I'll come and meet you straightaway."

20

"Prior to the twentieth century," Anthony began, speaking without a pause like someone who has prepared a talk, "paintings of nudes do not exist in the Spanish tradition. Goya's 'Naked Maja' is an exception. So too, and even more striking, is the 'Toilet of Venus' by Velázquez himself. The reason for this is obvious: in Spain it was the Church that commissioned works, and to a lesser extent the royal household. That means religious imagery, portraits and a few everyday pieces. In Italy or Holland, things were different. There the nobility and the wealthy commissioned paintings to adorn their salons, and, since they had a less strict moral code, they were delighted to see mythological topics with a profusion of naked females. Spanish painters of the time knew how to paint naked figures, but under the Counter-Reformation they only used that knowledge to paint the male anatomy: scenes of martyr-dom and countless crucifixions and descents from the Cross. In this respect, as in so many others, Velázquez found himself in a privileged position: as a member of the court he received private requests, and was able to demonstrate his art in every genre, including the mytho-logical: 'The Feast of Bacchus', 'Vulcan's Forge', and quite a few more. Among them was the 'Toilet of Venus', now in the National Gallery in London: the first and for many years the only female nude in the history of Spanish painting."

There were not many people in the Michigan café: no-one was at the counter, and only a handful of tables were occupied. The late risers had already had their breakfasts, and it was not yet the noisy aperitif hour. Two solitary customers were taking their time reading *A.B.C.* and *El Sol* respectively; a third customer was busy writing, a smile on his lips; an artillery officer was smoking, staring absent-mindedly up at the ceiling. Beside one of the windows, two middle-aged ladies were talking together non-stop; on the table, next to their big cups of milky coffee and the tin sugar-bowl, they had left their missals and carefully folded black mantillas. Anthony was impressed by the variety of places such as this Madrid offered. Not even the celebrated cafés of Vienna, where he had spent many hours between visits to the Künsthistorisches Museum, could compare to the ones in the Spanish capital. In Vienna, the cafés gave him an awkward feeling of theatricality and decadence; in Madrid however there was nothing anachronistic about them, and they were always buzzing with life. Unlike Vienna, in Madrid the café walls were not covered with mirrors, because the customers did not need them: in Madrid cafés they looked directly at each other, without any need to hide their curiosity. There was nothing wrong with this self-assurance, he felt, because in the Madrid cafés people forgot one another just as readily as they looked at them. It was all part of the gentle flow of things in that lively, generous and superficial city. Nevertheless, the euphoria his surroundings produced, the fact of being with Paquita and the chance to talk to her about his favourite subject did not make him forget that he was caught up in something that was vitally important for many people, starting with himself, since his career was on the verge of taking a completely unexpected twist if his first impressions were confirmed and he was not making an irreparable gaffe.

"In the 1640s, Velázquez was at the height of his fame," Anthony went on, trying to keep his voice neutral, "and in addition to his duties as court painter, he received and accepted commissions from the Church and from important figures among the Spanish nobility. One of his clients was Don Gaspar Gómez de Haro, son of the Marquis del Carpio, who succeeded the Count-Duke of Olivares as Philip IV's adviser. I don't know if you're aware of all these historical details – if not, it doesn't matter. What is important is that Don Gaspar was not only a very powerful man, but a passionate collector. He commissioned

Velázquez to paint a canvas with a mythological theme: a naked Venus in the manner of Titian. Despite the unusual nature of the request, to judge by the result Velázquez carried out the task with obvious relish. When the painting was finished, Don Gaspar prudently kept it in his palace, so that no-one else saw it until many years later, when all the protagonists of this story were dead and buried."

Anthony paused. He wanted to tell the rest precisely but carefully: he had no wish to offend the sensibilities of his beautiful companion with crude details.

"Don Gaspar Gómez de Haro," he went on, lowering his voice and his gaze, "was not merely an art connoisseur, but a man of licentious habits. As a man, he was more like Don Juan Tenorio than Saint John of the Cross, to put it mildly. Perhaps it was this weakness that led him to ask Velázquez to paint him a picture so incompatible with the morality of his age. However that may be, the main question is: who is the woman in the painting? Did Velázquez use just any model, or even a prostitute, to represent Venus? Or was the model, as some claim, one of Don Gaspar's lovers whom he wanted to immortalise on canvas? And what if, as others maintain, the woman in the painting was none other than Don Gaspar's own wife? Those who support this thesis argue as proof that the features of the Venus in the painting, reflected in the glass Cupid is holding, were deliberately blurred by the painter so that nobody would recognise them – something that would have been unnecessary if she were just a whore."

"And what's your theory?" the young woman asked.

"I prefer not to commit myself. The idea that an illustrious married woman would pose naked is odd, especially in Spain under the Inquisition, but it's not impossible. There are always exceptions to the rule. Don Gaspar's wife, Doña Antonia de la Cerda, was related to Doña Ana de Mendoza y de la Cerda, the Princess of Eboli, who is said to have been Philip II's lover. Both were women of great beauty, strong-minded and daring. Even so, I can't see the logic in such a compulsively unfaithful husband wanting a naked portrait of his wife, even if it was Velázquez who was painting it. It would have been much easier to have her painted in her clothes. Anyway, we will never know the exact truth: the history of art is full of surprises."

"I haven't the slightest doubt about that," said Paquita.

"I detect a hint of irony in your voice," said Anthony. "I'm probably boring you with my ramblings. But I must insist that you're wrong. Experts' debates and theories may seem dull, and my articles definitely are, but art itself isn't. Paintings mean things, just as much as poems or music do – important things. I know that for a lot of people an old painting is nothing more than a precious possession, a collector's item or an excuse to show off one's knowledge in order to advance in the academic world, and I won't deny that these factors exist and need to be taken into account. But above all, a work of art is the expression of something both sublime and yet at the same time deeply rooted in our beliefs and emotions. I prefer the barbarism of an inquisitor ready to burn a painting he sees as sinful to the indifference of someone who is only concerned with confirming its date, antecedents or sale value. To us, a painter, a client and a model from the seventeenth century are nothing more than entries in an encyclopedia. But in their day they were flesh and blood like you and I, and they poured their souls into these paintings for very deep reasons, sometimes spending fortunes on them or even risking their lives. And they never imagined that all of that would one day end up in a room in a gallery or in the corner of a basement."

"My word," she said, "yet again I have to ask you to forgive me. It's obvious that my relationship with you is one long succession of offences and apologies."

"It will stop being so when you no longer consider me as useless as a watchman's whistle, if that is the right expression. But I am the one who should apologise. I tend to get carried away when I talk about this topic."

"That's alright, it makes it more appealing. Carry on with your hypothesis."

"There is a lot of debate as to when exactly Velázquez painted the 'Toilet of Venus'. Everything suggests it was towards the end of the 1640s, because in 1648 Velázquez went to Italy and did not return until 1651, by which time the painting was already in Don Gaspar's palace. It may have been painted in Italy, where there was an abundance of canvases of naked women, but I don't think so. In Madrid there were also many similar paintings by masters such as Titian or Rubens, even in the royal collections. Although they were not on public display, as keeper of the Crown's artistic heritage Velázquez was familiar with them. I'm convinced the 'Venus' was painted in Madrid before his stay in Italy, probably early in 1648, and in the strictest intimacy."

As though this phrase had activated a spring, the artillery officer leapt from his seat. The waiter ran over to help him on with his greatcoat, which was hanging from a stand. Handing the waiter a coin, the army man headed for the door. As he passed their table, he gave the Englishman a sideways glance, and then stared more openly at Paquita, who had lowered her gaze. The officer bowed in mid-stride and left the café. Anthony thought his companion looked uneasy, but did not think it wise to ask her to explain what it was all about.

"In November 1648," he continued, "Velázquez travelled to Italy a second time on the orders of Philip IV. The aim was to acquire works of art to add to the royal collections. However, this time the trip lasted longer than expected: two years and eight months. The King grew impatient and called his favourite painter back, but Velázquez kept delaying his return. During his prolonged stay in Italy, he painted very little: in Rome he did portraits of Pope Innocent X and prominent members of the Vatican curia. While convalescing from some fevers he also painted two tiny, melancholy paintings of the Villa Medici. The rest of the time he spent travelling round Italy, meeting artists, collectors, diplomats and patrons, buying paintings and sculptures and making sure they all reached their destinations. His wife and two daughters stayed behind in Madrid. When Velázquez finally came back to Spain he was a weary, dispirited man. In the decade between the return from Italy and his death on 6th August 1660, he only painted portraits of the royal family, among them 'Las Meninas'."

"Well, that's something at least," said Paquita, who appeared to have recovered from the incident with the artillery officer.

"Yes, of course. It's an extraordinary painting and it shows that Velázquez was in full possession of his faculties, at the height of his creative capacity. But if that's so, why did he paint so little?"

"Do you think the 'Venus' brought him bad luck?"

"I think that after painting that picture, or while he was painting it, Velázquez went through a tremendous personal crisis he never really recovered from. What's more, I think the real cause of the crisis lies in the painting itself. I've been arguing over this for years with an English expert, an old Cambridge professor who's now a curator at the National Gallery. He supports . . . a different theory from mine. He doesn't like women, and perhaps that's why . . . Well, let's not dwell on that. It's Velázquez's personal problems that matter here, not mine."

"Perhaps they coincide," said Paquita, "and you can tell me about them if you wish. It's easier to talk of one's own worries than to wait for Velázquez to come and paint them."

"No, no, I'll do no such thing. We can't stray from the question. Look, I'll tell you what I think happened: in 1648, Don Gaspar Gómez de Haro commissioned Velázquez to paint a naked woman representing Venus. His own wife or somebody else, that doesn't matter for now. Velázquez accepted the commission. He painted her not once but twice. First as Venus at her toilet, with her features carefully blurred in the glass so that nobody could identify her; and then, also naked, with her features clearly painted and without resorting to the subterfuge of mythology. Obviously this second painting was for himself. It never appeared in the inventory of Don Gaspar Gómez de Haro's possessions. By painting this second picture, Velázquez was running a great many risks. If its existence became known, there would have been a huge scandal: the Inquisition could have become involved, and in the best of cases he would have lost the King's favour. Ever since he arrived in Madrid and pushed out the former court painters with his innovative style, there had been no shortage of enemies plotting his downfall. Then there is Don Gaspar Gómez de Haro himself. If the relationship between painter and model had gone beyond the purely professional and entered the realms of romance or something even worse – as the painting appears to indicate – whether it is the portrait of his legitimate wife or his lover, a bloody revenge is called for: we are in the Spain of Calderón and the principles of honour, and Don Gaspar is powerful. Only an unbridled passion could have led someone as naturally sedate, almost apathetic, as Velázquez was to commit such a folly."

As he grew carried away with his account, Anthony had gradually been raising his voice, and now he paused to regain his composure. Watching him, Paquita's brow furrowed and her eyes misted over. Oblivious to this, Anthony drew his hand across his face and went on.

"Velázquez was aware of his position. Being an intelligent man and realising his passion was doomed, he decided to put distance between himself and Spain. He had no difficulty persuading Philip IV to send him on an official mission to Italy; and so off he went, on the King's orders, taking the second portrait with him."

"A poor substitute," said Paquita.

"But better than nothing. Besides, to Velázquez reality and painting often merged into one, although that is another story. What concerns us here is that when he returned, his passion cooled by the lengthy absence, he left the compromising canvas in Italy, probably in Rome. Over the years someone acquired it, brought it back to Spain, and now it's there, a few metres from this café, waiting for—"

"Waiting for Anthony Whitelands to make it known to the whole wide world," Paquita interrupted him.

This time the young woman's tone of voice did succeed in alerting the Englishman.

"Of course," he said, "although first we have to settle a few details. Are you angry?"

"Yes, but not with you. All the men who cross my path seem to be dreamers. But let's leave that. It's not me who is important here, but Velázquez."

Her voice quavered, and with a sudden movement of her head, as though something else had caught her attention, she turned her face away. Disconcerted by this abrupt change, Anthony did not know how to react. A few seconds later, she turned back to him. Again her eyes were misty with tears, but she said in a steady voice:

"Yesterday, in front of the Christ of Medinaceli, I begged you not to authenticate that painting. At the time I believed I was offering you something valuable in exchange. I see now that for you I am worth less than the picture, or what the picture signifies. Nothing will make you turn from your path, and I do not reproach you for that. I am not humiliated at being defeated by a woman who died three hundred years ago, and of whom we know only the face and a fair proportion of her anatomy, but you must understand that it makes me feel rather odd."

"I can't understand properly if you won't explain the reason for the way you behaved," said Anthony.

"Let me have your handkerchief."

Anthony passed it to her. Paquita dabbed at invisible tears and handed it back.

"A few minutes ago," he said, seeing that she did not seem to want to add anything more, "you asked me to tell you my concerns. I'll do so briefly. For a few years now, my life appears to have come unstuck. I am in a rut professionally and personally, and there is no sign that the situation is about to change. I've seen too many similar cases to have any illusions: brilliant studies, great expectations, a few years of splendour, and then nothing: stagnation, repetition, mediocrity. I'm following the pattern: I've left my youth behind, and now I'm going backwards, like a crab. Then all at once, in the most unexpected way, I'm given a unique opportunity, not just in my life, but in the history of art in general. It involves risk, borders on the illegal and, as if that were not enough, powerful emotional factors come into play. And yet, if in spite of everything this turns out well, if just this one thing turn out well, I would achieve something far beyond satisfying my ridiculous academic vanity. I would gain prestige. And money – yes, enough money to purchase my independence and my dignity. At last I would be able to stop begging . . . Have you any idea what that means, Señorita Paquita?"

"All of us women know that, Señor Whitelands. But don't worry, I'm too proud to insist. I understand your reasons, of course, as you would understand mine if I revealed them to you. But I cannot – not yet. I can however offer you some clues. You'll have to deduce the rest, and then we'll see if you are as good at unravelling the present as you are at following the ins and outs of the seventeenth century."

While they were talking the original customers in the café had gradually been leaving, and their place was taken by a fresh, noisier set of people. Anthony called the waiter, paid, and they left. The wind had dropped, and high in the clear sky the sun was spreading a warmth that heralded spring. The first buds were appearing on the trees. Without exchanging a word they walked to the side gate of the garden, then came to a halt while she searched for the keys.

"Earlier," said Paquita, with the gate already ajar, "I said I would ask a favour of you. You haven't forgotten, have you?"

"No. Tell me."

"At seven this evening José Antonio Primo de Rivera is holding a meeting at the Europa cinema. I want to go and I want you to go with me. Meet me at six on the corner of Serrano and Hermosilla. We can take a taxi from there. Can I count on you?"

"It will be a pleasure."

"We'll see about that. I think you'll find it an instructive experience, anyway. At six then. Punctual as an Englishman."

21

By common accord between all those concerned, the miseries that the vicissitudes of history, misrule of the nation, and conflicts between opposing groups had heaped on Spain in 1936 were momentarily suspended at the aperitif hour. The elegant cafés of the Salamanca neighbourhood were overflowing with upper-class customers, as were the greasy bars in Lavapiés with shop assistants and workmen. As Anthony Whitelands made his way back to his hotel, his mind was on a variety of matters. For the first time since his arrival in Madrid, he was happy with the way things were going. In his opinion, the recent conversation with Paquita in the Michigan had taken a favourable turn: she had dropped both her mocking attitude and the mystery of their previous encounters; he had been able to express his points of view without any vanity or nervousness – in short, without committing any error he would now have to regret, and without making a fool of himself as he had done before. The future of their relationship might still be unpredictable, but at least it would be more normal. The opportunity she was offering him that same evening was proof of this change of attitude: not only was it a demonstration of trust, but also perhaps an invitation to take their relationship into another area, permission to enter into direct competition with a rival whose superiority it would be childish not to recognise, but whom it was not impossible to get the better of with a little ingenuity and patience. However, all this was relegated to the back of Anthony's mind in comparison with the incredible importance of the Velázquez painting he had become involved with. This excited him to such a degree that it was only his naturally reserved character and strict upbringing that prevented him from behaving like a lunatic in the middle of the street. He was striding along, waving his arms about and, without realising it, muttering phrases or random words that attracted the attention of several passers-by. He was eager to reach his hotel, where he intended to write down the maelstrom of ideas whirling around in his head, partly in order to sort them out, and partly to relieve his overflowing brain. With this in mind, and although he felt the pangs of hunger, he ignored the siren calls from the restaurants and cheap cafés he was racing past.

Barely a hundred yards from his goal, he heard a voice behind him. When he turned round, he found himself face to face with Higinio Zamora Zamorano.

"What!" he exclaimed. "You again! Isn't this one coincidence too many?"

Higinio Zamora laughed and said:

"You're right. It would be some coincidence if it were. But it isn't: because I've just come from your hotel where I went to find you and the gentleman in reception told me you weren't there."

"I see. And may I know why you came looking for me?"

"You may, you may. In particularly, since your humble servant here was the one who came to see you. But it's not something to be talked about in a minute standing here: it deserves a good stew and a bottle of Valdepeñas."

"I'm sorry," said Anthony. "I can't allow myself a meal today."

"Oh, my dear sir, I fear I did not properly convey my meaning. I'm doing the inviting."

"It's not that. I have work to do, and need to get back to the hotel at once."

Higinio Zamora's eyes smiled, but his face was still serious.

"Well, if you really have to work, don't go to the hotel. There's a cove in the lobby who has the look of a policeman, and when I asked after you, he looked me up and down from top to toe. From which your humble servant deduces that he's awaiting for you. Could that be so?"

"It could."

"In that case, give him the slip and let's go and have that stew. I can see your mouth watering the moment I mention it. And don't be worried about me being indiscreet: I won't ask why they're keeping an eye on you."

Anthony did not have to think it over for long: whether the person waiting for him in the hotel was Captain Coscolluela or someone else sent by Lieutenant-Colonel Marranón, it would be wise not to show up: he had too much to hide. And if they took him off again to the offices in the National Security Headquarters, he would have to forget about his appointment with Paquita, and the opportunity to go with her to José Antonio Primo de Rivera's meeting.

"Alright, let's go, but I insist on paying my share."

"That's not a Spanish custom," said the other man, "but I accepts."

Leaving the hotel behind, they walked for a while until Higinio Zamora went into an eating house. The Englishman followed him. There were quite a few people inside, but in the monastic silence the only sound was the clatter of plates. The waiter pointed them up towards the mezzanine, where they sat at an empty table. It was soon covered with dishes filled with cabbage, chick peas, pork fat, sausage, potatoes and black pudding. A fat woman wearing a grimy apron ladled soup into earthenware bowls, and a lad brought them wine. Serving himself some of everything, Higinio Zamora began to tuck in with great gusto. When Anthony saw his companion was not ready to talk to him, he did the same. The food was delicious and, although nothing special, the wine went well with it, so that their cheeks were soon crammed and their eyes gleamed with satisfaction. Higinio Zamora chose this moment to lay his knife and fork on his plate, wipe his mouth with a care that betrayed a certain degree of good manners, and to say:

"First and foremost, allow me to repeat, even if this is the first time I am mentioning it, that nothing what I am about to say to you is out of self-interest towards me or my person."

When Anthony waved vaguely to show he was listening, his companion went on:

"I'll speak to you in all confidence. As far as I can tell, you may be a lord or the King of England, but here you're more lonely and lost than a reconnaissance plane. Don't go getting offended – I mean it as a friend, like."

"I'm not offended, but I have no idea what you mean. What I am is my own business."

"Perhaps in your own country. Here everything belongs to everyone. If someone is happy, everyone celebrates; if they're sad, we all share their sadness."

"What if someone wants to be left in peace and not have anyone interfering?"

"Then they're in trouble. Look, I'll tell you how things really are: whatever they say, this is not a poor country. This is a country of poor people. I don't know if you can see the difference. In a poor country, everyone gets by as best they can with whatever they have. But not in Spain. Here what people have is important, but more important still is what their neighbour has or no longer has. But that is not my point. My point is your personal situation, not the money you may have. And that's where you are suffering. You may fool everyone else by looking like an antiquated dummy and with manners to match, but you don't fool Higinio Zamora Zamorano 'ere. I've seen you for what you are. I mean with regard to La Toñina. Don't be afraid, I've no intention of blackmailing you – I've already told you it's all the same to me. Besides, you've done nothing wrong; quite the contrary. What I am talking about here is that poor family: Justa, Toñina and that poor fatherless mite, the child of sin. You heard what Justa said: they're all alone in the world. Well now, the girl is willing, clean, one of the most discreet persons I know and nobody's fool. And yet, if something isn't done, she faces a bitter future. You on the other hand have got fine prospects, but your present situation is a mess. Chance has thrown the two of

181

you together. Do you catch my drift?"

Anthony, who until now had been only half listening and had carried on eating, now laid down his knife and fork, stared at his companion, and said:

"Are you trying to sell me the girl, Señor Zamorano?"

The other man put down his glass of wine and raised his eyes to the ceiling with the resigned expression of an adult trying to explain something very simple to a not very bright child.

"Oh!" he said. "Buying and selling! As if there was nothing in the world but buying and selling! You people see everything like salesmen. Before we had to argue about how our meal would be paid for, and now this. No, señor, Toñina is not for sale. She is not like that. If her father was alive, there is no way she would be doing what she does. She would have studied, she would be a respectable young woman; she might even have gone to university. But her poor father met a sad end in a good cause, and society abandoned the two of them. They have had to try everything to avoid starving to death. Does that make the poor girl second-hand goods?"

"I never said anything of the kind. You're the one insisting."

"And you're the one who doesn't understand a thing," Higinio Zamora replied gently, almost affectionately. "That's the problem. Not the problem between you and me, but between Spain and the world: you don't understand the proletariat. You see them as uneducated, as people who can't talk properly and always have a threatening scowl on their faces, and so you think: God help me! If the workers ask for something, if they demand a right or a pay increase, you get frightened. They're going to strip the shirt off my back, you tell each other. Of course, there's some truth in that. But it's not just money the proletariat wants. They want justice and respect. And as long as you lot can't understand that, there'll be no harmony or social peace, and the violence will only increase. You've seen what is going on in Madrid and the rest of the country: the workers are burning churches. I don't agree with it, but tell me this: who built them?"

Pausing to down another glass of wine, he continued in the same didactic tone:

"If the workers rebel, instead of asking the reason, they get the police let loose on them. If that's not enough, it's the Civil Guard, and if necessary the legionary troops. With arguments like them to back you up, you have no need to be right. Remember what happened in Asturias. But the proletariat has one thing on its side: it is never-ending. Look around you and listen to the voice of the people: it thinks the time is ripe and knows it won't get another opportunity, so the revolution is bound to break out. When the Republic was declared in 1931, everyone said: about time, that's the end of injustice. That was years ago, and today everything is the same: the rich are still just as rich, the poor just as poor. And if anyone complains, wham! with the billyclub, and stand up straight! Either the workers seize wealth and power by force or there'll be no worthwhile changes here. You've seen what's happened in Russia. Is that paradise on earth? I couldn't say, but at least in Russia they've got rid of all this nonsense."

He fell silent once more and glanced around to see if there was any reaction to his speech. Seeing that the customers at the adjoining tables were carrying on eating unconcernedly, he himself attacked the rest of his stew with a ferocity that had been absent from his rant. The Englishman took advantage to say slyly:

"And the Bolshevik revolution will not take place if I set Toñina up in a flat?"

"Very funny," replied Higinio Zamora, rather hurt by Anthony's insinuation but determined to stay cheerful. "I see you didn't understand me. Not just when I was talking about the situation, but when I explained all the rest. But look, we all know no-one can stop the course of history: neither you nor I can do anything on that score. What we can do is sort out that poor young girl's problem. I'll be honest with you: that's the only thing I'm worried about, and I don't know what to do. I feel really bad about it. I promised to look after that family, but I haven't managed to do a thing. When it comes down to it, Justa has lived her life. But, for the love of God, that poor girl has never known anything but humiliation and hardship."

His voice quavered, and tears welled up in his eyes. Thanks to his vague resemblance to Velázquez's "Menippus", Anthony had arbitrarily attributed to him the intellectual characteristics of the legendary philosopher of antiquity. Now, faced with this sudden display of sentimentality, he felt far more awkward than he had a moment earlier when his companion seemed to be trying to blame him for the Bolshevik triumph.

"Control yourself," he whispered. "Someone might hear you."

"I couldn't care less. They can't arrest anyone for crying. And I'm sorry to go on so, but whenever I think of that poor unfortunate . . . the life she lives is indescribable. And the future awaiting her is beyond words."

"Well, come the revolution, perhaps things will be sorted out for her."

"Ha! I said the revolution was bound to break out, not that it would triumph. On the contrary, with things as they are, at the first sign of trouble they'll bring the big guns out onto the streets. And if they're the ones who win, everything will be far worse than it is now. That's what I'm most afraid of."

Anthony sneaked a look at his watch. They had finished the stew, and he needed to hurry if he was to return to his hotel and get to his appointment on time.

"I can understand your frustration," he said, trying to adopt a conciliatory tone, "but the solution you are seeking is not in my power. I'm a foreigner, I'm only visiting, and I'll be going back to my own country in a few days."

Higinio Zamora dried his tears and looked at the Englishman with renewed interest.

"Bah," he said forcefully, "we can worry about the details when the time comes. I mean the fact that you're leaving isn't an obstacle, far from it. It would be good to get her out of Spain. In England that girl would be in her element. She has it in her to be a respectable young lady; besides which, she is hard-working, honest and very grateful. She never forgets a favour. Yes, I know," he went on solemnly, as though this aspect disturbed him far more than Anthony's evident astonishment, "I know a plan like this contradicts Marxist principles. A worker should not look for his own salvation but must help save all his class. But I'm convinced that if Marx had known the girl he would have made an exception. As for the child, just think: with an English education, plus a Spaniard's innate bravery – why, he could become a British Army officer in India, no less."

There was no way he was going to convince Anthony. The Englishman had been taught to show complete respect for any person, whatever their origin or social status, but this same principle was based on a rigid view of social rank, so that his companion's pretensions seemed to him not only absurd but intolerable. To Anthony, Higinio Zamora's ramblings were sheer madness. However, since Higinio had remained calm and apparently had nothing to gain personally from the matter, the Englishman decided not to pay too much attention to what he had said. Perhaps, he thought, the poor man needed to get it off his chest. The important thing now was to bring their conversation to a close, and the only way for him to do that was to adopt a sympathetic attitude and to agree with him in the vaguest terms possible.

"Rest assured I will try to think of a viable way of fulfilling your wishes without prejudicing my own situation," he said pompously, "but now I really must take my leave. And I've had second thoughts about what we agreed at the start: I'll pay."

This suggestion, which he had hoped would favourably dispose Higinio to him, produced the exact opposite effect. The Spaniard rejected his offer and insisted on paying for everything – especially as he had been so bold as to ask such a huge favour and had received such a positive response. Fearing fresh complications, Anthony accepted, and before the other man could settle the bill he stood up, shook hands with him and rushed out of the restaurant. In the street, he set off for his hotel as quickly as his bloated stomach would allow. At a safe distance from his goal, he halted, then renewed his approach with great care, just in case the man Higinio Zamora had mentioned was still on guard outside. Finally, when he could not see anyone suspicious close to the hotel, he almost ran the last few yards, took his key from the receptionist and shut himself in his room.

The atmosphere inside was conducive to work: the stove gave off a pleasant heat, while the oblique rays of the pale setting sun filtered in through the window. Anthony took out his notebook and pen, sat at the desk and got ready to write down the observations that had been delayed by his meeting and the enormous meal. However, almost at once he folded his arms across the desk, laid his head on them and fell asleep. Without being aware that he was sleeping, he dreamt that he could hear the sound of a large crowd singing the "Internationale" down in the street. The window framed a red sky into which thick columns of black smoke were rising. It was obvious that the revolution had broken out, and that therefore his life was in great danger. With the implacable logic of dreams, he saw himself dragged along by the whirlwind of events. There's no escape, he thought. They'll force me to dress in rags, let my beard grow, and shout: all power to the soviets! This vision produced a spasm of physical anxiety: he began to sweat profusely and his stomach started to burn. He wanted to run away, but his muscles refused to obey the orders from his brain. He awoke with a sour taste in his mouth, and the great fear that he had slept beyond the time for his appointment. His watch reassured him that this was not the case. Putting away his book and pen once more, he splashed water on his face and hair to at least tidy up his outward appearance, put on his coat and hat and left his room and the hotel as quickly as he could. The lamplighter was just lighting the lamps in the square.

As he ran towards his meeting point, he recalled the details of his nightmare. He reflected that Higinio Zamora's prophecies over their meal must have impressed him more than he had realised at the time, when he had merely thought them outlandish. Perhaps I'm walking on the edge of the abyss, he told himself.

22

This sense of foreboding was still weighing heavily on Anthony Whitelands when he arrived out of breath at the agreed corner. Paquita was waiting for him beside a taxi in Calle Hermosilla. More to avoid being recognised than to protect herself from the cold, she was wearing her coat lapels turned up, with an elegant lilac-coloured cloche pulled down over her eyes. When she saw him hurrying towards her, she took a hand out of her mink muff, briefly signalled and got into the taxi without waiting for him. Anthony followed, and closed the door behind them. The taxi pulled away, and for a few minutes they sped along in the conspiratorial silence of people on their way to commit a crime.

They drove from Cuatro Caminos down Bravo Murillo through the melancholy twilight of a winter's evening. As they drew closer to their destination they passed increasing numbers of people heading to the meeting on foot, overflowing from the pavements into the road. The taxi was forced to go more and more slowly, and often had to brake sharply: to judge from the look of the crowd, it did not seem a good idea to sound the horn. Eventually, the taxi driver said he could go no further. The only explanation he gave was that he wasn't one of them. Anthony paid, and Paquita and he got out to continue on foot. As the throng was growing ever denser, Paquita held tightly to Anthony's arm.

"We're not heading into a trap, are we?" asked the Englishman.

"Don't be a scaredy-cat," said Paquita. "Anyway, it's too late to change your mind. Are you frightened?"

"Only for you."

"I can look after myself."

"That doesn't mean anything, it's just a cliché," said Anthony, secretly offended at being called a coward. "Besides, I am safe whatever happens: I'm a British subject."

Paquita gave a low laugh.

"The meeting has been banned by the police," she said. "We're breaking the law."

"I'll claim I was seduced by your charms."

"Would you say a thing like that?" she said, only half joking.

In spite of this banter, Anthony was not entirely confident of their position. He kept sneaking glances to his left and right to see if there were any police about, but despite his tall stature he could not make out any uniforms. Perhaps the presence of the Assault Guard would have been counter-productive, he thought, or possibly they were waiting until everyone was shut inside a building to lay into them. But if there are no police and other groups attack us, who is going to restore order? he wondered. After much deliberation, he decided there must be a company of guards concealed near the cinema, ready to intervene at the first sign of violence. This possibility reassured and alarmed him in equal measure.

The cinema occupied the whole of a three-storey building. The billboards facing the street had been covered with black cloths on which were printed the names of Falange members killed in street clashes or ambushes. Reading the lengthy, dismal list robbed Anthony of the last shreds of his good humour. The cinema doors had been flung wide open and people were forming long queues, closely super-vised by blue-shirted youngsters trying to discover any possible agents provocateurs among the crowd. Everything was being done in a very serious, orderly fashion. Anthony and Paquita lined up and made their way into the foyer. There everyone was being directed either into the stalls or to the upper floors. They found themselves being pushed hither and thither until a stocky, swarthy man with slicked-back hair and a pencil moustache came over. The emblem of the yoke and arrows on his blue shirt and the revolver at his belt helped lend him a definite air of authority. Despite this, he could not conceal his nervousness. Without so much as glancing at the Englishman, he looked anxiously at Paquita.

"No-one told us you were coming," he said.

"I know. I'm here incognito," she replied. "I've come to accompany an international observer."

The official looked Anthony up and down suspiciously. Recovering from his surprise at Paquita's white lie, Anthony adopted a nonchalant, almost dismissive air. The Falangist looked away and said:

"Alright. I'll take you to a box."

"No," Paquita hastened to object. "He mustn't know I'm here. We'll find somewhere to sit. Above all, don't say a word to him."

"As you wish. There are still seats at the ends of the stalls. But get a move on, it's going to be a full house."

They found two seats together at the end of a row not far from an emergency exit. Anthony was relieved at this, because he wanted a way out he could use in a hurry as soon as trouble started, and without losing face in front of his companion. Finding a seat was getting more difficult by the minute: the cinema was full to overflowing, with people standing in the aisles and gangways. All the boxes were crammed as well.

In the centre of the stage stood a long table draped in a black cloth. The gap between stage and stalls was filled with a line of blue-shirts carrying the Falange banners. The atmosphere grew more and more heated. Finally, twenty minutes after the announced time, a loud cheer went up as three speakers stepped onto the stage. Anthony recognised Raimundo Fernández Cuesta and Rafael Sánchez Mazas, but not the third man. He was a tall, bald fellow with an athletic build. Paquita whispered that he was Julio Ruiz de Alda, the legendary aviator who had crossed the Atlantic ten years earlier in a seaplane, and was one of founders of the Falange. By now the three speakers had sat down at the table and were waiting for silence to be restored. After a few moments, Fernández Cuesta stood up, took the microphone and called out: "Silence!" The audience calmed down at once, and Fernández Cuesta himself was the first to speak.

"As you all know," he began, "the reason for this meeting is to take stock of what happened in the recent general elections. The Popular Front emerged victorious: a further step towards casting Spain into the arms of Marxism. Moreover," he went on, silencing the howls of protest with a gesture, "if the coalition on the Right had won rather than the one on the Left, the end result would have been the same, because elections are a wretched sham whose sole aim is to legitimise the appropriation of power by a bunch of corrupt good-for-nothings who have sold our country down the river."

"That man is going to get us all arrested," Anthony whispered in Paquita's ear.

"Don't be nervous," she replied. "This is only the beginning."

"That is why," the orator continued, "for the elections the Falange chose not to ally with either bloc. We stood alone, well aware that we would lose, because we do not care about losing in a contest we have never believed in. We stood in the elections so that we could spread propaganda; that was the only reason." Pausing for dramatic effect, he went on in a lower voice: "However, that effort was also in vain, because those who understand us hate us, and those who should love us do not understand us. Because we are neither on the Left nor on the Right. We possess the impulse for radical change that is seen on the Left, and the sense of nation of the Right, but we do not share the hatred of the former or the egoism of the latter."

These paradoxes led both the majority of the audience and the orator himself rather to lose the thread. He continued in the same high-flown language, but without much argument. The public did not want to lose its enthusiasm, but its show of support became increasingly less spontaneous. Fernández Cuesta went on haranguing them excitedly and with extravagant gestures, and ended by crying "Arise, Spain!" The audience responded with a loud ovation.

The next to speak was Rafael Sánchez Mazas. Unlike the previous speaker, he had a weak voice and spoke in the flat tone of a preacher no longer convinced that his sermons had any effect. His ideas though were more substantial. To Anthony it seemed as if he were not trying to enthuse his audience, but to convince them. This made him feel sympathy towards Sánchez Mazas, although he considered the effort was misplaced, since every Spaniard present was already a convert to the ideology in which they were being instructed.

"When the Falange announced it would fight the elections on its own," said Sánchez Mazas, "some said we were like penniless stray cats without a home. What no-one mentioned was that they were trying to drown us at birth, because we were being killed off all over the place. It is true however that we are poor. Poverty is the Falange's strength: because we are poor, the Falange understands and defends the rights of the poor, the agricultural labourer, the sailor, the soldier, the village priest. We want to be the defenders of the people, not the praetorian guard of those who speculate in high finance or big business. The socialists say they will increase the daily wage, that Spain will live better under them. That may or may not be true. The only certainty is that they are not really concerned about Spain. Against their narrow interests, the Falange is proposing something different: a united destiny and a great redeeming purpose. Justice free from influences, pure justice: that is what we want, in order to help bring about Spain's rebirth!"

There was also loud applause when Sánchez Mazas finished speaking, but the audience's initial ardour was cooling noticeably. Doubtless they had heard the same message many times throughout the electoral campaign.

Julio Ruiz de Alda, the next to speak, won applause and cries of support thanks to his austere dynamism and the native noble courage of a military man from Navarre. It was essential, he said, for Spain to shake off the torpor that democratic rule had lulled it into. For that reason, the Falange was ready to take power by any means, legal or illegal. Only in this way, he asserted, within a few years – two, three, four, but no more – will the new generations bring to Spain the national syndicalism that will make our Fatherland great.

Shouts of encouragement and applause rang out again. Anthony glanced at his watch: it was gone half past eight; surely the meeting would soon be over. Since everyone was well wrapped up because of the cold outside, and the cinema was full, the heat was stifling. Although slightly disappointed, deep down Anthony was pleased: he had never been to a fascist meeting before, but now he saw that, apart from the occasional rhetorical excesses, their arguments were not as far-fetched as he had been led to believe. If things carry on like this, we'll get out of here with no problem, he told himself. At that moment, a stirring in the audience led him to think everyone was about to leave the auditorium in an orderly fashion. But then Raimundo Fernández Cuesta took the microphone once more and bawled into it:

"Attention! The National Chief!"

A tremor seemed to shake the foundations of the Europa cinema as José Antonio Primo de Rivera stood up to speak. The entire audience got to their feet and raised their arms in salute. Swept along by this shared impulse, Anthony also stood up, but did not salute. A gruff voice called out from the row behind:

"What's the matter? Don't you salute?"

"I'm not authorised to do so," Anthony said, turning round and exaggerating his English accent.

This explanation apparently satisfied his challenger. Anthony turned back again and looked across at Paquita. By then everyone had lowered their arms and the audience was sitting down again in an expectant silence, so that he had no chance to see whether or not

193

she had also defied the general sentiment. José Antonio had reached the table and was embracing and slapping the backs of the other speakers. Then he moved to the centre, leaned forward, and immediately launched into his speech.

"Those who have addressed you before me have already spoken about the reason for our meeting here today. It is not complicated. The Popular Front has won the elections. Spain is dead. Long live Russia!"

This brief declaration brought a huge roar from the audience. Everyone had recovered their fervour in an instant. Despite feeling despondent about this unexpected turn of events, Anthony was also able to appreciate the extraordinary circumstances that the quirks of fate had landed him in. Only a week before, all he had known of contemporary Spain was what little the British press deigned to inform its readers of; he had not even heard of the Falange or José Antonio Primo de Rivera. Now though, not only did he know about the party, its ideology and its main leaders; not only had he met and become friends with its founder and National Chief; and not only because of this had he attracted the attention of National Security Headquarters, but he was also competing with José Antonio for the favours of the fascinating young aristocrat sitting next to him and straining upwards as she listened expectantly to the words of the extraordinary, vehement and plainly deranged man who at that moment was publicly proclaiming the need and duty for the Falange to stage a coup d'état. Of course, a week earlier, in contrast to the tumultuous life he was now leading, Anthony had been enjoying a pleasant existence in London. Whereas now . . .

"Or did anyone sincerely believe," José Antonio went on once silence had been restored, "that our society's problems can be solved by calling on its citizens every two years to place their voting papers in an urn? Let's not delude ourselves! On April 14, 1931, when the Republic triumphed over the Monarchy, it was not a form of government that came to an end, but the social, economic and political basis on which that government was constructed. Azaña and his minions were well aware of that. Their aim was not to replace a liberal monarchy with a bourgeois republic, but to replace the destroyed state with another one. What is this new state we can expect? It can be one of two things: either a socialist state that imposes the so-far triumphant revolution, or a totalitarian state which achieves internal peace by making everyone's interests their own . . ."

Possibly, thought Anthony as applause and cheers for José Antonio, the Falange and General Primo de Rivera repeatedly interrupted the speech, he would be happy to change places with me: he could leave the stage and sit where I am, next to Paquita, listening to the nonsense spouted by a madman intoxicated by his own rhetoric. What does that fellow want? Does he really believe in what he's saying, or does he do it to impress her? And she herself? What does she think? Why did she bring me here? To show me José Antonio's best side or his worst? And why does she care about my opinion anyway?

"Let's not deceive ourselves, or leave things for another day!" José Antonio went on, his ardour rising to new heights. "Our only duty is to embark on a civil war, with all that entails. There is no middle ground: Spain must be Red or Blue! And you may rest assured that faced with such a choice, our strength will triumph in the end. And then we will see how many rush to pull on their blue shirts. But the first, those of the difficult hours, will still reek of gunpowder, will still bear the scars . . . and yet from their shoulders will sprout the wings of empire!"

He could not say any more: the entire audience stood up again, raised their arms and began to intone the "Face to the Sun" anthem.

"Let's go," said Paquita, grabbing Anthony by the arm.

"Now?"

"Now or never. They're all standing up, and in the midst of all this noise they won't notice a thing."

Paquita was right: they passed under the forest of raised arms out into the side passage, made their way to the foyer, put on their coats and went out into the street without anyone intercepting them. Night had fallen, and the street was unusually empty, as if the traffic had been cut. A cold wind whipped up the political pamphlets strewn about the pavements. The Englishman imagined enemies lurking in every dark corner.

"I don't like this calm," he said. "Let's find a taxi and get away from here as quickly as possible."

From the building they had left they heard the muffled sounds of the last verses of the anthem, followed by martial cries. As they walked down Bravo Murillo they saw a dense mass of workers coming towards them. They looked fierce and hostile. Paquita pressed closer to her companion and rested her head on his shoulder. He understood what she was doing, and the two of them continued on their way like two lovebirds lost in a world of their own. The human tidal wave swept over them and passed on almost without touching them. As soon as the danger had passed they separated and walked on more quickly. In Cuatro Caminos a detachment of Assault Guards was redirecting the traffic. Since no taxi was in sight, they went into Tetuán station and took the metro to Ríos Rosas, where they alighted and hailed a taxi. Anthony gave the address of the Castellana mansion. When the taxi pulled away, Paquita settled in the seat, sighed and said:

"Well, now you've seen him. Tell me sincerely what you think."

"Sincerely? That your friend is as mad as a hatter," Anthony replied.

Paquita gave a sad smile, and reflected for a moment until she replied in a faint voice:

"I won't be the one to contradict you. And in spite of that, I'm bound to him by feelings much stronger than reason. For good or ill, my destiny and his are linked. Don't take me literally: my declaration has no practical consequences and never will have. Fate has decided that our destinies will run on parallel lines without ever meeting. To go into details would be painful for me and boring for you. But I'm not blind. I am perfectly aware that José Antonio's ideology is inconsistent, that his party has no programme or social base and that his famous eloquence consists of speaking with great conviction without saying anything concrete. As for the others: Ruiz de Alda is nothing more than a symbol; Raimundo Fernández Cuesta is a lawyer with no political nous, and Rafael Sánchez Mazas is an intellectual, not a man of action. None of them has the authority or strategic sense to lead a revolutionary movement. José Antonio does possess those qualities, but he detests using them. He would quit if it weren't too late: too much blood has been spilt to back out now. Yet it's madness to carry on. If, due to some unforeseen course of events, the Falange were to come to power as it hopes, José Antonio's future would be no different: at best, others would use him; at worst, his own allies would do away with him."

Realising that if he said anything Paquita would fall silent, but that if he kept quiet she would be unable to halt the flow of her innermost thoughts, Anthony said nothing, and his companion obligingly rushed on.

"You must be wondering why I am telling you all this; why I made you come to the meeting and why I trust you. First and foremost, I'm doing so because before long you are going to have to make a crucial decision, and I want you to do so fully aware of all that's involved. Secondly, because I appreciate and respect you, and, although as you have seen I have no scruples about it, I prefer not to be regarded as a manipulative woman. Twice now I've said I was willing to return your favours, and I never go back on my word."

The taxi pulled up outside the mansion, and Anthony was glad not to have to reply immediately to this vague offer. He waved a hand in the air; Paquita took one of hers out of her muff and extended it to him.

"Goodnight, Anthony," she whispered, "and thank you for everything."

"It was nothing," replied the Englishman, then added in all seriousness: "For a moment I thought you were going to pull out a pistol."

"I don't carry a weapon," said Paquita, smiling, "and I don't think I need one with you. Don't make me change my mind."

She shook hands, opened the taxi door, and stepped out. Before Anthony could do the same to say a proper goodbye on the pavement, she had already gone through the gate and was disappearing into the gloom of the garden. Realising there was no further purpose in him being there, he gave the taxi driver the address of his hotel, and spent the rest of the journey pondering what Paquita had said. His personal experience up to this point had led him to believe that Spanish Fascism was a solid, united movement. Now this image had been demolished by someone whose opinion he had no reason to doubt. Despite the arrogance, even megalomania of its leaders, the Falange was a small, marginal group held together by the oratory of its founder and by the ever-present thrill of physical danger, which prevented its members making any cool assessment of the situation. And although none of this affected him personally, the conclusion profoundly depressed the Englishman.

23

"Sorry to bother you at this time of night, Don Alonso, but I thought I ought to inform you that the individual in question has finally been located and arrested. He's being brought here at this very moment."

At the far end of the line, Don Alonso Mallol, the director-general of Security, sighs as he hears Lieutenant-Colonel Marranón's report: he is pleased at the news, but it will doubtless mean he will be unable to have a quiet dinner at home, as planned. He replies:

"I'll be there in twenty minutes."

Lieutenant-Colonel Marranón hangs up and rolls a cigarette, frowning. He is not happy either about having to get a mackerel sandwich sent up from the café downstairs. The cause of all this fuss will have to pay for their bad tempers, he thinks, lighting the cigarette and straightening the papers on his desk in order to give his boss a good impression. He calls his secretary Pilar in and tells her what is going on. The plump shorthand typist raises her sturdy arms resignedly. She does not seem annoyed, although for years her husband has been unable to work because of a chronic illness, meaning that the weight of earning their livelihood, doing the household chores and looking after an invalid has fallen on her shoulders. Doing overtime is very inconvenient: she will have to call a neighbour and ask her to deal with supper and her sick husband until she gets home. Yet the plump stenographer never complains or loses her good humour. The same cannot be said of Captain Coscolluela, whose temper is growing worse by the day. The captain is a man of action; he was used to combat and the military life, but now because of his wound he has to be patient for long hours at a time, and to waste his energies in annoying paperwork.

Don Alonso Mallol appears in the office sooner than expected. He is wearing an elegant navy blue overcoat with black velvet lapels and a bowler hat. When he received the call he was at an event in the Ateneo, and to avoid the traffic in the city centre chose to walk the short distance to Security Headquarters. That afternoon Catholic students demonstrated in Puerta del Sol against the ban on religious teaching, and some stragglers are holding everything up, he explains as with the colonel's help he leaves his coat and hat on the stand.

"What I want to know is if they're already Catholics, why do they need to be taught it?"

"What they want is to avoid studying and cause trouble," the lieutenant-colonel agrees.

Señor Mallol and his subordinate sit down. The director-general takes a cigarette from his cigarette case and offers one to the colonel, but not to Pilar. Inserting his own into a long holder, he lights it and does the same for Marranón. The two men smoke in silence for a while.

"So where the devil had our man got to?" Señor Mallol eventually asks.

"You're not going to believe it, Don Alonso. To the Europa cinema, listening to Primo and his fascist chums! When he was arrested he denied being there, but one of our agents saw him going in together with the Duke of La Igualada's daughter."

"Great heavens, that hothead drives them all crazy! What does she do to them?"

"What women always do, Don Alonso: she gives them false hope."

Señor Mallol smiles faintly and asks if the meeting had not been banned. Yes, permission had been refused, but the Falange had ignored it. The cinema owner alleged he had been forced to accept. At the last moment, the Deputy Interior Minister had decided not to send in the police so as to avoid any serious trouble. As it turned out, the remedy was worse than the illness: at the end of the event, there were clashes with the socialist youth organisations. Several people were hurt and one died of gunshot wounds: an eighteen-year old Falangist from Ciempozuelos who worked in a pharmacy there.

A loud knocking at the door interrupts the colonel's report. In come Captain Coscolluela and Anthony Whitelands, escorted by two uniformed guards. When she sees them, Pilar takes out her shorthand notebook and checks the tip of her pencil: from now on, everything said could be a matter of record. The Englishman appears to be shaken, but still shows traces of imperial arrogance. Before he can say a word, Don Alonso Mallol stubs out his cigarette in an ashtray overflowing with butts, shakes the holder, puts it in his jacket pocket, and then stands up.

"Señor Whitelands?" he says, holding out his hand. Anthony shakes it without thinking. "I don't believe we've been introduced. Alonso Mallol, Director-General of National Security. I'm sorry to have to meet you in such circumstances."

"Might I ask . . . ?" Anthony stutters.

"Don't make things worse, Vitelas," the lieutenant-colonel cuts in. "We're the ones who ask the questions here. But if you want to know why you've been arrested, I can give you various reasons."

"I merely want to ring the British Embassy," says Anthony.

"Nobody will be there at this hour, Señor Whitelands," says Mallol. "There'll be time enough for that. First let's talk. Be so good as to take a seat."

Closely watched by the two guards, Anthony hangs his coat on the stand next to Mallol's, then sits in the same small wicker armchair he occupied the first time he was here. Pilar draws up her chair in order to be close to those who will be speaking, while Captain Coscolluela flops into another, suppressing a groan: after so many hours waiting, his wounded leg is painful. Anthony realises he does not have many friends in the room. Lieutenant-Colonel Marranón waves an arm; the Assault Guards salute with much creaking of leather and clashing of metal, turn on their heels and leave the room. Their boot heels thump along the corridor outside. Then an ominous silence falls, eventually broken by the director-general, whose voice is neutral but betrays a touch of exasperation.

"Señor Whitelands, since you yourself attended a meeting of the Falange at the Europa cinema today, you will be aware that we have much more important things to attend to than keeping an eye on you. If all of us here are spending our precious time on this, there must be some other reason for it: do you follow me? If that is so, I'll get straight to the point. You have heard what kind of things were said in that cinema, not once, but over and over again. You have seen how the audience reacted. You know of the existence of the fascist movement in Europe, and its aims: sedition, seizing power by violent means, civil war if there is no other way and, ultimately, the imposition of a totalitarian regime. They do not hide their intentions or simply blow hot air: look at Italy, Germany, and the countries that want to follow their example. However, despite the seriousness of the threat, that is a matter for the Spanish government, not for you, or even for me. Fascism is politics, and I am concerned with public order. Do you smoke?"

Anthony shakes his head. The director-general offers round his cigarette case, performs the little ceremony with his holder once more, breathes in the smoke and then goes on.

"José Antonio Primo de Rivera is a fool," he says. "but he doesn't know it, and that's the problem. As the son of a dictator he grew up like a prince, surrounded by fawning courtiers. Later, when those who had raised his father to the heights pulled the rug from under him, he could not accept it. That took him into politics. He is good-looking, a brilliant orator, and lives surrounded by a clique of silly little rich kids who laugh at all his witticisms. In normal circumstances, he would have been a successful lawyer, made a good marriage, and this madness would have passed."

He pauses, sighs, and then goes on.

"As it is, he fell in love with that girl, things didn't work out and that pushed him over the edge. Then again, the political and social situation in Spain only serves to encourage his madness, with obvious results. This very evening, at the end of the meeting in the Europa cinema, there were clashes in the street with the usual outcome: one Falangist dead – a poor eighteen-year old lad. José Antonio fills their heads with fantasies, sends them out to die and doesn't turn a hair. You must have seen the list of dead Falange members; perhaps you would also like to know how old they were: the majority were youngsters who did not even understand the ideas they were sacrificing their future for. Primo de Rivera sees that as poetic. I see it as sinister."

At first Anthony listens carefully, but his attention wavers when he hears of José Antonio's frustrated love affair with Paquita – from the director-general's insinuations, it must be her he is referring to. What can have gone wrong with their relationship? The question bothers him, but this is not the moment to lose himself in speculation: he himself is in a difficult position, and he will need all his ingenuity if he is to emerge unscathed and without revealing too much.

The room has gradually filled with smoke. Pilar coughs and has to stop taking notes. The lieutenant-colonel gets up and opens the window. A blast of cold air sweeps in from the dark interior courtyard, together with the desolate clack of a typewriter. After a minute the lieutenant-colonel decides they have had enough fresh air and shuts the window again. Mallol continues with his explanation.

"In addition to being irresponsible and off his head, Primo de Rivera is quite obviously an idiot. He visited Mussolini and Hitler to ask for their blessing and aid. Both of them received him with open arms, but soon got the measure of him and politely brushed him off. Mussolini sends him a monthly allowance that is barely enough to pay his administrative costs. Hitler doesn't give him a penny. He's offered his services to the extreme Right and the extreme Left, with similar results. The socialists received him with a hail of bullets; the anarchists listened to him as if he were a lunatic, and when they grew bored, slammed the door in his face. Gil Robles has turned him down as well, and although a lot of the military are attracted by Fascism, they would never dream of turning to the Falange if they were to carry out a coup: they don't need the feeble help of a group of inexpert novices, nor are they willing to take orders from a lunatic like him. As if that weren't enough, they remember that José Antonio was cashiered from the Army for punching General Queipo de Llano. That's no way to win over the high command. For his part, José Antonio is scornful of the generals: he thinks they didn't defend his father because they were cowards or simply because they betrayed him. The upper middle classes consider him one of their own and look kindly on him, but when it comes down to it, they won't commit themselves or give him any funds. After all, José Antonio has promised to end class privileges and to nationalise the banks. As things stand, the only way out for the Falange is to take to the streets on their own to try to seize power, then wait for the Army to back them up. Of course if they did that, it would get them nowhere. If the armed forces stage a coup they'll do so when they are good and ready, not when the Falange decides to do so. And the Falange don't have the wherewithal: they don't have any weapons, or the funds to buy them with."

The director-general of Security falls silent so that Anthony can assimilate all that he has said and draw his own conclusions, then moves on from the general to the specific.

"The Falange has always been desperately trying to get its hands on weapons, and this effort has been redoubled since the recent elections. Apart from Mussolini, they receive money from a few senseless rich people. Naturally, these weapons have to be bought abroad, and with foreign currency. Some of their rich backers have money deposited outside Spain, but they guard it jealously. If anything were to happen, those deposits would allow them to live comfortably. A very few of them are willing to sacrifice everything for the cause. The most conspicuous among these is your very good friend the Duke of La Igualada."

This revelation leaves Anthony dumbfounded, not so much because of the duke's ideology, but because of the fact that he had deliberately concealed it from him. His reaction does not go unnoticed by the others: the director-general and the lieutenant-colonel exchange knowing glances. While Señor Mallol ceremoniously lights another cigarette, the lieutenant-colonel takes over.

"In the past, the Duke of La Igualada was a fervent supporter of Primo de Rivera's dictatorship. He was his close friend, and when he was toppled, the duke transferred his allegiance to the son. He has always protected and helped José Antonio, both financially and through his position: in the years when he was ostracised, the duke received him in his home like one of the family. Then things became complicated—"

"But that's another story," Señor Mallol interrupts him. "We have other priorities. Everything points to the fact that the Duke of La Igualada is intent on getting a large sum of money out of Spain to buy arms with. His eldest son has been travelling in France and Italy for a month. The reason for the trip is said to be for him to undertake supposed art studies; the real one is for him to contact fascist groups to organise the purchase and despatch of weapons as soon as the funds come through. The duke has no accounts in European banks, and according to reliable reports he has not sold anything or raised any capital in Spain. But he is up to something."

"And at this precise moment you arrive, the most innocent man in the world," the lieutenant-colonel says sarcastically. "You visit the duke, go for a blowout with José Antonio, sweet-talk the daughter, and yet you know nothing of what we are talking about."

"We know that an art dealer in London by the name of Pedro Teacher got in touch with you," the director-general says. "Did he go and see you on the Duke of La Igualada's behalf?"

"Who told you about Pedro Teacher?" asks Anthony. "That is a private matter, related to my profession."

This time it is Captain Coscolluela who replies from his corner.

"For several years now, Pedro Teacher has been a contact between fascist groups in Britain and Spain. Didn't you know that?"

"How could I? He himself said nothing about it. Pedro Teacher is well known in the tiny British art world, and I don't get involved in politics. I had no reason to suspect that behind his visit lay some international intrigue."

"So you don't deny that you spoke to Pedro Teacher in London a week ago?" asks the lieutenant-colonel. Pilar listens intently and straightens up in her seat in order not to miss any of the reply.

"You know that as well as I do. Let's not waste any more time, gentlemen. Pedro Teacher came to see me on behalf of a Spanish family to ask me to value that family's collection of paintings. Neither Pedro Teacher nor subsequently the people concerned made any attempt to hide the possible reason for this valuation: given the current instability in Spain, they are considering the sale of a part of their possessions with a view to moving abroad. It goes without saying that I have never been in any way involved in this decision. I was asked to make a valuation; that is part of my profession."

"You admit you took the commission," says the lieutenant-colonel.

"Of course. I am a specialist in Spanish painting, and I was tempted by the possibility of enriching my knowledge by looking at a collection which I thought would be interesting. Besides, I had no other pressing engagements in England, and so I was pleased to have the excuse to return to Madrid."

"As you yourself said, that was a week ago. Isn't that a long time to carry out a valuation?"

"Not in the slightest. A painting cannot be valued lightly. A lot of factors have to be taken into account, some of them artistic, others to do with materials – chemicals, for example. Or documents. In addition, every painting has its own history, and it all helps determine its authenticity and, ultimately, its value. It is not simply a question of deciding whether a painting is authentic or a fake. Apart from forgeries, there can be changes due to clumsy restoration work, mistaken attributions, copies made by the painter himself, or it may have been done in the artist's workshop, and so on. The duke has a large collection, with works from many different periods. To tell the truth, a rigorous and exhaustive examination would take months, perhaps an entire year. I hope to do it quickly, but not in the twinkling of an eye."

This thoughtful exposition is greeted with due deference, and then immediately dismissed by his interrogators, who are far too wily to allow themselves to be led into territory they know little about, and which has little to do with what concerns them.

"What would be your rough estimate of the value of the duke's painting collection?" asks the director-general.

"That's impossible to say," the Englishman replies. "Obviously, its economic value depends on many imponderables. Anyway, don't get me wrong: assessing monetary value is not part of my expertise, and in this case I was not asked to do so. As an expert, I confine myself to authenticating a work or, if it is anonymous, attributing it to a painter or school, a period or its place of origin. This of course has economic consequences, but they come later."

"Did you recommend the sale of any particular work to the duke? To anywhere in Europe: you are in contact with gallery owners in England and other countries."

"I've already told you, I'm not an art dealer. I won't deny that during our conversations the topic of a possible sale came up. I said that I was against the idea. His excellency the duke can confirm what I have just told you."

"Señor Whitelands," the director general insists, "are you sure that, in the light of what we have been saying, you are not hiding anything we should be aware of? Do you have any evidence that the duke is proposing to sell anything important outside Spain? The question could not be clearer; I beg you to respond equally clearly. Yes or no?"

Anthony has already made up his mind, and so has no hesitation in responding.

"No."

This emphatic answer is followed by a calm silence. As if they were expecting exactly this, none of the others shows any sign of confusion or impatience. Don Alonso Mallol gets up, walks round the small room, then addresses the stenographer.

"You can go home now, Pilar, and thanks for your cooperation."

"Always happy to oblige, Don Alonso," she says, closing her notebook and putting it in her bag. She takes out a pencil box and puts away her pencil. "I'll bring you the typescript tomorrow morning."

"Don't go to any trouble, there's no rush," says Señor Mallol gently.

Pilar nods her head slightly to all of them, Anthony included, and leaves the office. Señor Mallol turns to the Englishman.

"I also thank you for your collaboration, Señor Whitelands," he says, shaking his hand before speaking to the lieutenant-colonel. "Gumersindo, I'll leave this to you."

"Yes, don't worry, Don Alonso."

Seeing everyone else stand up, Anthony does the same and walks over to the coat stand.

"Can I go now?" he asks, about to put on his raincoat.

"No. You are under arrest for attending a banned gathering. You will be taken to the cells here in Headquarters, and in due course we will decide whether you should appear in court or if, as a foreigner, you will be deported. Captain Coscolluela will accompany you. I don't think we will need any guards. We can fill out your details tomorrow. By now there won't be anybody left to take your photographs."

"What! You're going to lock me up?" Anthony wails. "I haven't even had dinner!"

"Nor have we, Señor Vitelas," replies Lieutenant-Colonel Marranón. "Nor have we."

24

When he woke up, Anthony could make out a dim brightness beyond the small, narrow cell window. He calculated it must be around six in the morning. Since he had been unable to make out the face of his watch all night, he had no idea how long he had slept. Probably very little. From the moment of his incarceration, when he heard the sinister clang of the metal doors shutting as Captain Coscolluela left, Anthony Whitelands had gone through stages of bewilderment and then panic, and finally settled into a lengthy period of reflection. Obviously, his situation did not look good: the law was on the side of those who had arrested him, and his own lack of collaboration meant that they had no inclination to renounce any of the advantages that this legality gave them. Seen from this point of view, his immediate future looked grim. And he was tormented by doubts as to whether he had acted correctly, both from a practical and an ethical standpoint.

After much debate on the pros and cons of his decision to lie, he finally decided he had done the right thing, or at least had not made a huge mistake. In the first place, the affair he was caught up in only involved him indirectly; he had no reason to choose one side or another in the complex power struggle going on in Spain: it was not his country, and he knew nothing more about what was going on than the versions each side had given him, and they were both fragmentary and utterly partial. Out of principle, he was in favour of those who represented the upholding of political legitimacy and the established order, and yet the arguments put forward by the Falangists did not seem to him so outlandish. He felt little sympathy for the tough attitude of the government officials, who were backed by the power of the state; the Falangists on the other hand, with their easy nature and youthful vigour seemed to irradiate the romantic aura of the underdog. Not to mention Paquita, of course: would she forgive him if he betrayed José Antonio and her family, if he cared more about saving himself than being loyal to her?

And finally, if he told the truth, what would happen to the painting? The government would probably find some legal subterfuge to seize it and hang it in the Prado. That would be an event of world importance, and Anthony Whitelands would play no part in it. Of all the misfortunes facing the Englishman, this seemed to him the most terrible.

However, all this deliberation got him nowhere. In denying the evidence to the director-general of Security, he had simply been trying to gain time to think, but now his thoughts, far from offering him a possible solution, only confirmed his fears. They would not let him out of here unless, in exchange for his freedom, he offered them some important revelation. But what could he reveal? Any lie would be discovered immediately, and would only make things worse: his adversaries were no fools. On the other hand, telling the truth would not do him much good either. He was in no position to bargain. Thwarting the duke's plans, whatever they might be, would not make things much better for him: at most, a quiet deportation rather than a trial and a lengthy period in jail. The prospect of being sent to a Spanish penal institution filled him with justified terror: even if he survived the test, his personal and professional life would be left in ruins.

His spirits were not lifted by the hunger he felt, the tiredness produced by a long and eventful day, the freezing cold cell, the gloomy silence, the darkness into which he was plunged and the ruthless attacks from fleas and bedbugs. The place stank, and all he had to lie down on was a cement block. When, overcome with exhaustion, he finally managed to fall asleep, he was surprised to find himself within a pleasant dream. He was in London, strolling through Saint James's

Park on the arm of a beautiful woman who at times looked like Paquita, at others like Catherine, his forsaken lover. It was a fine spring morning, and the park was crowded. Everyone they met – distinguished-looking men and women – greeted them effusively in a way very untypical of the English. Some even stopped to pat him on the back or dig him conspiratorially in the ribs. Anthony saw these expressions as a desire to show their affection and approval: London society was giving its blessing to his unconventional relationships, and giving its unreserved approval. When he awoke, the memory of this tranquil imaginary stroll only served to deepen his misery: a perverse fantasy had offered as reality something that could never happen.

As day dawned, the basement of Security Headquarters gradually filled with voices, footsteps and the clanging of doors. But no-one paid him any attention, as if those responsible for locking him up had forgotten his existence. This sensation depressed Anthony far more than any possible threat. His hunger and thirst had become unbearable. By ten in the morning he had no strength left, and decided to give in. The thick wooden cell door had a square opening in its upper half, crossed by two solid metal bars. Anthony pressed himself against the opening and began shouting to attract the guards' attention. When nobody responded, he gave up. A short while later, he tried again. It was not until his third attempt that somebody roughly asked what he wanted.

"Please, find Lieutenant-Colonel Marranón or Captain Coscolluela and tell them that the English gentleman they arrested last night is willing to talk. They will understand. And for the love of God, be quick about it."

"Alright. Wait here," said the guard, as if Anthony had any other choice.

More than an hour went by, during which Anthony was plunged into the deepest despair. He no longer cared what Paquita or anyone else thought of him; deportation or any other humiliation seemed to him preferable to this uncertainty. At last he heard the sound of a key in the lock, and the imposing figure of an Assault Guard, shotgun slung over his shoulder, appeared in the doorway.

"Come with me."

Struggling to keep up with the guard, Anthony walked back along the way he had come the previous evening. The two men came to a halt outside an office door; the guard opened it and stood to one side. The Englishman's head was spinning from the torments he had suffered and from the despicable act he was about to commit. He went in without raising his eyes from the floor, and stayed head down until a voice he immediately recognised jerked him out of his submissive attitude.

"For heaven's sake, Whitelands! What scrape have you got yourself into now?"

"Parker! Harry Parker!" exclaimed Anthony. "Thank the Lord! How did you find me?"

"It was quite simple," replied the young diplomat. "I went to look for you this morning at your hotel, and the receptionist told me you had been brought here. For goodness' sake, Whitelands, I had to create an international incident for them to let you out. What did you do this time? You've become public enemy number one."

"It's a long story."

"Don't tell me now. We have to hurry. People are waiting for us."

"For me? Who? Where?"

"Where do you think? At the bull-ring? At the embassy of course. We'll take a taxi."

"But I can't go to the embassy like this, Parker. Look at me: I've spent the night in a cell, I've got fleas all over me."

"Well, at least you're sober now. That's something: the last time we met you were completely sozzled. Come on, there's no time to lose," Parker added, cutting short the other man's protests. "Either you come with me to the embassy as you are, or I leave you here. There's a certain

Captain Cocohueco who seems to have it in for you. A serious-looking man. Lame. Military bearing. You decide."

"Very well," said Anthony, quaking at the very mention of Captain Coscolluela's name, "but on one condition: we must stop at a bar so that I can get a drink of water and something to eat."

By now they were out in the street. Paying no attention to his compatriot's pleas, the young diplomat was waving his arms about to hail a taxi. One soon pulled up, and Harry Parker pushed Anthony inside.

"There isn't a moment to lose," he repeated. "You can get something to eat at the embassy: some tea and porridge. How does that sound?"

Anthony felt faint, but after his night in the cells and the tragic thoughts that had kept him awake, the sense that he was safe made up for any further inconvenience.

"Parker, I . . . I haven't yet . . . I haven't yet thanked you . . ." he said as he sat back in the seat. He immediately fell fast asleep.

He was awakened by somebody shaking him.

"Wake up, Whitelands. We've reached the embassy. Are you sure you haven't been drinking?"

They got out of the taxi, went into the embassy, climbed the marble staircase, knocked on a door and entered after receiving permission to do so. Anthony was surprised and shocked to find himself in a spacious, elegant drawing room with heavy curtains and walls lined with green silk, presided over by an enormous oil portrait of His Majesty Edward VIII. Seated on a sofa close to the hearth were two middle-aged gentlemen, in the impeccable outfits of career diplomats. Another man in a pinstripe suit was walking up and down on the thick carpet, absent-mindedly puffing on a pipe. None of them made any attempt to greet the newcomers. Still smoking his pipe, the standing man shot a disapproving glance at Anthony's bedraggled figure, frowned, and then continued his pacing. Anthony tried hard to look dignified and resist the urge to scratch as hard as he could to stop the itching caused by all the parasites he had brought with him. Harry Parker, who had obviously forgotten about the promised breakfast, introduced the men in the room, although they barely deigned to acknowledge Anthony. One of the two diplomats was David Ross, first secretary at the embassy. He conveyed to the others the ambassador's regrets at not being able to attend the meeting: he was tied up with other matters. The other diplomat was Peter Atkins, the embassy's cultural attaché, whom David Ross had asked to be present given the nature of the meeting. The gentleman with the pipe was Lord Houndsditch. Lord Houndsditch, explained Harry Parker to Anthony in a whisper, worked in British Intelligence, and had arrived by aeroplane that same morning. Apparently he had hit bad weather crossing the Channel. Since he himself was not introduced, Anthony concluded the others all knew who he was and the situation he found himself in. Otherwise there was no reason for him to be there. After a few moments of obligatory awkwardness, the first secretary motioned for Anthony to take a seat.

"A glass of port?"

"No, thank you."

"A whisky then?"

"No, thanks. I haven't had breakfast yet."

"Oh."

There was another brief silence. Standing beside Anthony's armchair, Harry Parker suggested it might be useful, if everyone agreed, to explain to Mr Whitelands what was going on. After a moment's consideration, the first secretary gave a reluctant sigh that something so obvious needed any explanation, then began to explain.

"A few days ago," he said, "you, Mr Whitelands, rang our counsellor, Mr Parker here, and arranged to meet him in the Ritz Hotel. At that meeting, you handed over a letter which Mr Parker was to give to a certain person if certain things happened. On that occasion, Mr Parker detected signs that you were under the influence of alcohol or other toxic substances, and put your behaviour down to you taking temporary leave of your senses. The next morning however, he informed me of what had happened, and the two of us opened and read the letter."

Hearing this, Anthony jumped in his seat and turned towards the young diplomat, who was regarding the scene with a sedate smile on his face.

"Parker! How could you do such a thing? I spoke to you in the strictest confidence, and you swore to me that—"

"I didn't swear anything, Whitelands. And don't worry about confidentiality. We've kept the secret as far as possible," the other man replied. "You must realise I had no other choice. I am a diplomat, and anything that might affect the interests of the Crown, you know . . ."

"Mr Parker does not owe you any explanation, Mr Whitelands. He did the right thing, that is to inform his superiors of the conduct of a British subject in Spain, given the suspicion that this conduct could be harmful to relations between our two countries. In addition, in case it has slipped your mind, we have just with great difficulty obtained your release from the Spanish Security Headquarters, where you were under arrest," Clearing his throat, he went on: "My personal impression of the contents of the letter was not favourable; I mean I tend not to believe a word it says. However, with things as they are in Spain, I decided it was best to take every precaution. In short, I contacted the Foreign Office. Now our cultural attaché Peter Atkins can fill you in on the rest."

The cultural attaché began to speak with as little enthusiasm as his predecessor. He explained that while the first secretary was warning the Foreign Office of an allegedly fraudulent transaction and its possible diplomatic consequences, he, as cultural attaché, made a call to the person to whom the letter was addressed, a man by the name of Edwin Garrigaw, a curator at the National Gallery in London, and read him the letter. Mr Garrigaw, a person of unimpeachable character and a renowned authority in his field, had asked him to repeat the contents of the letter, and then asserted that the painting mentioned by Mr Whitelands must of necessity be a fake. Without calling into question either Mr Whitelands' knowledge or his probity, Edwin Garrigaw was convinced that Whitelands' powers of judgment must have been affected by circumstances that were impossible to determine without closer knowledge of his behaviour. In consideration of which . . ."

At this point, Anthony could not contain an explosion of anger, paradoxically brought on by his exhaustion and lack of food.

"This is intolerable!" he shouted, rising from his chair and pointing an accusing finger at the others in the room. "You have behaved in a manner that is a betrayal of your positions and the fact that you are gentlemen. Not only have you betrayed the trust I placed in you, but you have placed something that is mine by right in the hands of a rival, causing me incalculable material and moral damage! Edwin Garrigaw . . . some authority! That man is a pompous cretin! In Cambridge he was known as Violet! And I'll tell you something that ought to make you blush: ten years ago, he had the temerity to take on Adolfo Venturi and Roberto Longhi over the attribution of a painting that was supposedly by Caravaggio. Can you credit it? Venturi and Longhi! It goes without saying that they made mincemeat of him. But it seems that fellow never learns. I've seen the painting with my own eyes, gentlemen! I . . ."

His outburst subsided as quickly as it had erupted. Anthony collapsed back into his armchair and hid his face in his hands, his body wracked by a fit of sobbing. The diplomats looked on in horror, staring at each other without the slightest idea of how to resolve this embarrassing incident. Finally, Lord Houndsditch stopped his pacing up and down, confronted Anthony and said in an even, resolute tone:

"Mr Whitelands, kindly leave these distressing emotional outpourings for some other occasion. They are out of place here, as are your accusations. These gentlemen have done their duty as diplomats and Englishmen. You on the other hand have put your personal interests before those of your country. I have also read that famous letter, and this is my conclusion: if the claims there are false, then you are either a fraud or a lunatic; if they are true, you are an accomplice to an international crime. So stop behaving like an idiot and listen carefully to what I am about to say. Thanks to you I have had a very unpleasant journey. Don't make it even more disagreeable."

When Anthony had succeeded in bringing his fit of hysterics under control, Lord Houndsditch brought a chair up close to him and sat astride it. Grasping his pipe by the bowl, he pointed the stem at Anthony's nose and peered at him inquisitively.

"Does the name Kolia mean anything to you? Have you heard it in recent days?"

"No," Anthony replied. "Not in recent days, or ever. Who is he?"

"We don't know," said Lord Houndsditch, raising his voice for everyone to hear. "Gentlemen, that's the nub of the question. Kolia is the code name of a Soviet agent who is operating in Spain, but that's all we know. He could be Spanish or a foreigner, a man or a woman, anything. We have no information about his identity or what he is up to. Our informer has only been able to send us a coded message in which he tells us that the Soviet Union's ambassador in Spain was recalled urgently by the Komintern for a lightning visit to Moscow. To the Kremlin and the Lubianka, the headquarters of the N.K.V.D. As a result of that visit, the N.K.V.D. gave Kolia precise instructions . . ."

At this, Lord Houndsditch lapsed into a glowering silence. When this seemed to be going on forever, the first secretary plucked up the courage to ask:

"So then what?"

"So then nothing," declared Lord Houndsditch, as though the question was inappropriate.

A wall clock struck one. Everyone in the room apart from Anthony checked that their watch showed the right time. Lord Houndsditch rubbed his hands together.

"It must be almost time for lunch, don't you think?"

"Whenever you wish, Lord Houndsditch."

Given the new direction taken by events, Anthony was uncertain whether it was better for him to go unnoticed or to try to clarify his situation. In the end he decided to draw attention to himself with a discreet cough. Lord Houndsditch shook his head and exclaimed:

"The devil take it, Whitelands, I'd almost forgotten about you. Well, as time is short, I'll tell you what you must do. To recapitulate, this is where we stand; you are involved in the sale of a fake painting . . . for heaven's sake, don't interrupt me. Of a painting mistakenly attributed to someone called Velázquez."

"Forgive me, Lord Houndsditch, but—"

"Be quiet, Whitelands. I couldn't give a damn about your opinion: I work for British Intelligence, not Sotheby's. I mean to say that the government of His Majesty," he continued, pointing to the august portrait of the monarch with his pipe, "is interested in the operation from a non-artistic point of view. Is that clear? Let me go on: it appears that the proceeds of the sale would be used to buy weapons for fascist groups in Spain. The Spanish intelligence services, if anything worthy of that name exists, are also aware of this. Now, gentlemen, pay attention. What I am about to say has to remain within these four walls. In His Majesty's name, Whitelands, I order you to continue with the sale as if the painting were genuine, and to make sure it is valued as highly as possible. Do I make myself clear? Officially, we have no knowledge of any of this wheeler-dealing. If the Spanish authorities discover the operation and decide quite rightly it is illegal, you are the one who will face the consequences. We will not step in on your behalf; we will deny all knowledge of the facts, or even that we have been in touch with you. We cannot act in any other way: England does not meddle in Spain's internal affairs. Besides, England may not have friendly relations with fascist governments or groups, but neither does it adopt a hostile attitude towards them. Live and let live is the motto of our foreign policy."

He puffed furiously on his pipe, shook the bowl over an ashtray until a dottle of tobacco and saliva fell out, put the pipe in his pocket and added:

"However, everything points towards an imminent Bolshevik revolution in Spain, and although this will still be an internal matter, it is not something that England can permit. A Communist country only a few miles from our coasts and with the ability to control the Straits of Gibraltar is unthinkable if the balance of power is to be maintained in Europe and the Mediterranean basin. Until now we have kept an entente with the fascists, and nothing suggests a change of attitude on Mr Hitler's part. Mussolini is a puppet, and is busy with his ridiculous war in Abyssinia. Our real enemy in the Soviet Union. Whether we like it or not, in Spain we have to support the fascists against the Marxists. I think I have made myself crystal clear. Any questions?"

Since it was none of their business and the orders came from a higher authority, the diplomats expressed their complete agreement with what Lord Houndsditch had said, and declared that they understood perfectly. Anthony said nothing either. His choice was plain: either obey Lord Houndsditch or lose the embassy's *de facto* protection and immediately fall into the clutches of Lieutenant-Colonel Marranón. Since he was also still convinced that the Velázquez was authentic, anything related to the discovery of the painting that was associated with his name could only be favourable, whatever the ultimate aim of its sale. Basically, as far as he was concerned events had taken a positive turn: seeing that from now on he was acting on explicit instructions from the British government, he could count on it supporting, however discreetly and indirectly, both himself and his plans.

"What is my current position with regard to the Spanish police?" he wanted to know.

"Go and ask them," replied the first secretary. "We've done enough by setting you free. In my view, they'll leave you in peace. They locked you up to see if you would talk, but they don't gain anything by keeping you behind bars. They prefer you to be on the outside so that you can lead them to what they are looking for. Bear that in mind. They don't know anything about the painting: that gives you the advantage."

As he was saying this, the first secretary stood up to leave the room with the others. They were all in a hurry to go and have lunch, but no-one more so than Anthony, who stood up too and, seeing that nobody apparently wished to say goodbye to him, headed for the door. Harry Parker went with him, to make sure he left the embassy without any fuss. In the doorway, however, a doubt suddenly struck Anthony. He stopped and turned back towards Lord Houndsditch.

"Excuse me, Lord Houndsditch, but there's one thing that's not clear to me. What role is Kolia playing in all this?"

"Kolia? I told you before: we have no idea. But there's one thing of which we are sure: Kolia is your counterpart. If we know about the sale of the painting and the Spanish authorities suspect something, then it's obvious the Russians are aware of it too. Naturally, they have no desire to see the fascists receiving help in either funds or weapons, and they will do all they can to prevent it. That's why they've brought in Kolia."

"I understand," said Anthony. "And how could Kolia prevent the sale?"

"What a silly question, Whitelands!" Lord Houndsditch exclaimed. "The usual way: by eliminating you."

25

A heaped plate of lentils with sausage and half a loaf of white bread, washed down with a carafe of red wine, were not enough to relieve the gloom produced by Lord Houndsditch's ominous words. While Anthony was satisfying the hunger accumulated from the day before, he could not get rid of the feeling that he was being pursued by a faceless killer. Anyone, anywhere and at any time, could stab him in the back, shoot him at point-blank range, strangle him with his tie or put poison in his food or drink. And so while he ate and drank warily, Anthony wondered for the hundredth time whether he should leap onto the first train and return to England. The only reason he did not do so was the despairing conviction that he was caught up in an international intrigue, which meant there was nowhere on the planet he would be safe from the conspirators if they decided to get rid of him, whether as a reprisal, to guarantee his silence or out of mere distaste. He told himself that the only way to escape alive was to finish the task that had brought him to Madrid as quickly as possible. Only once his presence was no obstacle to his enemies' plans would they leave him in peace.

With this vague sense of consolation, he finished his meal and started on his way back to the hotel. He walked briskly along the busy streets, constantly glancing to right and left, and occasionally spinning round in order to catch anyone attacking him from behind. He himself was aware how absurd his conduct was, since he had no idea what his potential assailant might look like. In his feverish imagination he had decided that the murderer looked like George Raft, and so he peered at the passers-by, trying to identify the actor's features and the dapper outfits for which his characters were famous. This eccentric behaviour helped him forget his fear, and he was driven on by the desire to reach his hotel so that he could wash, shave, and change his clothes: if he were to meet a tragic death, at least he ought to die looking presentable.

Passing the well-stocked window of a grocer's shop, he came to a halt, went in, and bought a range of foodstuffs. He did not want to be outside after nightfall, and was buying provisions in order to shut himself up in his room and resist the siege. He bought bread in a bakery, wine in a tavern. Abundantly supplied in this way, he reached the hotel without any untoward incident.

As was becoming the custom, the receptionist looked at him with disgust, justified on this occasion by his lamentable appearance. But at that moment the Englishman could not care less what anyone else thought of him. Nodding coldly to the man, he held out his hand for his room key. The receptionist handed it to him, directing his gaze as he did so at something or someone behind Anthony's back. Anthony whirled round, trying desperately not to cry out in fear. The sight that met his eyes was no cause for alarm.

A young girl dressed in rags was sleeping in one of the foyer armchairs. Anthony asked the receptionist what that person had to do with him.

"That's for you to know," the receptionist said. "She came here late last night asking after you, and hasn't budged since. I was going to call the police, but then I thought you already had more than enough problems on that score, and I didn't want to add fuel to the fire."

Anthony knelt down in front of the girl so that he could see her face. He was astonished to recognise Toñina. As though she had glimpsed his reaction in her dreams, she opened her eyes and stared at the Englishman with a look of immense gratitude. Anthony leapt to his feet as if he had seen a tarantula.

"What are you doing here?"

Toñina rubbed her eyes and smiled.

"Higinio Zamora came to see me. He told me to come to this hotel, and that you would know what it was about. He said that if you weren't here I should wait until you returned. I've been here since yesterday. I was beginning to think you had gone back to your own country."

"Higinio Zamora told you to come?" asked Anthony. "Did he say why?"

"He told me you would take me with you to England."

As she said this, she pointed beneath the chair. Anthony was astounded to see a bundle wrapped in a scarf.

"Listen, Toñina," he said, trying to stay calm and express himself as simply and clearly as possible, "I've no idea what Higinio Zamora told you, but whatever it was, there's no truth to it. Yes, we did have lunch together yesterday, at his insistence. He was very ill at ease, and during the lunch he spouted lot of nonsense. In order not to upset him still further, I chose not to contradict him. Later on, more important events led me to forget our conversation. Besides, it wasn't up to me to clarify any possible misunderstanding. If Higinio Zamora got the wrong end of the stick, that's his problem, not mine. You understand what I'm saying, don't you?"

Toñina said she did. Reassured, Anthony headed for the staircase leading to the bedrooms. Reaching the first step, he turned to see if Toñina had left the hotel, but found her right behind him, bundle in hand. Either she had not heard his explanation or she had not understood it; or she had understood but had no intention of accepting that it had anything to do with her. Anthony realised he had to act decisively and unambiguously: the only solution was to grab the girl by the throat, drag her out into the street and send her on her way with a kick up her scrawny backside. That was the only language these people understood. Perhaps the receptionist would deplore the use of violence in the hotel lobby, but he would grasp the situation and stand by him. This thought encouraged Anthony, so he put his hand on Toñina's shoulder and looked her up and down.

"You haven't eaten since yesterday, have you?" he asked. When she nodded silently, he added: "I've got provisions in this bag. Come up to my room and I'll give you a sandwich. Then we'll see."

He spoke to the receptionist, who was watching all this with great curiosity.

"I'm in my room, and don't want to be disturbed for any reason," he said.

The receptionist raised his eyebrows and looked as if he was about to protest. When she saw this, Toñina climbed three steps to be on the same level as the Englishman, and whispered in his ear:

"Give him a tip."

Anthony hastily took out a five peseta coin, went over to reception and left it on the desk. Without a word, the receptionist put it in his pocket, then stared up at the ceiling mouldings while Anthony and Toñina ran upstairs.

In the room, Anthony handed the bag of food over to Toñina, begged her to leave something for supper, collapsed onto the bed fully clothed and fell asleep at once. When he woke up, the room was in darkness; night had fallen, and the only light was the pale glow from the street lamps. Toñina was curled up beside him, fast asleep. Before lying down, she had removed his clothes and shoes and covered him with the sheet and blanket. Anthony turned over and fell back into a deep sleep.

He was awakened from this peaceful interlude by a loud knocking at the door. When he asked who was there, a man's voice replied:

"A friend. Open up."

"How do I know you're a friend?" asked Anthony.

"Because I say so," replied the voice. "It's Guillermo. Guillermo del Valle, the Duke of La Igualada's son. We met at my parents' house, and I saw you the other night with José Antonio in the Happy Whale."

Their voices had also woken Toñina. Realising what was going on, and perhaps accustomed to similar scrapes, she jumped out of bed, hid her scanty possessions under it, picked up the clothes strewn on the floor, then climbed into the wardrobe. Anthony put something on and answered the door.

Guillermo del Valle thrust his way into the room. As on previous occasions, he was dressed with scruffy elegance. Smiling broadly, he shook Anthony's hand.

"Forgive me for receiving you in this mess," said the Englishman. "I wasn't expecting visitors. In fact, I told them in reception I was not to be disturbed on any account."

"Oh, yes," said the newcomer, his smile giving way to a boyish laugh, "the fellow at the desk didn't want me to come up, so I showed him my pistol and convinced him. I'm no thug," he said quickly, seeing the Englishman suddenly turn pale. "In normal circumstances I would never have bothered you. But I had to speak to you."

Anthony closed the door, pointed to the only chair in the room, quickly pulled the cover up over the bed, and sat down on it.

"Don't bother," said Guillermo del Valle. "I'll only take a few minutes of your time. Are we alone? Yes, I can see we are. I meant, can we talk and be sure no-one will overhear us? As I told you, it's a matter of extreme urgency."

Judging that this was hardly the moment to admit there was an adolescent prostitute hiding in the wardrobe, Anthony invited the newcomer to explain what it was all about. Guillermo del Valle said nothing for a few moments, as if suddenly having doubts as to whether he had been right to come. With a hesitation that revealed both his natural timidity and the insecurity typical of his tender years, he began by apologising for any unpleasantness in their previous meetings. He said he was always tense in his parents' home, because they insisted on still treating him like a child. Family pressure had pushed him into studying Law, though he had no vocation for it and got no pleasure out of it. By temperament he was a poet, not like the Romantics, but in the line of Marinetti and the Italian Futurists. Poetry and politics were all he could think about. Perhaps that was why he did not have a

226

girlfriend. At university he had joined the S.E.U., attracted to it initially by its Falangist ideals, and then by its leader's magnetic personality. He dedicated his spare time now to working at their Centre, helping with administration and propaganda. He hastened to add that this bureaucratic activity did not prevent him from taking part in public events that often turned violent.

"As for what brings me here," Guillermo del Valle continued, "I'll try to explain as best I can. I still haven't really got it clear in my mind. But if you listen until I finish, you'll understand the cause for my concern, and also why I came to talk to you."

Pausing once more, he drew his hand across his face, still casting anxious glances towards all corners of the tiny room.

"I'll come straight to the point. Something strange is going on at the very heart of the Falange. I suspect we have a traitor among us. I don't mean that we've been infiltrated by the police. We take that for granted: we wouldn't be up to much if the Interior Ministry didn't take the trouble to keep a close watch on us. We have a lot of members, and it's impossible to guarantee the loyalty of each and every one of them. As I say, that's not important, and I wouldn't have come to see you for such a trifling matter. I'm talking about another kind of betrayal."

Now that he had revealed what his concern was, Guillermo del Valle calmed down and continued speaking in a friendly, even confidential manner. Despite being so young and inexperienced, he was in a remarkable position to be able to appreciate all the inner workings of the party in which he was so active: he saw José Antonio not only in his role as the dynamic leader, sure of himself, his ideas and his strategy, but also in his smaller family circle, in the company of Paquita. There, José Antonio was more human, showing his indecision, his contradictions and his moments of weariness and discouragement: weaknesses he could not afford to demonstrate even to his closest friends. This had allowed him to appreciate the loneliness of the Chief.

As he listened to him, Anthony was able to detect, beneath the veneer of a rich, pampered young man with boyish looks and a nonchalant air, the same perspicacity and feverish intelligence he had found in his sisters. This awareness put the Englishman on his guard: in the past few days he had often felt he was the two women's plaything, and he did not want to repeat that experience now with this youngster.

"I understand what you're saying," he said, "but what does that have to do with betrayal?"

The young Falange activist got up from his chair and paced up and down the room, careful not to get too close to the window.

"Don't you see?" he exclaimed. "Somebody is trying to get rid of José Antonio so they can take over the reins of the revolution, or perhaps strangle it at birth."

"That's just your supposition, Guillermo. Are there any facts to back it up?"

"That's the point," said Guillermo del Valle excitedly. "If I had any proof, even a single fact, I would go straight to the Chief and tell him about it. But if I go empty-handed, with mere suppositions, what would he make of it? He would be angry and make sure I was given a dose of castor oil. And yet I know my intuition is correct. Something important is going on, something that will have tremendous consequences for the movement and for Spain."

Anthony took his time responding, in order to emphasise the difference in his attitude.

"That's the endemic problem of you Spaniards," he said, spreading his arms wide as if trying to include the entire nation. "You have the intuition, but you lack the method. Even Velázquez suffered from the same fault. Can you believe that despite all his training and despite having spent several years in Italy, he never managed to grasp the basic laws of perspective? As you said a few moments ago, you yourself have legal training, but instead of behaving like a lawyer, concentrating on the known facts and the truthfulness of the testimonies, you think and act like a poet. Nowadays it's fashionable to say poetry is a form of knowledge, but I don't agree, at least not in matters of this kind. On the contrary, I think we have to make sure logic comes first if we don't want to fall headlong into chaos. We have to coexist in a world of conflicting interests, and coexistence is based on a collective respect for norms that are both explicit and the same for everyone."

He paused, then added with a level smile that was intended to compensate for his hectoring tone:

"I'm afraid with ideas like this I'll never join your ranks."

"I'm not asking you to do that," replied Guillermo del Valle. "I came to ask you to do one specific thing. You may wonder why it was you I came to. It's very simple: because you are a foreigner, someone who has recently arrived and is not staying long, which means you are in no way related to my concerns. You have no links with the Falange or any other political movement in Spain. At the same time, I think you are intelligent, honourable and a good person. What's more, I believe I noticed there was a feeling of sympathy between José Antonio and you, as well as that indefinable sense of harmony that can create a friendship between people with differing, even conflicting, ideas and temperaments."

"Let's get down to brass tacks then. What do you want me to do?"

"Talk to him. Without mentioning my name, of course. Warn him. The Chief is very sharp; he'll understand how serious it is straight-away."

"Or he'll have them give me a dose of castor oil," said the Englishman. "Your intuition about my relationship with José Antonio is as arbitrary as your intuition about everything else. The political situation is extremely complex; it's no surprise that those who have to decide the future of Spain should feel anxious and uncertain. If in the midst of all this confusion I come along and spread fear and suspicion, either José Antonio will not listen to me, or he'll think I'm a lunatic. Or an agent provocateur. But in spite of that," Anthony added, seeing the other man's childlike face fall on hearing these words, "I will try to speak to him if the right opportunity arises. I can't promise any more than that."

This ambiguous promise was enough to make the young Falangist's face brighten again. He leapt up from his seat and shook the Englishman warmly by the hand.

"I knew I could count on you!" he exclaimed. "Thank you! In the name of the Spanish Falange and in my own name, thank you, comrade, and may God bless and keep you!"

Anthony tried to cut this effusive outburst short. Since he had no intention of keeping his promise, and was planning to leave Spain as soon as he could, the young man's sincere gratitude weighed on his conscience. Guillermo del Valle understood the need to terminate their interview, and, adopting once more that martial curtness favoured by the Falangists, which had until now become overwhelmed by his poetic passion, he said:

"I will trouble you no longer. Simply one final request: don't mention anything I said to my parents. Farewell."

The moment he had gone, Anthony ran over to the wardrobe. Overcome by the lack of oxygen, Toñina lay motionless on the pile of clothing. Anthony picked her up, laid her out on the bed, flung the window wide open, then slapped her cheeks until at length a faint gasp told him she was still in the land of the living. Relieved, he covered her in a blanket to protect her from the cold night air, then sat to wait in the same chair from which the impassioned Falangist had tried to involve him in yet another intrigue, be it real or imaginary, that was apparently vital to the future of the nation. Anthony had come to Madrid to value a painting, but without knowing how seemed to have become the collision point for all the forces in the history of Spain. The Englishman was reflecting on how unenviable his position was when Toñina opened her eyes and stared all around her, trying to remember where she was and how she had got there. Eventually she smiled apologetically and murmured:

"I'm sorry. I fell asleep. What time is it?"

"Half past nine."

"It's very late . . . and I bet you haven't even eaten."

She tried to get up, but Anthony kept her in bed, insisting she rest. Then he shut the window, brought the chair over to the table and consumed the rest of the provisions and most of the wine he had bought that afternoon. By the time he had finished, Toñina was asleep again. Taking out his notebook, Anthony prepared to write up the notes he still had to finish, but did not manage to get down a single word. An intense weariness produced by all the events of the past few days suddenly overtook him. He put away his pen, closed the notebook, took off his clothes, switched off the light and slipped into bed, gently moving the girl to one side. I'll get rid of her somehow tomorrow, he thought to himself. For now though, in his desperate situation, the warm presence of this sleeping body next to him gave him a comforting if illusory sense of protection.

26

From the bright light filtering in through the shutters, a drowsy Anthony realised it must be late. According to his watch it was half past nine. Toñina was still sleeping like a baby next to him. Going over in his mind all that had happened the previous day, and trying to weigh up the situation, Anthony got up, washed, dressed and slipped silently out of the room. At reception he asked to use the telephone, and dialled the Duke of La Igualada's number. The butler answered, and informed him that his excellency could not come to the telephone. It was an urgent matter, the Englishman insisted: when could he speak to the duke? Ah, the butler was not in a position to give an answer; his excellency had not informed the servants of his plans. All the butler could suggest was that the gentleman keep trying at regular intervals. Then he might be in luck.

Disappointed, Anthony returned to his room. He found Toñina fully dressed and about to leave. She had carefully made the bed and done her best to tidy up the rest of the room. The sun was flooding in through the open shutters.

"If you don't mind, I'll be gone a few hours," she said. "I have to look after my son. But I can come back sooner if you want me to."

Anthony snapped back that she could do what she liked so long as she left him in peace. Toñina slipped out, head bowed. As soon as he was on his own, Anthony began pacing the room like a caged beast. Twice he sat down with his notebook, and twice he got up again without having written a single word. Another attempt to get in touch with the duke ended with a curt dismissal from the butler. Anthony racked his brains trying to understand the reason for the duke's sudden change of attitude. Could he possibly be aware that the police knew of his plans, and preferred to wait for a more favourable moment to carry them out? But if that was the case, why had he not told him so, rather than keep him out of it? If the duke had any doubts about his loyalty, Anthony needed to reassure him as quickly as possible.

With all these thoughts whirling round in his brain, Anthony found it impossible to stay cooped up in his room. After a night's restorative sleep, and with the sun high in a clear blue sky, he considered the previous day's fears as childish. Although he had no reason to question the truth of what Lord Houndsditch had said, it now seemed to him unlikely that a Soviet secret service agent would concern himself with someone so politically insignificant. And even if their paths did cross, nothing was going to happen in broad daylight in the midst of all the crowds in the city centre. There was nothing left of the provisions he had bought the day before. And as though he did not have enough to cope with, he now had an extra mouth to feed.

Out on the pavement, Anthony was immediately pleased with his decision. He felt as if he had left his worries behind in the gloomy hotel lobby. It was only when he reached Plaza Santa Ana that he realised the change that had taken place in the weather over the past few hours. In this part of Madrid, which had few trees or plants, the arrival of spring was heralded by subtleties of light and atmosphere. It was like the change of a state of mind.

After breakfasting on coffee and a roll, the balmy spring-like atmosphere encouraged Anthony to stride out on foot. Almost without meaning to, he found himself outside the Prado once more. If he had to leave Madrid, he did not want to go without saying goodbye to his beloved paintings. As he climbed the steep staircase to the entrance, he was struck by a disheartening thought: perhaps this would be his last opportunity to study works of art in whose company he had known so many moments of ecstasy. If the madness incubating in every sector of Spanish society did degenerate into the armed conflict everyone was predicting, who could guarantee that the countless artistic treasures scattered throughout the country would not succumb to the maelstrom?

Oppressed by this gloomy speculation, Anthony walked through the gallery. He did not notice that a man in a mackintosh, wearing a little Tyrolean hat, was following him at a distance, hiding in a recess or behind a pillar if the person he was following stopped in front of one of the paintings. On the one hand this caution was justified, because at that time of day there was nobody else in the entire museum, but at the same time it was unnecessary, because Anthony was not even paying attention to the paintings he paused in front of. It was only when he came to the first work by Velázquez that he abandoned his reflections and concentrated on the here and now. This time he was irresistibly drawn to two singular characters.

Diego de Acedo, known as "The Cousin", and Francisco Lezcano, would have occupied a place in this world equal to or somewhat lower than that of a dog if Velázquez had not ushered them triumphantly into immortality. Acedo and Lezcano were two dwarves who were part of the substantial number of buffoons in Philip IV's court. The paintings in which they appear are large, one metre high by eighty-five centimetres wide. The portraits of the princesses Margarita and María Teresa are the same size. The painter's gaze is unchanging, whether his models be dwarves or princesses: a human gaze, without flattery or compassion. Velázquez is not God, and does not feel compelled to judge a world that is already made, for good and ill; his mission is simply to reproduce it as he finds it, and that is what he does.

It is obvious that Lezcano is an imbecile; probably Acedo is as well. Despite their lack of intelligence, or perhaps to emphasise it, the two buffoons are shown doing things that require a minimum of knowledge and learning, two qualities they do not possess: "The Cousin" is holding open a tome almost as big as he is; Lezcano has a pack of cards in his hands, as if he is about to deal them out. The page Acedo is holding open looks as though it has writing and even an illustration on it, but this is merely one of Velázquez's customary tricks: close to, the writing and the drawing are no more than a shapeless blur. The buffoons fill most of the canvas; to the right of each painting the Sierra de Guadarrama is sketched in; the presence of the mountains and the absence of any other reference points places the dwarves in the country-side; the light implies it is late afternoon; taken as a whole, the canvases suggest neglect. In the background, the majesty of the mountain peaks; in the foreground, the symbols of smallness and destitution.

Anthony is so captivated by these characters that without realising it his lips start to move as if he is talking to them. At this moment Acedo and Lezcano seem to him the only beings capable of under-standing and sharing his dejection in the face of a catastrophe that will destroy everything in its path, beginning with all that is beautiful and noble, and will show no pity for the weak. This is not my country, the Englishman murmurs, looking first at one and then the other of the dwarves. It would be absurd to link my fate to that of people who are not relying on me, who don't even know of my existence. It's impossible to say I'm fleeing when I'm beating a wise retreat.

The dwarves make no reply. They look straight ahead of them, but not at the voyeur; probably at Velázquez himself as he paints them, or at infinity. Anthony is not surprised by this indifference: he did not expect anything else. To him, the dwarves seem like the people of Madrid, mute companions in a march towards the abyss.

When Anthony turns round to head for the exit, still absorbed in the parallel world of painting, he becomes aware that a man in a mack-intosh and a little Tyrolean hat is striding towards him. This brings him back to earth with a bump: this must be the dreaded Kolia, heading towards him with criminal intent. As in a nightmare, terror paralyses Anthony's legs. He wants to cry out, but no sound emerges from his throat; an instinct for self-preservation makes him raise his arms and wave them around wildly to protect himself and ward off the aggressor. Seeing this, the other man comes to a confused halt. He politely doffs his hat and exclaims in a mannered English:

"For the love of God, Whitelands, have you gone mad?"

Panic gives way to astonishment in Anthony's muddled brain.

"Garrigaw? Edwin Garrigaw?"

"I didn't know how to locate you, and I didn't want to go through official channels, so I came to the Prado. I knew I'd find you here sooner or later. And I told myself that what the heck, a visit to the gallery is worth all the bother of the journey."

Once he had recovered from his shock, Anthony was filled with a blind rage.

"I hope you weren't expecting a warm welcome," he growled.

The elderly curator shrugged.

"Where you're concerned, I don't expect a thing. Yet you ought to be grateful to me," Pointing to the buffoons, he added: "Couldn't we talk without these two poor wretches looking on? I'm staying round the corner from here, at the Palace Hotel. We'll be quiet and comfortable there."

Anthony hesitated. He would have loved to send this pompous meddler packing, but common sense told him not to make an enemy of a world authority in the field, someone who could be of great help to him or could cause him a host of problems. After a moment's thought he waved his hand resignedly, then headed for the exit, followed by Garrigaw. They crossed the Paseo del Prado without uttering a word. They found a quiet corner in the hotel's splendid rotunda, took off their coats and sat in two spacious armchairs. The tense silence continued until the curator said, almost in a whisper:

"For Heaven's sake, Whitelands, don't be so damned suspicious. Do you really think I want to steal the glory of discovery from you? Think about it: I'm a curator at the National Gallery, if I may be immodest I am figure of universal renown, and I'm going to retire very soon. Would I risk a lifetime's reputation for an adventure with such an uncertain outcome, and, if I may say so, of doubtful legality? And if I should decide to commit such a travesty, would I come expressly to see you to tell you of my intentions?"

Anthony waited a few moments before replying. At the far end of the room, the syrupy sounds of a harp mingled with the hum of conversation.

"Don't be such a hypocrite, Garrigaw," he said at length, coldly and calmly. "Would you have me believe you left your office in Trafalgar Square and your tea at the Savoy simply to talk to me about a painting you haven't even seen? Don't make me laugh. You have come to take a piece of the cake with you, if not the whole thing. You sought me out because I'm the only person who can lead you to where the Velázquez is hidden. Fortunately I didn't give any details of that in my letter. Otherwise . . ."

A waiter came up to see if they wanted anything. Edwin Garrigaw ordered a coffee; Anthony wanted nothing. When the waiter had left, Garrigaw adopted a hurt expression.

"You've always had a mean streak, Whitelands," he said, with no trace of anger in his voice, more like someone describing a piece of furniture. "You had it as a student, and it's grown worse with age. And with the lack of professional success, if you don't mind my saying so. But listen closely to me now: I don't want anything to do with that painting. It's a fake, Whitelands, a fake. I'm not saying it's a forgery or a deliberate fraud: possibly its current owners think it is authentic, perhaps they are acting in good faith. But it is not a Velázquez. And I haven't abandoned my routine to rob you of anything, Whitelands. A few days ago, a member of our embassy here in Madrid called me to explain what was going on, and read me a letter you yourself had written. I set out at once with one single aim in mind: to prevent you committing an irreparable folly. Because in spite of your personal shortcomings and your naivety, I judge you to be a competent professional, and I have no wish to see your career ruined or to see you become the laughing stock of the academic world. You can believe me or not, but I'm telling you the truth. I've dedicated my whole life to our profession, Whitelands, and I love it. Art has been and continues to be my passion and my reason for living. And although I have never enjoyed polemics, I also love my professional colleagues. You are my family, my . . ."

Garrigaw was so moved by his own words that a lump came into his throat that prevented him continuing. To conceal his confusion, he took a scarlet handkerchief out of his jacket pocket and patted his forehead, chin and cheeks with it. Then he peered at the results of this operation on his handkerchief.

"The climate in Madrid always cracks my make-up," he explained as he folded the handkerchief and put it back where it belonged. "It's too dry. It also cracks paints. I trust you took that into account."

The waiter returned carrying a tray on which were a cup of moka, a small jug of milk, a sugar bowl, a spoon, a linen napkin and a glass of soda water. Garrigaw smiled with satisfaction. Regretting his previous refusal, Anthony took advantage of the waiter being there to order a whisky and soda. Then, while the curator was delicately sipping his coffee, he said:

"You haven't seen it. The painting, I mean. You haven't seen the painting, and I have."

Garrigaw wiped the corners of his mouth like a dainty damsel before deigning to reply.

"I don't need to. I'm an old hand, and I've met similar cases. The Devil sits at the crossroads and offers wonderful things to any traveller willing to sell their soul. It all ends up in sad disillusion. The Devil's nature is to deceive. I've experienced the same temptations: Mephistopheles has displayed his gaudy wares before my eyes too. Smoke and mirrors, Whitelands, smoke and mirrors."

"But you haven't seen the painting," Anthony insisted, although with less conviction this time.

"That's precisely why I know it's a fake, and that's why I'm here. If I had seen it, I might have been blinded by the trickery as you were. It's the easiest thing in the world to see what you want to see. If that were not the case, men would not marry women, and humanity would have died out thousands of years ago. Darwin perceived that clearly. Oh, Whitelands, Whitelands, how many examples have we seen, how many of our colleagues, even the most sensible and level-headed among them, have been discredited thanks to an irresistible desire of theirs? All those hasty attributions! All those mistaken datings! All those symbolic interpretations, those revelations hidden in a detail of a landscape, or in a fold of the Virgin's cloak! The desperate urge to uncover and interpret what by definition is mystery and ambiguity!"

Leaning forward, he patted Anthony on the knee with a gesture that was both slightly mocking and paternal.

"Face the facts, Whitelands: when we evaluate a work of art, fifty per cent corresponds to reality, and fifty per cent to our tastes, our prejudices, our education and, above all, to the circumstances. And if we don't have the work of art in front of us and we're relying on memory, the weight of reality is reduced to a mere ten per cent. Memory is weak, it idealises, it's slipshod, our thoughts swap information. For amateurs, these transfers are unimportant; it may even be that subjectivity is essential in the visual arts. But we are professionals, Whitelands, and we have to fight against the ways emotion can deceive us. Our task is not to make sensational discoveries, not even to interpret or value. Our task is simply to analyse the canvases, the pigments, the stretchers, the crackle, the sale invoices – in short, anything that can help establish reality and avoid chaos."

Sinking back into his seat, he brought the tips of his fingers together and went on:

"A short while ago, in the Prado, I was observing you. I was some way off, there wasn't much light, my eyes are not what they used to be, and yet I'm convinced I saw you talking to Diego de Acedo and

Francisco Lezcano. I'm not someone who would reproach you for that. I've often poured my heart out to painted images, with more emotion and sincerity than either men or angels can expect of me. In front of some paintings I have burst into tears, not out of aesthetic emotion but to unburden my soul, to make a confession, as psychotherapy or whatever you will. There's nothing wrong with that, as long as we realise what these momentary outbursts are. But in the cold light of day we have to keep emotion under lock and key, and put our trust only in facts, in first-hand verification, in comparisons . . . In what circumstances did you see the painting, Whitelands? On your own, or with someone? For several hours, or only a few minutes? What documents have you examined? And what about X-rays? No-one can run the risk of theorising these days without first taking X-rays. Have you done that? Don't say a word, Whitelands; I know the answer to my questions. And you still insist on contradicting me?"

The whisky had been brought. Anthony took two generous gulps. Encouraged by its warmth, he responded:

"I'm not contradicting you, Garrigaw. You're the one who's come from London to make me undergo this sort of academic lobotomy disguised as rigour and method. As far as your questions are concerned, I'll tell you one thing: I may have good or bad answers to them, but you have none, because you haven't seen the painting and are thrashing around like a blind man. What you're expressing has nothing to do with wisdom or experience, still less with fellow feeling. What you're expressing is nothing more than the fear that I'll triumph in a way that will completely expose your lengthy career of opportunism, bogus scholarship and stabbing others in the back. That's why you came here, Garrigaw: to get in my way, and, if you can't stop me, to have your name associated with the discovery and steal part of what belongs entirely to me."

The elderly curator pursed his lips, raised his eyebrows amusedly and gave a low whistle.

"Have you got everything off your chest now, Whitelands?"

"Yes."

"Thank God. Now describe the painting to me."

"Why on earth should I?"

"Because I am the only person who can understand it, and you're dying to tell someone about your blasted picture. At this precise moment you need me more than I need you. So far you've only demonstrated how on edge you are. That's natural. In your place, I'd be climbing the walls too."

Garrigaw's calm response helped to ease the tense verbal fisticuffs and restore the old relationship of master and disciple.

"One metre thirty centimetres tall by eighty centimetres wide. The background is a dark ochre colour, with no landscape or other additional element. In the centre is a naked female, leaning to her left. Her right hand is holding a blue cloth across her lap. The pose is somewhat similar to the 'Danae' by Titian, which Velázquez could have seen in Florence during his first visit to Italy. The woman's features are clearly defined, and are not those of any of the models we know Velázquez used. The palette is identical to that of the 'Rokeby Venus', and there can be no doubt that it's the same woman."

"Don Gaspar Gómez de Haro's lover?"

"Or his wife."

"Are you joking, Whitelands?"

"It's always been suggested that the Venus in the painting could have been Gómez de Haro's wife, Doña Antonia de la Cerda. That's why Velázquez blurred the face of the woman reflected in the mirror."

"Oh, please! That theory is nothing but the work of squalid minds! No noble, especially not a Spanish one, would allow his legitimate wife to pose naked or would ever commission any such thing. There are no precedents . . ."

"No human conduct needs precedents to be possible. There are no precedents for a painter like Velázquez either."

"I can see where you're heading: the painter enamoured of his model, a secret painting, impossible loves, revenge . . . Pure fantasy! Are you really willing to stoop so low just to win a slice of fame? You're with a colleague now, Whitelands, so don't try to sell me this cheap gewgaw."

"My theory is not so outlandish," Anthony said, determined on this occasion to ignore the insults and to take advantage of the other man's knowledge. "Spanish society in the Golden Age was much more liberal than that of England; it was nothing like the gloomy image the 'black legend' would have us believe. Spain was much closer to Italy than any other country. Lope de Vega or Tirso de Molina's comedies, and even the Quijote, show the lax customs in Spain, and even Calderón's savage code of honour is an implicit recognition of the fragility, rashness and ardour of women. If we are to believe the literature of the time, they were cultured and determined; they were not intimidated by the idea of undertaking risky exploits disguised as men. In my opinion, events went like this: a libertine nobleman, married to an intelligent and unconventional woman, commissions a painting on a mythological theme, but which is basically the portrait of a sensual, uninhibited naked woman. The painting is never meant to leave Don Gaspar's private apartments, and so his wife has no problem taking part in the game. We cannot dismiss the idea that she could be an accomplice in her husband's licentiousness rather than a virtuous, unwilling victim. After all, the painter is Velázquez; to be painted by him not only flatters her vanity, but guarantees her a preeminent place in the history of art. If the 'Rokeby Venus' really is Doña Antonia de la Cerda, even you must agree she is an extraordinarily beautiful woman, and not exactly a blushing maid. Anyway, let's not get sidetracked. A powerful mutual attraction arises between Doña Antonia de la Cerda and the painter. In secret, Velázquez paints a second nude portrait, and this time he does not hide the model's face. It's the only way in which he can keep forever the woman he loves, to prolong a relationship doomed to be short-lived. To avoid complications he departs for Italy, taking the painting with him. If he left it in Madrid, someone might discover it. Two years later the King calls for his painter, and Velázquez returns to Spain. The painting remains in Italy. Some time later, a cardinal acquires it and brings it back. The painting remains hidden among a substantial family collection, and only now surfaces. What is so implausible about a story like that?"

"There's nothing implausible; but there's very little that's real. It's all the fruit of your imagination. It could have happened like that, or in the exact opposite way: the painting could have been done by another painter, Martínez del Mazo for example."

Anthony shook his head: he had already considered and rejected that possibility. Juan Bautista Martínez del Mazo was born in Cuenca in 1605. He was Velázquez's best disciple and assistant, and in 1633 he married his daughter, Francisca. On Velázquez's death he was appointed a royal painter. Works by Martínez del Mazo were frequently attributed to Velázquez. Anthony himself had written an article analysing the differences between the two painters.

Garrigaw shrugged.

"I won't go any further. I won't argue any more either: I can see it's impossible to try to convince you. Let's leave it at that. I came here to see you, but listening to your nonsense is not the only thing I can do in Madrid. I'll stay a few days, look up some things, visit friends and colleagues. I might even get as far as Toledo or El Escorial. And I'll try to see a bullfight; I just love those bullfighters. If you need anything from me, leave a message at reception. I know you will."

27

Leaving the Palace Hotel, Anthony Whitelands could make out green buds on the branches of the deciduous trees. This timid proclamation of spring irritated him immensely: any excuse was valid to externalise the anxiety he was feeling after his conversation with Edwin Garrigaw, not so much because of the insults as for the undeniable effect the other man's arguments had had on his own convictions. And yet there was no way he could show any weakness now, still less give up. If his fear of committing a tremendous mistake led him to abandon his efforts, what could he expect? A return to his dissatisfaction with the narrow world of academia, with its tedious research and sordid rivalries. It would take as much courage to carry on as to back out now. Not to mention his fear that the cunning Garrigaw would himself run the risk he was encouraging Anthony not to take, and end up claiming all the glory. Because, as he knew only too well, in normal circumstances Edwin Garrigaw rather than Anthony Whitelands would have been the perfect person to judge the authenticity and value of such an important painting. It was only the turbulent political situation in Spain, and above all the long-standing animosity between the mannered, splenetic Garrigaw and the devious Pedro Teacher that had led to a second-rank expert being chosen instead. Doubtless it was for this reason that, as soon as Garrigaw learnt he was being usurped, he had travelled to Madrid ready to use his prestige and wiles to regain his position. But I'm not going to let him get away with it, Anthony told himself.

With this firmly in mind, and clutching a large bag of provisions he had bought at the same grocer's shop as the day before, he entered the hotel and asked for his room key.

"I gave it to the young lady," the receptionist said. "She's waiting upstairs for you."

Anthony failed to notice the receptionist's respectful tone, or that he used the term "young lady" to refer to Toñina, whom he imagined must have returned after fulfilling her maternal duties, determined not to leave his side a minute longer than necessary. But when he tapped on the door, precariously grasping the bag in his other hand, the person who opened was none other than Paquita del Valle, the Marchioness of Cornellá.

"Good morning, Mr Whitelands," she said, amused to see the effect her presence had on him. "Forgive my being so bold. I wanted to talk to you, and I thought it better not to wait for you down in the lobby, where anyone could see me. The receptionist was kind enough to give me your key. If I'm in the way, just say so, and I'll leave."

"Not at all, don't even think it," stammered the Englishman, depositing the bag of provisions on the table and hanging up his coat and hat on the stand. "The fact is, I wasn't expecting . . . The receptionist did mention something, but of course I didn't think it was you . . ."

Paquita was standing by the window. She was silhouetted against the strong spring sunlight, which brought glints to her long, wavy hair.

"Who did you think it was?"

"Oh, no-one. It's just that . . . recently I've been receiving a lot of unexpected visitors. You know: the police, people from the embassy . . . Between them, they're driving me crazy."

Surveying the desolate panorama of the hovel he was staying in, Anthony could not help recalling the splendid salon at the Palace Hotel, and could picture with painful precision how elegant and comfortable the bedrooms there must be. Yet again he was made aware of how disadvantaged he was when it came to the decisive moments of his life.

"But please don't remain standing," he added, in an attempt to bring some dignity to their meeting. "Take a seat. Although I only have one chair. This room is not . . ."

"It's perfectly adequate for what I've come for," she interrupted him, still standing in the window.

"Ah."

"Don't you want to know why it is I've come?"

"Yes, yes, of course . . . It's just that, I'm sorry, it's because of the surprise. As you can see, I bought some food . . . this way I can work uninterrupted . . ."

The young marchioness shifted impatiently.

"Anthony," she said quietly, deliberately changing to a less formal way of addressing him, "you don't have to give me any explanation for your behaviour. And don't try to change the subject. I came because a few days ago I asked a favour of you, and offered you something in exchange. I'm here to keep my side of the bargain."

"Oh . . . but I've done nothing."

"The order of the factors does not affect the product," said Paquita, apparently refusing to let logic get in the way of her determination. "I am keeping my promise, and you will have to do the same. Does it seem such a bad deal to you?"

"Oh, no," said the panicking Englishman. "It's just that . . . in all honesty, I never took you seriously."

"Why? Do you generally not take women seriously, or is it only me?"

"No, neither is the case . . . but as it was someone like you, an aristocrat . . ."

"Don't talk nonsense!" exclaimed the young Marchioness of Cornellá. "The aristocracy may be the symbol of tradition and rank conservatism, but we aristocrats do whatever we like. The bourgeois have money; we have privileges."

It occurred to Anthony that the obtuse Garrigaw should have heard this simple, direct assertion, and applied it word for word to Doña Antonia de la Cerda. But he knew he could never make any reference to this or anything else that might happen in his room.

"What about . . ." he began.

". . . him?" she said, with an ironic smile that the Englishman could not see as she had her back the light. "He will never know, unless you tell him. I'm counting on your chivalry; besides, an essential part of our bargain was the fact that you are not going to stay in Spain a minute longer than necessary. Let's not waste any more time. I've told them again that I was going to Mass, and it won't be long before someone starts to suspect my sudden religious fervour."

Paquita's sardonic tone was not the best way to arouse the Englishman's ardour. He was also only too well aware of the absurdity of the situation and of the dire consequences for everyone that this adventure was bound to have. But these doubts counted for little compared to Paquita's physical presence in the tiny room, where the atmosphere seemed to have become charged with electricity. Velázquez must have felt something similar towards Don Gaspar Gómez de Haro's wife, putting his social position, his artistic career and his life at risk, thought Anthony as he threw all caution to the winds and flung himself into the arms of the adorable marchioness.

Half an hour later, she picked up her bag from the floor, took out a cigarette case and lit a cigarette.

"I've never seen you smoke," said Anthony.

"I only do so on special occasions. Does it bother you?"

There was a slight catch in her voice, which Anthony saw as a trace of tenderness. But when he moved to embrace her, she gently pushed him away.

"I'll finish my cigarette and be on my way," she murmured, staring up at the damp patches on the ceiling. "As I already told you, I can't be away long. Not to mention the police: if they're keeping you under surveillance, they will have seen me come in, they'll see me leaving, and they'll put two and two together. Of course by now that doesn't really matter."

Anthony understood her last sentence and the sadness with which it was spoken: her relationship with José Antonio Primo de Rivera doubtless meant that all precautions against police surveillance were in vain. The fact that the young marchioness was immediately thinking of another man hurt his pride, but he could understand it.

"Will we see each other again?" he asked, without much hope.

"Possibly," replied Paquita, stressing each syllable. "To see each other . . . yes, perhaps we could see each other again."

She got up, the cigarette still between her teeth, and started to get dressed. At that precise moment there was a loud knock at the door. Anthony's heart leapt into his mouth. The list of people who might be lurking out in the corridor was long and frightening: the dreaded Kolia, José Antonio himself, Captain Coscolluela, Guillermo del Valle. Trying to stay calm, he asked who was there. Toñina's voice responded. Anthony gave a sigh of relief: her presence was more of a nuisance than a danger, and he was sure he could sort things out.

"It's the chambermaid," he said to Paquita in a low whisper, and then shouted: "I'm busy, come back later!"

"I can't wait, Antonio," the girl said anxiously on the far side of the door. "I've brought the baby and have to change his nappy!"

At a loss, the Englishman instinctively turned back towards Paquita. She had finishing dressing and was sitting on the bed to pull on her stockings. Shrugging her shoulders, she continued calmly putting on stockings and shoes. When she had finished, she stood up, turned round and began to stare out of the window. Anthony, who had tucked the sheet round his waist, went to open the door. He paused with his hand on the doorknob, hesitated for a few seconds, then said:

"Wait!" Crossing the tiny room, he stood beside Paquita and murmured: "It's a long, ridiculous story of absolutely no importance whatsoever."

Without deigning to look at him, Paquita tossed the cigarette on the floor and crushed it beneath her shoe. Then, as though talking to herself, she muttered:

"My God, what have I done? What *have* I done?"

Anthony put his hand on the shoulder pad of her coat, but she brushed it off violently.

"Don't touch me, Mr Whitelands," she hissed, and headed for the door.

Outside, the baby had started howling. The marchioness opened the door and stood looking at Toñina, who was cradling her child and singing him a lullaby. Paquita steered her way round them and walked off, head held high. Recovering from her surprise, Toñina held Anthony back just as he was about to pursue the marchioness down the corridor.

"Antonio, you're stark naked!"

Anthony flung the sheet to the floor and stamped back into the room, muttering curses in English. The baby was still howling. Toñina picked up the sheet and came into the room, closing the door behind her to avoid any scandal. Dressing as quickly as he could, the Englishman stopped to look daggers at her and shout:

"Damn you and that repugnant creature!"

"Forgive me, Antonio, forgive me! The gentleman downstairs didn't tell me . . ."

As she was saying this, she protected her baby just in case Anthony's curses were followed by blows. Seeing her react in this way, Anthony's anger evaporated. Hastily putting on his jacket and shoes, he ran out of the room and down the stairs, until he arrived panting in the lobby. Paquita was not there or out in the street. Anthony came back in again and raised his hands enquiringly towards the receptionist. Feigning ignorance of the farce he himself had created, the receptionist informed him that the young lady had left the hotel and hailed a taxi. Without going back for his hat or coat, and with his shoes still undone, Anthony called another taxi and told the driver to go to the mansion on Castellana.

Not far from there, while all these dramatic events were taking place, more responsible for them than the waspish receptionist, although much less aware of how things had turned out, Higinio Zamora Zamorano was heading for Justa's place to learn what the result of his initiative had been. The good woman could not tell him anything, and even if she had known of the fatal chain of blunders, neither she nor Higinio would have concluded that their plan was a disaster. With a view of life and its eventualities in which political slogans and the wit of *zarzuela* comic operas were of equal value, Higinio and Justa knew that they had little to hope for from his attempt to place Toñina, but that, compared to nothing, this little was a lot. Two life stories spoilt from the start by a fateful conjunction of social obstacles and personal failings had taught them to consign grand concepts and noble sentiments to the world of the cinema and novels in instalments. Having survived almost by miracle into old age, they put all their faith in the fortuitous and unavoidable commitments born of the petty guilt and ungovernable weaknesses of human nature.

"Don't worry about the girl, Justa," Higinio Zamora had said when he told her about his conversation with Anthony Whitelands. "The Englishman is a good man, and if at first he mistreats and beats her, that only means he'll be more likely to look after her later on."

Justa could not have agreed more, convinced as she was of Higinio Zamora Zamorano's wisdom. And here he was now, very proud of himself as he climbed the dark staircase and knocked gaily on her door with the knuckles of one hand while clutching in the other a bouquet of violets he had bought from a flower-seller in the street. Justa answered at once, and this promptness as well as her attitude, rather than any glimpse he had of her face from the gloomy landing, instinctively put him on his guard.

"You have a visitor, Higinio," she said, tilting her head to one side and hiding her hands in the folds of her ragged cotton dressing gown.

Higinio stepped inside, peering suspiciously at the figure staring at him from the far side of the room.

"I'm Kolia," said the visitor.

Higinio and Justa exchanged apprehensive glances.

28

At one extreme of the vast social spectrum – far from ordinary folk or the sub-species that is the urban proletariat, its natural enemy – the traditional aristocracy is governed by an accommodating philosophy equally superficial and incoherent, but just as effective, as the rough-and-ready ethical code of the working man. As marked as anyone else by the circumstances of their birth, the nobility are bound by an unavoidable mental servitude that prevents them reflecting on their conduct, themselves or the world – if those three things are not one and the same. Even if they were capable of such reflection, they would be unable to modify their received ideas or their way of life. They are obliged to sacrifice their finest qualities on the altar of irrationality, dogma and negligence, and instead with iron discipline cultivate defects which strengthen their position to the extent that it is precisely their position which allows their faults to be further cultivated. Rebellious without a master, and fickle without choice, the irresponsibility governing their actions leads them to live in constant indecision: their initiatives lead nowhere, their thoughts inevitably become frivolous, and their passions, free from all consequence, degenerate into vices.

Don Alvaro del Valle, Duke of La Igualada, Marquis of Oran, Valdivia and Caravaca and a Spanish grandee, feels the weight of this crushing inheritance on his shoulders now that he is faced with a historic juncture. Since he lacks neither intelligence, imagination nor spirit, and is capable of good judgment, he plots and schemes, and yet in the end the determinism of his social position leaves him back where he started, and obliges him (to himself and to the world) to play the role of a simpleton who has lost touch with his time and his reality.

It is in this mood that he is peering out of his study window. As if trying to comfort him, the garden is showing the first green buds of spring. Still staring out of the window, the Duke murmurs:

"What you are asking of me goes against my conscience."

This declaration is received in silence by the three men behind him. One of them, as if he had known from the start that their mission was useless, is keeping out of it. The second man looks across expectantly at the person who until now has been their spokesman. This one says, in the understanding tone he has employed since the start of the meeting:

"Sometimes the Fatherland demands such sacrifices, Alvaro."

The person talking must be close to fifty years old. He is tall, distinguished-looking, with coarse but intelligent features. His penetrating gaze and metal-rimmed glasses give him the air of an intellectual, which to a certain extent he is. By profession a soldier, when the Republican government dismissed him from the Army for no real reason, he earned a living writing for various newspapers and wrote a chess manual that won praise from the experts and favour from the enthusiasts. Rehabilitated, he occupied important positions in Spain and the Protectorate. Though he is not suspected of any sympathy for a coup, the Prime Minister does not trust him, and has sent him to Pamplona to keep him away from Madrid. The Duke of La Igualada and he are old friends, and as friends they have often aired their political differences vehemently but with mutual respect. It was he who had called a few days earlier from Pamplona to ask whether the rumours he had heard were true. Taken aback, the duke had simply given him the official version.

"I'm trying to sell some of my possessions in order to raise funds in case I have to remove my family from here."

"That's not what I've been told, Alvarito."

It was after this short conversation that the duke had concluded that, were a conflict to break out, he would be at odds with both sides, and so, much to Anthony Whitelands' bemusement, had decided to postpone the sale of the painting. Now, taking advantage of a lightning visit to Madrid, the general is paying a visit to the anguished duke, together with two other prominent generals, to get information and to call him to order. So far the duke has resisted them without openly opposing them. Faced with his stubborn silence, another of the generals restates their request in military language:

"What has to be done, will be done. Full stop."

From the beginning of this meeting, this general has remained distant, curt. He does not hide his disgruntlement at all this pussy-footing around, and in his exasperated tone there hangs a vague threat. Yet when it suits him, no-one can act as calmly as him. Like the others, he is in Madrid to take part in a conclave of generals; for him, this has meant a long journey, because a short while previously the Azaña government had posted him to the Canary Islands. After his first intervention, he has said almost nothing throughout the meeting with the duke. His only comments have been to cool the others' impetuosity, advise caution, cast doubt on the possibility of moving from words to action. He is the youngest of the three and the least martial in appearance. Short, paunchy and with already receding hair, his face is puffy, his voice squeaky and high-pitched. He does not smoke, drink or gamble, and does not run after women. The fact that despite everything he enjoys enormous prestige both inside and outside the Army speaks volumes for his professional abilities. Azaña has always trusted him because of his extraordinary organisational capacities, and because he felt that despite his profound conservatism, a punctilious sense of duty will prevent him from moving against the Republic. And so it has proved until now: on several occasions he has been invited to join plots to stage a coup, but he has always refused, or at least not explicitly expressed his support. His caution, which contrasts so strongly with his courage and decisiveness in combat, annoys his comrades-in-arms all the more because they need him. Everyone agrees he has to be with them; the problem is no-one knows whether he is, or up to what point. At all events, they have tried and will continue to try up to the final moment to win him to their cause. Even the Falangists, who detest his prosaic style and his apparent lack of ideals, have made him offers through trusty intermediaries, though with disappointing results: he has not deigned to reply to the Falangists and has shown his irritation with the intermediary for meddling. He does not listen to any offers and does not make any. He gives orders, carries out those he is given and says that nothing else is his affair. Just in case he changes his mind, he has been sent to the most distant and untroubled region of Spain's chaotic geography. On the surface he agrees and is even happy with this, but it is possible that deep inside he has already condemned those who aim to keep him out of political life.

The first general tries to tone down the conversation.

"It's not only the money, Alvarito, it's the social prestige of our actions, were they to take place . . . You are a national figure."

When he hears these fawning expressions of deference, the third general slumped on the sofa clicks his tongue mockingly. Military and spruce in aspect, he is the opposite of his plump companion: temperamental, a troublemaker and libertine, with a corrosive wit. Older than the other two, whom he considers his inferiors, he has also made a name for himself in Africa, but started out in the shadow of the bitter colonial war in Cuba. He considers it puerile, not to say effeminate, to calculate the cost of an action in terms of effort or losses. In order to keep him busy and contented, the previous government appointed him Inspector General of the Customs Police, a post that is well paid and not very onerous. This means he has to travel all over Spain, and this, added to his easy-going, jolly character, has made him the ideal go-between for the scattered military leaders.

Now the three of them have met in secret in Madrid with fellow generals to take a decision and, depending on what this is, to coordinate movements and set dates. But the meeting has only served to underline their differences. Nearly all of them agree on the need for a military intervention to put an end to the current chaos, prevent the disintegration of the Spanish state and forestall the Red conspiracy orchestrated by Moscow. Beyond this however there are conflicting opinions. Many of them are in favour of not waiting any longer; the more the inevitable uprising is delayed, the better the enemy will be prepared. A minority are against action, considering this too hasty. All of them can recall the fate of General Sanjurjo, who rebelled a couple of years earlier and is still living in exile in Portugal.

A coup is no easy matter. Firstly, it is not certain that the Army is unified: some generals are committed republicans; others are not, but their code of honour prevents them from rebelling against a government legitimised at the ballot box. Many middle-ranking officers in direct command of troops are left-wing or support sectors on the Left. And finally, there is no absolute guarantee that the troops will obey, or how effective that bunch of little lambs with no combat experience will be. The generals who have served in Africa see a simple solution to this: the Legion will stage the coup, then if necessary the regular army can be brought over from Morocco; the Moors are loyal and would be delighted to wage a colonial war in reverse. However, this manoeuvre does not resolve the most serious aspect of the question. The frequent nineteenth-century military coups took place in an agricultural, not to say feudal, Spain, with an isolated population that lacked education and was indifferent to politics. Today the opposite is true. If the coup meets with armed resistance and develops into a fully-fledged civil war, a united and competent army will doubtless win pitched battles but will be unable to control the cities and industrial centres, particularly if, as seems likely, the Civil Guard and the Assault Guard are unwilling to join the uprising. If this proves to be the case, the irregular forces on the extreme Right will have to come into play: they are numerous, experienced in street fighting and keen to see some action. However, the drawbacks are obvious: since they are not part of the military structure, the members of these groups obey their own leaders and nobody else. One of the generals present at the duke's mansion has been negotiating with the Carlists in Navarre and has learned his lesson. In return for their collaboration, the Carlists had a long list of demands, some of them reasonable, others outrageous. In addition, these hard-won agreements are only temporary because of the constant bickering in the Royalist camp. In the end, the general has reached the conclusion that, even if they share common objectives, these paramilitary organisations that are strong on ideology but weak on discipline are the opposite of the Army. In spite of this, he has reached a tentative pact with the Carlists. The relationship with the Falange is more difficult. None of the generals present feels the slightest sympathy for the party, and still less for its leader, from whose lips they have heard repeated insults against illustrious military figures for not supporting the dictatorship of Primo de Rivera in its day. José Antonio considers the Army guilty, through action or omission, for his father's downfall, and has no qualms about expressing his disdain in words and deeds: a few years earlier, one of the generals now present was punched by him in public, before witnesses. The aggressor was cashiered from the Army, but for the victim the shame of the insult is still raw. Although they have no personal reasons for disliking him, the other two generals regard José Antonio Primo de Rivera as a good-for-nothing, whose ineptitude has allowed a group of rich young men who were poetic dreamers to degenerate into a gang of uncontrollable bandits. Since the Falangists have no funds or effective support, if the generals decide to launch them onto the streets they will have to supply them with weapons. This implies a sizeable investment and a great risk, because there is no reason to believe that once they have outlived their usefulness, these squads will allow themselves to be disarmed. This as well as other considerations is what has brought the three generals to the study of Don Alvaro del Valle, Duke of La Igualada, to try to win his support with pompous phrases, obsequious praise and veiled threats.

His excellency the duke is torn between scruples and self-interest. After all his wavering, the last thing he wants is to end up confronting both sides in the conflict.

"I'm a simple man, Emilio," he says to his friend plaintively, playing for time, "a man of the countryside. Politically, what interests me is respect for tradition, love for Spain and concern for my family."

"All that does you honour, Alvaro, but the present situation calls for more. From all of us, but from you in particular: you have a name and a position. Your titles of nobility have been in the *Almanac of Gotha* for centuries."

As susceptible as anyone to the prestige of coats of arms, but horrified at seeing a brigadier-general soft-soaping a civilian, the slumped general raises his eyebrows and clicks his tongue again. He does not understand that his colleague is not lowering himself willy-nilly: times have changed in this respect too, and faced with the growing threat from the fascist countries, England and France are following events in Spain with great concern. They could intervene directly or indirectly. Any condemnation from the League of Nations would complicate the future of the state that emerged from the coup. It is vitally important for the plotters to emphasise the conservative nature of their enterprise, to distance themselves from Germany and Italy's expansionist tendencies, to make it clear they are driven solely by a desire to reestablish order. Gaining the support of Spain's most prominent families and clergy is not paying undue homage to the nobility, but a strategic manoeuvre on the eve of battle.

However, this move by the skilled chess player falls short of its aim. The duke peers out of the window once more: the wind is rustling the tree branches and there are dark clouds on the horizon: typically changeable March weather. Perhaps his unsubtle comrade is right, thinks the general, and diplomacy is pointless; in that case, they will have to take the extreme measures the situation demands, and face the consequences. While he waits for a reply from the duke, he mentally draws up lists of those to be shot. The duke implores God for a miracle to save him from his dilemma, even for a few moments. His prayer is immediately answered. The double doors to the study burst open, and the duchess sweeps in like a whirlwind. Standing in the middle of the room, she only realises her mistake when it is too late. Despite her confusion, she is the first to react: she starts to withdraw, murmuring excuses that drown out the clicking of the generals' heels. The duke quickly takes advantage of the situation.

"What's the matter, Maruja? It must be something very important for you to waft in like a ghost without knocking. As you can see," he rushes on, without waiting for her explanation, as though this did not interest him, "I'm in a meeting. You already know Emilio. These gentlemen . . . are accompanying him."

He carefully avoids giving their names, and the old family friend kisses the duchess's hand. Of the other two, one obeys protocol with a solemn bow of the head; the third, a vulgar show-off, strokes his moustache and says in a hollow voice:

"We were just advising your husband to leave affairs of state in the hands of others and dedicate himself to cultivating flowers in his garden to offer to you, your grace."

Slow on the uptake as well as hard of hearing, the duchess cannot follow this nonsense, and yet she grasps what is going on and the danger involved. She casts her husband a warning look, which he interprets correctly: do as they say, and get rid of them. Then, speaking out loud and with an urbane smile on her face, she says:

"Forgive me, Alvaro. And you gentlemen as well. Without meaning to, I've burst in where I'm not wanted, and for a mere trifle. Carry on with what brought you here, and pretend you never even saw me."

With this the duchess leaves the room, without saying goodbye or offering them something to drink. In the doorway she waves and purses her lips in order to rob her appearance of any importance, and closes the door behind her. But her intervention has been a catalyst. Of the three generals, Emilio Mola and Gonzalo Queipo de Llano have been completely disarmed. Only Francisco Franco seems unmoved, still keeping his own counsel.

29

Refusing the glass of cheap rum Justa offered him, Kolia managed to seem neither polite nor scornful. This offhand attitude, so unexpected in someone seen as a ruthless N.K.V.D. agent, terrified Higinio Zamora Zamorano far more than any show of malice.

"I simply did what I was told to do," he said, almost pleadingly. "Snitch the Englishman's wallet and hand it over to their embassy to alert them to the fact that he was in Madrid. After that, he kept coming back to our humble abode. He's crazy about the girl."

The Soviet agent toyed with the little bunch of violets Higinio had left on the table. His lack of interest cut short the romantic fantasy Higinio was about to launch into.

"And how did the people at the embassy react?" he wanted to know.

"When I was there, as if it was routine. Naturally enough. But they've talked to him several times, and are keeping their eye on him. When he was taken prisoner at National Security Headquarters, they lost no time getting him out."

"They don't want him to blabber. Nor do we. What do we know about why he's here?"

"Your humble servant knows nothing at all. He himself told me he was only in Madrid for twenty-four hours, yet he's still here, and it seems he's got no intention of leaving. I couldn't tell you whether it's the English or the coppers who are keeping him."

"There might be other people involved," muttered the spy. "No matter. The important thing is to act. Otherwise we won't be able to do a thing. Where is he now?"

"At this very moment, he's in the hotel with the girl. Like I said, he's crazy about her."

The agent's cold eyes once again cut Higinio short. In order to show how advantageous the situation was, Higinio told him about the young Falange activist's visit to the hotel room. Toñina had climbed inside the wardrobe, heard their entire conversation, and the next morning had reported back to him, without leaving anything out. She had also pretended to faint in order not to worry the Englishman. The girl was very quick, and with a bit of help could make a future for herself anywhere but in Spain. Kolia cut him short yet again; he had listened carefully to Higinio's account, and was now deep in thought. After a few moments he got up and started striding round the miserable room. A strong smell of boiled cabbage seeped in through the cracks in the window frame from the courtyard below. As offhandedly as before, he motioned to Justa to leave. She did so, casting Higinio an apprehensive glance as she went. The object of this doom-laden warning shuddered once more.

"The important thing now," said the spy once they were alone, "is for him to complete his task. To eliminate the obstacles to the sale of whatever it might be."

"But I thought . . ."

"Things have changed. Orders from the top. Once the matter is settled, we give him the chop."

"The Englishman? Does he really have to be bumped off? He's not to blame for anything."

The heartless spy repeated his languid gesture and sat down again.

"Once the job is done he's no use to us, and he knows too much."

"He won't say a thing, I can guarantee it: he's crazy about the girl."

Kolia drilled him with a cold, penetrating look.

"What about her?" he said. "Can she be trusted?"

"Toñina? For the love of God! She'll do what we tell her to."

"She better had."

The spy had been tearing off the petals from the bunch of violets. Scattered on the oilskin tablecloth and lit by the feeble light of a bulb dangling from a greasy cord, they looked to Higinio like something from a cemetery.

"You're surely not thinking . . ." he whispered, quivering like quicksilver.

"I don't think anything. I only carry out orders. But get this into your head: don't play around with the Central Committee. Do your duty and, when I say so, take care of the Englishman. It won't be difficult: he trusts you. If you don't have the guts, tell me and I'll find someone else to do it. But don't breathe a word about this."

At the same hour, far from the courtyard and without the slightest suspicion of the merciless sentence passed on him by the Lubianka agent, Anthony Whitelands asked the taxi driver to pull up a hundred metres before the mansion. He was determined to cover the last part on foot, protected by the trees and bushes of the verdant Paseo de la Castellana. No precaution was too great if, as experience had taught him, he really was at the centre of several concentric circles that were all keeping a close watch on him and on each other. He had already been seized by José Antonio's personal bodyguard, and it had only been the rapid and friendly intervention of the Chief that had prevented a tragic finale. He also knew that Spanish National Security were tightening the net around the Duke of La Igualada and anyone who had any contact with him or his family. Yet none of this could lessen his determination to speak to Paquita and clear up the misunderstanding.

His cautious attitude proved justified: two cars were parked outside the mansion, their drivers smoking and chatting on the pavement. The vehicles' as well as the drivers' appearance led him to dismiss the idea that they were either Falangists or members of the security forces. To think there might be fresh protagonists in the confusing drama he was caught up in made him feel giddy, and so he left all consideration of this for later and continued his stealthy approach. A small detour allowed him to reach the side street without attracting the drivers' attention. Once there, he hugged the wall until he came to the iron gate. When he tried to open it, he found it was locked. The wall was too high for him to see over into the garden, but by gripping protruding stones he managed to heave himself up and raise his head over the top. The garden was deserted. Through the study window, he could see the duke's silhouette. To avoid being spotted, he quickly jumped down, and in doing so scraped his right hand on the wall's rough edges. Tying his handkerchief round his hand to staunch the blood, he carried on down the street in search of a better observation post. A shadier part of the garden allowed him to clamber up the wall again and peer inside, protected from anyone's curiosity by a row of cypresses. From there he could see the rear of the mansion, with a back door that gave onto the most secluded part of the garden. A staircase descended to a paved rectangle in which stood a summer house designed to provide shade during the hottest months of the year. Inside it were a marble table and half a dozen wrought-iron chairs. The wintry bareness of the surrounding vine and the abandoned state of the summer furniture gave the place a melancholy air.

All at once Paquita came rushing out of the back door. The coincidence of her appearance and Anthony's reason for being there brought him up with a jolt. He struggled to get a better view without revealing his presence or losing his precarious balance. Neither the distance nor the obstacles nor his own consternation prevented him from noticing how profoundly agitated the young woman looked.

Anthony was not mistaken. A short while earlier the duchess had also come across her daughter, and her maternal feelings had suffered a violent and painful shock. Prevented since childhood by her social condition and an unrelenting education from applying her natural intelligence to any of the practical aspects of life, Doña María Elvira Martínez de Alcántara, by marriage Duchess of Igualada, had graciously accepted her domestic, decorative role. She had developed a notable ability to detect frivolity in all its many guises and to respond to them precisely and rapidly. More recently however, the fateful turn of events in Spain since the declaration of the Republic had brought with it a radical change in her attitude. Her former perspicacity was now employed in glimpsing any sign of an impending drama in the smallest detail. A short while earlier she had been wandering aimlessly through the mansion when she had run head first into Paquita who, to judge by the way she was dressed, had just come in from the street. The duchess had instantly perceived the distress the younger woman was trying to hide beneath the distant, rather flippant attitude that characterised their relationship. A mixture of maternal instinct and social awareness told her not to enquire directly if something had happened to her daughter, but she detained her on the slightest of pretexts. Paquita could only hold back her feelings for a few moments; after that she burst out sobbing, then ran off to shut herself in her room. The duchess's female intuition led her to suppose she could guess the cause of such heartbreak and, incapable of choosing between doing something and nothing at all, she went to find her husband, bursting in on the generals' plotting. The voices and sounds of doors opening and closing warned Paquita there were other people in the house. Anxious to avoid a family scene until her troubled spirit had calmed down, she fled from her bedroom to seek refuge in the garden.

Perched up on the wall, Anthony watched as she closed the back door, glanced left and right to make sure she was alone, and then walked slowly, head down, over to the arbour, sighing deeply, her body shaking as she went. A swing hung from the stoutest branch of an ancient elm. The young marchioness went over to it and gently stroked the ropes, as if that innocent contraption brought back the naïve pleasures of an irretrievably lost childhood. Seeing her so sad, Anthony felt the urge to jump down into the garden and run to comfort the unfortunate young woman. The only thing that stopped him doing so was his certainty that the cause of her sorrow was probably what had just happened between the two of them in the hotel room. He was puzzled by this, however: he could not understand the rapid switch from her initial boldness and self-assurance to her current despair. As he saw it, the untimely arrival of Toñina had not been enough to justify such a dramatic change.

But this paralysis of bewilderment was short-lived. A stern shout from behind shocked him so much he almost fell off again.

"Get down from there this minute, you numbskull!"

Without thinking about it, more from fear than from any instinct for self-preservation, Anthony pushed forward to get off the wall and escape from whoever was shouting at him, and plunged headfirst into the garden. The soil beneath a clump of myrtle bushes that had been composted for spring softened his fall. Bruised but intact, the Englishman crawled to hide behind a hedge. All this happened so quickly that when Paquita looked in the direction the noise and the voice had come from, she saw only the head and shoulders of a stranger at the top of the wall. She had been so wrapped up in her own predicament that the sudden apparition of a purple-faced man only disturbed her still further. She cried out and, paying no attention to the interloper's plea for her not to raise the alarm, ran back to the rear door of the mansion. It was already open. Alerted by her cries, the butler rushed out, brandishing a shotgun. With all the speed and acumen of a hunting dog, he raced down the steps, looked all around him until he discovered the intruder, and was about to pull the trigger when a shout from Paquita halted him.

Still pointing the gun at the man, the butler ordered him to put his hands up. The prowler replied that if he did that, he would fall off. He made this sensible objection looking first towards the house and then almost at once turning his head, because it also applied to the drivers who, on hearing the shouts, had left their vehicles and were running down the side street calling on him to surrender.

This situation could have lasted some time if the duke and the three generals had not appeared from the house after a few moments. To his master's silent enquiry, the butler pointed his double-barrelled shotgun towards the intruder on the wall.

"Good Lord!" exclaimed the duke when he saw the extraordinary figure. "Who is that fellow, and what's he doing there, half in and half out of the garden?"

"I don't know, your grace," the butler replied. "But if your grace gives me permission, I'll blow his head off and then we'll see."

"No, no! I don't want any scandal in my house, Julián! Least of all today," he added, pointing to the three generals at his back.

With this, the situation seemed to be drifting towards an impasse until, emerging from his apparent indolence, General Franco took the initiative. He went over to the wall and addressed the intruder in his high-pitched, commanding voice.

"You, whoever you may be, jump over the wall into the garden at once!"

"I can't," replied the other man. "I'm a war invalid, general sir."

"General, sir?" Franco exclaimed. "So you know who I am?"

"I wish I didn't, general sir, but I know only too well. I had the honour of fighting under you at Larache. I was wounded, promoted, decorated and retired from active service. At present I am attached to National Security Headquarters. Captain Coscolluela, at your orders as ever, sir. And please, tell these men out here not to shoot."

In order to prevent his colleague taking the lead in everything, Queipo de Llano's stentorian voice rang out.

"Put your weapons away, you dunderheads! Do you want the whole of Madrid to find out? And you up on the wall, where did you say you were posted?"

"To National Security Headquarters, general sir, under the command of Lieutenant-Colonel Marranón," replied Captain Coscolluela.

"Well, blow me down! What did I tell you? That bastard Azaña is having us followed."

"Not you, general sir," Captain Coscolluela protested. "I'm following an Englishman."

"An Englishman?" said Mola. "An Englishman in the Duke of La Igualada's house? Do you think we're fools?"

"Not at all, general sir."

"Well," said Queipo de Llano, "perhaps it's not such a bad idea having him shot. If he's spying on us or if he's here for some other reason, our names will come out when he gives his report."

Frowning, Mola thought this over, stroking his chin.

"Will you do that, captain?"

"No, general sir. I only have to report on the Englishman's movements."

"So who is this blasted Englishman?" asked Franco. "A spy?"

"No, general sir, he's a professor or something of the sort."

For their own reasons, the Duke and Paquita, who were both watching this interrogation, abstained from corroborating what the captain was affirming. From his hiding place, Anthony watched the development of this farce that he had set in motion and in which everyone but him was playing a role. Even though having Paquita so close to him clouded his judgment, he realised that for the moment at least it would be impossible to talk to her on his own, and that it was absolutely necessary for him to get away from the mansion before he was discovered or before Captain Coscolluela succeeded in convincing the generals he really did exist.

If he managed to get round the group under cover of the hedge, perhaps he could take advantage of the confusion to slip behind the summer house, climb the steps and dash in through the back door, which had been left open. Once inside, with a bit of luck, he could find the door to the basement where the painting was kept, hide there and wait for nightfall. Then he could return to the garden, climb back over the wall and escape.

It was a hare-brained plan, but the first part turned out to be easier and more successful than he could have hoped: everyone in the garden was staring at Captain Coscolluela, and he, although Anthony had to pass his line of vision for a short stretch, only had eyes for his former commander, who at that precise moment was haranguing him fervently.

"Listen to me, Captain! Whatever administrative post you may hold, you are still an officer. An officer of the Spanish army! Do you understand me? Yes? Well then, you will know who to obey and who not to obey. Not merely because of the authority vested in our rank, but because an order that goes against our interests is an unworthy order, one that an officer in our glorious Army should not carry out. Spain is in danger, captain! International Communism is only waiting for an order from Moscow to launch the revolution and annihilate Spain! Captain Coscolluela! A Spanish officer owes his loyalty to Spain and Spain alone, and we three here represent Spain."

"Beware of imitations!" added Queipo de Llano, in a slightly mocking tone that mortified the speaker. "And don't forget that any wall can be used by a firing squad."

As this ominous threat rang through the air, Anthony reached the door, slid through the gap and found himself in a square lobby with a corridor leading further into the house.

30

Fearful, silent, and in a tearing hurry, Anthony Whitelands scurried along the corridors of the mansion. His anxiety only increased when he realised that the further he went the more lost he became, and the further he was from any hypothetical salvation. The time he had gained was running out. Any moment now he could find himself confronted by the fearful butler or the formidable trio of generals. He was just regretting not having obeyed the order from Captain Coscolluela, whom he now saw as representing all the advantages of legality, when the sound of footsteps led him to seek refuge wherever he could. Fortunately, among the extravagant décor that characterised this courtly residence there was no shortage of curtains, and a thick one in scarlet velvet now allowed him to hide where he could hear, though not see, everything going on in the passage.

Before long he heard the sound of someone crying, and his heart leapt – it could only be Paquita. He resisted his fervent desire to appear before her, take her in his arms and offer her his comfort and his love, not only because he was still convinced he was the involuntary source of her despair but because he heard other, more determined steps heading towards the same spot from another part of the house. The surprise encounter startled the two protagonists, both of whom had been even more caught up in their own concerns than the Englishman.

"Oh, Father Rodrigo!" he heard Paquita exclaim. "You scared me! I wasn't expecting to see you . . . but you're heaven-sent."

Father Rodrigo's harsh voice answered.

"I can't attend to you now, daughter. More serious matters are calling me."

"Surely not more serious than saving a soul, Father?" pleaded the young woman. "I'm asking you for the love of God: hear my confession."

"In the middle of a corridor? Daughter, the sacrament of penance is no laughing matter."

The stern priest seemed to think this put an end to their meeting, but Paquita insisted, unwilling to listen to reason.

"At least tell me one thing, Father. Is it true that love can redeem a sinful act?"

"Divine love, perhaps, but not human love."

On hearing the word confession, Anthony pricked up his ears behind the curtain.

"But what if a young woman, carried away by an irresistible love for a man, were to commit a sin; wouldn't it be easier for her to obtain the Almighty's forgiveness? Isn't it God who has placed the capacity for love in our hearts that leads us to forget ourselves, Father?"

Hearing this, Anthony had to restrain himself in order not to throw all caution to the winds and reveal himself. The strict father confessor reacted very differently.

"Daughter, now you are frightening me. What grave mistake are you about to commit?"

"The mistake has already been made, Father. I love a man, and have reason to believe he feels the same. Yet powerful reasons prevent our love from following the usual paths. He respects me and, since he is a paragon of virtue, he would never consent to anything that would damage my honour and virtue."

"Well then, daughter, where is the sin in that?" asked Father Rodrigo.

"You see, Father, I . . ." stammered the young woman, ashamed at her sense of guilt and fearful of being chastised, "in order to rid us of the obstacle that prevented him consummating our love outside the norms of morality and convention, I decided to lose my virtue . . ."

"Abomination! What am I hearing?"

"You've known me since I was a little girl, Father," Paquita continued in a faint but determined voice. "For as long as I can remember not only have you been my mentor and guide, but there have also been bonds of friendship between us. That is what I am appealing to now, Father: forget your precepts for a moment and listen to my pain and confusion with earthly ears, as my friend and counsellor. I will not hide anything from you: a few hours ago I gave myself to a man. I deliberately chose someone for whom I do not feel the slightest attraction or respect, someone I can wipe easily and painlessly from my memory. I coldly deceived him as to my motives, and with feigned frivolity led him to—"

The priest interrupted her account with a loud roar.

"Paquita, it's not a father confessor you need, but a man in a white coat. You have forgotten not only religion, but your family name. When you behaved as you say, did you think of your family's honour as well as of eternal damnation? Not to mention the man whom you induced to commit sin. Paquita, your act was depraved, and in your words and attitude now you are not showing the slightest remorse. And you still think I should grant you absolution?"

"But Father—"

"Don't call me Father. I'm not your father, and you are not my daughter. You've always been rebellious and proud, precisely the marks of Lucifer. I'm not surprised to see you are now possessed by the Evil One. Get away from me, and away from this house. You have a younger sister whose innocence could be tainted by your very presence. Go somewhere where no-one knows you, do penance and pray to the Lord for His grace and mercy. And now I am going: I have more important things to do than to listen to your depraved ramblings."

The priest was beating his retreat, with Paquita's plaintive cry still in his ears:

"Remember, Father, that what I said is under the secret of the confessional!"

This admonition was of little use to Anthony Whitelands, who was more crushed than angered by the humiliating revelation. It was of less use still to the motley pair that was Higinio Zamora Zamorano and Justa, who at that very moment were opening the door to Toñina, carrying the child of sin in her arms and the bundle of clothes over her shoulder.

"Toñina!" her mother exclaimed. "What are you doing here?"

"And with all your belongings!" added Higinio. "Come on, tell us what happened, because if that fop has done the dirty on you, he'll have Higinio Zamora Zamorano to reckon with."

"Don't get so worked up, Higinio," Toñina replied calmly, depositing her bundle and the baby on the table. "And you, Mother, don't look so sour. The Englishman is not a bad sort, and it was me who chose to come back. I for one have no wish to get involved in that game."

Toñina went on to tell them what had happened at the hotel. When she had finished, Higinio waved his arm airily.

"That's nothing, you booby," he said categorically, without losing his proverbial good humour. "That's what Englishmen are like: as cold-blooded as lizards. They can hunt you and kill you, then deny the whole thing. And those society girls are pretty much the same: yes, they wear combs and veils when they go to Mass, but they don't have an ounce of decency in them. And that one in particular is the worst of all. Now the fascist has shown her the door, all the men in the Puerta de Hierro Club will be having their way with her."

Justa had picked up the baby and was rocking it in her arms.

"Even so," she said, "the girl is right to be offended. As the song says, even the poor have a heart."

Toñina pulled a face.

"It's not how you think," she said. "The marchioness stained the sheet."

"What did you say?"

"I saw the blood with my own eyes."

Higinio called for quiet: he needed to think this over. He strode around the room, frowning deeply and with his hands clasped behind his back. Every so often he came to a halt, the frown lifted and a slight smile played around his tight lips. They could hear him murmuring to himself. "Well now, well now," and immediately afterwards, "perhaps that's the answer." Then he would set off again, with the two women casting him respectful glances. Oblivious to this decisive moment, the baby honoured it nevertheless by bursting all the eardrums in the building with his loud howls.

Meanwhile, in the corridor of the ducal mansion, the object of this deliberation, condemned by her spiritual director and unaware that her confession had been heard by the very same victim of her deceit, was drying her tears, cursing to high heaven and then going on her way, upset but impenitent.

After waiting cautiously for a while, Anthony poked his head out. Seeing the coast was clear, he continued with his pointless advance. He had scarcely taken a few strides when the sound of footsteps and voices obliged him to hide a second time. Since there was no handy curtain to duck behind this time, he pressed himself up against the wall, trusting that the deep shadow thrown by an angle of the corridor would help him go unnoticed.

Soon the Duke of La Igualada and General Franco were so close to him that he could have reached out and touched them. As he held his breath, he heard the latter say in a rasping voice:

"One thing is certain, your grace. It is the Spanish Army that will decide. And only us! If this young friend of yours and his gang of cowboys want to play a part in anything, they'll have to be completely subordinated to the militia and will act when and how they are ordered to, with no disputes or objections. If they don't, they'll have to face the consequences of their lack of discipline. The situation is serious, and we cannot allow any arbitrariness. Tell your protégé exactly what I've told you, your grace. I won't deny that I appreciate those lads' patriotism, and I can understand their impatience, but this matter is for the Spanish Army to resolve, and no-one else."

"That's exactly what I'll do, General, don't worry," said the duke, "but General Mola had led me to understand . . . his point of view on this . . ."

"Mola is a great soldier, an exemplary patriot and a wonderful person," said Franco, lowering his voice, "but sometimes he lets his emotions run away with him. And Queipo de Llano is reckless. As I said, the situation is serious, and someone has to keep a clear head and steady nerves. The victor in the coming war will be the one who succeeds in keeping order in his ranks."

The pair had moved on, and Anthony was creeping in the opposite direction, when he saw the two other generals coming towards him. He darted back into his dark corner. From there he could make out Queipo de Llano's wine-soaked tones.

"Emilio, if we wait for that tortoise Franco to make up his mind, we'll be here forever! Too much caution will give the advantage to the Bolsheviks. Then we'll really have a fight on our hands. Believe me, Emilio, the first blow counts double."

"It's not easy coordinating so many people. There's a lot of indecision and caution."

"Let's forget about coordinating, then. Send the Carlists out into the streets, Emilio. If there's slaughter, that will make people's minds up. Essentially, everyone agrees. What's holding them back are personal arguments or quarrels. Not to mention that some of them are scared stiff. Or they have personal ambitions: Sanjurjo wants to lead the uprising and so does Goded. Franco meanwhile will scoop the lot on the sly if we're not careful. If you don't take command, Emilio, we won't get anywhere, I'm telling you."

"I'm listening, Gonzalo, but there's no point rushing things. You want to settle everything by blasting away, but this is a complex issue."

General Mola suddenly came to a halt, and his companion, who had his hand on his arm, bumped into him. Worried he had offended the person who tacitly at least held the greatest authority among the triumvirate of conspirators, Queipo de Llano looked inquiringly at Mola. The latter raised a finger to his lips, calling for him to stay silent. Then he stretched out his arm and pointed to something barely visible on the floor of the gloomy passageway.

"Good Heavens! What's that?"

Mola adjusted his glasses and bent forward.

"It looks like a bit of bloody cloth," he said, avoiding touching it.

"A servant must have dropped it."

"In such a posh place? No chance of that, Gonzalo."

"What do you make of it then?"

"Let me think," said the expert chess player.

Anthony realised with horror that this disturbing find was none other than his own handkerchief. He had been wearing it wrapped round his hand ever since he had grazed himself on the wall; but so much had happened to him since then he had completely forgotten about it and had not noticed it fall to the floor.

The two generals were still perplexed.

"Do you think we're being spied on?" said Queipo de Llano, reaching into his pocket and pulling out a pistol.

"I don't think so, and put that toy away, for God's sake!"

"Perhaps that lame fellow's story wasn't as absurd as it sounded."

"Let's investigate. You go back that way, and I'll carry on. If there's anyone snooping, we can surround him and overpower him. If you see Franco, tell him what's going on."

Although his brain and his limbs were paralysed with fear, Anthony realised that if he stayed where he was he would soon be discovered, and so he tiptoed after Mola. Soon afterwards, without knowing how, he found himself in the hallway. The front door was close by, but the memory of the guards posted outside dissuaded him from trying to leave by it. Crushed by anxiety and doubt, his eyes fell on "The Death of Actaeon". Anthony had always been disturbed by that painting, and in his present circumstances it was doubly unsettling. A lengthy period of Christian civilisation, followed by centuries of bourgeois culture, had relegated Greek mythology to the realms of poetic imagination: beautiful tales with a vague metaphoric dimension. Now however, the image of the proud hunter condemned to a cruel death, torn to pieces by his own dogs merely for having unwittingly come into fleeting contact with an attainable but merciless goddess, seemed to him to have a lot in common with his own experience. Titian had been commissioned to paint it, but once it was finished he decided to keep it for himself: something more powerful than interest, integrity or obedience prevented him from depriving himself of constant contact with it. He kept it in front of his eyes throughout his life. Perhaps the sublime Venetian painter had also had an unforgivable encounter and been struck by the fatal arrow, thought Anthony.

A sudden noise from the corridor put a stop to his daydreaming. Realising that this complicated his position still further, but clueless as to how to avoid another equally fatal encounter, he ran upstairs and hid on the dark landing of the first floor of the mansion.

31

Nightfall came early, and the Duke of La Igualada's mansion was enveloped in gloom as from his hiding place Anthony strained to hear his pursuers' brief instructions from the hall he had just left to seek refuge on the upper floor.

"If anyone has really got into the house, which I doubt," said the grim butler, "he cannot have left again without being seen. I propose we make a thorough search, room by room. You look on the ground floor. The servants have been warned in case he tries to slip into the kitchen, larder or laundry. I'll take care of the bedrooms."

The generals accepted the butler's orders without demur, recognising the temporary authority of someone who knew the terrain.

Feeling cornered, Anthony wondered whether he should surrender and throw himself on the duke's mercy. Surely he would not allow any kind of violence against someone who was, in a manner of speaking, working for him, especially in his own house – provided of course that he did not know what had transpired between his daughter and the Englishman. Even so, the duke's protection would only be of limited value. Nothing could guarantee the life of someone who had been a direct witness to a military conspiracy at the highest level.

This line of reasoning led Anthony to conclude that he should continue to do his best to escape without being spotted. He was retreating quickly, keeping his eyes fixed on the staircase where at any moment he expected to see the butler and his shotgun appear, when a hand gently gripped his arm and a cheery, surprised voice said:

"Tony! What are you doing lurking here in the dark? And what's all that noise?"

"Lilí!" whispered Anthony, once he had recovered from the shock. "Don't shout. They want to kill me."

"Here, in our house? Who's after you?"

"I'll tell you later. For now, for heaven's sake, help me!"

As quick as ever to react, Lilí took charge of the situation and led Anthony into the room she had emerged from a few moments earlier. She followed him in and closed the door. The Englishman found himself in a large white-walled room with a small balcony that opened onto the orange glow of sunset. The austere furniture consisted of a desk, two chairs, a chintz armchair and a bookcase full of books which, to judge by their spines, were mostly educational. On the desk lay an open notebook, an inkwell, a pen, a blotter and other writing materials.

"This is my study," Lilí explained. "I was doing my homework when I heard noises, so I went out to look. What's going on?"

"They're searching the house from top to bottom. They're looking for an intruder and they think it's me," Anthony gabbled. "Can you hear the doors slamming? They'll be here in no time."

"Don't worry. Come with me."

A door in the wall led into a small, square bedroom, occupied by a painted iron bedstead, a bedside table, a wardrobe and a prayer stool. On the table stood a brass candlestick, and hanging from the wall above the bed was a fine antique carving, probably from Valencia, showing the Virgin with an infant Jesus. There was a loud knocking at the door, and the sound of the butler's gruff voice.

"Señorita Lilí! Open up!"

"Hide under the bed," Lilí told Anthony. "I'll get rid of him."

Anthony did as he was told, and from the floor heard the two of them talking.

"What's going on, Julián? And why the shotgun?"

"Don't be frightened, señorita, it's only a precaution. Did you see or hear anything strange?"

"Nothing. What am I supposed to hear? I've been studying for hours, bored stiff. Father Rodrigo will be here any minute to test me on what I've learnt."

"Alright then. Make sure you lock the door and don't open it to anyone you don't know."

A moment later, Lilí reappeared in the bedroom.

"You can come out now. I've locked the door as he told me to and shut the lace curtains to the balcony. You're safe here, and you can leave once all the fuss has died down. We'll find a way. And Father Rodrigo isn't coming; he's fighting his own war."

Anthony crawled out from under the bed and brushed himself off. Lilí was sitting on the edge of the bed, swinging her legs. She patted the counterpane for the Englishman to sit next to her. He did so, and she stared at him intently.

"You're the intruder they're looking for. If not, you wouldn't be hiding. What are you doing here? We weren't expecting you today."

Without waiting for a reply, she went on:

"It's because of Paquita, isn't it? Don't lie to me like you did last time. You've been with her. You smell of her, and a short while ago she smelt of you. I heard her crying. And now all this commotion . . . Oh, Tony, what do you see in her that I haven't got? Just look: because of her, they want to shoot you. But here I am, protecting you. I don't know what from, but I'm protecting you."

"And I'm truly grateful, Lilí. As for the rest, I can explain—"

"I don't want explanations, Tony. I want you."

Taking his right hand in hers, she continued to gaze at him, and then said, a sob in her voice:

"I don't know if as they say there will be a revolution any day now. But if there is one, the first thing they'll do is kill us all, just like they did in Russia. I'm not scared, Tony, but I don't want to die without ever having lived. I'm a woman, but what do I know about life? A bit of arithmetic, the tributaries of the Ebro, and Bécquer's verses. Is that fair?"

"Oh, things don't necessarily have to be as bad as you paint them . . ."

"You don't know that and nor do I. But if it happens – and rest assured, something terrible will happen – if it happens, I don't want to be like one of those saints in my prayer book, with the palm fronds of their martyrdom in one hand and a finger in their mouth. I don't want to be a saint, Tony, I want to be a normal person, to know what that means. And if that's a sin, so be it. I didn't create it. How can it be sinful to desire what my body, my mind and my soul are calling out for? And how am I supposed to ignore a desire I feel inside at all hours of the day and night, especially when Father Rodrigo never talks about anything else but the temptations of the flesh?"

Anthony struggled with his fear and his scruples. An ex-wife, a lover, a few adventures and a close study of Mannerist painting had taught him not to underestimate the anger of a woman scorned, particularly in a tight situation like the one he found himself in.

"My dear Lili, I can understand your problem," he said, stroking her hand in as detached a way as possible, "but I'm not the person you need to resolve it."

With childish ease, Lili went from hollow licentiousness to innocent simplicity.

"On the contrary, Tony," she said, "there's no-one more suitable than you. For a start you're a Protestant, so if what we're going to do is a sin, it won't affect you."

Anthony got up and went over to the window. He was shocked to the core by the devious moral attitude the two sisters displayed. Only a few hours earlier Paquita had used a similarly specious argument, and although she had later confessed her guilt and shown remorse, the way both of them twisted moral precepts was proof not only of their lively intelligence but of a profoundly misguided upbringing. For no apparent reason, this thought saddened Anthony greatly.

"Your argument is nonsense," he said coldly.

Lilí looked at him even more seriously.

"It's not nonsense, Tony; it's just an excuse. I decided to take this step a long time ago. I'm not doing it blindly: I've often heard adults talking about it, and I've seen the animals on my father's farms . . . But I could not do it just like that. Then you appeared. I don't mean now, but the first day you came home. As soon as I saw you in the hall, lost and studying that ghastly picture, I said to myself: that's him, heaven has sent him. From that moment on I've been trying to convey my feelings and intentions to you, but to no avail: you don't understand a thing. You're a ninny; I love you all the same, but you're a ninny. I'd almost given up hope, then all of a sudden this evening fate brings you to my door at the point of a shotgun. How am I supposed to interpret that?"

"You're not," the Englishman said icily.

He pulled back the curtain slightly and peered out into the garden. Perhaps he could jump from the balcony without any great risk: it was not too high, and there was not much light. Then he could race across the garden to the wall, climb it and reach the street. If he ran from there to Paseo de la Castellana, there would be lots of passers-by about, and they would not dare kill him in front of so many witnesses. Or perhaps they would. Yet if he stayed where he was, sooner or later they were bound to find him. If in addition they discovered him with Lilí, he did not give much for his chances of coming out of this alive.

While he was considering all this, he opened the window a little way to calculate the height. Right underneath he heard Father Rodrigo's harsh tones:

" . . . and not to stray from the path of righteousness. God revealed it to me, and you have made your decision, your grace. The steep and narrow path . . ."

The Duke of La Igualada's voice was a scarcely intelligible low murmur:

282

"But where will that path lead us, Father? Just because it is steep and full of thorns does not make it the right one."

"You should not trust those military men, your grace."

"But aren't they seeking the salvation of Spain?"

"Your grace, when they speak, Spain means one thing; to us, it means something completely different."

Silently closing the window, Anthony dropped the curtain and went back to Lilí, who was still perched on the bed.

"What you're asking is impossible. Put yourself in my place."

"I can't put myself in your place, just as you can't put yourself in mine. We each have to decide for ourselves."

"But you're still a child, Lilí."

"How old was Mariana de Austria when she was married to Philip IV? You should know: Velázquez did a portrait of her."

Anthony could not help smiling.

"She was fourteen," he admitted. "And Princess Margarita married at fifteen."

"You see? By then we are already women."

"If you mean that you can make a scene and complicate men's lives, I quite agree. But that's starting the wrong way round."

"Tony, if you don't think I'm attractive tell me straight out, but don't treat me like a child. I'm not one, and you know it. If I were, I wouldn't be able to read what you're thinking in your eyes. Do as you like. And don't worry: whatever your decision, I won't do anything to harm you. I love you, Tony."

It was pitch dark by the time Anthony dropped down from the balcony to the garden. He reached the wall without any problem, looked for a projecting stone, and managed to haul himself up without grazing himself as he had the last time. Before jumping down into the street, he turned back to survey the mansion. Everything was quiet; all the windows were dark or had their curtains drawn. By the dim light of the outside lamps he thought he could make out Lilí's silhouette on the balcony, watching to see if he had escaped successfully.

He ran as fast as he could out of the side street and into Paseo de la Castellana. There he went on running through the crowds until he was completely out of breath. A taxi was passing by; he hailed it and gave the address of his hotel. His first impulse had been to head for the embassy to ask for asylum, but then he thought it would be shut, and concluded it would be better to return to his hotel and call Harry Parker from there. They would surely come and fetch him and offer him protection in return for the invaluable information he had about the direction of future events in Spain, obtained by chance but at considerable risk. Nothing could interest British Intelligence more than first-hand, trustworthy information about an imminent military coup and the identity of its leaders.

Aware of how scruffy he looked, he strode defiantly over to the receptionist, told him he wanted to make one or more telephone calls, and enquired whether anyone had asked for him or called while he was out.

"Anyone? My word, since you signed in it's been like Carnival in here."

The day's extraordinary events had exhausted Anthony. Feeling close to collapse, he asked the receptionist for a glass of water. The man took a jug from under the desk and gave it him. The cool water with a hint of aniseed immediately revived the Englishman.

"You shouldn't overdo it," said the receptionist, his ironic tone laced this time with a dose of sympathy. He went on to list all the comings and goings. "First the floozy left with the brat, and took all her stuff with her. Or it might have been all your stuff, but that's none of my business. Then that young gent from the other day turned up, the comedian with the pistol. Seeing you weren't here, he left in a huff without saying a word. He'll be back. And about an hour ago the gentleman of the first day put in an appearance."

"The first day?"

"With all that's been going on you've probably forgotten him. The first day you were in the hotel a very elegant gentleman came to see you, a foreigner in fact. He spoke impeccable Spanish. He expressed great interest in you, but then never came back. Until today. He was very upset that you weren't here and left a phone number. He said you were to call him as soon as you arrived."

"Didn't he leave his name?"

"No. He just left his number and a scent so strong I almost fainted."

Anthony recalled the mysterious visit and also that he had mentioned it to Harry Parker in one of their conversations. The diplomat said he knew nothing about it. Perhaps he was lying. The only way to resolve the issue was by calling the number the anonymous visitor had left. Anthony decided to postpone the call to Harry Parker, in case something new came out of the other. As far as Guillermo del Valle was concerned, it would be best to do nothing. At that moment Anthony could not give a damn what happened in the ranks of the Falange, and the last thing he wanted was any fresh contact with the Duke of La Igualada's family.

When he called the number the receptionist had given him, a quavering, unfamiliar voice replied. When Anthony said who he was, the other person started speaking in English.

"I need to see you urgently," he said. "It's not a good idea to speak on the phone. I'll be waiting for you in an hour in Chicote. Don't tell anyone. Come alone."

"How will I recognise you?"

"I'll recognise you, and you'll know me when you see me. In an hour. Chicote. I have to hang up."

32

Chicote was not far from the hotel, and since the meeting was not due for another hour, Anthony was able to wash and change, and even found time to wolf down a substantial squid roll in a Plaza Santa Ana bar, because he had not had a thing to eat all day.

Then he walked down Calle del Príncipe, Sevilla and Peligros, deliberately reaching the agreed meeting point five minutes late so that he could observe the locale from outside and discover who had arranged to meet him there. He was busy doing this when someone behind him said in English:

"I'm here. You're late. Don't turn round. Let's go in."

Chicote had become one of the most popular haunts of the bohemian Madrid of the Second Republic, which had come into existence at the same time. That night was no exception, and the number of customers milling about led Anthony to obey the order without fearing a trap. Once inside, he turned round to see his companion's face. To his surprise, he immediately recognised Pedro Teacher.

"Why didn't you tell me from the start it was you?" he asked.

"Don't say my name!" the unctuous art dealer hissed. "I'm here incognito."

"With a bowler hat and a monocle? Why all this mystery anyway?"

Pedro Teacher pushed him on without answering. They fought their way through the crowd until by some miracle they found an empty table. Pedro Teacher hung his coat and hat on a stand, and tucked his monocle away in his top pocket. He looked very agitated, and could not stop glancing around in all directions. When the waiter came over, he ordered two dry Martinis without consulting Anthony.

"They prepare them very well here," he said. "The best in Spain."

"O.K. Now explain all this nonsense to me. What are you doing in Madrid?"

"Desperately searching for you," replied Teacher. "Listen. Shortly after you left London, persuaded by me if you remember, something unexpected happened. As a result the operation I had envisaged took on another aspect, one which, if you'll pardon the melodramatic expression, became lethal."

"Lethal for me?" asked Anthony calmly: after all that had happened to him since arriving in Madrid, nothing could shock him.

"Lethal in general, but I'm afraid to say, doubly lethal in your case. Caught in the crossfire in both the metaphorical and the literal sense of the word. Because of which, as I was saying, my sense of honour impelled me to come looking for you. I arrived a day later than you and at once discovered where you were staying, thanks to contacts I have at the nerve centres, if I may use that term, of the government administration. Madrid holds no secrets for me. As dealer to the most illustrious families in Spain, there are few circles or places where access is denied me. And among all the homes whose doors are wide open to me, that of our mutual friend the Duke of La Igualada occupies a special position. And his delightful family, of course. If, as I suppose, you have visited the mansion on Castellana, you will have noticed the varied and exquisite collection of paintings they possess, the majority of which were offered and sold by Pedro Teacher himself."

The waiter broke into this monologue with the two Martinis, but when Anthony reached out to take one, Teacher intercepted him.

"I'm sorry, Whitelands my friend, but they're both for me. You may order whatever you wish, but I need a tonic to lift my spirits. Risk is part of an art dealer's job, but not this kind of risk. Your health."

After Teacher had downed the first drink in two gulps and was savouring the second one glassy-eyed, Anthony decided it was high time to stop beating about the bush and to discover the real reason why he had followed him and arranged for them to meet. In response, Teacher wiped his lips with the back of his hand and took up his story.

"So I went to look for you in your hotel and found you weren't there, if you'll pardon the non sequitur. I went back the next day, but could not even get near the place because it was so closely guarded. Since then I've spent all my time trying to catch up with you. To no avail: when you weren't being arrested by the police, you were in the embassy, and when you weren't there, you were with the Falange. Not to mention the gang of pimps and whores in whose company you seem to like to spend your spare time. Which of course is none of my business."

"In which case, let's leave my leisure activities out of this and get to the point. Why are you looking for me, Mr Teacher?"

This reproach reminded the art dealer he ought to be cautious: he peered timidly all around him, dabbed with a linen handkerchief at the sweat pearling on his brow and upper lip and said in a whisper:

"I can't tell you."

"And that's why you brought me here?"

"It's here that I can't possibly tell you. People are listening."

"Nobody is listening to us, Teacher. They're busy with their own affairs. And if that weren't enough, in this country not even the director of the British Council understands English."

"Don't be so sure. Madrid is swarming with foreign spies! Swarming, Whitelands! It's only natural. In no time at all, the future of the world will be decided right here. The decisive battle between Good and Evil. Armageddon."

"That may well be," said Anthony, noticing his companion growing increasingly agitated the more Martini he consumed, "but I'm too tired to waste time listening to your drivel. If you're not going to tell me anything, I'll return to my hotel and go to bed. Armageddon can start without me. Goodnight."

"No, no, don't go!" Pedro Teacher pleaded. "I've got something of the utmost importance to tell you. After all, that's why I came all this way. But nobody must hear us."

"Whisper it in my ear."

"Not on your life. They would read my lips: there are spies who have that skill. Let's go to another bar. No, that's no good: it would be the same there. And out in the street we could be followed, photographed even . . . I've thought of a better idea. Come to my place. I have a simple apartment here in the centre, where I keep some of my stock-in-trade, and where I can receive clients in complete privacy. It's a little jewel, Whitelands – you'll love it. And it's very secure. Because I store valuable paintings there, I've installed the most modern and efficient safety devices. I can't give you the address out loud, but I'll write it on this paper napkin. Memorise it and then burn the napkin. No, don't burn it. That would attract attention. Eat it. No, that would give rise to comments too. Alright, it's up to you how you dispose of it. I'm leaving now. We mustn't be seen going out together. Wait a quarter of an hour then come to the address on the napkin. Have you got that?"

"Of course. As clear as day. But there's no way I'm going anywhere. How do I know you're not laying a trap for me? You yourself spoke of a lethal risk."

"I find your insinuation offensive, Whitelands. We're Englishmen, colleagues, gentlemen."

"That's no guarantee."

"Be reasonable. I've spent days looking for you to warn you of a great danger. Don't reject the hand I'm offering. We might not get another opportunity. Does the name Kolia mean anything to you? Ah, I see you're raising your eyebrows. I can tell you a lot more about him and how you can thwart him. I can also clear some things up about the disputable and disputed provenance of a certain painting . . . So, I'll expect you in fifteen minutes. Do as you see fit."

Slipping his monocle back in place, he stood up, took his coat and hat from the stand and walked out stiff-legged. Anthony read the address. It was at the nearest end of Calle Serrano, not far away. While he was mentally picturing the route to take and wondering whether or not to go, the waiter came over with the bill for the two Martinis. This demonstration of Teacher's confusion and brazenness reassured Anthony about the art dealer's intentions. No crook would have done anything so clumsy. Anthony paid and left the bar.

The night was still wintry, but the temperature had risen over the past few days and so the walk did him good and helped clear his mind. The previous few hours had gone by in a whirl, and now Anthony felt physically and mentally exhausted, with no willpower left. He was convinced he had reached the limits of his energy, and had lost interest in everything to do with his journey. Even the Velázquez painting now seemed to him something too distant and too fraught with danger. Although it was still tempting, the prospect of this imagined professional triumph could not match his fervent desire to return to the tranquillity of his work, his home and his orderly daily life back in England. Whatever revelation Teacher was promising, his mind was already made up. He would go back to England the next day without consulting, informing or saying goodbye to anyone.

Going round the Cibeles fountain, he went past the bar in whose basement the Happy Whale functioned. That was where José Antonio Primo de Rivera and his comrades met to drink whisky and debate the intellectual issues of the day. Anthony had fond memories of the night he had been invited to take part in their discussions, even though he had little wish to meet José Antonio again after the deceitful, not to say outrageous, way Paquita had used him as a stepping stone towards her mating with the Falange's National Chief. By now Anthony had reached Calle Serrano, and was reminded of the conversation he had had with Paquita in the Michigan a few days earlier. On that occasion he had talked to her about Velázquez, and she had opened up to him about her personal problems. A bond had been formed between them, but that was now snapped forever. Would they ever see each other again? It did not seem likely.

Absorbed in these memories and thoughts, Anthony arrived late at the address Pedro Teacher had written on the napkin. By the time he came to a halt in front of a massive wooden door, his watch showed exactly eleven. Set into one side was a much smaller door that had a bronze lion's head knocker on it. Before knocking, Anthony pushed at the door, which opened to his touch. He stepped inside, after looking all around him: there was no-one in the street and he was almost certain no-one had followed him or was watching him. After so many days under surveillance, this sudden freedom seemed like a bad sign. Despite this, he carried on into the entrance. Thanks to the street lighting, he could make out a switch on the wall: he pressed it and a bulb in a gilded brass wall-fitting lit up. Shutting the street door behind him, Anthony climbed a wide staircase with thick wooden boards that were shiny from use and creaked beneath his feet.

The door to the apartment on the second floor where Teacher said he lived was also ajar. Warily, Anthony crossed the threshold. The hallway was in darkness, but at the end of the corridor he could make out a dim glow. There were no pieces of furniture, carpets or paintings either in the hall or in the passage. Creeping along the corridor in order to catch whoever might be there unawares, Anthony soon found himself in a spacious room lit by an oil lamp. The bare walls and sparse furniture confirmed his suspicions: no-one was using the apartment as a home, office or art gallery. This realisation alone would have been enough to make Anthony aware of the mistake he had made if another discovery had not showed him just how foolish and naïve he had been.

33

Pedro Teacher was dead. Dead as a doornail: that much was clear. Only a short while before he had described the situation as lethal, and now he was proving it by his own example. His body lay on its back in a pool of blood in the middle of the room. The legs and arms were outstretched, as if he had collapsed on the spot. He was still wearing his coat; the bowler hat had rolled a metre from the head of its former owner. Next to his face, the lens shattered but still intact, lay the monocle.

Spurred on by his survival instinct, Anthony found himself out on the landing again before he had even attempted to weigh up the situation. He heard the sound of footsteps climbing the stairs. Looking down, he saw armed men rushing up towards him. Some of the neighbours were opening their doors, peering out, then darting back and shutting themselves in. It would have been useless to call on them for help; besides, Anthony was so weary he could not even think. What will be, will be, he told himself. As this was passing through his mind, he was surrounded by four individuals who urged him not to offer any resistance. The mere thought of it made him smile involuntarily.

"Is there anyone else?" they wanted to know.

"A dead man inside. To whom do I have the pleasure?"

They made no reply, but bundled him into the apartment and shut the door. One of the men trained his gun on him while the other three quickly searched the rooms, guns at the ready. When they had completed their search, they made a call from the telephone on the wall in the passageway. The response at the other end was immediate, as if someone had been expecting the call. The conversation was over in two monosyllables. After he hung up, the man who had telephoned relayed it to the others:

"We're not to touch a thing. He'll be here in five minutes."

Still keeping their eye on him, the four men rolled cigarettes and lit up. Anthony tried to work out whose hands he was in. Following what to him seemed like an eternal wait, the arrival of Lieutenant-Colonel Marranón and an assistant provided the answer. His appearance would doubtless have allayed the Englishman's fears if the new arrival had not immediately strode over to him and punched him hard in the face. The blow and the shock knocked Anthony to the floor. From there he gazed up at his attacker more in sorrow than in anger.

"Son of a bitch! If it weren't for that blasted republican insistence on legality I'd put a bullet in you right now!" roared the lieutenant-colonel.

His assistant, who was much calmer, had gone down on his haunches next to the body, carefully hitching up the tails of his coat so that he would not get any blood on them. From there he gave his preliminary report:

"The body is still warm. He was shot point-blank in the thorax region, with a large-calibre weapon. The coat and his dark suit make it hard to say exactly where the point of entry was, but he must have died instantaneously. The neighbours would have heard the gunshot, but in the current situation they'll keep mum."

This reasoned report helped calm the lieutenant-colonel down.

"Was it you?" he spat at Anthony.

"No! How could it be me?" Anthony protested. "I'm an art historian and couldn't kill a fly; I couldn't even think it. Besides, where's the weapon?"

"How should I know? You could have thrown it away or hidden it. No murderer waits for the police gun in hand. Do you know the victim?"

"Yes," said Anthony. "In fact, I was with him less than an hour ago, in Chicote. He arranged to meet me there to tell me something important, but he was frightened someone might overhear. To avoid that he told me to come here, but when I arrived he was already dead."

"Nothing fits," growled the lieutenant-colonel. "Where exactly are we? This looks to me like a safe house, somewhere for terrorists, gangsters or foreign agents to meet."

"As you can imagine, I didn't know that. He described it to me completely differently. I walked here from Chicote. If Captain Coscolluela has been following me as he usually does, he can confirm that."

"Captain Coscolluela was killed this afternoon," the lieutenant-colonel said curtly. "And I ought to do the same with you. Claim you were trying to escape. Because of you I've lost my best assistant. And now they've rubbed out this fellow, who could have provided us with information."

"Pedro Teacher?"

"Or whoever he is. We've been tailing him since he arrived in Madrid, but he's a slippery character. If you hadn't left a napkin on the table with this address on it, we would never have found him. Of course, he's not much use to us now."

Now that things had calmed down somewhat, Anthony could tell from the lieutenant-colonel's face just how weary he was. At that moment, he turned away from Anthony to talk to his men.

"Two of you stay here until the magistrate comes to remove the body. The rest of you, come with me. This numbskull is coming with us to the National Security Headquarters. We'll get him to talk one way or the other."

On the way to headquarters, Anthony asked for details of how Captain Coscolluela had been killed. The lieutenant-colonel, who after his initial outburst had recovered from his distaste for the Englishman, coldly told him what had happened. The captain's lifeless body had been found around six o'clock that afternoon on wasteland near Retiro park. The evidence suggested he had been shot somewhere else and dumped there later. In the lieutenant-colonel's view, it was plain who had committed the crime: a few days earlier a law student affiliated to the Falange had been killed in a street battle, and his comrades, as was their custom, had in this way avenged his death. The attack was part of the terrorist campaign the Falange was launching to prepare the terrain for a military uprising.

"Do you have any proof for what you're saying?" asked Anthony once he had finished. "Any eyewitnesses? Has the Falange admitted responsibility?"

"There's no need."

Anthony Whitelands took a decision.

"When we reach your office, I'll tell you where and when I saw poor Captain Coscolluela for the last time. And I suggest you call the Interior Minister. He'll want to hear it."

While this conversation was taking place, in an apartment at 21 Calle Nicasio Gallego, where the Falange had its centre of operations, a visit by Father Rodrigo, an old acquaintance of the Marquis of Estella, and the news he had brought, had led to an urgent meeting of the Political Junta being called.

"I heard it as clearly as you can hear me now: for the moment they are going to do nothing."

The party's secretary-general, Raimundo Fernández Cuesta, sounded concerned but conciliatory:

"The situation could change at any moment. As things stand now..."

"What if things don't change?" said Manuel Hedilla.

José Antonio Primo de Rivera cut the argument short by slapping the table with the palm of his hand. When he spoke, he was deliberately downbeat.

"Comrade Hedilla is right: nothing will change. Mola and Goded have got water in their veins. And Franco is lily-livered."

"That leaves Sanjurjo," José María Alfaro pointed out. "He's got guts, and we're with him."

"Ha," snorted José Antonio, "neither Franco nor Mola are going to bring Sanjurjo back from Portugal to hand him the commander-in-chief's baton. They all want it for themselves. It's a dogfight. By the time they all agree, it'll be too late."

The Political Junta was split, and the foreseeable revelations Father Rodrigo had brought straight from the mansion on Castellana only exacerbated their differences. The moderates considered it absolutely necessary to unite with the Army, even if that meant the Falange played a subordinate role in any uprising. The hardliners were in favour of seizing the initiative. Others, who were more thoughtful, insisted they were all missing the point: whoever took the first step, if the Army intervened the generals would take command, and the Falange's ideology, spirit and political programme would necessarily be distorted in the short or long term. Some of those who held this view preferred to stay out of things and wait for a clearer opportunity in the future. For an uprising against the Popular Front government to take place and the Falange not to do a thing was an odd, almost obscene idea: not even those in favour of this strategy dared suggest it openly, knowing this would be seen as cowardice and indecision. It was only occasionally and indirectly that one of them hinted at the idea of staying neutral.

José Antonio Primo de Rivera was wrestling with his doubts. As the National Chief of an authoritarian party, he had no need to consult with or to be accountable to anyone over his decision. Deep down however he was not a political leader but an intellectual, a jurist trained to examine the facts from every angle. His fanaticism was rhetorical. Having known them since childhood, he was more aware than anyone that the generals, with their patriotic pomposities, were simply carrying out the wishes of Spain's landowners, financial bourgeoisie and aristocracy. Many officers, including some of the highest rank, admired the Falange's youthful energy; but this admiration was no more than a nostalgic throwback to what they once had been or would have liked to be, before they got caught in the swamp of automatic promotions, the mud of mediocrity, easy living and petty rivalries. With few exceptions, the generals behind the coup were mediocre, lightweight and, when it came down to it, just as corrupt as the government they were proposing to overthrow. But what was the way out of this dilemma? José Antonio asked himself. A year earlier he had thought up a plan which would have altered the balance of forces. Taking advantage of a change of government that nobody agreed with, he had planned a march on Madrid similar to the one Mussolini had led on October 28, 1922. The entry into Rome of the serried ranks of Fascist militants, with their black shirts, imperial ensigns and banners flapping in the wind, had left a lasting impression on him when he had seen it on a cinema newsreel at the age of nineteen. On that occasion the people had acclaimed their new leader; King and Church had recognised him as such, and the Italian army, which had previously looked down on him, was forced to submit. Both Mussolini and Hitler had fought in the Great War, but neither of them had followed a military career; even so, unlike the centuries-old tradition of dictatorships in Spain, in the two preeminently totalitarian countries the Army obeyed civilians and their doctrines, and not the other way round. In 1935, with the threat of a Popular Front government looming, José Antonio had wanted to achieve something similar in a march on Madrid from Toledo with thousands of Falangists and the military cadets from the Alcázar. Thousands more would join them along the way, and he was counting on the support of the Civil Guard. But the plan never came to fruition: it was torpedoed at the last moment by some of the high-ranking officers. José Antonio Primo de Rivera knew their names, and in particular that of the person who, as chief of the general staff, had had the last word: Franco.

"I'll tell you what we will do," he said finally. "I'm going to give the military an ultimatum. Either the uprising takes place now, with the Falange as its spearhead, or the Falange takes the lead, whatever the consequences. That way, we will have warned them. They will be the only ones responsible before God and history for the outcome."

He then asked José María Alfaro to call Serrano Suñer. When he came in, he told him:

"Ramón, I want you to organise a meeting for me with your brother-in-law as soon as possible. If it can be tomorrow, all the better."

As the meeting broke up, Father Rodrigo trotted after José Antonio like a lapdog.

"Don't trust the military men, your highness. They will not fight God's war, but their own."

34

At the age of fifty-six, Don Manuel Azaña looks much older. He is plump, balding and pale, with an ugly, sour expression. His eyes behind thick lenses are two slits that are drowsy or cunning depending on who is describing them. Anthony Whitelands has only seen him in photographs or caricatures in the right-wing press, where he is portrayed as a toad, a tadpole or a snake. Now Anthony is brought before him in the president's office. He has once again told the story he first told to Lieutenant-Colonel Marranón in General Security Headquarters, and then to Don Alonso Mallol and Don Amós Salvador, respectively the director-general of Security and the Interior Minister. The latter has called the Prime Minister, and, despite the lateness of the hour, Azaña receives them immediately, listens carefully, and when the Englishman has finished, studies him closely.

"Are you sure the painting is by Velázquez?"

Both Anthony and the others are taken aback by the question. Azaña grimaces in what is meant to be a complicit smile.

"Don't take offence. I'm grateful for what you've told me about the conspiracy and the generals, but as you well know, that comes as no surprise to me. But the painting was not part of my calculations. Señor Whitelands, I don't know much about art. My passion is literature. If I could be someone else, it would be Tolstoy or Marcel Proust. Well, that's what I would say now. When I was young I wanted to be Rudolf Valentino."

He smiles again, this time more naturally. When he received the call, he had been about to go home. Now he has realised it is going to be a lengthy meeting, and is adapting as best he can to this unforeseen setback.

"I spent a long time in Paris," he says, still addressing the Englishman because the others already know this, "before the Great War. The Studies Extension Commission gave me a grant to attend some courses at the Sorbonne. In fact, I was only interested in the art and intellectual life of that great city. And the girls, as you can imagine. I would visit the Louvre every day and spend an hour in one of the classical antiquity rooms or sit gawping at a painting. Then I would go back to my room and try to write down my impressions. Forgive my ramblings," he says, including everyone in the room with a sweep of his arm. "It's late, and I've had a very long and tiresome day. You must be tired too. I'll soon be finished. As I was saying, I went to the Louvre every day. I was fascinated by Italian painting, above all the Venetian school. For that reason I once went to a talk on Titian by a compatriot of yours, a professor from Oxford or Cambridge. A middle-aged man, good-looking, elegant, rather mannered in his gestures. He gave a false impression of being timid, but he knew his subject and was very intelligent, as well as being astonishingly erudite, unlike our pompous so-called experts. I was so impressed by him I can still remember his name: Garrigaw. His entire talk concerned a single painting: 'The Death of Actaeon'. It was not on show in the Louvre or any other gallery. Apparently it belonged, and doubtless still does, to some fortunate individual. All we had for his lecture was a fine copy, on which the professor showed us the different details of that curious mythological episode. As you can imagine, I was fascinated by the fable and the way it was portrayed. I don't know whether you can picture it: young Actaeon goes out hunting and by chance comes upon Diana naked; the unforgiving goddess fires an arrow at him. He is turned into a deer, and is immediately ripped to shreds by his own pack of dogs, without being able to do anything to prevent it. To paint the fable, Titian chooses a midway point in the tale: the essential has happened, or is about to happen. Anyone who doesn't know the beginning or end of the story will remain in the dark. Possibly at the time Titian painted the picture,

Greek mythology was common knowledge. I doubt it. It must have been some other reason that led him to choose this precise moment over any other. The moment when the mistake has taken place, and the arrow has been fired. The rest is a matter of time: the outcome is inevitable . . . Please be patient with my digressions. Often, in the solitude of this office, at this time of day when I'm overwhelmed with tiredness and – why deny it? – have lost heart, I take refuge in the memory of earlier days – I'm not sure they were any happier, but at least they were less complicated – my childhood in Alcalá, the Augustinian school at El Escorial, Paris before the war . . . and not long ago when I was daydreaming like this, I remembered the lecture on that painting by Titian."

He pauses to light a cigarette, and studies his respectful audience through half-closed eyes. Then he goes on, much more animatedly:

"Many people think we are in precisely the same situation now. The irreparable mistake has been committed, the arrow has left the bow; all that's left is for our own faithful hounds to tear us to pieces. But I'd like to see it differently. In fact, I'll go further. I think that the arrow that could kill us is the defeatism everyone has fallen prey to. There has never been such a widely shared consensus as the one we're witnessing in Spain now. The unanimous conviction that we're rushing headlong into disaster. I ask myself if I'm the only one who doesn't agree, and tell myself I'm not. Last month's elections proved that, and during the campaign we had an opportunity to judge the general mood."

Lost in his own thoughts, Anthony is unaware of this, but what Don Manuel Azaña says is true: during the election campaign he spoke to several mass rallies. Despite his lack of personal charisma and his reputation as an intellectual; despite the erosion of many years of political intrigue during which he and his party have committed serious mistakes; he was demonised by the Right and reviled by the Left, but the voters still supported Azaña, and the masses acclaimed him because they saw in him the last chance for agreement and conciliation. At his final public address, held on the outskirts of Madrid in a place that was hard to get to and in bitterly cold weather, with a government boycott against it, half a million people turned up. Azaña's policies are straight-forward: to consolidate the Republic, not to throw overboard all that has been won so far, not to increase the country's problems or to make life worse for ordinary citizens. In order to carry out these policies, he can count on solid support in parliament and from the vast majority of Spaniards, even if, as he knows only too well, that majority support is of little use against guns or artillery. Even so, he still believes that common sense will prevail, that the Spanish nation's instinct for self-preservation will win out. He also believes, because he has seen the birth and development of the Second Republic from the inside, that deep down no-one wanted to reach the point they have arrived at now. The relentless compromises of electoral pacts and day-to-day politics have forced the socialists to take a more radical stance in order to prevent the workers leaving their U.G.T. union for the C.N.T., where the anarchists are able to maintain the purity of their principles thanks to them rejecting any idea of collaboration and a constant display of irresponsibility. As a result, driven on by a revolutionary rhetoric which in Azaña's view is frivolous, the socialists feel obliged to seize power just as the Bolsheviks did in Russia. They dismiss any further compromises, pointing, not without reason, to the brutal repression against the working class by both the Monarchy and the Republic. In the current situation however, their decision is suicidal. The Right is more sensi-ble: it is defending the interests of a minority and therefore does not have to please the exasperated masses who are clamouring for palpa-ble, immediate results. The Right can wait, because it is not going hungry, and will only turn to armed rebellion if it cannot see any other way out. Right-wing groups, like the Carlists or the supposed fascists in the Falange, are a handful of extremists whom their masters keep on a short leash by depriving them of funds. As for the Army, Azaña knows what's what: not for nothing was he Minister of War in the first Republican government. Contrary to widespread opinion, Azaña thinks that the military have no wish to topple a Republic which in the end belongs to them too. When they had the chance to defend the Monarchy – the restoration of which they are now calling for on the quiet – they didn't lift a finger, and they won't do so now to bring down the Republic. Leaving aside the generals who fought in Africa, who really frighten him, the others are characterised by incompetence, laziness and the labyrinths of hierarchy. The present-day Spanish Army is an old-fashioned, indolent and disorganised institution; it has few material assets and low morale. In 1898 it played a lamentable role in Cuba and the Philippines and now, to regain its dignity with regard to itself and the nation, it has taken on the role of arbiter in Spanish politics. All in all, however, the balance of forces is delicate, and where there's confusion, the resolute triumph.

"Couldn't it be by Martínez del Mazo?" asks Azaña.

Pleased to have the opportunity, Anthony Whitelands gets ready to explain why not. In the name of all his colleagues, the Interior Minister protests.

"Shouldn't we be concentrating on more urgent and weighty matters?"

The president of the Council of Ministers replies amiably.

"My dear Amós, there's time enough for everything . . . or for nothing. Right now, that painting intrigues me. Antonio Primo de Rivera is a regular guest in the house where it's on display, and several coup-mongering generals just happen to be there as well. The obscure art dealer who started the process of selling it has been found dead in an empty apartment owned by a Swiss import company. He did not have time to reveal a secret to Señor Whitelands here, whom he had followed from London for reasons unknown. The British Embassy is so interested in the matter that they alert their intelligence services, who send out one of their top men. And this evening one of our own intelligence agents is assassinated, a man who by chance was last seen in the Duke of La Igualada's house on the day of the conspiracy. This might just be a string of coincidences, it's true, but if it isn't, that painting has got a baleful influence that puts Tutankhamun in the shade."

"In that case," insists Amós Salvador, the Interior Minister, "wouldn't it be better to take the bull by the horns? I'll get a warrant drawn up immediately, and we can seize the painting. Then we'll see."

Glad at last to hear a concrete proposal, Lieutenant-Colonel Marranón leaps from his chair to give the relevant instructions. Azaña signals for him to sit down again.

"I confess the same idea had occurred to me, and I find it tempting for several reasons," he says. "In the first place, I'd really like to see the painting. And if it is by Velázquez, I'd love to get it out of that basement and put it on show in the Prado. But we cannot do anything that smacks of illegality. In the current situation we have to be doubly careful. As far as we can tell, Don Alvaro del Valle has not committed any crime. It's no crime to have a valuable painting, or to speak to citizens of whatever political persuasion. We'll keep an even closer watch on them, and if they try to smuggle the painting out of the country or if we can catch them out committing a misdemeanor, then we'll nab them. Until then, we're bound hand and foot."

"But they've killed one of my men," moans the lieutenant-colonel.

"That unfortunate incident affects us all," replies Azaña, "and I feel it twice over: as a citizen, and as head of government. Every violent death brings us a step closer to the abyss. If we cannot put a stop to this, soon there'll be no going back. But what I said about the painting is also true of the murder. We'll start an investigation to find out what happened, and the full weight of the law will be brought to bear on those found guilty; but that's all. It won't be easy. If, as Señor Whitelands has just informed us, the captain recognised the plotters, they are the prime suspects, but it's obvious they will have covered their tracks. The fact that the body appeared on wasteland rules out any idea that he was shot by accident in a street fight. But we can't act on suspicion, especially against generals who at the moment of the crime were officially hundreds of kilometres from Madrid. However that may be, it seems as though the conspiracy is in its final stages. Yet I insist we must not forget the death of that man Pedro Teacher. Both he and Captain Coscolluela were closely following Señor Whitelands. There must be a connection we can't spot."

He falls silent and lights another cigarette. He looks at his watch: it's very late. Seeing this, he realises just how tired he is. The others look pale and bleary-eyed as well. Azaña sighs and goes on.

"Gentlemen, as I've just said, we are on the edge of the abyss. At the moment, no-one can make their mind up to advance. But all that's needed is a push to pitch the country into catastrophe. And I'm convinced that if and when that push is given, it will be by what in historical terms is an insignificant event, something that future generations will see as a mere anecdote, and will have to magnify in order to understand why a nation plunged into a fratricidal war when it could have avoided it. And I can't get that painting out of my head, damn it!"

He pauses for a long while, then adds:

"As I said, for the moment our hands are tied. But there is nothing to stop us asking Señor Whitelands here to continue investigating on his own behalf. He has told us he is determined to return to London as quickly as possible, and in view of what has happened, that seems to me perfectly reasonable. Not even with the authority I enjoy as head of government would I venture to suggest that he postpone his departure until after he has had one last meeting with the Duke of La Igualada. But if he did so, perhaps he might uncover something new that would allow us to disentangle all this mystery."

Unable to control his growing anxiety, Lieutenant-Colonel Marranón cannot help protesting loudly.

"With all due respect, I don't think that's a good idea. The mission is highly risky. Those people stop at nothing, and I've already lost one assistant. This isn't how we're going to prevent the threat of a coup, for heaven's sake!"

Anthony is strangely moved to detect, perhaps mistakenly, that the lieutenant-colonel is concerned for his safety. But it is Don Alonso Mallol who replies.

"They wouldn't dare touch an Englishman."

"That won't stop them. Pedro Teacher was English too. And the embassy won't get involved over a meddling private individual. It could get us into trouble though."

Azaña intervenes.

"Everything has its advantages and disadvantages, but the discussion is pointless. The final word rests with Señor Whitelands."

Señor Whitelands, to everyone's astonishment, not least his own, has already reached a decision.

"I'll go to that house," he announces, "whether you want me to or not. I realise I can't just leave Spain with things as they are. I mean regarding the painting. I'm an art expert, and I have a reputation. That is more important than caution."

He does not mention any further reasons, which are no business of the others in the room.

"I'll keep you informed as best I can," he continues. "And don't worry about my embassy. I won't tell them a thing or turn to them for help. I know they wouldn't pay me any attention anyway."

The meeting breaks up. The goodbyes are brief: everyone is sleepy. A car drops the Englishman close to Plaza del Angel, so that he can walk the last part on his own and nobody will see who brought him. The receptionist is asleep in his chair, head on his arm, arm on the counter. Anthony takes the key without waking him, and goes up to his room. He is so tired he is not surprised to find Toñina in his bed, sound asleep. He undresses and clambers in beside her. Toñina half opens her eyes, takes him in her arms without a word and makes up with tenderness for the inexperience of youth. After his emotional rollercoaster with Paquita and Lilí, her simple caresses are a soothing balm.

35

Anthony Whitelands began the day with what, despite having been in Madrid for only a short time, he now regarded as a ritual: breakfast in the usual café, a quick glance at the daily newspapers, a stroll to the mansion on Castellana. The butler opened the door with his habitual gruffness. His gypsy features betrayed no surprise or hostility, as if the fearsome butcher of the previous evening had existed only in the Englishman's imagination.

"Be so kind as to come in and wait in the hall while I inform his excellency."

Left on his own again with "The Death of Actaeon", Anthony wondered how Velázquez would have dealt with the dramatic scene if he had been commissioned to paint it rather than Titian. Well-versed in the magnificent shows of ceremony that held together the floating republic of Venice, Titian had made use of the profound classical culture that had been built up in the city since the Renaissance to portray the irrational, disproportionate punishment meted out by a goddess who was a captive to her own limitless power. Diana dominated the scene, like the merciless forces that rain down on mankind: illness, war, destructive passions. Velázquez was not unaware of the calamities that govern our world, but he refused to portray them on canvas. Most likely he would have depicted an accidental witness to Actaeon's dreadful fate, reflecting in his features the astonishment, terror or indifference one would feel when faced with the terrible event he had seen and would carry with him forever, without having understood it or how he could convey to the world its meaning and what it had taught him.

As though a fickle fate were also presiding over the course of his actions, Anthony's reflections were interrupted by a quavering but happy voice.

"Tony! You're back! Thank God! Aren't you in danger anymore?"

"I don't know, Lilí. But I had to come at any cost."

"To see me?"

"I won't lie to you: you're not the reason I'm here. But since we've met, I want to take advantage of our meeting to clarify what happened yesterday."

Lilí came up to him and pressed her hand over his mouth.

"Don't say a word. You Protestants always think you have to say unpleasant things. You believe that something bitter or wounding or brutal must be the truth. But things are not like that. Miracles and fairy tales are not an illusion. They express a hope. Perhaps Heaven is only a hope too. Even so, it helps us live. Truth cannot be an illusory hope. I'm not asking you for an explanation, I don't reproach you for anything, I'm not demanding anything of you. But you can't rob me of hope, Tony. Not today or tomorrow, but perhaps some day, things will be different. At that moment, if I've survived and you call me, I'll go wherever you say and do whatever you want. Until that moment, whether real or imaginary, finally arrives, all I ask of you is an affectionate silence. And that you don't tell a soul about it. Do you promise?"

Before Anthony had time to reply, Don Alvaro del Valle and the butler appeared in the hallway. Although there was nothing intimidating about their attitude, Anthony felt suddenly uneasy. Until then he had been as determined to come to the mansion and confront the duke on his own ground as he had been in Azaña's office the previous night; but now he began to wonder what he was doing there, and how to proceed. Apparently the duke was not certain of how to receive him either. In the end, his host decided to come straight to the point.

"What brings you here, Mr Whitelands?"

This direct question made things easier.

"Your grace, I've come to be paid what I'm owed."

Lilí was still in the hallway. She had begun to leave when her father and the butler arrived, but remained on the lookout in the doorway in case the Englishman should need her. Seeing this, the duke shot her a reassuring look.

"That seems reasonable," he said to Anthony. "Let's go to my study. Nobody will disturb us there."

Taking this as his responsibility, the butler nodded.

Entering the study, Anthony's gaze was inevitably drawn towards the window from which he had first seen Paquita in the garden, in the company of a mysterious suitor. In that same garden she had given him a fleeting embrace, and it was there he had surprised her a few days later in the depths of despair. Now, bathed in the warm morning sunlight, the garden seemed abandoned. A flock of sparrows was flitting between the ground and the tree branches. The two men sat as they had done on previous occasions. Anthony immediately took the lead.

"When it was first suggested I come here, I was offered remuneration, and you yourself later ratified this commitment on several occasions. I have tried from the start to fulfill my task, and I think I have done so, as far as possible, loyally, conscientiously and competently. It is not only fair, but correct that I should be rewarded. We professionals not only have a right to be compensated, but have to defend that right for all our profession. I am against the whims of amateurs: to decline payment implies declining responsibility. Because of your position, you, your grace, think and act according to different principles, but I am sure you understand and approve of what I am saying."

"Without a doubt."

"Possibly, but the preamble seemed to me necessary in view of what I am about to say. I was engaged to value some paintings. It turned out that nothing was as it seemed. Unwittingly, I have become an essential or incidental element in a conspiracy whose aim and scope I still do not fully comprehend. That is what I meant when I spoke of receiving payment. I want the explanations I am owed. Give me them, and I will leave. And you can keep your money – it's of no interest to me."

The duke was silent for a long while, then said:

"I can perfectly understand your curiosity, Mr Whitelands. And I can assure you there are several questions I would also like to ask you . . . although I'm not so sure I would like to hear the answers. But perhaps for the sake of harmony it would be better for us to remain in mutual ignorance, don't you think?"

Anthony's heart sank, but he immediately told himself that the duke could not know anything specific about the events he was referring to, or he would not have expressed himself in such a calm, roundabout way. If the duchess had been present, things would have been more hazardous, but man to man he still had room for manoeuvre.

"The events I was referring to," he said, trying not to flush as he began to lie, "go beyond anything personal. As far as that is concerned, nothing untoward has happened. But allow me to begin at the beginning. Who is Pedro Teacher, and what role does he play in this farce?"

The duke seemed relieved to hear this question. Doubtless he had been expecting something more delicate, and so had no qualms about giving Anthony a full reply: Pedro Teacher was an art dealer thanks to whom the duke, together with several other aristocratic Spanish families, had acquired works of art, especially signed paintings by well-known figures.

"Pedro Teacher has access to interesting works, and sells them at reasonable prices. He has a select clientele in London and here in Madrid. I've bought a few paintings through him, and sold or exchanged others advantageously."

To judge from his way of speaking, either the duke knew nothing of the art dealer's death or he was a consummate liar. Anthony decided it was the former, and said:

"And now Pedro Teacher is collaborating in the sale of the Velázquez you keep in your basement."

"You know that as well as I do. The operation required someone I could trust. I mean professionally as well as personally and politically. Pedro Teacher does not fulfil those requirements. His political opinions are well known, and he is not highly enough regarded as a Velázquez expert. Any judgment he came to would not have been above suspicion. That is why he turned to you."

"Did Pedro Teacher know what the proceeds of the sale were for?"

"More or less. Pedro Teacher fully supports our cause. I mean the cause of those of us who want to put a stop to the current chaos and prevent the Marxist hordes taking over Spain."

"I don't understand. Pedro Teacher is English, or virtually so; he has a thriving business in London. The fact that he has established commercial and even friendly links with people in another country is not enough for him to want to get involved in the daily politics of that country to the extent that he runs serious risks both in Spain and in England."

"You are doing so."

"Against my will."

"Yesterday, as I believe, you tried to climb the wall into my garden, and today you have once more ventured into the lion's den. Don't tell me you did those things against your will. It often happens that the most rational and materialist of men feels a sudden impulse and almost without realising it cheerfully throws all thought of his personal security, his prerogatives, everything regarding his well-being, right out of the window."

"Your grace, I'm not someone like that. It's the Marquis of Estella you're talking about."

The duke closed his eyes, as if his reaction to hearing that name required him to reflect for a while and put his own thoughts and feelings in order. When he reopened them, there was a glint there that contrasted strongly with his innate melancholy expression.

"Ah, José Antonio!" he said, glancing knowingly at the Englishman. "I hear that you and he got on very well. I'm not surprised. No-one can remain immune to his magnetism, not even those who would like to see him dead. You're an intelligent, honourable, and – although you try to deny it – irredeemably idealistic man. José Antonio realised this from the start, and told me so. Like all true leaders, he has the capacity to judge people at first sight, to read in their minds and hearts what they are trying desperately to hide from the world, and often from themselves. Oh, if only I had that ability! But it's no use, I'm blind when it comes to trying to decipher anyone else's intentions."

Rising from his armchair, he began pacing round the room. He felt riven by contradictions and the hard choices he had to make; he needed to comment on them to somebody but had no-one around him he could trust to listen and understand. In those turbulent days, nobody was in any mood to pay attention to ideas or personal problems that were not their own. Thanks to his being a foreigner and his easy-going attitude, Anthony had become the perfect recipient for many people's intimate confessions, and the escape valve for the passionate outpourings of others. Only now that it was too late was he beginning to wake up to this characteristic, which had led to so many misunderstandings over the past few days. And now the duke, himself caught up in this mechanism, could not help pouring his heart out.

"In its day I was an ardent defender of the Primo de Rivera dictatorship. I knew Don Miguel intimately, and I was sure he did not take the reins of power out of personal ambition, but because he was aware this was the only way to save the Monarchy and everything it stood for. By then the Marxist plot had already infected our social body, due to complacency from our lethargic ruling classes and with the blessing of those same intellectuals who are now tearing their garments and denouncing the Republic. No-one was as sorry as I was to see the fall of Primo de Rivera, because in everyone's cowardly acceptance of it, starting with the Army's, I could clearly see the signs of what was to come. After Primo de Rivera had been toppled and forced into exile, I became a second father to José Antonio, not just because he was the son of a friend fallen on misfortune, but because I could satisfy some of my own rage in the passion with which he defended his father. The recklessness with which that lad was capable of confronting – verbally or with his fists – much more powerful individuals or institutions compensated in part for my own lack of courage."

The duke sat down again, passed his hand over his face and lit a cigarette. Then he went on in a weary voice, as if saying all this brought him pain rather than relief.

"Naturally, neither I nor anyone else could prevent what happened next. I mean the affection that grew up between Paquita and José Antonio. In normal circumstances, I would have liked nothing better than to have him as my son-in-law, but with things as they stand, there was no way I could approve of their relationship. José Antonio's life has been marked by violence from the start, and everything points to it having a violent end. I don't want my daughter to become the Pasionaria of the Right. I am by nature flexible and accommodating, but on this matter I stayed firm. And both of them curbed their impulsive natures and accepted my decision. I know how much they have suffered as a consequence, but I'm not sorry. The course of events in Spain has only reaffirmed my conviction, and there is always the hope that things will improve."

"And as long as they don't, you supply José Antonio with weapons or the money to purchase them."

"I have no choice. Without weapons to defend themselves, he and his comrades would have been killed long ago. José Antonio has a historic mission to fulfil; I cannot divert him from his path, but I'll do all I can to protect him."

"You know the use to which the Falange puts those weapons."

"I have a vague idea. Nobody tells me, and I don't ask. In the end, it doesn't matter: weapons have only one purpose. In this case, the chance to trade blows and keep the enemy at bay."

"Don't be naïve," said Anthony. "The Falange isn't interested in simply surviving. What they want is to install a fascist state in Spain. José Antonio rejects the Monarchy. He supports a kind of syndicalism very close to socialism. I've heard him enthusiastically and eloquently defend this ideology both in public and in private."

The duke shrugged.

"Yes, I know about that. My two sons have turned out to be fervent Falangists and fill my ears with their slogans day and night. I'm not too worried about them. If one day the Falange were to impose their beliefs, they would soon return to the fold. In Italy too the Fascists were meant to eat children raw, but now Mussolini goes arm in arm with the King and the Pope. The Bolshevik revolution, the one coming from below, is irreversible; the one from above on the other hand is pure rhetoric, because it is not nourished by the class struggle and does not engage with it."

He stubbed his cigarette out in the ashtray, lit another, and began walking up and down again, talking to himself as if he were alone in the study.

"That is exactly what I'm trying to convince the generals of. They're very blinkered, suspicious of anything they don't understand or cannot control, and they're stubborn as mules. That's how they have been trained, and I won't deny that this gives them strength, but at decisive moments these qualities become a hindrance. They detest José Antonio because even though he is not part of the military establishment he has more authority and more prestige than any general, and the Falange squads are more disciplined, more courageous and more trustworthy than the regular troops. It's because of this rather than any ideological differences that they have it more in for him than the real enemy. They'd be only too happy to put all the Falangists up against a wall.

They won't do so, because José Antonio enjoys far greater support than he appears to. Patriots and those who believe in order are with him; it's only the violence surrounding him that prevents them showing it more openly. Because of that, the military put up with him in spite of themselves, but try to marginalise him indirectly. They put pressure on us to withdraw our support for the Falange and so choke the movement to death, or to wait for them to fall one by one for lack of weapons and funds."

He turned to Anthony with the expression and gestures of a lawyer pleading in court.

"It's a grave mistake that I'm trying in vain to disabuse them of. If they agreed to join an alliance with the Falange, they would not only gain a formidable ally when it came to the time for action, but they would also have the theory of state they lack. Without José Antonio's doctrinal support, the coup will be nothing more than a silly military adventure: the stupidest among them will come to power, and it will soon be snuffed out."

"Have you told José Antonio all this?"

"No. José Antonio despises the military. He blames the Army as an institution for having betrayed his father, but he can't see that the same Army that left the father in the lurch is ready to do the same with the son. He possibly senses there may be some manoeuvring going on to sideline the Falange, but nothing more than that. If he knew what the generals are really planning, he would probably do something rash. That's why I prefer not to tell him anything."

"What do you mean by 'rash'?"

"Start the uprising himself. The idea's been in his head for some time. He thinks that if the Falange seizes the initiative, the Army will be forced to back them up whether they want to or not. He cannot see that Mola and Franco would be capable of letting the Falangists get slaughtered without batting an eyelid, and then use that as a pretext for re-establishing order by force. That is my dilemma, Mr Whitelands: if

I listen to the generals and leave the Falange defenceless, I'll be committing a crime; but if I provide them with the weapons they need, I may be committing a greater one by sending them to a certain death. I don't know what to do."

"And while you hesitate, Velázquez stays in the basement."

"That's of no importance whatsoever now."

"It is to me."

The duke was still on his feet. Anthony stood up as well. The two men paced the study. As he passed the window, Anthony thought that out of the corner of his eye he glimpsed a figure stirring in the garden. When he stopped to look properly, he could not see anyone, and thought he must have been taken in by the shadow cast by a passing cloud or a branch tossing in the breeze.

"Your grace," he said, still striding up and down, "I'd like to make you a proposition. If I succeed in dissuading José Antonio from starting the uprising and convince him to submit to the Army's command, would you authorise me to reveal the existence of the Velázquez? It's not a lot to ask: I will give up any profit that could come from its legal or illegal sale, in Spain or abroad. As you said, perhaps I am an idealist, but my ideals are not political: I don't aspire to change the world. As part of my studies, I know enough about history to be aware of how all attempts to improve society or human nature have ended up. But I do believe in art, and I'm ready to sacrifice everything for it, or almost everything: I'm no hero."

While he listened to the Englishman's proposal, the duke had carried on pacing up and down, his hands clasped behind his back, staring at the carpet the whole time. All at once he halted, looked intently at Anthony, and said:

"I was afraid for a moment you were going to include my daughter as part of the bargain."

The Englishman smiled.

"To be honest, the thought had occurred to me. But I have a great respect for Paquita, and I would never use her as part of any deal. She has to feel the same as I do, and I have no illusions on that score. The Velázquez will be reward enough."

The duke spread his arms wide in approval.

"You are a gentleman, Mr Whitelands," he exclaimed.

Hearing this praise from a father who knew nothing of what had happened between him and his two daughters, Anthony could not help blushing.

"But how do you think you can convince him?" asked the duke. "José Antonio is not someone who gives in easily."

"Leave it to me," said Anthony. "I've got an ace up my sleeve."

36

Doña Victoria Francisca Eugenia María del Valle y Martínez de Alcántara, Marchioness of Cornellá, better known by the very Spanish diminutive Paquita, felt more uneasy with every hour that passed since the moment when she had left her honour and virtue in the arms of an Englishman. Nothing that had happened since then had succeeded in restoring her peace of mind. When she had sought refuge in the calm isolation of the garden, she had found herself in the midst of a violent dispute between three generals in civilian clothes and a soldier with a war wound whose head was bobbing over the garden wall. Her attempt to obtain absolution and spiritual guidance from Father Rodrigo had come up against his unshakeable intransigence. This painful incident had been followed by an unpleasant search of the mansion for a possible intruder, one whose identity Paquita was sure she could guess, making her more anxious still. When order had finally been restored, the family dinner had been worse even than the disturbances it followed: visibly bewildered, her father had picked at the different courses merely for politeness' sake; her mother had claimed she was slightly indisposed, and had not eaten a thing; her brother Guillermo had tucked in heartily as usual, but mechanically and in a sullen silence; and lastly, Lilí, usually the life and soul of the family, seemed to be the saddest of them all, completely caught up in her troubles, and ate the least of any of them. Halfway through the meal, Father Rodrigo had joined them. He said he had been visiting a gravely ill person. Without bothering to conceal his irritation, he muttered a few short prayers, nibbled at a piece of bread, sipped a little wine and then quit the table and the room, pausing only to glare at Paquita in utter contempt.

That night the young marchioness hardly slept. As she tossed and turned, she tried in vain to rein in the whirl of ideas and emotions swirling pitilessly round her brain. Whenever she dozed off, her dreams were like the projection of an obscene, delirious film, shot by the Devil himself. At dawn this witches' Sabbath began to fade, to be replaced by a desolate sense of sadness and an imprecise feeling that she struggled to define as she lay waiting for the light of day to rescue the world from darkness. And of all the torments she had suffered, this indefinable sensation was the worst. She spent the best part of the morning trying to drive it away. Twice she came across Lilí in the mansion corridors, but her sister, instead of rushing up to her, throwing her arms round her and smothering her cheeks with kisses while she poured out the thousand childish notions fluttering through her madcap mind, did nothing more than glance furtively at her out of the corner of her eye, with something that looked incomprehensibly close to hatred.

Towards midday Paquita found the house so oppressive she decided to go out. Her state of mind led her to want to be alone, but she thought that if she mingled with a mass of people, this silent contact with anonymous men and women busy going about their own affairs, comforted by their joys or preoccupied with their problems, would help her put her own situation into perspective. She already had her coat and gloves on, and had taken up her handbag, when the house-maid came into her bedroom. A woman was asking for the Marchioness of Cornellá. The butler, when he saw her ragged appearance, had sent her round to the tradesman's entrance, and now she was waiting in the kitchen. She had not wanted to give her name or reveal the object of her visit. She had simply given the marchioness's name and expressed not so much a wish to see her as a need to talk to her urgently. She did not seem to be either crazy or dangerous; she was carrying a heavy bundle and cradling a tiny baby in her arms.

Paquita's first impulse had been to tell them to send the girl away at once, but mention of the baby made her think again. As it seemed only prudent not to let this stranger into the house, Paquita went to meet her below stairs, where her bedraggled aspect had led her to be confined. In a small room next to the kitchen, a plump woman was starching and ironing a shirtfront embroidered with a crown and a gothic monogram. Paquita asked her to leave, and it was there, standing up, that she had her talk with Toñina.

"Perhaps . . ." Toñina began after clearing her throat several times and starting and stopping just as often, "perhaps madam remembers yesterday, when we met in that foreign gentleman's hotel room. I . . ."

"I remember it well," Paquita interrupted in an exaggeratedly haughty tone, as if to make clear from the start that this coincidence and anything it might imply did not establish any complicity between them or do anything to reduce the gulf separating them.

Toñina understood it as such, but appreciated the valour implicit in the admission. She had been worried she might come up against a flat denial from Paquita that would have ruined her plan.

"Thank you," she said, lowering her voice. "I only said it to . . . I mean that I haven't come to explain nothing, but for another reason. I myself, if you'll excuse me, am a whore. By that I mean I know my place. Forgive me for bringing the baby with me. I had no-one to leave him with. My mother looks after him, but today she couldn't . . . So it was down me here . . . what I mean to say is that I myself am leaving Madrid on the quiet. I don't know if I'll be back some day. Nobody knows I'm going: only me, and at the moment you, your ladyship."

Hearing mention of the baby, Paquita could not prevent her eyes straying to the shawl it was wrapped in. In among the folds, she could make out pronounced eyebrows and puffy, graceless features. She was strangely moved by his far from angelic appearance. In order to recover her composure, she straightened up and snapped:

"Just tell me what brings you here."

"It's on account of the English gentleman. I didn't know who to turn to apart from your ladyship."

"I don't have anything to do with that person. I hardly know him."

Toñina recalled the bloodstain on the sheet, but realised this was not the moment to mention it.

"And I'm not saying anything different. Madam is perfectly free to know or know not who she pleases. But if no-one intervenes, he's going to be killed. This evening. Everything is in place, and the order's been given."

"The order?"

"Yes, your ladyship, the order to kill him. And I wouldn't want nothing to do with that. Begging your pardon, ma'am, but the Englishman has always behaved well towards me. In his treatment of me, and when it came to pay. And with the child too. He's a good man."

"Why do they want to kill him then?"

"Why else, ma'am? Because of politics."

The laundry room was damp and steamy, and since there was no furniture in it apart from that necessary for its function, the two women remained standing. Paquita had kept her coat on to show that their conversation had to be brief. Toñina still held the sleeping baby in her arms.

"There's not much I can do unless you're more precise," said Paquita angrily. She would have preferred not to know anything about all this, but now there was no going back.

"There's not much more I can tell you," replied Toñina. "Your servant here only knows half the story and doesn't want to get anyone into trouble. I can't give you any names. A couple of days ago a man came to our house. I didn't see him. In secret they call him Kolia. Does that mean anything to your ladyship?"

"No, who is he?"

"An agent of Moscow. Higinio . . . I mean, a friend who's been like a father to me, is in the Communist Party. Sometimes he gets orders and has to carry them out to the letter. Kolia came to tell him to bump off Antonio. Antonio is the English gentleman."

"I know that. What else? Tell me everything."

"I wasn't there. When I got back, Kolia had left. My mother and Higinio were arguing. They shut their mouths in front of me, but I could hear them from my room. They were very worried and they were shouting. Higinio has never killed anyone. It's never even occurred to him. He's kindness itself."

"But this time he'll do it."

"If the party tells him to, there's no way out. Obedience to the party is everything. That's the only way we can achieve our goals – Lenin said that."

Hearing that name, the baby opened his eyes and began to moan.

"He's hungry," Toñina announced.

"Do you breastfeed him?" asked Paquita.

"No, ma'am. He's too big for that. He eats bits of bread dipped in milk if possible; if not, bread and water."

"I'll ask them to warm some milk. Do you like cocoa?"

"Oh, ma'am, at home we don't have such extravagances."

Paquita went into the kitchen, where the heat mingled with the smell of stew. She felt faint, but resisted the temptation to take off her coat. She gave the necessary instructions, then slipped back into the laundry room.

"Where were we?" she asked.

"This evening I was supposed to take the English gentleman to a place near Puerta de Toledo, where Higinio and possibly some of his comrades will be waiting to finish him off. But I don't want to be part of it, that's why I'm for the hills. Of course if I don't do it someone else will, unless your ladyship puts a stop to it. But madam has to promise she won't go the police with the story. I don't want anything to happen to Higinio. Do you promise?"

Paquita was finding it hard to breathe. Her head was spinning: she needed fresh air and time to think.

"Come on," she said, "let's get out of here."

As she opened the door, Paquita almost collided with a uniformed maid who was about to come in, carrying a tray. Paquita told her to follow them, and the three women took the baby out into a narrow, shaded part of the garden, where a cool breeze was blowing. Paquita led the small procession to a sunny corner where a bench and a stone table stood next to a marble statue framed in a niche of clipped cypresses. This peaceful nook was visible from the mansion windows, and Paquita wondered how she would justify the scene if anyone spotted them. The women in the household often did charity work, and Paquita herself had several needy families in her charge, but she had never brought any of them home, still less sat down to chat with them in the garden at this time of day. Life was becoming very complicated for the young Marchioness of Cornellá.

The maid put the tray on the table. On it was a bowl of cocoa and a plate with a Viennese roll and some slices of sausage.

"The roll is for you," Paquita said to Toñina once the maid had withdrawn. "I thought you might be hungry. If not, you can take it for your journey."

"Thank you, ma'am," said Toñina, trying to spoonfeed the baby with the cocoa.

Since this process proved too difficult to allow them to talk, Paquita took advantage of the lull to reflect. First of all, there was no guarantee the tale she had just heard was true. She did not know the person telling it, someone who had openly confessed to her degrading profession. Probably, thought Paquita, this was all part of a plan to extort money from her. This little hussy had surprised her coming out of Anthony's hotel room, and was hoping to make money from it. But as it was only her word against Paquita's, she was trying to get her involved up in some cock and bull story. The best thing would be to summon the butler and have the woman and baby thrown out into the street.

"I still don't understand," Paquita said out loud. "To send an agent from Moscow just to kill a man must mean that man has done something very important."

"I don't know what to say, your ladyship. I only know bits and pieces. When he's drunk too much or gets horny, pardon the expression, the English gentleman is always talking about a painting. I've no idea if it's got anything to do with that or not, but I'm mentioning it in case it serves as a referendum for your ladyship."

Paquita's suspicions evaporated when she heard this clear proof of the extent to which Anthony trusted the woman now in front of her.

"Wouldn't it have been easier simply to warn the English gentleman directly of the danger, rather than coming to someone like me, who hardly knows him?" she asked.

"Easier, possibly," replied Toñina, "but it would have been no use. The English gentleman can be a bit slow over certain things."

Paquita could not help smiling at this. Their shared view of Anthony suddenly brought the two women closer. After a moment however, things returned to normal.

"Apart from that," Toñina continued, "there's the risk involved. Betraying the party may be bad for the future of the proletariat, but it's far worse for the present of anyone who does it. I'm running enough of a risk just by coming to see your ladyship. And if I'm not there, who's going to look after this little bundle of joy?"

At the mention of such a dramatic eventuality, the little bundle threw up all the cocoa he had swallowed, and started to howl plaintively.

"Have you any idea where you'll go?" asked Paquita, turning away and giving her to understand that this question marked the end of their conversation.

"To Barcelona, like all the others."

Paquita opened her bag and took out some banknotes and a visiting card.

"Take this," she said. "You'll need it. And if when you're in Barcelona you want to change your life, go to the home of the Baron de Falset, show him this card, and tell him you were sent by his cousin Paquita from Madrid. He'll help you. But if you prefer to wait for Lenin's prophecy to come true, that's your affair."

She accompanied Toñina and the baby to the side gate. Before she left, Toñina attempted to kiss her hand in gratitude, but Paquita quickly withdrew it and hastened their goodbyes. Closing the gate, she began to wander among the myrtle bushes, trying to resolve the emotional, intellectual and practical mess she found herself in. She could never have suspected that at that very moment the object of her concerns was only a short distance away from the mansion.

Immediately after his talk with the Duke of La Igualada, Anthony Whitelands had gone out into the street, found a telephone, called the house he had just left, and asked to speak to Guillermo. Fortunately, as usual, the young master had not yet gone out. On the previous evening he had stayed working late and now, bathed and dressed, he was ready for breakfast. When he came on the line, Anthony identified himself and asked if they could meet in the Michigan. Guillermo arrived soon afterwards. While he was tucking into a prodigious breakfast, Anthony enquired whether he had found out anything new about the supposed traitor in the Falange ranks. Since there was no news in that respect, the Englishman wondered Guillermo still thought it would be a good idea for him to talk to José Antonio about the matter. Guillermo was all for it, and so Anthony asked him to set up the meeting.

"Look for somewhere discreet, at whatever time suits him, and give me the details. I won't be armed, but tell him he can bring his gun but not his gunmen. We have to talk alone."

Guillermo del Valle tried to carry out his mission as quickly as he could, but came up against more problems than anticipated. When he arrived at the Falange headquarters on Calle Nicasio Gallego around two in the afternoon, they had no news of the Chief. He had called a meeting of the National Council for seven that evening, but no-one knew where he might be found before then. Guillermo del Valle left the Centre and went to Anthony's hotel to tell him what had happened. When the receptionist informed him that Señor Whitelands had left some time before, without mentioning where he was going, Guillermo del Valle wrote a brief note saying he would pass by the hotel as soon as he knew anything, although he thought it unlikely he could arrange a meeting for that day, as Anthony had wished. National Council meetings usually lasted for several hours, and when they were over its members went for dinner and then to drink and argue at the Happy Whale until the early hours.

This delay disconcerted the Englishman. He went up to his room expecting to find Toñina there, and her absence only made him all the more irritated. Unable to concentrate on anything demanding intellectual effort, and at a loss what to do with his time, he collapsed onto the bed and soon fell fast asleep.

When he awoke, it was already dark. He went down to reception and asked if anyone had left a message. The receptionist said yes, someone had. More or less an hour earlier, a gentleman had called and asked the receptionist to tell Señor Whitelands from him that he would like to meet at eight at a specific location. The gentleman in question had an English accent and the address he had given was almost impossible to understand. Anthony presumed it must have been an official from the embassy. When the receptionist showed him the address he had written down, Anthony did not recognise it.

"Is Calle de la Arganzuela far from here?"

"Quite a way," said the receptionist. "You'd do best to take a taxi or the metro to Puerta de Toledo. Calle de la Arganzuela is down that way."

37

An independent mind and the ability to reach a decision fearlessly and to stick to it had been her defining characteristics from the cradle on. These qualities had won the admiration of those who knew her well, and occasionally the mistrust of those only acquainted with her. If she had been born into a less socially constrained family, she would doubtless have received the influence of the Free Teaching Institute, would have embraced the principles of the incipient Spanish feminist movement, and, like so many women of her time, would have belonged to the Lyceum Club. Denied these outlets for her development, she had poured her considerable abilities into supporting her family. She was too intelligent not to realise what a waste this was: she often felt diminished, and had on several occasions embarked on crazy adventures simply in order to release some of the pressure threatening her mental well-being. She was the eldest of four children, but being a woman excluded her from the rights and responsibilities of being the first-born. In practice she exercised these rights, because her father was conscious of her talents and relied more on her judgment than on his sons', but this tacit endorsement from one so steeped in the ancient Spanish patriarchal tradition was generally seen as a weakness, which not only robbed it of all value, but at one fell swoop slammed shut the doors it opened.

Such was the woman who paraded her distress along the neat paths of the garden of a mansion in Paseo de la Castellana one early afternoon in March 1936, searching in vain for a convincing answer to her dilemma. The aforementioned qualities seemed to have deserted her just when she most needed them. She was so confused that she did not hear someone skipping towards her, and was startled to hear a cheerful, tender voice call out:

"What's wrong, Paquita? I've been watching you from my balcony for ages, and you look so nervous!"

Paquita was immensely relieved when she saw that the person asking the question was none other than her sister Lilí. Although their age difference at stages in life marked by rapid and crucial changes had prevented any real friendship developing between them, in the present situation the sisters' natural affection was complemented by an affinity that stemmed from both the similarities and the differences in their characters. Like Paquita, Lilí was intelligent, lively and resourceful, and yet her temperament was more thoughtful, more passive and less romantic. Paquita adored Lilí, in part because she saw herself reflected in many of her attributes and partly because she sensed that her sister was in some ways superior to her: a greater intellectual capacity for considering fundamental questions, a greater control of her emotions, and a capacity for altruism of which she imagined herself incapable. Given all this, Lilí's sudden appearance could not have been more timely: sooner or later the barrier of age had to come down, and this was the perfect moment. Paquita had become aware that her sister was somehow now a fully grown woman capable of understanding her dismay.

"Oh, Lilí, I'm in such a terrible mess," said Paquita. The fact of openly expressing her anguish in this way to a twin soul brought tears brimming to her eyes.

Lilí embraced her sister. All traces of animosity had vanished from her face. Her eyes were shining with a strange new glow that Paquita, totally absorbed in her own suffering, failed to notice and would have been unable to interpret had she done so.

"Come," said Lilí, "let's sit on that bench over there and you can tell me what's worrying you. I don't have much experience of the adult world, but I am your sister, I know you and love you more than anyone, so that should help make up for my ignorance."

They walked arm in arm over to an iron bench under a pergola, as far away as possible from the one that still bore the traces of the recent passage of a sick baby. They sat down, and Paquita poured her heart out to Lilí. She told her everything: her love for José Antonio and the duke's stubborn opposition to a union he knew would be plagued with dangers and disappointments; José Antonio's noble acceptance of this decision, convinced as he was of the role history had reserved for him, aware that he was predestined to a heroic, premature death – even though this manly acceptance was also due in large part to the fact that, in addition to being a patriotic paladin and candidate for martyrdom, he was an inveterate whoremonger. In addition, although José Antonio was susceptible to the just demands of modern women and had no qualms about incorporating a full reply to the question in his political programme, he only saw the problem from an intellectual point of view. In practice, he would never have consented to having a socially unacceptable relationship with the woman he loved: he was a revolutionary in many respects, but at the same time he was a stout defender of the reactionary Catholicism that was central to what he saw as the essence of Spain. So it was that Paquita, seeing the days, months and years pass by, found her resignation changing to exasperation, and her exasperation to open revolt. When chance brought into their narrow family circle a good-looking, discreet foreigner destined soon to disappear from their lives forever, Paquita dreamed up a wild plan.

When her sister reached this point in her story, Lilí could not help letting out a heavy sigh. Paquita took it as a token of condolence; smiling sadly, she clasped her sister's hands between hers and tried to calm her childish fears. Against all expectations, she explained, the experience had not been so awful. The Englishman had shown both consideration and a certain amount of passion, and demonstrated an enthusiasm that was truly contagious. When all was said and done – and Paquita could not help blushing to the roots of her hair as she confessed this – the experience, far from being painful or humiliating, had turned out to be quite pleasant.

"May God forgive me," she exclaimed, "and you too, my beloved Lilí, for setting you such a bad example. You're still a child, and this kind of thing has never even occurred to you. I'm only telling you because I'm desperate and there's no-one else I can confide in."

Paquita was so caught up in her memories and disturbed at the consequences of her actions that she failed to notice the change in her companion's attitude: Lilí had withdrawn her hands, straightened up and turned her head to one side. Behind half-closed lids, her eyes were cold.

"Yet the worst came later," Paquita went on.

Aware that she had committed a sin that would lead to her eternal damnation if she were to die all of a sudden, she had turned to Father Rodrigo for absolution. The priest's reaction had forced her to understand she had committed an abominable sin not only in the eyes of God, but also in the eyes of men. Too late she realised she would never be forgiven, and that she would never be able to tell José Antonio about her despicable act.

"A moment ago a poor woman from the gutter came to see me, bearing with her the fruit of her excesses," Paquita added, casting a sideways glance at the bench where that particular fruit had left its disgusting mark, "and while I was talking to her from the height of my supposed honour, I asked myself what difference there was, or rather, what difference there is, between that wretched woman and myself. But the worst, Lilí dearest, the worst of it is . . ."

At this point, Paquita's words were interrupted by a loud sigh, followed by heartfelt sobbing. In Lilí's mind meanwhile a battle was being fought between the impulse to embrace her sister and offer her the solace of her affection, and a secret rivalry over the Englishman. In the end, she did not move, but simply waited. Regaining her composure, Paquita made a strenuous effort to face up to a truth she did not have the courage to admit, still less put into words. As often happens with noble souls ruled by an ardent desire for perfection, she suffered dreadfully when she felt she was being humiliated by ordinariness.

"I love him," she whispered. "It's absurd, it's pathetic, but I've fallen in love with Anthony Whitelands."

Lilí closed her eyes, but remained serene. After a while she cleared her throat and said:

"What will happen now to José Antonio?"

At that very moment, the person in question was busy with something far more transcendental.

Two years earlier, Ramón Serrano Suñer, José Antonio's intimate friend and political associate, had married Zita Polo, a beautiful woman from a good Asturian family, whose sister Carmen happened to be married to General Francisco Franco. Determined to pursue to exhaustion any possibility of an alliance with the Army that would leave the Falange free to act on its own over the coup and guarantee the future acceptance of his bold programme of social reform, José Antonio had asked Serrano Suñer to help set up a meeting with Franco. Suñer was as quick to agree as he was pessimistic as to the outcome of any such meeting. Ten years younger than Franco, tall, good-looking, elegant, likeable and an excellent dancer, Serrano Suñer was the exact opposite of his drab brother-in-law: in spite of this, the two of them had an excellent relationship. Franco scrupulously respected family ties, and in his own case valued what they could offer in terms of social advancement to a military man with no personal fortune and more talent than renown. Aware of the friendship and political ideas that Serrano Suñer shared with Primo de Rivera, he chose to ignore them. He appreciated his brother-in-law's intelligence and political ability, and considered that his faithful support could prove mutually advantageous in the near future. He also knew of his valuable international contacts, particularly with Count Ciano, Mussolini's right-hand man: access to these potential allies could be vital when it came to deciding who would emerge as the sole leader of the rebellion. Unlike some of the other conspirators, who thought their duty would be done when public order was re-established, the unity of Spain safeguarded and the Monarchy perhaps restored, Franco knew that the general leading the coup would end up controlling the country's destiny, with or without the King, and he was not prepared to hand over this mission to Mola, Sanjurjo, Goded, Fanjul or any of the drunkards strutting around the guardrooms. That was why he agreed to meet Primo de Rivera, even though this meant postponing his return to the Canary Islands, which he had left in secret, and although he was not prepared to make the slightest concession to someone he considered a good-for-nothing, and even less to the Falange, which he saw as a hindrance that would have to be got rid of sooner or later.

The meeting took place that same morning in Serrano Suñer's parents' home. For José Antonio it turned out to be not merely ineffective but extremely frustrating. In spite of his apparent control of every situation and his brilliant oratory, José Antonio was timid outside his circle of friends. Franco on the other hand had an unshakeable self-assurance. Patient and crafty, he knew how to turn his innate caginess to his advantage, which meant he won every argument by boring his opponent or wearing them down. On this occasion, he received José Antonio with a great show of friendship, but before the Falange Chief could explain why he had come to see him, he launched into a story about how in the Canary Islands, where the climate was so pleasant and the landscapes so beautiful, but there was little for a military man to do, he had embarked on an intensive study of the English language. Since he knew from his brother-in-law that José Antonio had a profound knowledge of that tongue, he did not want to pass up the opportunity to ask him to clear up some difficulties he found with a language that was so rich but yet so different from Spanish. José Antonio politely attempted to resolve the general's linguistic doubts, and then tried in vain to steer the conversation back to the urgent matters that had brought him there. Franco however persistently turned the conversation towards irrelevant matters, or responded evasively, and insisted in peppering all his utterances with the English word "nevertheless", whether or not it was appropriate. At first disconcerted and then annoyed, José Antonio grasped that the astute general was poking fun at him. Following several hours of useless toing and froing, the Falange's National Chief and the general said goodbye politely but coldly, and never saw each other again.

The dashing Marquis of Estella would have been even more discouraged if he had known that while he was beating his head against Franco's brick wall, the woman he loved and who he thought loved him was describing to her sister the whirlwind of her emotions in terms that were highly unfavourable to him.

"I haven't the slightest doubt that God has punished me. Thinking I was committing the sins of the flesh, I have sinned by manipulating another person. I wanted to use a man for my ignoble ends, and God used him to humiliate me. I have fallen in love with Anthony, but can never be his."

"Why not?" asked Lilí, her voice no more than a squeak.

Paquita had spent the night reflecting on this, and so was able to supply all the details.

"First and foremost, he's English. It's true he likes Spain a lot, and doubtless would not mind staying to live here in Madrid. But no-one would want to do that on the eve of a Bolshevik revolution. And if I went to London with him, Papa would disinherit me."

"Paquita, that's so unlike you! Yesterday you were willing to unite your destiny with José Antonio's, with all the dangers and sorrows that implies, but today you're daunted by the idea of living on a professor's salary," said Lilí with a touch of scorn that happily her sister did not notice.

Paquita lowered her gaze and wiped a tear from her cheek.

"Oh, Lilí, if it were only a question of money! But it's more complicated than that; above all it's a question of honour. To begin with, he doesn't have the slightest idea about the real nature of my feelings. In order to overcome his resistance, I pretended to be a woman of easy virtue. Now he must think that I do what I did with him with anyone I happen to meet. How can I possibly convince him otherwise after what happened between us? And secondly, with things as they are, I can't abandon José Antonio. Even though our love is impossible, he counts on me. To know that I love him offers him moral support whenever he feels anguished or weak faced with all the hatred his person and his ideas arouse. If I abandon him now, what consolation will he have left? Then again, our relationship is an open secret; if the rumour starts to spread that I've betrayed him with a foreigner, who on top of it all seems to be rather a ninny . . . Oh, Lilí, I hate to think what use the press would make of news like that! No, no, I've turned it over and over in my mind, and there's no other way out: I'll have to sacrifice myself. I'll behave as if nothing has happened. I won't tell a word of what I've just told you, not to Anthony or José Antonio, nor to anyone: it will be a secret between you and me. You won't betray me, will you, Lilí?"

"For heaven's sake, Paquita, how could you doubt it?" Lilí replied. After a short silence, she added in a different tone: "But in return for my silence, tell me something that's beeen puzzling me."

"What's that?"

"Who exactly is Anthony Whitelands, and why did he come to Madrid, and to our home in particular?"

Unable to refuse her sister's reasonable request, Paquita revealed to her the existence of the Velázquez in the basement, the decision to sell it abroad, thanks to Pedro Teacher and Anthony Whitelands, and the vicissitudes of the operation. Lilí listened in silence to the explanation, then finally cried out:

"Is that all there is to the great mystery? A painting by Velázquez? What a let-down."

Paquita smiled and replied:

"It might not seem much to you, and if I'm honest, I have to agree. But apart from being worth a fortune, that painting is extraordinarily important in helping to understand the life and work of the greatest painter of all time. At least, that's what our dear friend Professor Whitelands says. To him there's nothing so valuable in all the world, not even me. When he speaks about the painting, he forgets everything and turns into a marvellous being, as if Velázquez himself were re-incarnated in him. Or perhaps I see him that way through a lover's eyes. In all honesty, I'm only sorry he can't see his life's great dream come true: to win fame for having discovered a masterpiece like the one that's hidden only a few metres from where we're sitting."

Lilí leapt up from the bench and waved her arms about in vehe-ment protest.

"Sorry? Paquita, that man has robbed you of your honour and ruined your life! Instead of feeling sorry for the disappointment in his professional career, you should be thinking of how to kill him."

In the midst of her agony, Paquita could not refrain from bursting out laughing.

"Lilí, you're so funny! You're such an adorable creature!"

Then just as suddenly she turned serious again, and added:

"In fact, we ought to be making sure of the opposite. That poor woman you saw me with just now had come to warn me that the Marxists are plotting to kill Anthony. She didn't tell me why, but she did say when, and gave me some idea of where. At first I thought it was like the plot from some cheap novel, but in the end I was convinced she was telling the truth. Apparently she was meant to be the one to lure him to where his murderers are waiting, but at the last minute she was unable to go through with such a terrible plan. As far as I could understand, she and Anthony also had something going on between them. Nothing serious."

"So what are you going to do?" Lilí asked impatiently.

"The truth is, I've no idea. That's what I was thinking about when we met. Then when we were talking about other things, it completely slipped my mind. Logically, my first idea was to go to the police, but that woman forbade me to do so, both for her own safety and perhaps for Anthony's too. The way things stand, it's possible that instead of protecting him, the police will cover up for the assassins. And if we rule the police out, there's only one person I can think of with the means and the courage to help. But I can't bring myself to ask such a favour of him: I'm scared that if the two of them get together, then what happened between us will come out."

Lilí had sat down on the bench once more. She was staring at her sister with her head on one side, cupping her face in the palm of her hand as if she were trying to identify the real Paquita in this silly, confused person she had in front of her. I can't believe this is what love is, she seemed to be thinking to herself. She had also felt its sting, but her response was very different.

38

The dramatic events that occurred in rapid succession from that moment on were due in good measure to the crossed paths of the protagonists involved, partly to the climate of fear and violence evident throughout Spain, and partly to an unfortunate conjunction of mistakes and coincidences.

At around six that evening, Anthony Whitelands left his hotel to go to the meeting with the person who had called, even though he did not know that person's identity or the reason for the encounter. This carelessness could be seen as stupidity, were it not for the confusion in which his recent sentimental experiences had left him, and the nervousness he felt at his imminent confrontation with José Antonio Primo de Rivera, which he saw as being extremely important.

Following the receptionist's advice, he walked down Calle Carretas to catch the metro at Puerta del Sol. As soon as he set foot outside the hotel, two plain-clothes policemen began to follow him, sent by Lieutenant-Colonel Marranón with strict instructions not to lose sight of him for an instant. After what had happened to Captain Coscolluela, the lieutenant-colonel had put two men on the job: a perfectly reasonable move that proved fatal in practice.

Anthony got off at Sol station to change lines. Not being familiar with the Madrid metro system, he had to go back and forth through the tunnels until he came to the right line and platform. This central station was very busy, and despite his height, the Englishman's abrupt changes of direction meant the policemen lost track of him. After a few minutes of desperate searching, they thought they had found him again, but as this was the first time they were following him and they were not as well acquainted with his appearance as Captain Coscolluela, they got the wrong man, and tailed him without realising their mistake, because each of them thought the other knew what he was doing. By the time a casual comment made their error obvious, half an hour had already elapsed. Since by now it was impossible to pick up his trail again, they opted to return to the hotel, inform their superior officer from there, and wait for the Englishman to reappear. Their false trail had taken them some way out of the centre of Madrid, and although they took a taxi, they only arrived back at the hotel at ten minutes past seven, a few minutes later than Guillermo del Valle.

He had spent the afternoon in the Falange headquarters, situated at number 21 Calle Nicasio Gallego, where he was hoping to meet José Antonio to arrange a meeting between Anthony Whitelands and the National Chief, as the former had requested. The National Council was due to meet at seven, and Guillermo was sure that José Antonio would arrive in advance, but this was not the case. At around six thirty, Guillermo del Valle heard Raimundo Fernández Cuesta announce that José Antonio had called to tell him he was delayed by some personal business, and that the council meeting was postponed until further notice. In the course of the conversation, José Antonio told his friend and comrade that the postponement was unimportant, because the meeting had been called to analyse the interview he had had that morning with General Franco, and unfortunately that interview had not left any glimmer of hope that there might be an agreement on collaboration between the Falange and the Army. As a result, the party needed to re-examine its policies as a whole, something which required careful preparation. So the meeting of the National Council could wait. At no point in the call did José Antonio say where he was calling from or mention what kind of personal business he was having to deal with.

When he heard the meeting was cancelled, Guillermo, who had promised to keep Anthony informed of his efforts, called the hotel.

The receptionist informed him that Señor Whitelands had gone out. Guillermo did not think it wise to tell the receptionist why he was calling, but instead decided to pass by the hotel himself on the way home. Night had fallen by the time he left Falange headquarters, and a cold wind was blowing; the hotel was too far for him to walk. He was standing on the pavement wondering whether to take a taxi or use public transport when two comrades came out of the Centre. Wearing bright blue Falange shirts bearing the yoke and arrows symbol embroidered in red, they asked him what he was doing there. When he explained, one of his comrades, who had a car, offered to take him back to the hotel. Guillermo del Valle was happy to accept the lift, and the other Falange member decided to accompany them. They parked the car in Calle Espoz y Mina, and the three of them strode into the hotel, startling the receptionist. Since Anthony had not returned, Guillermo del Valle wrote a note telling him of the postponement of the meeting and therefore of the appointment with José Antonio. He put the note in an envelope, sealed it, and handed it to the receptionist. The three Falange activists then cheerfully stepped out into the square. Just at that moment, the two men who had lost track of the Englishman in Sol station turned up outside the hotel. Nervous because of the probable consequences of their failure, they were taken by surprise at the sight of the three young Falangists. Believing they had fallen into an ambush, they instinctively pulled out their guns to defend themselves. Confused by this gesture from seeming civilians, Guillermo's two comrades also drew their weapons, and the four of them opened fire at the same time. More concerned not to be hit than to aim properly, all their shots flew harmlessly into the air. Guillermo's two companions quickly took to their heels, as the Falangists had been ordered if possible to avoid any street battles in order to prevent casualties and politically damaging reprisals.

Guillermo del Valle had no experience of this sort of skirmish. He was no coward, but lacked the capacity to react quickly with a cool head. While the others were shooting, he had stood there, paralysed. By the time he recovered and pulled out his own weapon, he was facing the two policemen alone. Seeing him point his gun at them, they both fired at him before he had time to pull the trigger. He collapsed to the pavement with several gunshot wounds.

Oblivious to this terrible incident of which he was the indirect cause, Anthony Whitelands left the metro and after walking for a while found himself in the grounds of the fish market close to Puerta de Toledo. By this time of night, there was no activity around the market, apart from the cats and rats fighting over stinking remains under the street lights. Clouds of flies buzzed through the icy night air, which the stench from the fish and seafood rendered unbreathable. Anthony looked in vain around this Dantesque wasteland for anyone who could tell him the way to Calle de la Arganzuela. At one end of the market stood a row of parked lorries. His feet sinking in the muddy tyre tracks, Anthony walked over to them, hoping perhaps to find a driver asleep in his cabin, but they were all empty – hardly surprising, given the nauseating stink all around them.

He finally found the street he was looking for by the unpleasant and tiring expedient of covering the area on foot. When he finally reached the corner of Calle de la Arganzuela and Mellizo, it was eight minutes past seven.

While he was searching for the street, it occurred to him that all this was rather odd. Until then he had been reassured by the fact that, according to the hotel receptionist, the person on the telephone had been English: no threat could come from a compatriot. Now however, Anthony could not help wondering what kind of Englishman could have chosen this desolate, sinister spot as a meeting place, unless he was trying to avoid any attention from the police.

His destination turned out to be a narrow, ugly newly built house, with small barred windows. The street door was shut, and there seemed to be no bell. Next to it was another larger wooden door which probably gave access to a commercial establishment – a workshop or warehouse. As this other door was also closed, Anthony decided to give up and head back into town. After all, the receptionist had probably made a mistake when taking down the address. He had only taken a couple of steps when the larger door swung open a little, and a voice whispered:

"Come in."

Anthony stepped inside, and found himself in a large, almost empty space. By the light of the naked bulbs dangling from the ceiling, he could make out rough, bare walls, iron beams and a grimy skylight. At the far end were stacks of cardboard boxes, and to one side stood a dilapidated automobile stripped of its wheels. There were also four men dressed in overalls and wearing caps. Three of them were fierce-looking, and were smoking furiously. The fourth was the one who had opened the door. He was now standing apart from his companions, with his cap pulled down over his eyes and his head lowered to avoid being recognised. This was unsuccessful because Anthony, despite the lack of light, immediately recognised him and turned to him for an explanation.

Higinio Zamora Zamorano gazed down at the floor and shrugged his shoulders.

"You'll have to forgive me, Don Antonio," he muttered, not looking him in the face.

"This doesn't make sense," protested the Englishman. "To make me come to this godforsaken hole at this time of night . . . I thought we had resolved the Toñina affair once and for all."

"It's not that, Don Antonio. The girl's got nothing to do with this. The comrades and myself have brought you here to kill you. Believe me, I'm really sorry."

"To kill me?" said Anthony, dumbfounded. "Oh come on, stop this nonsense! Why would you want to kill me? To rob me? I've got nothing on me. My watch and . . ."

"Don't insist, Don Antonio. It's orders from above. Your humble servant and these comrades is party members. Comrade Kolia gave us the order to proceed, in other words to carry out the execution. For the cause."

"What cause?"

"The cause of the international proletariat, Don Antonio, what else?"

One of the others interrupted him:

"Cut the sermon, Higinio. We're here to do the job, not have a natter. The sooner we get it over, the better."

He said this without anger or harshness. It was plain that none of them particularly enjoyed the mission entrusted to them.

"Holy Mother of Christ, Manolo!" Higinio exploded. "It's one thing to execute someone in the name of the October Revolution, it's something different altogether to slaughter a fellow like a pig. After all, Don Antonio here is no enemy of the people. Ain't that right, Don Antonio?"

"It's not up to you to deliver the verdict, Higinio," another of the men protested.

Anthony decided to try to steer the debate back to less theoretical considerations. He still could not entirely believe they intended to kill him, but they must have had a powerful reason for setting him such a complicated trap.

"Couldn't it be a misunderstanding?" he suggested. "I don't know who Comrade Kolia is, and he doesn't know me. We've never seen each other in our lives."

"You can't be sure of that. Comrade Kolia's identity is a secret. Besides, that's not the point. Comrade Kolia's orders are not up for discussion, and that's that!"

"Well said," agreed the fourth man, who had been silent until now. As he said, this, he jumped down off a crate, and Anthony realised he was a dwarf. It was only then that he understood that this act of summary justice was not a farce, but the brief prelude to his own death. This idea was met with a strange sensation of calm apathy. It did not seem to him ridiculous that a trajectory begun in the lecture halls and libraries of Cambridge and continued in the galleries of the Prado should, after several years of work, scant success, a few failures and a modest dose of hopes and fantasies, come to a close in a Madrid blindly given over to violence and hatred, at the hands of a gang of ruffians who were the perfect incarnation of the Spanish baroque.

"Let's get on with it," he heard Higinio Zamora say. "I just need a few moments with Don Antonio to settle some details relating to my goddaughter. It's never a good idea to leave loose ends in family matters. The comrades here," he added for the Englishman's benefit, "all know about you and Toñina."

Anthony meekly followed Higinio. He wondered what "details" could possibly matter in the final seconds of his life, but did not object. Once they had reached the door, Higinio Zamora grasped his arm and, pretending to be talking to him in secret, whispered in his ear:

"I've left it open."

It took Anthony a moment to register that he meant the door. The years spent studying had not completely ruined his reflexes, so that without pausing to think he gave Higinio Zamora a hefty push. Either Higinio's weak frame could not resist, or he pretended to fall: this distracted his comrades just long enough for Anthony to be able to pull the door open, leap through and rush off down the street. Rapid footsteps, oaths and a gunshot told him his pursuers were hot on his heels. His lengthy strides allowed him to stay sufficiently ahead of them for their hastily aimed gunfire to miss him. He was soon in the flat ground outside the market. This made him an easy target, despite the dim lighting. He ran in a zigzag towards the lorries, still closely followed by three of the men, while the dwarf was naturally enough left to bring up the rear. When he reached the parked vehicles, Anthony tried without much hope to hide behind them. He heard the dwarf shout:

"Cut off his escape! I'll look under the lorries!"

Fearful, out of breath, Anthony no longer felt calmly resigned to his fate, but could sense panic taking hold of his limbs. He closed his eyes, and what seemed to him a long period of time elapsed until the sound of a racing engine forced him to open them again. The beam from a car's headlights swept across the open ground, scattering rats and cats. The vehicle entered the market at full tilt, screeched round in a semi-circle and came to a halt alongside the parked lorries. A hand pointing a gun appeared out of the driver's side window. Anthony recognised the unmistakable mustard-yellow Chevrolet. He ran bent double towards the door being held open for him and jumped inside. The Chevrolet shot off again, raising a cloud of dust and mud, leaving Higinio Zamora and his comrades gesticulating wildly and firing aimlessly in its wake.

When they had got some distance away, the car slowed, and its driver turned towards Anthony, an ironic smile on his face.

"Would you care to tell me what you're doing in a mess like this? What are you trying to do: become a hero?"

"Look who's talking," said the Englishman.

39

In contrast to the violent events in the desolate Puerta de Toledo, the shootout in Plaza del Angel attracted a large crowd from the lively bars in nearby Plaza Santa Ana. Among them were two doctors, who immediately offered to examine Guillermo del Valle's body. They pronounced him still alive, although his pulse was very weak. The same policemen who had shot him helped the doctors carry him inside the hotel, leaving a pool of blood on the pavement. They laid him out on a table. The receptionist did everything he was asked to do, trembling and sighing the whole time, muttering to himself that he had always said that something like this was bound to happen with all the comings and goings in the hotel. His natural agitation was made worse by the prospect of a lengthy interrogation and the probable loss of his job.

It was not long before two Assault Guards appeared on the scene. They shouted at the curious onlookers and brandished their batons to encourage them to disperse. By now one of the doctors had telephoned the Clinical Hospital, and an ambulance was on its way. The policemen called Lieutenant-Colonel Marranón to inform him of what had happened. In turn the lieutenant-colonel called the Interior Minister and then hurried to the scene. By the time he got there, the ambulance had already taken the young man away. When the lieutenant-colonel asked if anyone knew who the victim was, nobody could answer: he had not had any documents on him, and only the receptionist said he had seen him before on a couple of occasions, explaining the circumstances.

"Damn and blast him," growled the lieutenant-colonel, "nothing can happen in this country without that devil of an Englishman being mixed up in it! Do we know what happened to him?"

No-one there had any idea. The lieutenant-colonel would have blown his top if he had had any inkling of where Anthony Whitelands was at that very moment and who he was with. While he was trying to locate him, the hotel telephone rang. The lieutenant-colonel answered in person. It was Don Amós Salvador, the Interior Minister. He had been told what had happened, and had taken the appropriate measures. He had also discovered victim's name: Guillermo del Valle, the son of the Duke of La Igualada, the man who wanted to sell the Velázquez painting. The young man's comrades had returned to Falange headquarters to report what seemed to them, not without reason, an unprovoked attack. A Falange leader had called the victim's family to give them the sad news.

"The duke's on his way to the hotel," said the minister. Get rid of the idiots who caused this mess as quickly as possible, and think up a more or less plausible story. And afterwards, don't stay out in the street: there could be fireworks tonight."

The lieutenant-colonel dismissed the two agents, but not before he had heaped insults on them: in the space of only a few hours they had made two huge mistakes, each with grave consequences. A short while later, the Duke of La Igualada appeared in a chauffeur-driven car. He was accompanied by his daughter Francisca Eugenia and Father Rodrigo.

Naturally enough, the news of what had happened had caused a great commotion in the Paseo de la Castellana mansion. Grief-stricken and indignant, the duke had told the rest of the household, apart from the duchess, who, to the amazement of both family and servants, had left the house alone, without telling a soul or indicating where she was going. The lateness of the hour excluded the possibility that she had gone to visit someone or was attending church, usually her only reasons for going out. Too upset to make any further enquiries, the duke, Paquita and Father Rodrigo left for the hotel as quickly as they could, leaving Lilí in the mansion with the delicate task of informing her mother as soon as she reappeared. Their other son, who was travelling in Italy, was being sought by the consular authorities.

Taking advantage of the anguished father's consternation, the lieutenant-colonel did not bother with any explanations, excuses or condolences, but sent him and his companions straight to the Clinical Hospital. He had already contacted the duty doctors: Guillermo del Valle was undergoing an emergency operation, and was in a critical state. Before getting back into his car, the duke turned to the lieutenant-colonel.

"I understand two people are responsible for this," he said between gritted teeth.

Marranón met his gaze.

"That's correct, your excellency: the person who gave an eighteen-year old a gun, and the person who supplied the money to buy it."

Without giving her father time to grasp what the lieutenant-colonel meant, Paquita gently pushed him into the car and gave the driver the address of the hospital. She was very pale, and in the opinion of the lieutenant-colonel, who knew of the relationship between the young woman and José Antonio Primo de Rivera, but had never seen her before and was now studying her closely, there was a mad glint in her eye. From the depths of the already moving automobile, Father Rodrigo, arm outstretched, shouted an "Arise, Spain!" that implied an excommunication.

When the car eventually reached Atocha, a surgeon came out of the hospital to greet them. He was still wearing a bloodstained gown. He explained concisely and briskly that the young man was already out of the operating theatre, where they had done everything humanly possible, but that the outlook was not encouraging. However, he added, softening his tone and his expression, they should not lose hope: medicine was far from being an exact science; God had the last word, and in the course of a long career he personally had witnessed more than one miracle.

Hearing this word, Paquita became even more tormented. Nuns emerged from the operating theatre carrying bowls whose contents they tried to hide, all the while muttering prayers under their breath. It was not a good omen. The doctor accompanied the duke to the dying man's bedside, with Father Rodrigo scurrying after them. The priest had brought all he needed to administer the holy oils. Paquita stayed behind and withdrew into a remote corner, where she fell to her knees and began to pray fervently.

The day had been especially intense for the unfortunate young woman. That afternoon she had poured out her heart to Lilí in the mansion garden, but the relief of unburdening herself to a sympathetic listener had only served to lift the fog that had until then prevented her from fully appreciating the seriousness of the situation. If she wanted to save Anthony, whose life – if what Toñina had said was true – would soon be in serious danger, she would have to act quickly and with no thought for the possible consequences. A crisis brought out the best in Paquita. She went back into the house, found a telephone, called the Falange headquarters and asked for José Antonio. A woman from the Female Section who answered the calls told her that the National Chief was not in the building, and was not expected until much later.

Paquita still had her coat on. She rushed out into the street, hailed a taxi, and told the driver to take her to number 86 Calle Serrano. She got out, paid the fare and went into the luxurious foyer. Seeing her enter, the caretaker got up and doffed his cap. A middle-aged maid opened the apartment door. When she saw Paquita she started back in surprise and apprehension, but soon recovered, and bobbed her head.

"Your ladyship, what an honour!"

Paquita waved her glove.

"No need for flattery, Rufina. Is he in?"

"No, Miss."

"Is he coming home for lunch?"

"He didn't say."

"It doesn't matter. I'll wait for him. Are you going to keep me standing out here in the cold?"

The maid stepped aside, a troubled expression on her face. Paquita passed by without looking at her, then went into the room adjacent to the hall. The furniture was large and noble, but the different styles suggested they were heirlooms of disparate provenance. Paquita saw a photograph of herself in a silver frame on a console table.

Two o'clock had just struck on a wall clock when the master of the house came in. Paquita was idly glancing at a volume of poetry from the library. When he saw her, the man's face suddenly brightened, but quickly became sombre again.

"I came to tell you something," said Paquita straight out. "Something you need to know."

José Antonio took off his overcoat and dropped it on a chair.

"You can save yourself the bother," he said curtly. "I already know. That pet rat in a cassock you keep at home couldn't wait to come and tell me. Unless there's something you wish to add."

Paquita opened her mouth, then closed it again. She was about to confess her sudden love for the Englishman, but before she could say a word, as if a powerful beam of light had dispelled the darkness around her, she realised what a mistake she was about to make. This revelation made her smile. Now she was the one who looked down at the floor. When she raised her head, tears blurred her vision of the man standing before her, who was staring bemusedly at her.

"It was a moment of madness," she murmured, as if to herself. "I have only ever loved one man. I'll never be able to love anyone else. I've behaved like a fool, and now it's too late to put things right. I didn't come to ask you for forgiveness. I'd be happy if you just lent me your handkerchief."

José Antonio hastened to pass it to her, but avoided all contact. Paquita dried her tears, and returned it to him. All at once she could barely contain her laughter as she thought of Anthony Whitelands. The memory of what had happened between them in the hotel bedroom now seemed to her like a scene out of a comedy film, where the emotions and actions are simply devices to entertain a public familiar with the conventions of farce. Seeing her sudden gaiety, José Antonio was even more bewildered. Paquita became serious again.

"I'm sorry," she said. "There's nothing funny about it. It's just that I feel so ridiculous. But that's not important. The fact is, I came to ask a great favour of you. It's something that's weighing on my conscience. That man, the Englishman . . . they want to kill him."

"A jealous husband, no doubt."

Paquita pouted, as if her pride had been hurt.

"Keep your sarcasm for the girls at the Rimbombín café," she said. "You and I know each other too well for all this pretence."

"Who told you they want to kill that fellow?"

"I simply know they do. Apparently it's orders from Moscow."

"That's his problem. It's nothing to do with me, and if they dispatch him, I won't be going to his funeral."

Ignoring his anger, Paquita took one of José Antonio's hands between hers.

"Silly, I only did what I did for you," she cooed. "You'd be stupid if you didn't take advantage."

José Antonio pulled his hand away and stepped back.

"Paquita, you're going to drive me mad!"

The young marchioness blushed. She could not believe what she was doing, and was astonished she felt no shame. She had probably started on what Father Rodrigo called the downward spiral of sin: once you were on the slippery slope, nothing but the grace of God could arrest your fall. But this was no moment to lose herself in theological debate: God's grace could wait.

A few hours later, the small yellow Chevrolet ploughed through the streets of night-time Madrid carrying José Antonio and the Englishman. The driver pulled up when they came to the Central Post Office in Calle Alcalá.

"Let's have a drink," José Antonio said cheerfully. "I'll allow you to buy. After all, you owe me something."

It was still early, and there were only three couples in the Bar Club, canoodling in the darkest corners. José Antonio and Anthony sat at a table, and a waiter soon came over. The two men did not speak until they had downed their first whiskies: José Antonio merely looked the Englishman up and down with a scowl lightened by a touch of irony. Anthony was nervous: he was up against an opponent who held all the cards but one – the ace on which his future and perhaps his life itself depended. Eventually he took the plunge:

"Why did you bring me to this bar?" he asked.

"To talk. I've heard that you wanted to see me for some important reason. As you can imagine, it's not easy for me to find a gap in my timetable."

"I realise that and I won't keep you long," said Anthony. "But tell me one thing: how did you find me?"

"One of your little girlfriends warned Paquita, and she came to enlist my help. Since I knew what you two had been up to, I refused. But, as you know, Paquita's powers of persuasion are irresistible."

Anthony grew alarmed. He was not expecting the conversation to take this turn.

"Did she tell you?"

"That doesn't matter. We'll talk about Paquita later. For now, I want to hear your fantasy."

Feeling less sure of himself, Anthony picked up the thread of the conversation again.

"A few days ago a Falangist whose name I'm not going to reveal came to see me. He thought he had uncovered a case of rank betrayal in your party and begged me to inform you of it. My being a foreigner gave me a supposed neutrality, and that, in his view, would make my account more credible. I told him that precisely because I was neutral I was reluctant to get mixed up in Spanish politics, especially since we had no incriminating evidence. He understood my position and promised to find the proof we needed, and since he was insisting so much I agreed to talk to you as soon as he had it. He tried to get in touch with you on several occasions, but without success. I didn't see him again after the first time. The only meeting we had was in my hotel bedroom."

Seeing their empty glasses, the waiter came over to ask if they would like another drink. José Antonio handed him a banknote and told him to bring the bottle of whisky, ice and a soda siphon, and not to disturb them again. Once all this had arrived, the Englishman continued:

"A few days later, a half-English, half-Spanish art dealer by the name of Pedro Teacher asked to meet me in Chicote and wanted to pass me some vital information. He was killed before he could do so. Before this I had been warned of the presence in Madrid of a secret N.K.V.D. agent code-named Kolia. Pretending to be friendly, Spanish Communists on orders from Moscow had been following me from the first day. This so-called Kolia decided to settle matters once and for all, and so earlier tonight I was duped into going to a remote, sinister location where a gang of thugs would have finished me off if it hadn't been for the loyalty of the one who had befriended me and for your arrival in the nick of time."

He paused, took a drink, then went on.

"From the outset I've been asking myself if there might be any link between those apparently unconnected episodes and the original reason for my being here. And I've reached the conclusion that there is. I have to say that Police Headquarters, the Interior Minister and the Prime Minister himself agree with me. I won't beat about the bush:

the traitor in the Falange, Pedro Teacher's assassin and the mysterious Kolia are one and the same person: you. Don't deny it: you're a Soviet agent."

Instinctively, José Antonio looked around the room to make sure no-one had heard the Englishman's words, then fixed his piercing gaze on him, and said:

"I've been called many things, but this is a new one. Might I know what your suspicions are based on, or have you simply joined the fashion for accusing me without proof?"

"I've got no documentary evidence, if that's what you mean. To satisfy your curiosity, I can only offer you the deductive process that has led me to this conclusion. It's as follows: as far as nearly all Spaniards are concerned, the political situation is untenable. A coup is inevitable. It only remains to be seen if it comes from Right or Left. Both sides are ready, and only a lack of unity on either side of the spectrum is holding them back. The military are the best prepared and possibly the most motivated, but they're procrastinating: they don't know if they can count on the unanimous backing of the general staff and the officer corps, they don't trust either the loyalty or the competence of their troops, they aren't clear about what the ultimate objective of the rebellion is to be, and above all, they can't agree on who should take command. While they are arguing, the Left is acquiring arms and getting organised. But they find it even harder to coordinate their forces. Caught between these two blocs, the fascists are a small group without any real support, few in numbers and with no clear ideas: they don't want to know anything about Soviet socialism, but at the same time they don't want to be part of the reactionary obscurantism that the Army, the priests and the rich represent. When it comes down to it, the Falange are nothing more than shock troops, with more show than substance. They survive thanks to gangsterism and two or three empty concepts. 'A unified destiny in the universal! Spain: one, great and free!' Ridiculous phrases and slogans that only sound good when they are shouted out loud, especially if the person shouting them is a handsome, brilliant, audacious young lawyer who also happens to have a title of nobility. Which brings us to the heart of the matter. The young lawyer is a brilliant orator and an attractive public figure, but as a politician he is useless. He can galvanise audiences, and yet nobody votes for him. He doesn't care about that, because it's other things that really interest him: going to the swimming pool at the Puerta de Hierro Club, making conquests with easy women, discussing literature with his friends. He says he went into politics to defend his father's memory and to save the Fatherland, and this is to some extent true: he is motivated by a kind of sentimental, pasteboard filial piety and patriotism which amount to nothing more than vanity. Being a trained lawyer and a young aristocrat, he loathes the brutality of the lower classes, and yet he cannot prevent his party from sliding slowly into thuggery. The capitalists use him unscrupulously to stir up public opinion, the workers' unions scoff at his plan to put an end to the class struggle, and meanwhile he has to stand by and watch as day after day his followers are mown down in meaningless street battles. His project, if there ever was one, has slipped from his grasp, and the vibrant speeches sustaining it may still enthuse those who hear them, but leave him not only bored but disgusted. Am I on the right track?"

"There's one thing missing," said José Antonio, his eyes half closed, drawling his words as if talking to himself. "The young lawyer in your story had an impossible love. Out of devotion and respect, he did not want to put the woman he loved on a ship that was drifting aimlessly: nor did he want that love to be perverted. Something had to be saved from the violence, deceit and betrayal. In the end, that sacrifice proved useless. His great love was perverted anyway, at the first opportunity, in the most stupid fashion and with the most unworthy person. But let's leave that for now."

The couples had left the bar; the two men were alone with the waiter. This unusual situation would have alerted them if they had not been so wrapped up in their exchange.

"Disillusioned with the idea he has given everything for," Anthony went on, pleased at the impact his words were having on his interlocutor, "disillusioned with all those who should have joined his ranks but had failed to do so, either out of self-interest or cowardice, disillusioned with the people of Spain, who won't listen to him, the young, brilliant lawyer decides to blow the country that has repaid his sacrifices so poorly to smithereens. He contacts the Soviet secret service with a proposal: if Moscow supplies him with the means, he will hand them the revolution on a plate. He will use his reduced but enthusiastic squadrons to launch an uprising throughout Spain. Faced with a real fascist threat, the socialists and anarchists will lay their differences aside: the result will be the people's revolution. Anything rather than allow the corrupt liberal system to continue or the military to install a regime at the service of high finance and the landowners. Too much innocent blood has been spilt for everything to end up as inspiring rhetoric and unviable empires. You are either Kolia or his contact in Spain."

"Fantastic!" roared José Antonio delightedly.

"Yes, it's not bad, but for the plan to succeed, two essential things have to happen: first, the Falangists must have no idea of their role in the pantomime; and secondly, it has to be carried out as quickly as possible, before the right-wing groups reach agreement, or before some unexpected event brings matters to a head. Of course, as usual things have not turned out as expected. The international situation is evolving rapidly; Stalin is worried by Hitler's warlike intentions, and prefers not to fall out with the European democracies. Better to postpone any sideshows. Moscow gives orders to back the Spanish Republic to the hilt. The young lawyer's plan is in tatters. But since he has already taken the first step and for him there can be no going back, he chooses to carry on with the uprising without any outside help, finding weapons and funds wherever he can. A young Falange member uncovers some irregularities; incapable of believing they have come from the National Chief himself, whom he adores, he asks me to talk to you. To put a stop to this, you give orders for me to be eliminated. Afterwards you'll take care of the informer. I manage to escape, and you bring me here to find out how much I know and to complete the business."

Anthony suddenly stopped. His mouth was dry, and his head was spinning. The whisky bottle was empty. He could see José Antonio's watery, amused eyes staring at him. A few seconds later, the latter exclaimed:

"My dear Anthony, you're completely crazy! And you say this is what you told the director-general of Security?"

"Yes, and Azaña in person!"

José Antonio could not help bursting out laughing. Anthony did the same. The two men were chortling, slapping each other on the back. They pounded their fists on the table, sending the bottle and glasses flying, unable to contain the attack of hilarity. The bond of friendship uniting them in spite of their rivalry came to the fore again.

The waiter approached, grim-faced.

"Excuse me for interrupting. There's an urgent telephone call for Señor Primo de Rivera."

40

After what seemed to her a suitable length of time, Lilí telephoned the hospital to ask how her brother was getting on. She finally managed to speak to Father Rodrigo. The boy was still alive, but the doctors had given up all hope of saving him, and the dreaded moment could arrive at any time. The duke would not move from his son's bedside, and Paquita, who could not bear the anxiety, rushed in and out of the hospital room with loud protestations of grief. Stunned by the news, Lilí's anguish was made worse by her mother's mysterious disappearance. A short while earlier she had sent the butler out to look for her in the streets around the mansion: he took the shotgun with him, hidden beneath the folds of his coat.

An hour later, he returned without any news of the duchess. It was a very tense night, and in Paseo de la Castellana he had not come across anyone who might have seen her. Lilí preferred not to contact the police; all she could do was wait and trust in providence. Instructing the servants to inform her if there was any development, she shut herself in her room. She could not keep up her pretence of calm. But far from comforting her, these familiar surroundings only increased her unease: everything there reminded her of her recent encounter with the Englishman. Perhaps at that very moment he was dead too. In her unbridled adolescent fantasy she saw him stretched out lifeless, killed by a gunman's bullet or butchered with a knife. Perhaps his very last thought had been of her.

Among those who thought they knew her best, Lilí was regarded as level-headed, with a positive attitude to life; someone happy to celebrate, although slightly immature and naïve. In fact, she was quite the opposite. Her situation was made worse by the fact that her cold, analytical brain and her passionate, rebellious heart had combined to lead her secretly to reject all the religious teachings she had received. Now, deprived of the comfort of prayer and belief in divine intervention, at the end of her tether after all her recent intense experiences, she thought she was going mad.

At ten past eleven, someone knocked on her door. Lilí covered her ears so as not to hear this herald of devastating news, but then recovered and went to answer. The maid told her that her father was on the telephone. Lilí ran to it. The duke was barely audible, and was so excited he could hardly get the words out. Sobbing and spluttering, he told her that her mother had arrived at the hospital ten minutes earlier. She had pushed past Father Rodrigo, who was trying to prevent her from going into her son's room, and threw herself on Guillermo, calling his name and smothering him with kisses. At that precise moment, the miracle had occurred. Guillermo del Valle opened his eyes and smiled when he recognised his mother's face. The doctors, astonished at this reaction, which was completely inexplicable in medical terms, found they had to attend to Paquita, who had fainted. Lilí was the only element missing from this scene of utter joy.

"Come as quickly as you can," cried the duke. "Join us in giving thanks to God. And tell Julián to come with you. It's dangerous out in the streets tonight. Apparently there's been more shooting, and buildings set alight."

Lilí had just put the telephone down when it rang again. As she was so close to it, she picked it up herself. An unknown man's voice asked for Paquita.

"She's not here. Who's calling?"

"A friend," said the voice at the far end of the line. "Just tell her the Englishman is safe and sound."

Lilí collapsed onto a chair. The maid asked if she was feeling alright. After a few moments Lilí said she was, and told her to gather all the staff in the music room. Once they were all assembled, she told them of Guillermo's miraculous recovery. When the murmurs of contentment had died away, she asked them to say the rosary to give thanks to God for the grace he had granted, and instructed the butler to find a taxi in which to accompany her to the hospital. Then she went back to her bedroom to dress for going out.

It took twenty minutes for Julián to return to the mansion in a taxi. Due to the disturbances in parts of the city centre, many taxi drivers had stopped working to avoid getting caught up in incidents that could result in damage to their vehicles.

"They burn your taxi and you're done for," their driver told them.

As proof of his warning, the night sky was red with flames.

It was after midnight by the time Lilí finally arrived safely at Atocha, and was able to enter her brother's hospital room. The atmosphere was one of retrained joy. Although the youngster's life was out of danger, he was still under observation, and there was no call for them to be too optimistic as yet: a relapse could not be ruled out, and the after-effects of the wound and the desperate last-minute operation were yet to be determined.

Lilí shared her family's delight, then took Paquita aside and told her of the telephone call about Anthony. Paquita received the news with complete indifference: it was obvious the Englishman no longer interested her. Lilí could not help wondering what had caused this abrupt volte-face, and also where her mother had got to during the lengthy period between her disappearing from the mansion and reappearing at the hospital.

The answer to this last question was as simple as it was extraordinary, and requires a brief digression.

Still not yet sixty years old, Don Niceto Alcalá Zamora had concluded that his active participation in politics was almost over and done with. He had been the first elected president of the Second

Republic, and had occupied that position of highest responsibility throughout the five years of its troubled existence. Conservative and Catholic, he had had to struggle with extremists on the Left and Right, with the workers' movements, the demands of the nationalists, with pressure from the Church and Army who saw him as the guarantor of public order, with a press only too happy to blame all the country's woes on decisions he made and, worst of all, with the intrigues, jealousies and petty-mindedness that went hand in hand with power. It had been impossible for him to please everyone; in fact, he had ended up with almost everyone against him, and yet he was proud of the fact that, thanks to his tenacity, capacity to negotiate and ardent rhetoric, he had safeguarded democracy from his detractors' plots and extremist fantasies. Now however he saw the end of his period in office fast approaching. Neither he nor his methods were to the taste of the Popular Front, still less to Manuel Azaña. The idea of relinquishing his post and possibly politics altogether saddened him but did not leave him in despair: he was pessimistic about the future because he could see disaster looming, and he did not want to preside over the funeral rites of a regime for which he had given his all, and which he had saved *in extremis* on many occasions. On top of all this, one of his daughters was married to a son of Queipo de Llano: if there was an uprising, the war would invade his home. As with all politicians, the idea of resigning broke his heart, but at his age, and with the added problem of the onset of blindness, the thought of retirement increasingly filled him with pleasure rather than melancholy.

That night he had been about to finish work when an aide-de-camp announced there was a lady outside who insisted on seeing him. There was a ducal crown on her visiting card, and when an assistant read him the name, the President gave orders for her to be shown in at once. His failing vision allowed him to make out the blurred outline of the Duchess of La Igualada and, with the agility of someone who knows every inch of a room he has worked in for years, he managed to skirt furniture and assistants and kiss the hand of his much-loved friend.

"Marujín!"

"Niceto!"

He dismissed the staff and invited her to sit down. The duchess and the president were both from Priego, a town in the province of Córdoba. A youngster of extraordinary intelligence, perseverance and dedication, Alcalá Zamora had left Priego to study at university, go into politics and eventually reach the nation's highest office. Slightly younger than her childhood friend, the duchess had left their town soon afterwards to receive a meticulous education at a boarding school run by the nuns of the Sacré Coeur in Seville, after which she had married Don Alvaro del Valle, Duke of La Igualada. Before they had gone their separate ways, Niceto and Marujín had not only shared the games and escapades of childhood, but also begun the innocent flirtations of puberty. Since those days they had met from time to time, always constrained by the demands of protocol and ceremony.

"You're as pretty as ever, Marujín. Time seems to stand still where you're concerned."

"I've already heard that you're as blind as a bat, Niceto. I look a fright. Besides, the worst thing that can happen to a woman has just happened to me. That's why I'm here."

Alerted by this unexpected declaration, Don Niceto Alcalá Zamora stroked his moustache and said affectionately:

"Tell me what's upsetting you, my dear."

The duchess waved her gloved hand; the charms on her bracelet tinkled.

"I've come to ask a small favour of you. It's something just between the two of us, Niceto. I escaped from home by the back door to get here; no-one knows where I am, nor should they ever know. Not to protect our reputations: we're too old for any gossip. No, because of what I'm about to ask of you."

"If it's within my power, you know I'll do it."

"I want you to put the Marquis of Estella in jail. Promise me you'll do it, Niceto, for the sake of our old friendship."

"Primo's son? Goodness gracious, I'm often sorely tempted, believe me. That boy is a good-for-nothing. Perhaps it's not his fault: he lost his mother when he was five, and then his father was always out on the town . . . But what you're asking is beyond my powers, Maruja. I'm not a dictator. I have to show respect for the republican rule of law, in what I say and even more in what I do."

The duchess went from light-hearted banter to profound distress in the blink of an eye. For some minutes the President of the Republic heard her sobbing and could dimly make out a bulky figure heaving in front of him. His pleas and expressions of affection gradually restored the desolate mother's power of speech.

"That little upstart marquis is the source of all my troubles," she said. "Only yesterday I caught my daughter in floods of tears. She didn't want to tell me the reason, but a mother doesn't have to be told certain things. That marquis has been prowling around her for some time. Paquita is a fully-grown woman: she has a good head on her shoulders and her feet on the ground, but she is a woman. And the Devil teaches third-rate Don Juans a ton of tricks."

"Maruja, we cannot be certain he has done anything wrong. And if no-one files a complaint, we have no reason to arrest him."

"Certain! I am the Duchess of La Igualada, and my word is more than enough! But there's more. That man has brainwashed the whole family with his ideas: my husband wants to throw away our inheritance, my eldest son is in Rome, paying court to that gesticulating clown, and my youngest is running round Madrid dressed in blue like a plumber. It will all come to nothing, I know. But Niceto, you're the President of the Republic. Get that monster out of my life!"

Fearing another deluge of tears, Alcalá opted for a balanced judgment.

"Don't cry, Maruja. Here's what I'll do. I'll instruct the police to arrest him on any excuse. With the things he gets up to, it won't be hard to find some misdemeanour. And once we've got him behind bars, we can think of the next step. Leave it to me."

Before the duchess had time to weigh up his offer, the aide-de-camp entered in a state of great excitement. Without apologising for bursting in on them, he went over to the president and whispered something in his ear. Alcalá Zamora blenched.

"Maruja, my dear friend," he said in solemn tones, "I've got some bad news for you. I've been told that your son Guillermo has been wounded in a gun battle. I don't know how seriously. At this moment he is being attended to at the Clinical Hospital. Your place now is by his side. He needs you. I'll make sure an official car takes you there. And please, keep me informed."

He pressed a button, assistants appeared, and, after a brief farewell, the distraught duchess left. As soon as he was on his own, Alcalá Zamora asked for a call to be put through to the Interior Minister. When he came on the line, the president instructed him to find and arrest José Antonio Primo de Rivera. Taken aback, Don Amós Salvador dared raise an objection.

"Legally, that would be no problem, sir. But putting the National Chief of the Falange in jail would be a ticking time bomb. His followers would take to the streets. And we couldn't lock them all up."

"Round up a few of the leaders. You know, cut their numbers. In this country it's no disgrace to spend time behind bars. I was arrested in 1931. Put them in Modelo prison, and if they make a fuss, get them out of Madrid and send them somewhere quiet: to Lugo, Tenerife, Alicante, wherever you like. That way they'll be protected, not least from themselves."

41

Anthony Whitelands woke with a start. His companion had squirted a jet of soda water into his face. He found it hard to remember where he was until, after wiping his glasses, he recognised José Primo de Rivera's frowning, solemn face. They were still in the Bar Club on Calle de Alcalá. Seeing that he had come round, José Antonio said:

"Bad news. Guillermo del Valle has been killed."

They were the only ones left in the bar; even the barman seemed to have disappeared. Anthony quickly recovered his wits.

"Guillermo dead?" he said incredulously. "It was you! Guillermo del Valle was the Falangist who came to see me. The one who had discovered the existence of a traitor. Now I understand! Tonina heard the conversation when she was hiding in the wardrobe in my hotel room. Then she pretended to faint, and ran off as soon as she could to tell Higinio Zamora everything. That scoundrel Higinio sent his moll to keep an eye on me . . ."

"Don't talk any more rubbish. Even if there were any basis to your fantasies, I wouldn't touch a hair on the head of a brother of Paquita's. Guillermo was killed by two men working for your friend Lieutenant-Colonel Marranón. Now there's a warrant out for my arrest. They've already taken in my brother Miguel and other Falange leaders. There are patrols out looking for me all over Madrid. They'll be here soon. The barman must have given them the tip-off. That's why he's vanished."

"What are you going to do? You could still escape."

"No. I'm the Falange National Chief. I am not going to hide. If they want to arrest me, they'll have to face the consequences."

With that, he took his pistol out of his jacket pocket. Anthony was terrified.

"You're not going to shoot it out with the police?"

José Antonio smiled, removed the clip from his gun and laid them both on the table.

"I'm not that crazy. I'm going to leave my weapon here so that they can't say they shot me in self-defence. I don't want any more violence. Believe it or not, I've always rejected the use of violence. God knows the trouble I've had trying to restrain the justified indignation of my comrades in the face of attacks from the socialist mobs – with the authorities' collusion, I might add – and to prevent the Falange sliding into that abyss. Unfortunately, I have had to accept reality and allow them to use weapons to stop us being crushed like insects. I'm sick and tired of it. Perhaps you're right, perhaps there are more than enough reasons for me to turn my back on my own creation. I wanted peace and reconciliation, but no-one would accept me. I've given my life for Spain, and Spain has rejected me. I've defended the working class, and the working class, instead of listening to me, does nothing but attack me. No-one pays me any heed. And yet, I could have achieved what no-one has done or will do: to get beyond the senseless class war and lay the foundations for a new Spain, a homeland for all. All my efforts have been in vain: Spaniards prefer to continue with their anachronistic ideologies, obscurantist demagoguery, the rule of local bosses disguised as democracy, and their savage vendettas. What's the difference between parading an image of the Sacred Heart in procession and burning one? This is a reactionary country up to its neck in misery, lethargy and lack of hygiene."

Laying a hand on Anthony's shoulder, he went on in a more personal tone.

"Go home, my friend – this is no place for you. Go back to the green fields of England and tell them what you've seen: explain my struggle, my aspirations and the obstacles I have had to face."

Anthony shook his head and waved an apologetic hand.

"I'm sorry," he said, "but I'm afraid I'm not going to do that. I'll go back to England exactly as I came: without taking sides. Not that I am indifferent to what is going on here – quite the contrary: the situation leaves me in despair, and even more so when I consider what's just around the corner. But that's not my problem. Nobody asked my opinion when they were laying the foundations or setting their objectives or defining the rules of the game. So don't expect me to deliver a verdict now. My involvement is strictly personal. If they're waiting for you outside, I'll go with you. Not because I think as you do, but because we came in together and we drank together. If they intend to shoot, perhaps they will think twice when they see you are with a British subject, or perhaps not. But I have absolutely no wish to hear about the reasons why you are all so keen to massacre one another."

Calle de Alcalá was blocked off. There were only two black cars drawn up outside the bar, and half a dozen Assault Guards posted in doorways with shotguns.

When José Antonio Primo de Rivera and Anthony Whitelands came out of the bar with their hands in the air, Lieutenant-Colonel Marranón stepped out of one of the vehicles and came over to them.

"I was wondering what had become of you," he said to the Englishman. "You're both under arrest."

"On what charges?" asked José Antonio.

"Carrying firearms without a permit."

"Neither I nor this gentleman are carrying any weapons," Anthony protested.

"Damn it, Vitelas, don't force me to invent something! I'm putting you behind bars; tomorrow the judge can decide what to charge you with. You come with me. Señor Primo can go in the other car."

José Antonio extended his hand to the Englishman.

"I don't think we'll ever meet again."

Anthony shook his hand, and looked him in the eye.

"If they hadn't come to arrest us, would you have killed me? Tell me the truth."

José Antonio smiled, shrugged and walked over to the car, escorted by the six guards. With one foot on the running board, he turned and raised his arm in farewell. Anthony and the lieutenant-colonel got into the back of the other vehicle. A policeman sat facing them.

"What did you talk about?" the lieutenant colonel asked as they pulled off.

"Basically, about women."

"I thought as much. Have you heard what happened to that lad, the brother of the woman you've been talking about?"

"Yes. Is he dead?"

"Not a chance. Toffs are like cats: throw them off a roof and they land on their feet."

Anthony settled back in the leather upholstery. He sighed deeply and closed his eyes. When he opened them again, they had pulled up at the door to his hotel. The cobbles had been hosed down, so there were no traces of blood left in Plaza del Angel.

"Aren't you arresting me?"

"No, not you. I don't ever want to see you again. You're a pain in the neck. Plus you stink of whisky. You have to be smarter, less reckless and less of a womaniser to get mixed up in international affairs. Your train leaves Atocha station tomorrow at two in the afternoon. Don't miss it, and don't even think off getting off before you've crossed the border. The Civil Guard has your description, and they have the bad habit of shooting first and asking questions later."

Anthony groped his way up to his room and collapsed fully dressed onto the bed, but did not manage to fall asleep until daylight crept through the shutters. He was awakened by someone shaking him roughly. Accustomed by now to this kind of treatment, he did not turn a hair.

"Who are you, and what are you doing in my room?" was all he wanted to know.

"Don't you remember me, Whitelands? Harry Parker, from the embassy. I learned you were leaving, and came to take you to the station. We'll all be relieved when the train pulls out with you on board."

"For God's sake, Parker, the train leaves at two this afternoon, and it's only ten to nine."

"That's right, there's just enough time. There are a few loose ends to tie up. Get dressed and pack. I've got a car waiting outside. Hurry up. We can have a coffee near here. With *churros*, if you're quick."

Too exhausted to object, Anthony did as he was told. He came down suitcase in hand; as he was settling his bill, he realised it was a different receptionist: this one was equally rude and even more distant. One of the glass panels was missing from the revolving door, but all the shards had been swept up. Leaving the case in the embassy limousine, they ate a frugal, silent breakfast in Plaza Santa Ana. Both in the café and during the subsequent journey, Anthony could sense a certain unease in his compatriot, as though he were making an effort not to blurt out something important. They were dropped at the embassy front door.

"Leave your case," said the young diplomat. "We won't be long. There are some gentlemen who want to say goodbye to you. You already know them."

"What if I refuse to see anyone?" Anthony said defiantly.

"You'd put me in a tight spot, Whitelands, and you've already caused me more than enough headaches. Be a good lad: it's only a minute."

They went up to the elegant room presided over by the portrait of His Majesty Edward VIII, where Anthony had previously met Lord Houndsditch and the two embassy officials. A cheery fire was burning in the grate. Lord Houndsditch came over to greet the new arrivals.

"Delighted to see you again, Whitelands. You know David Ross, the embassy first secretary, and Peter Atkins, our cultural attaché. On this occasion, we are joined by . . . well, there's no need to introduce him."

To his surprise and annoyance, Anthony saw that he was referring to Edwin Garrigaw, the old, effeminate and mean-spirited curator. Anthony nodded towards everyone and then, at Lord Houndsditch's invitation, took a seat in an armchair. Lord Houndsditch addressed Parker, asking:

"Have you told him?"

"No, sir. I thought it better for you to tell him personally," the diplomat said.

Lord Houndsditch nodded, filled his pipe deliberately slowly, looked round at all those in the room as if seeking their moral support, cleared his throat and then said to Anthony:

"Very well, Whitelands, I won't beat about the bush. We have two pieces of news for you: one good, and one bad. I'll start with the bad one. Last night, while your friend the Duke of La Igualada's family were all gathered in the Clinical Hospital because of . . . you know, because of that badly wounded Falange chap . . . a sad incident, by Jove. Just because it happens so frequently doesn't make it any the less sad. Fortunately, in the end the lad pulled through. Back at Verdun in '17 I saw similar cases. Not many though, it has to be said. As I was saying, while the family was at the hospital, there was . . . well, there was a fire in the mansion on La Castellana. Arson? With things as they are, we shouldn't rule out the possibility, although given the circumstances of the blaze I doubt it. It looks more like a domestic accident: a short circuit, a cigarette not put out properly, something of that sort. Everything was in turmoil: the family was not there, the servants were on edge; that's how these things happen. Luckily no-one was injured. Somebody realised what was going on, the firemen came and dealt with the fire without any great problem. In fact, it was only the basement that suffered. Apparently they kept old bits of furniture, carpets, lots of junk down there. All that burns like tinder. Some paintings were also destroyed: irreplaceable ones, it seems. I'm telling you all this because I believe that at some point the supposed Velázquez was down there."

The longer Lord Houndsditch went on, the paler Anthony became. He stole a glance at Edwin Garrigaw and thought he saw a mocking smile on his lightly painted lips. He asked for a glass of water. Harry Parker offered him something stiffer, but neither Anthony's body nor his head could stand any further assault. While the young diplomat was pouring a glass from a jug, Lord Houndsditch went on:

"Don't take it to heart, Whitelands. That was the bad news. Our friend Garrigaw here can give you the good one. Whenever you wish, Edwin."

The elderly curator let a few moments pass so that he could savour the triumph of what he was about to reveal.

"The good news, Whitelands, is that the painting was not by Velázquez. No, don't lose your temper until you've heard me out. First and foremost, your honour and your academic prestige are safe. It was not a fake and, given the conditions in which you examined it, your attribution is understandable. I'll go further: your hypotheses were on the right track. I'm very impressed."

"Please, Garrigaw," said Anthony in the faintest of voices. "Explain what you mean."

"Alright, alright. If I'm not mistaken, you had identified the subject of the painting, a female nude, as Doña Antonia de la Cerda, the wife of Don Gaspar Gómez de Haro. Doubtless you were right, and if so, that would confirm the identity of the woman who posed for the 'Rokeby Venus'. That's an important discovery, Whitelands. If you can prove it, I predict a huge success for you in our grudging circle. But the second portrait, the one you saw, was not painted by Velázquez, but by his assistant."

"Martínez del Mazo?"

"No. Juan de Pareja. For those who don't know who I mean," he said, glancing round at the others, "let me just say he was a Moor, a slave acquired in Seville. For many years he worked in Velázquez's studio, from the start of his master's career in fact, and learnt the rudiments of technique from him. Velázquez appreciated him both professionally and personally, because he took him with him on his two trips to Italy. We don't know Pareja's exact date or place of birth," the curator continued with his lecture, "but he was younger than Velázquez. Endowed with a natural talent, he learned not only from his master but from the great Italian maestros he was able to meet and even get to know in Italy. He painted some portraits and religious topics; being a slave, he was not permitted to show them in his life-time, but now they are on display in the Prado, in Valencia, and even in galleries internationally. The two being so close, it's logical that Velázquez was a great influence, and this has meant that on various occasions works by Pareja have been wrongly attributed to him."

He paused for his listeners to fully absorb his last assertion, then continued in the same didactic tone.

"During the second trip to Italy, Velázquez painted Pareja. When he returned to Spain, the painting stayed in Italy. Nowadays it's in England, in Sir William Hamilton's collection. I've seen it, and I can assure you it's a painting of the highest order. You may have seen copies of it. If so, you'll know what Juan de Pareja looked like: unbelievably handsome. Dark-skinned, intense eyes, curly hair, proud bearing. They say Velázquez painted it as an exercise before he embarked on his portrait of Pope Innocent X. I do not agree. By 1650, Velázquez had painted many portraits of Philip IV and the royal family; he did not need practice and was not unsure of himself. He simply painted Juan de Pareja because he was fed up with painting cardinals, and because they were friends and allies. That's why he granted him his freedom. If in Madrid Velázquez had painted Don Gaspar Gómez de Haro's wife as Venus, it's likely that the model and the assistant got to know each other, and probably something more came of it. Juan de Pareja painted her in secret, as he did all his works. Possibly rumours started circulating in Madrid, and since the master was responsible for any crimes his slave committed, Velázquez and Pareja fled to Rome."

With this, he fell silent and stared at Anthony, waiting for his reaction.

"Where do you get this theory from, Garrigaw? You haven't even seen the painting."

"Pedro Teacher knew the whole story. He never told anyone, and I don't know how he found out. Following his death, the British intelligence services searched his gallery and his home in London. They discovered all the documentation. We heard about it this very morning. We don't know if the Duke of La Igualada knew, or believed in good faith that the painting was by Velázquez, but anyway, now that the painting has gone, it's of no importance."

David Ross, first secretary at the embassy, thought he should add what he knew.

"Pedro Teacher was an agent working for the Germans. We knew that for some time, and were on his trail. He worked for the Abwehr, run by Admiral Canaris. Possibly for other countries too. A double agent. Almost all of them are."

"Is that why he was killed?"

"I don't think so. Spies don't kill each other. They're colleagues. They help each other and collaborate, when it doesn't go against their own interests. The same with governments. If the counter-espionage service uncovers an agent, they try to convince him to turn their coat, and generally succeed. Spies are flexible, as their trade demands. A living spy is useful, a dead one is worthless. Sometimes their own government thinks it's a good thing to take them out of circulation. But, as I say, it's odd. We've no idea who killed Pedro Teacher, and still less the reason for it."

"He was about to reveal a secret to me when they killed him," Anthony suggested.

"Don't put too much store by that," David Ross replied. "He was a loudmouth. I'm sure he was trying to win your trust to get information out of you. He was worried about the sale of the painting. His relationship with the duke had cooled recently: he felt excluded from a deal he had organised so carefully."

"And Kolia?"

Lord Houndsditch spoke up.

"Our informants have lost all trace of him. And we still don't know his true identity. Perhaps Kolia was Pedro Teacher. He might also be any one of us here. Those blasted spies get everywhere. No matter. Forget Kolia. Now the painting has gone, you no longer interest him at all. Neither him, nor Moscow. Nor us, if you don't mind my saying so."

"But he tried to kill me."

"No," said David Ross. "If Kolia had wanted to kill you, you would not be here now. What happened at Puerta de Toledo was a pantomime. Higinio Zamora Zamorano works for us."

Harry Parker looked at the clock.

"Time is getting on," he said neutrally. "Perhaps we ought to be going, unless you have anything to say or ask, Whitelands."

Leaving his empty glass on a side table, Anthony got up from his armchair. His head was aching, his stomach heaving. Sensing his discomfort, Lord Houndsditch laid a hand on his shoulder.

"Parker is right. Go home, forget Madrid. It's a filthy, turbulent city; people don't know their place. And don't worry about your friend Primo; nothing will happen to him. Fascism is a pain, but it's not a problem. Russia is the problem. Sooner or later England will have to ally itself with Germany to face the Communist threat." He turned towards the portrait of His Majesty Edward VIII, and pointed his pipe. "That's how His Majesty sees it, and he does not hide his sympathy for Hitler. It's true Hitler is not a complete democrat, but politics makes no distinctions. That's why it's not for educated, sensitive people like you, Whitelands. Go back to London, to your paintings and your books. And ask Catherine to forgive you. She'll hurl insults at you, but she will forgive you. Women are a nuisance, but they're the best thing we have. Politics on the other hand is horrible. The Communists and the Nazis are monsters, and even we, who are on the good side, are little more than blackguards."

EPILOGUE

As they left the embassy, the sun was shining high in a clear blue sky. The air was warm, there were buds on all the branches, white and yellow flowers in the flowerbeds: the heralds of a magnificent 1936 spring. When they reached the limousine, Harry Parker glanced at his wristwatch and stopped Anthony as he was about to get in.

"It's still early," he said. "I thought you might like to pay a last visit to the Prado. If you promise me not to do anything silly, I'll drop you there and pick you up in an hour. The suitcase can stay in the car."

"Thank you, Parker," said Anthony, touched by this gesture. "It's very kind of you."

At the gallery, he nodded to the female attendant and headed straight for the Velázquez room. When he reached it, he stood in the centre, unable to make up his mind. He did not have much time, and he needed to concentrate in order not to waste an opportunity that might not come again for several years. But before he could direct his gaze to any particular work, he heard his name being pronounced softly behind his back. His heart leapt.

"You, here!" he cried. "How did you know where to find me?"

"There's no secret," she said. "I asked Mr Parker to bring you. This seemed to me like a good place to say farewell."

"Oh, yes, you're right. If we do have to say goodbye, nowhere better. Let's look round the room. If any painting interests you, I can tell you about it."

Paquita clung to his arm, and they began to walk slowly round the room, their heads close together.

"You must have heard about the fire in the basement," she said. "I'm really sorry, Anthony."

The Englishman shrugged his shoulders.

"Apparently I was lucky. If the painting really was done by a Moor, I would have looked a complete fool. For your family though, it must be a great loss."

"It doesn't matter. We're rich, and the fright we had over Guillermo has made us see how little material possessions are really worth."

"Perhaps you're right. How is Guillermo? And the rest of the family? I'm sorry I can't say goodbye to them."

"Guillermo is recovering admirably. If he doesn't suffer any relapse, we'll have him at home in a couple of days. As you can imagine, my parents are beside themselves with joy. Poor Lilí though has been badly affected. She's still a child, and all this excitement has been too much for her. She doesn't stop crying, and now she's saying that she is to blame for the fire. That's crazy, of course. We'll never know how it started. Anyway, Papa has decided to send her to Badajoz, to the estate of our relative the Duke of Olivenza. There she can forget this nightmare and regain her health and good humour."

Anthony opened his mouth to say something, but could feel the stern gaze of the Duke of Olivares on him. Painted on horseback, the duke seemed to be pointing his baton to show the path Anthony must take. The Englishman shook his head and said, "Poor Lilí!" then, to change the subject, he added: "And what about José Antonio? Have you heard anything?"

"Early this morning he saw Alonso Mallol, the director-general of Security. It was not a friendly chat: apparently José Antonio called him a cuckold. He's been transferred to Modelo prison; he's now charged with contempt of authority as well as the illegal possession of firearms. I'll go and see him tomorrow. I want to say farewell to him too."

"To say farewell?"

"That's right," the young woman said. "They'll let him out in a few days, but by then I won't be here. I'm leaving, Anthony. I came here not only to say goodbye, but to tell you something I think you should know."

They were the only ones in the imposing room of Velázquez paintings. Paquita paused, then went on:

"Yesterday was very strange. I've always thought I was a sensible person, and yet in a single day I changed my mind three times. In the morning I was convinced I was madly in love with you. I was at home, overwhelmed by that discovery, when the girl from the hotel came to see me – the one with the baby. She knew there was a plot to kill the kind English gentleman and came to warn me; she did not want to be an accomplice to the crime. She said she was leaving Madrid with her son. May God have mercy on her and the poor little thing. I made a great effort and went to José Antonio's apartment. The last thing I wanted at that moment was to see him, but I knew he was the only person who could save your life. But when I came face to face with him, I realised that my love for you had been no more than a fleeting moment of passion. There has been only one man in my life. Our involvement with each other was a mistake. We don't change our affections so quickly."

"You did so three times in one day," Anthony said, cut to the quick. "What was the third?"

"The final one," said Paquita solemnly. "When we were told what had happened to Guillermo, I realised we were all plunging into an abyss, and that something had to be done to save us. At the hospital . . ."

Overcome by the memory of that moment, she almost broke down, but soon recovered her composure, and went on:

"I don't want to be melodramatic. At the hospital I made a solemn vow. If my brother was saved, I would retire from the world. When God produced the miracle, it confirmed what I already thought. That all the ills that had befallen my family were a punishment for my sins. I don't

378

know if heaven and I are at peace now, but I at least know what path to take. A cousin of my mother's is Mother Superior in an enclosed convent in Salamanca. Once I've settled all my affairs, I'll go there. For the moment I don't want to take vows. It's too soon, and I've been hasty far too often recently. I'll spend a few months praying and meditating; I'll decide after the summer."

Anthony struggled to take in these disconcerting pieces of news. The three women he had become involved with were all changing their lives and where they lived: Toñina, Lilí and now Paquita. Madrid is going to be empty, and I'm to blame, he thought. Instead of saying anything, he led Paquita in front of the portrait of Mother Jerónima de la Fuente. Although it is a relatively large painting, the nun seems tiny, as though the passage of the years, asceticism and experience have made her shrink without in any way affecting her energetic character. Her eyes look weary, her eyelids are heavy and slightly reddened; her mouth is drawn in a stubborn line. In one bony, veined hand she is clutching a book; in the other she raises a long crucifix. She has momentarily transferred her gaze from the carving of Jesus on the Cross to the man painting her and also, throughout the centuries to come, to anyone who stops to contemplate the painting. She seems severe, but her gaze is one of piety and compassion.

"There are two identical portraits of her in Madrid," said Anthony. "Both of them are attributed to Velázquez. This is the better one; the other is in a private collection. Both have a slogan at the top of the canvas. It's been worn away by time, but is still clearly legible: BONUM EST PRETOLARE CUM SILENCIO SALUTARE DEI. It means 'It is a good thing to wait for God's salvation in silence'. In the other portrait, there is also a pennant with another phrase I can't remember in its entirety, but which says something like: 'His glory is my only satisfaction'. I'm afraid that in the solitude of your cell you're going to have to choose which of the two versions you'll follow."

Without a word, Paquita let go of Anthony's arm and left the room slowly but resolutely. Anthony did not even turn to look. He remained studying the portrait of Mother Jerónima for a while, then went over to the corner where "Las Meninas" was on display. This was where Harry Parker found him, after he had come into the gallery, concerned he had not reappeared.

"Time to go, Whitelands."

"Do you know something, Parker?" said Anthony. "After a lengthy silence, Velázquez painted this picture at the end of his life. His masterpiece and his last will and testament. It's a court painting in reverse: it shows a group of insignificant people: little girls, servants, dwarves, a dog, a couple of attendants and the painter himself. The figures of their Majesties, the representatives of power, are no more than a blurred reflection in the mirror. They are outside the painting and therefore outside our lives, but they see everything, control everything; they are the ones who give the painting meaning."

The young diplomat looked down at his watch once more.

"Whatever you say, Whitelands, but it's getting late and we mustn't miss that train for anything in the world."